Nine Lives *of* Kitty K.

*To Winnie Mulholland
who first told me Kitty's story.*

The Nine Lives of Kitty K.

An Unsung Heroine of the Goldfields

MARGARET MILLS

MARY EGAN PUBLISHING

Published by Mary Egan Publishing
www.maryegan.co.nz

This edition published 2020

© Margaret Mills 2020

The right of Margaret Mills to be identified
as the author of this work in terms of section 96 of the
Copyright Act 1994 is hereby asserted.

Designed, typeset and produced by Mary Egan Publishing
Cover designed by Anna Egan-Reid
Cover art © Greg Hepworth

Printed in New Zealand

All rights reserved. Without limiting the rights under copyright above, no part of this publication may be reproduced, stored in or introduced into a retrieval system, or transmitted, in any form or by any means (electronic, mechanical, photocopying, recording or otherwise), without the prior written permission of both the copyright owner and the above publisher of this book.

ISBN 978-0-473-54203-0

Introduction

The *Wakatip Mail* (as the local newspaper and other commercial enterprises of those days spelled the name) is well enough supplied with records, sometimes spurious, of the district's founding and supposed Māori antecedents, but there is little written about the next hundred years, especially from the view of families and women, when this should have been the easier to catalogue.

Credit then to Margaret Mills, who in the 1970s teased out the history of the colourful Kitty Kirk, which in turn references much of our past – from gold-rush Dunedin to the Wakatipu, Kingston, Kinloch, Bullendale, Queenstown and bits in between. We get insights into domesticity, horses (lots) and eventually Kitty's fall from grace and rather tragic demise. It's good, and important. Read the source material drawn from people who were on the spot.

Queenstown was lucky to have had Margaret. University educated, she came down from Auckland in the 50s, took up with Johnny Mills, an early ski-champion from a colourful family (his father was the town bookmaker in the days before the TAB). They had equally colourful children. Margaret, now 89, lives on Waiheke Island.

Michael Lynch, ex/*Otago Daily Times,* whose family has been in Queenstown since the beginning of the golden days.

BOOK ONE

Young Kitty

The First Life
Ireland 1855

Chapter One

Katy Lyons crouched on the floor, her arms flailing as she tried fruitlessly to ward off the blows her mother was raining on her head.

'Ye filthy little slut, ye know what ye've done to us! Ye knew well enough what ye were doing! Ye've taken cows to the bull often enough. Shame on yer head for the shame ye've brought on us!' Two more punches met their mark. 'And shame again for hiding it 'til it was too late to do anything about it.'

'Please Ma, don't hit me again, please, please…'

'I won't. Me arm's tired. But just wait 'til yer Pa gets home. Then ye'll find out what a hiding is. After that we're away to the Father for you to make your confession so he can round up the young bastard what did it. Ye'll be wed as soon as the Father can fix it.'

More tears. 'Ma, no! We're in love, we were going to run away but his Pa found out and he's sending him away to be a soldier. It's not fair and anyway, he's a proddy so I can't be wed.'

'What! Holy Mother! It gets worse! Here's Pa, he'll kill you!'

Lyons staggered into the bothy. 'Why all the snivelling? I've just had a grand time and ye missed it! The young lords have left for the army, both of them! Young Sir was in his uniform, Mr Arthur in his best clothes and their servants in new clothes, and with six of the Lord's best horses and all the people cheering and clapping and waving. It was a great show. And then I come home to two women howling their faces off. What in God's name is the matter with ye?'

'That brave young soldier has left our Katy with a bellyful of arms and legs. She's showing already and the pair of them only fifteen, isn't that enough to cry for? The shame of it! What'll we do?'

'I'll show ye what I'll do for a start' he snarled as he unbuckled his belt. 'First her, and then, Kathleen, it'll be ye for letting her. Young Arthur has gone the same way as his father and brother.' The belt began to fall. 'Ye must have known he'd drop ye in it. That's what they do. They marry rich English ladies, never Irish milkmaids, especially stupid ones.'

'Pa, he said he loved me, he promised to come back for me and he said his father had promised to look after me.' she wept. Her father laughed caustically. Kathleen sobbed harder, repeating over and over, 'What shall we do? It's the convent for ye. They'll take the babbie for the orphanage, that's what they'll do, and ye'll spend the rest of yer days scrubbing their floors.'

'With a bit of luck maybe I can belt it out of yer,' said Pa, and he started trying to do just that.

A knock came at the door and it was shouldered open by a tall, well-built man, his brown hair starting to grey at the temples.

'Mr Padraig—' Kathleen started to say, but the intruder interrupted her.

'Lyons, you can stop that right now. Katy, go out and get in the cart. You're coming with me, now.'

'Where?' she whispered tearfully, 'Where are yer taking me?'

'Somewhere where you won't be beaten up by anyone. Get your things and go outside.' And turning to her parents, he said, 'You won't ever see her again so you'd better make up a story about a sick aunt or maybe she's got a place as a milkmaid. Stick to your story and keep your gobs shut or you'll be evicted before you know what's hit you. Just be thankful that His Lordship promised to look after her and her brat, and he keeps his word.

'Now as for you, Lyons, before this we were planning to turn you out for a useless drunk who's turned a decent cottage into a pigsty. Women's work? Wasn't that your excuse? Your woman does the farming while you do nothing but drink and talk. She can keep the holding, it's now in her name. Get drunk again or lay a finger on her or your girls and you're out of here. Mrs Lyons, you have two years rent-free, and there are some bits of furniture to replace the bits your drunk of a husband sold. Any more trouble from him, tell me. He'll feel my fist and then he's gone. And if one word gets out, you'll have me to deal with.'

'Thank ye Mr Steward, but what are ye going to do with my Katy? I need her here.'

'You just sold her for two years' free rent. Katy will be well cared for. I know better than to tell you to get rid of your man, so you'll probably have more daughters unless I have to get rid of him for you. Look after them better than you looked after Katy. Don't worry about her, she'll be better off than you'll ever be.' With this he strode out to join Katy in the cart.

Early the next morning they pulled to a halt in front of a large grey building in a city. Katy, who had been exhaustedly dozing was amazed to see that there were similar buildings everywhere. Padraig bundled her out of the cart, up some steps and held her while he rapped at the door.

'Wait,' Katy cried. 'My things!'

'Don't you bother about that old stuff, Katy girl, there's a whole new life ahead of you. Throw away the old stuff and for the love of God please don't start crying again.'

At that the door opened and a woman stood there. She hastily put down the dust pan she had been carrying. 'Padraig! At this hour in the morning! What on earth are you doing here?'

'Let us in and give us something to eat and drink, we've been travelling for a night and a day. And please get Billy to tend to the horse. He needs a good feed, I've been pushing him.' He led Katy into a warm kitchen, lifted the kettle from the hob and began to brew tea. 'My sister, Maggie, will be back here in a minute' he said 'sit yourself down.'

Katy was nursing her cup of tea when she came in. She looked up and cried 'Holy Mother, there's two of ye!'

They both laughed. There were, indeed, two of them. Twins, as near to identical as a man and a woman can be, solid but not fat, both fairly tall, but Padraig had broad shoulders and an air of strength and determination while Maggie was all warm motherliness. Two pairs of grey eyes studied Katy.

Maggie ran to Katy and pulled her into her arms. 'What on earth are you thinking of, Padraig, and at this hour of the morning? There's more than tea called for here. Now you just bide here while I get this wee thing bathed and fed and into bed. They're getting younger are they not?'

'They surely are. But this one's not for you. We'll talk later. Now you get her sorted while I talk to Billy. I need the horse taken home tomorrow and a good fast ride brought back. I'll need it to be stabled for a while – what? Of course I'll pay. And I'll want a bed and a feed. Now. Let's be getting on with it.'

Maggie led Katy out, all the time talking soothingly. 'Now, we'll just get you into a warm bath, give you something nice to eat and settle you into bed. When you wake up we'll go and buy you some nice new clothes and I'm sure you'll feel a a lot better. How old are you? Fifteen? How far gone are you? You must have some idea. Come on my poor wee dear, you're cold and tired and hungry so it's into the tub with you. One of my girls will help you, but don't tell her anything, hear me? And don't tell anyone who got you preggy.'

Tired as she was, Katy could not stop staring around her. A bath at home meant a tin tub on the floor in front of the fire on a Saturday night, after her father and mother and before her sisters. Here it was a whole room with a bath in it. She watched while the girl tipped bucket after bucket into the tub. Then she was helped to undress and helped into the bath. Lulled by the warm water and the flow of comforting words, Katy finally stopped crying. She had her hair washed with scented soap for the first time in her life. When she was dried and dressed in a flannel nightdress she exclaimed, 'This is too big for me!'

'Silly, it's a nightie!'

'You mean I sleep in it?'

The girl laughed. 'Now, what else would you be doing in it?'

Katy kept quiet after that except for an occasional squeak as a comb was dragged through her matted hair, which was then plaited into a thick black braid. When she was wrapped in a dressing gown they went back to the kitchen where she was seated by the fire and given a thick slice of white bread, a cup of tea and a bowl of porridge with cream and honey on it before being tucked into the first bed she had ever seen.

Maggie picked up Katy's discarded clothes with the fire-tongs and tossed them into the fire. Padraig, who had already eaten, was sitting with a glass in his hand. Maggie looked at her brother and said, 'It's a bit early for that. This is breakfast, not dinner.' She looked at Katy. 'Now, tell me about this little beauty you've brought me.'

'Clean her up, dress her well, teach her some manners – you know the drill. I know I already told you she's not for you. I know it's a pity but I'm just too tired to talk now. We've been a day and a night in a cart behind a plodder so I'm away for a sleep too. There's too much to tell so it will have to wait. Sorry, Mags,' and he dragged himself off.

Mid-afternoon Katy appeared wearing the dressing gown. She greeted Maggie warmly then said, 'I can't find my things. This coat is lovely but it's too big and it doesn't button up, but it's the loveliest coat I've ever seen.'

When the girl looked at her, laughed and said, 'It's not a coat, it's a dressing gown,' Maggie snapped at her and told her that it wasn't so long ago she hadn't known what a dressing gown was and to be kind. She told her to get Katy a plate of stew and then find her something to wear. 'Something that will do for today, but something fit to go out in, because later we're going shopping.'

Padraig came in just as they went out. 'What, more tears?'

'You know they're all like that to begin with, and she's little more than a baby. Now get this inside you, you've got some talking to do.' She put his food in front of him and poured two cups of tea.

'She's not so much of a baby that she couldn't get into trouble with young Arthur. He's only fifteen too. Just following the family path, but he's got more heart. He got too attached. When he was told he was being sent to the Regiment, Arthur carried on something awful and said he'd find Katy wherever they put her and run away with her, so His Lordship promised that he would find her a nice place well away from here and tell him where she'd gone when he got home. And, unlike most other lords, our brother cares about his people, and he keeps his word.'

Maggie snorted. 'You know that it's you who cares about our people. And have you found that nice place for Katy yet?'

'As a matter of fact, we have. She's going to New Zealand.'

'What! She can't look after herself. She's too young, she's too pretty and she's not very bright. And I make her out to be maybe six months gone or more. Is this "caring for the people?" What are you thinking about?'

'It's complicated. The family has to get rid of her and the baby, right? There's another member of the family that has to be got rid of and that's Andy. So they're both going to New Zealand.'

'Are you crazy? What has Andy got to do with Katy? He's been disowned, and he's safely away in the army.'

'He's been up to his old tricks and deserted before he could be court-martialled, so he's a wanted man but not wanted by the family. To avoid scandal they're sending him to New Zealand.'

'Why are we talking about Andy when all I want to know about is Katy?'

'You're not going to like any of this at all, Maggie, but this is what's going to happen. You're going to be really angry but let me finish, understand? Andy now goes by the name of Jack Cameron, and we've got him under lock and key until the ship sails. Katy stays with you until the baby is born and you will teach her all you can, then she'll be married to Jack Cameron and they will sail away to New Zealand.'

Maggie exploded. 'That's the craziest thing I ever heard of! Why should Katy be sacrificed for that bastard?'

'You forget, Maggie, you and I are the bastards and look how well we were looked after. You got this house and I was trained for the steward's job that I hold for life. Katy will be given a remittance and so will Andy, and you know he won't touch her. If she were to be married to him before the baby was born and that baby was a boy, he would be first in line for the title until the young lord produces, and our sister-in-law won't stand for that. You will be very well paid for your part in it. Like it or not, that's what's going to happen.'

'No, that I understand, but Katy can't possibly go on a ship in her condition, and she can't go with him.'

'When we cooked up this scheme we didn't realise how far gone she is, or they would be on their way by now. They will be married as soon as the baby is born. Our George's English Ladyship wanted me to put them in the ground because it is all Katy's fault that her darling boy got sent to the army. George drew the line at that. I absolutely refused to have any part of it. She had an ever so well-bred tantrum and fired me. She doesn't know she can't do that. George simply can't run the estate without me and I was given the job for life. George is brilliant with horses and can race them and sell them. Her Ladyship's money is kept completely separate from the estate accounts but I manage both. Neither of them can count past their fingers, but as long as they can have whatever they want they are happy and ask no questions. The beauty of this plan is that I've made it plain that the money has to come from her account, not the estate account so that's why I've been chucking it around so freely.'

'Will you please stop telling me how clever you are and get to Katy. Can't you see that I'm worried about the girl and I think you are, too. Why can't she be treated the same way as our mother was? You aren't as hard as you pretend to be and I'm sure you must have thought of that.'

'I did, but Her Ladyship won't have it. Father was a grown man when he took up with Ma and she was a well-educated woman, having been a governess. Poor Father had to marry for money. His wife knew the score too. And she was ugly, so it really was a marriage of convenience because she couldn't get anything better. Also, they were all three in their twenties, not fifteen-year-old kids.

'Of course I want you to know the whole story. Katy being so far gone gave me a whole new set of problems. And I am trying to do the best I can for Katy. She'll be financially secure for at least the next ten years. I've had to keep Andy under lock and key until the baby's born. Her Ladyship won't have it any other way and she's the one who's paying. Katy has to learn to live in a decent house and how to manage one. First thing, teach her to stop saying "yer". You know the drill. You've trained enough girls to pass for ladies.'

'I suppose I'll have to do it if I want to feel better about Katy, she's such a pathetic little waif. I really would love to keep her, but I can see the problem.'

'You know that Andy will never touch her and he's bound to leave her pretty soon. There'll be a remittance for each of them in New Zealand and we've fixed it so he can't pick up his unless he takes her with him, so she'll know where to go and how to do it after he's gone. George has been sending shipments of horses to New Zealand so he's got an agent there who will handle it. Katy will be fine once you've taught her to be independent. Looking like she does, she'll probably marry fairly soon after he's out of the picture.'

Maggie was sadly shaking her head. 'It's a great story, Padraig. How can Katy marry again if she's married to Andy? There's too many holes in it, too many questions for even you to answer.'

'After a while Katy can tell people she's a widow. Just remember that this baby is family. Its father is our nephew. And George is its grandfather. Andy will be kept locked up until the baby has been born and baptised. Then Jack Cameron and Catherine Lyons will be lawfully wed in the Free Church of Scotland. They want immigrants so badly they offer free or cheap passages. He's very lucky George decided that a member of the family couldn't possibly travel steerage, so they'll have a cabin. They'll sail away to a new life in New Zealand and our family will be free of a wanted man with an unwanted woman and an unwanted child who will live happily ever after in a brand new country. It's a fairy-tale ending, isn't it? And it's perfect. They're looking for a single man, nicely dressed, not a shabby bearded middle-aged teacher with a young wife, and of course they won't expect a baby.'

A month later Katy went into labour. Maggie took charge, assisted by one of her girls, and a baby girl was born without complications. Padraig spent the time informing Cameron of the next steps. Padraig and Maggie would take Katy and the baby to be baptised by a Church of England minister who held the living from the family. Because of this he could be trusted to keep quiet and to keep the entry in the register hidden. Katy had yet to be persuaded that being baptised a Protestant would not land her in the fires of Hell. They hoped that, seeing the parson dressed like a priest and being told that the only difference between the two faiths was one was spoken in English and the other in Latin, she would accept it, and she did. The baby was baptised Catherine Margaret Lyons, to be called 'Kitty'. Padraig and Maggie were the god-parents. Then the happy pair (leaving the baby with Maggie, who was still resistant to the marriage) went to a different parish where John Andrew Cameron and Catherine Lyons were reluctantly joined in holy matrimony.

Padraig gave the bride away. Katy had been told that if she didn't get married her baby might be taken from her. She was given a copy of her marriage lines and told not to lose them. They went directly to the harbour, and along with Padraig and Maggie, they boarded the ferry to Scotland. On arrival they were met by the representative of the Free Church of Scotland, who administered the oath of loyalty to the Kirk. Cameron signed for both of them. Maggie and Catherine, as she was now to be known, were weeping copiously, and Kitty loudly joined in.

Maggie pulled Catherine into her arms. 'Goodbye, my wee

darling. I hope you have a long and happy life. Andy will leave you soon and when he does, remember your place and take up with someone who doesn't think himself your better. Always be true to yourself and take care of your money.'

As they stood on the wharf watching the ship make ready for departure, Maggie started to turn away but Padraig said, 'I'm not leaving until I can tell George that I saw them safely away over the horizon. Come on Maggie, you know she couldn't have stayed here, and you've done very well out of it. We all have.'

'So you say. But I've come close to hating you. Playing with a girl's life and enjoying it. I got really fond of her and I'll never know what becomes of her.'

'I know. I got fond of her too. But we'll hear from the agent when she picks up her remittances. I'm not as hard-hearted as you think. I hid some gold in the lining of her cargo trunk and told her she is not to touch it until Andy has been gone for a couple of years and she can pretend to be a widow. I've been told that women are in short supply over there, and with her looks I'm sure she'll be snapped up in no time. In a few months' time you can tell me how I could have handled it better. Come on Mags, it's nearly time we went. It'll be good to be home, and we have to try to put all this behind us.'

'It will that. But I'll never forget that wee girl. I just hope that our nephews keep their trousers buttoned from now on, but that's a faint hope.'

'Come on, Maggie, at their age were you any better? And remember how the family looked after you.'

Maggie looked at Padraig and laughed, and with a final look over her shoulder to make sure that the ship was finally out of sight, she took her brother's arm and together they walked out of Kitty's life .

On board the ship the Camerons coped by avoiding each other as much as possible. After finding that both the smell and sight of baby Kitty nauseated him, Cameron spent most of his time on deck. Whenever he could, he slept on deck, explaining to anyone, whether they were interested or not, that it was hard to sleep with a crying baby. Sometimes he would even pretend that he suffered from seasickness.

He did make several attempts to teach Catherine to read but decided that she was abysmally stupid. There was no conversation between them because they had nothing in common. Maggie had polished up Catherine's grammar in the little time they had, but Cameron still shuddered at the brogue and at the thought of her appearing in society as his wife. He thought he knew what people would think of him, and he was absolutely right. He had not yet realised that he wouldn't be accepted into any sort of society anyhow.

One day when he was attempting to teach her, he was shouting and she was crying when they were interrupted by a soft Scottish voice.

'Mr Cameron, Mr Cameron, that's no way to teach. You have to inspire confidence in your pupils. You were introduced to me as a teacher, but what I have just seen and heard leaves me in serious doubt.'

The speaker was a plainly dressed middle-aged woman who had been introduced to him as a fellow-teacher whose name was Miss Brodie. She had been on leave and was coming back to the colony to live with her recently widowed brother. She was returning to her teaching position and was looking to recruit more teachers. Cameron looked at her in horror and made a hasty departure, muttering, with memories of his own schooldays, something about only being used to teaching boys. From then on Miss Brodie took over Catherine's education. She also found it impossible to teach her to read, but she was very eager to learn other things and became strangely adept at arithmetic. Her ability to handle money when she had never before had any was something Miss Brodie simply couldn't understand. Catherine still couldn't recognise the written figures, but she did manage to learn to make a sprawling sort of X in case she had to make a signature.

Catherine was happy. She loved her baby and had begun to realise that she was a lot better off than she would have been had she stayed at home with her parents, beaten and shamed. No man would have married her, and Kitty would have been taken away and given to the nuns. She still dreamed of her young lover, and she hated Cameron with every bone in her body. She had not yet realised that she had power over him by the simple fact of knowing who he was. Also, she was beginning to enjoy her status as a married woman. Although she still cried for Maggie, she felt that she was gaining a friend in Miss Brodie.

That lady cornered Cameron on deck one day. 'Your wife is very far from stupid,' she said. 'She's actually quite bright. She suffers from a condition called "word blindness". There's no cure for it and incidentally, aristocrats can have it too, it's no respecter of persons. The interesting thing is, she is amazingly good with figures. She can do mental arithmetic as quickly as I can. She's obviously not of your class, and she's very young, but you should have thought of that a whole lot sooner. Now, show her bit more respect and a lot more kindness. Your attitude is drawing people's attention to you, and I imagine you don't want that. But, just remember, the eye of the Lord is on you always.' And she stalked off.

Cameron reddened with fury. Who did that upstart spinster think she was? Who did she think he was? At least she recognised him as a gentleman. If she did, others would. As he stood thinking about that, another passenger stopped and said to him in passing, 'Busybody Brodie having a go at you was she? Don't worry, you're not alone and the wrath of God hasn't smitten anybody yet. It's *her* eye you have to watch out for, not the eye of the Lord.' Laughing, he strolled on. For the rest of the voyage Cameron managed to avoid Miss Brodie, who was continuing with Catherine's education, coupling it with a lot of religious instruction.

The Second Life
Dunedin 1856

Chapter Two

When the Camerons disembarked in Dunedin, the capital of Otago, they were expecting a city. They looked at what they saw with some trepidation. Catherine knew she didn't want to live in a city, but this didn't look like one and she didn't think she wanted to live in this place either. Nor could Cameron see a city so both were confused. They saw dirt roads, wooden buildings and a lot of corrugated iron. Cameron asked a passing sailor how far it was to the city only to be told laughingly, 'This is it, mate.'

Cameron had had absolutely no intention of living with Catherine but realised that he was stuck with her until he found his feet or a way out of there, whichever came first. So it was up to him to find somewhere to live for the meantime. Now, waiting for their trunks to be unloaded, Cameron wondered how on earth he was to find somewhere decent to live in this dump. Magically, Miss Brodie appeared at Catherine's side.

'And where are you going to live, my dear?' she asked. Catherine looked at Cameron.

'I have to find something,' he muttered, not willing to meet Miss Brodie's eye.

She smiled. 'And you don't know where to start, do you? The cargo luggage won't be unloaded for some hours. I suggest you hire yourself a handcart for your cabin luggage then find yourself an agent. Get yourselves settled at least for tonight then find somewhere to eat.'

Cameron produced the address of the agent. 'Well, that's something,' Miss Brodie said. 'He's a very highly respected man, even if he is not of our church. Now for the handcart,' and she indicated a group of men standing a little way off. 'Freddy,' she called. 'This is Mr and Mrs Cameron. Could you please take them to Mr Burroughs and then wait to show them to their lodgings. And they'll want to hire the cart tomorrow, too.'

'Yes, Miss Brodie,' answered Freddy, touching his cap.

'Well, goodbye for now, Catherine, my dear, I'll catch up with you tomorrow and show you where to buy what you need and where to go to kirk. May God be with you.' She moved off to a waiting carriage.

Cameron turned to Freddy. 'Now my good man, if you will just load our things, we'll be off.'

Freddy, who had been tamping his pipe, looked up slowly and said, 'Who are you calling "my good man"? Now, you listen to me, my good man, you're hiring my cart, not hiring me. Put your clobber on the bloody cart. I'm only escorting you because Miss God's Eye told me to and you don't fall out with a Brodie.'

As they walked through the muddy streets to the agent's office, Freddy chatted to Catherine telling her what a great place Dunedin was. There was not a lot of work, he said, but if you were ready to work hard, you could do very nicely, but it wouldn't be so easy for someone who didn't want to take his coat off.

'My husband's a teacher,' said Catherine proudly, rather liking the thought of being a teacher's wife, even if she couldn't stand the teacher himself.

'Never had any time for them meself,' he answered, 'but Miss

Brodie may be able to sort him out as long as he does as he's told.' He laughed.

On arrival at the agent's, Freddy told them that he was away for a drink but would be back in an hour or so. Catherine and Cameron went in, and after being greeted by the clerk, they were told to sit down and wait. The clerk spent some time fiddling with some papers then announced that a cottage had been found for them, but it needed a bit of work. Some furniture could be provided, but they would have to sort things out for themselves. He advised them to find lodgings for the night and then start on things in the morning. Cameron, who seemed to have become permanently angry, started on the clerk, who, completely unruffled, said, 'You'll have to discuss it with Mr Burroughs. I can only tell you what's written here. He's with a client at the moment but he shouldn't be long.' And Cameron, fuming, had to be satisfied with that.

After ten minutes or so Burroughs appeared, ushering out a florid looking man perspiring into a check suit. 'All right, Mr Whelan, to finalise, your horses will be unloaded at high tide and your men will be there ready for them. If you have any problems be sure to let me know. And if I hear of a suitable man for you, I'll send him to you. Goodbye.' They shook hands and Whelan left.

'Mr and Mrs Cameron. Come on in to my office.' Burroughs looked almost as if he were Padraig's older brother: large, efficient, no nonsense. He was dressed in a well-tailored black suit. Catherine wondered if 'agents' and 'stewards' were the same thing.

'Take this chair, Mrs Cameron.' He pulled it out for her. 'Is your baby a boy or a girl? Kitty. That's very nice. I'm Mr Burroughs. I hope you had a pleasant journey. My instructions are to look after you. Welcome to Dunedin, and you too, Mr Cameron.'

Cameron started, 'I understand we are being put into an unfurnished house that needs repairs. That's not good enough. Unless I have some money, how are we expected to survive?'

'Steady on, Mr Cameron! There's a quarterly remittance for you and a separate one for Mrs Cameron. You can only collect yours if you are accompanied by your wife. This is a very unusual arrangement I must admit, but my instructions are most specific. I also understand you were given the first installment before you left Ireland and had all this explained to you.'

'Bloody Padraig!' Cameron burst out.

'Mr Cameron, I'll have no bad language in here. You'll have to find yourself employment as soon as you can. You are a teacher, I believe. I shall give you a letter of introduction to Miss Brodie. She or her brother will find you a place, but you'll have to be prepared to toe the line.'

'Oh, my God! I have already met Miss Brodie and she took a dislike to me, to put it mildly.'

'Mr Cameron, if you continue using bad language I'll have nothing more to do with you. If you always speak like this, it's no wonder Miss Brodie took a dislike to you. This is a Christian colony where blasphemy is not tolerated, and the Brodies are very influential here. In fact, the way you are behaving will see you permanently unemployed except as a common labourer. Any more bad language and I will have you thrown out. Now, apologise or this is the end of our acquaintance.'

'I'm sorry, Burroughs. The fact is that I'm practically at the end of my tether. But that fellow who left just as I came in was talking to you about horses. I was raised in a horse-breeding establishment and I heard you say you would find a man for him. Would I be at all suitable?'

Burroughs burst out laughing. 'Oh Cameron, you've just made my day. I think you could suit very well. Whelan is a publican who has imported some racehorses and wants to make a name for himself in the game. But the position just might see you right.' He laughed even harder. 'Whelan is very well off and wants to be someone in society. An unusual man, he is very aware of his social shortcomings, and the man he wants is a "gentleman's gentleman". Do you fancy the position? You are certainly qualified for it!'

Cameron was almost apoplectic and struggled to keep control of himself. 'I didn't come here to be made a fool of. Now just give me some money and I'll go.'

Catherine had been crying quietly and burst out, 'Please, please don't quarrel. Please Mr Burroughs, sir, I badly need somewhere to feed my baby and to put her down for a wee sleep. And I really, really want somewhere to live.'

Burroughs touched a bell on his desk. 'My dear, I'm so sorry, you were so quiet I almost forgot about you. And please don't call me "Sir".'

The door opened and a handsome woman came in.

Burroughs stood up. 'Violet, this is Mrs Cameron. She is just off the boat and we haven't got her accommodation sorted yet. Could you look after her and baby Kitty for an hour or so and then perhaps mind Kitty so I can show Mrs Cameron her cottage? I've sorted out a lodging for them for tonight but they need to know what they're going to want tomorrow to set themselves up.'

Mrs Burroughs was delighted. 'Kitty, is it? How lovely! May I carry her? Would she like a nice bath? Would you like a cup of tea, Mrs Cameron?' Catherine wiped her eyes, handed Kitty over then burst into tears again. 'Oh, thank you Mrs Burroughs, thank you. Please call me Catherine. You are so kind.' The men watched as the women went out, Mrs Burroughs chattering soothingly all the way.

'Now, Cameron, I have already explained the money situation to you. You were given your first remittance just as you left. You didn't go ashore anywhere so unless you gambled, you should have all of it left, minus what you paid Freddy.' He noticed the expression on Cameron's face. 'Oh, you haven't paid him. Well, you'd better attend to that forthwith or you won't be able to get anyone to help you or even speak to you. Freddy is quite a character and very popular here. Word gets around very quickly in a small community and you don't want to get off on the wrong foot. Jack is as good as his master, and sometimes he's actually quite a lot better.'

'But didn't you say that my wife gets a remittance too? What about that?'

'I know it's quite irregular, and I confess I don't understand it, but the wording is precise. Her money is to prevent her and Kitty from being a "burden" on you. In short, you have to become a provider, but she can provide for Kitty. Babies cost money, you know. I also understand that she has been taught how to manage a simple household. So I suggest you put your pride in your pocket and accept what you've been given, which, in my opinion, is extremely generous. And I repeat, you have to be accompanied by your wife when you collect your remittance. So take care of her.'

'Padraig has gone to no end of trouble to humiliate me hasn't he?'

'I don't who this Padraig is. I have only had dealings with His Lordship and up till now it has only been about his horses. Every page I have received about you or his horses has been signed off by him. He seems to be more concerned about your wife's welfare than about yours. I confess I really don't understand anything about it. You know a lot more about this than I do but just remember, I am merely an agent and as such, I am not employed by you. I am not the master of your destiny, you are. My job is to help you settle in here and to look after your wife and help her find her feet. Being an educated man won't help you much, so for goodness' sake, don't come the gentleman. And it might be a good idea to avoid Miss Brodie. She can be pretty unforgiving, so you're unlikely to get work as a teacher. Now, I have work to do. Go and make yourself comfortable in the outer office while you wait for your wife. Then I will show you to your cottage, which I know you won't like, but you'll have to get used to it – it's all you've got. You'll have to make a major effort to better yourself, and you'd better get rid of your attitude. Remittance men are at the bottom of the heap here, unless they can prove themselves. I'm sure that your wife knows all about you, so be careful how you treat her. After that I'll show you to tonight's lodgings. Your trunks will be sent to the cottage first thing tomorrow morning. Oh, and don't forget to pay Freddy. He'll be waiting for you, but you can dismiss him if you wish. I'll have the clerk make you a cup of tea while you wait.'

In about an hour Catherine came down. She was positively glowing. She was freshly bathed and dressed in a dress and coat that Burroughs recognised as having belonged to a daughter who had married and had left home. Kitty had been left with Mrs Burroughs.

'Mrs Burroughs is a really lovely lady,' she said.

The handcart loaded with their cabin luggage was waiting at the door. Burroughs stepped outside with them. 'I always take my constitutional at this time' he said. 'It's just a short walk, but bracing.' He offered his arm to Catherine, who, surprised, took it, leaving Cameron to push the cart.

'Please Mr Burroughs, what's a constitu... what you take? I haven't learnt many long words yet, but Miss Brodie says she's going to teach me.'

Cameron winced, but Burroughs laughed and patted her hand. 'Catherine, my dear, may I call you Catherine?' She smiled and nodded. 'A constitutional is a brisk walk that one takes for the good of one's health, and I endeavour to do it every day.'

'And "endeavour"? What's that?' Catherine asked. 'Do you mind me asking questions all the time?'

'Of course not. That's how you learn. You are very lucky Miss Brodie offered to teach you. "Endeavour" means "try".'

'Miss Brodie was very kind to me on the ship. But why don't you just say "try"? It's much easier.'

'I'm blessed if I know why. What you are saying makes a lot of sense. I suppose I must just like long words.' They continued chatting while Cameron, sulkily pushing the handcart, wondered at Catherine's ability to make friends. Granted, she was very easy to look at, and she was still very shy, but people seemed to like her. They were not put off by that atrocious accent and her appalling ignorance! How could anyone tolerate that? Women going all motherly over the baby he could understand, but Freddy and an educated man like Burroughs?

'Here we are,' said Burroughs, stopping at a small wooden building with a stone chimney and a corrugated iron roof.

'It's a hovel,' shouted Cameron. 'Am I supposed to live in that?'

'Mr Cameron, may I remind you that beggars can't be choosers. You're not a "gentleman" here. You will have to fix it up a bit, and if you don't know how to do that, you will have to learn. You have a lot more learning to do than your wife does. This is all you can afford until you start earning some money, so for heaven's sake stop moaning and get on with your life.'

Catherine, who had rushed inside as soon as they got there came rushing out again. 'Mr Burroughs, It's lovely. It's very dirty, but I can fix that. It needs some mending too but it's all right to live in if the roof doesn't leak. I went into the yard. It's big, there's already a hen house. Can I get some hens? Our trunks are here already. I can't wait to get started! I have the money that Mr Padraig gave me.'

Burroughs was smiling broadly 'Well, at least one of you is happy. My wife insists that I'm to take you back to have tea with us, then you have lodgings for the night. In the morning Violet will take you shopping. She'll enjoy that. She's been a bit bored since the daughter got married and left. Bring the handcart, Cameron. We'll need it in the morning. And don't worry, Freddy will be pushing it. You and I will have other things to worry about.'

They walked back to Burroughs' office with Catherine quietly planning. She would tell Mrs Burroughs about her illiteracy and ask her to make a list.

Burroughs was talking to Cameron. 'You're going to have to make some repairs to the cottage. Some of the timbers need replacing, and I have had some timber put there.'

Cameron said miserably, 'I can't do that sort of thing. I've never done manual work in my life. I wouldn't know where to start.'

Burroughs looked at him and shook his head. 'You're a pretty poor specimen aren't you? By the stamp of you, you've been a cavalry man. You have the bearing and the arrogance. Can you shoe a horse?'

'Of course I can, if I have to. What's that got to do with it? Is there a job with horses going?'

'No, there isn't. But you must be able to hammer a nail in straight so you can start to patch up the woodwork. Luckily for you the roof doesn't leak, nor does the tank, and I had the chimney swept. The cottage needs smartening up and the grounds need clearing. The garden needs digging, some pickets in the fence will have to be replaced, that sort of thing, but nothing too onerous. As I see it, you can do it yourself or you can pay someone to do it and I'll deduct that from your remittance. Or you can pay rent, also deductible from your remittance, and I, as your landlord, will order the improvements. The last option will be the most expensive, as the rent will be related to the improvements and will increase accordingly.'

Sunk in misery, Cameron said, 'You're remorseless, Burroughs.'

'Mr Burroughs to you. No, Cameron. I'm a businessman. Like you I came here with nothing but an education, but I was prepared to work with my body and scrimp and save until I found an opening in business where I could use my brain and a certain amount of native shrewdness. Remittance men like you are two a penny here and either sink or swim, but I wasn't one. I had to do it all myself and to begin with I could only find hard manual jobs. It took me a long time, but now I'm very comfortable. You can do the same if you put your mind to it. My job as an agent is to look after my employer's best interests, not yours. Here we are. My wife is insisting on giving you tea. For some reason, in the colonies, "dinner" is the midday meal, "tea" is the evening meal. "Supper" is a hot drink and a biscuit just before you go to bed. Now, I expect you to behave and show respect for my wife. Treat her as a lady, act like the gentleman you used to be.'

They went inside, Catherine racing ahead to see her baby. They had never been apart before.

During the meal Cameron behaved impeccably and Mrs Burroughs found him absolutely charming. Burroughs treated him like a gentleman, while he hid his inner amusement. Mrs Burroughs insisted that Catherine and Kitty should stay the night 'so as not to disturb the wee angel' and the two women went upstairs. Burroughs was enjoying himself. He had to admit that Cameron, however much he disliked the man, was an entertaining conversationalist, so he kept up what he saw as his charade, handing out port and cigars. Eventually he sent him off with the address of the lodging house and then went to bed chuckling.

The next morning Freddy arrived promptly and accompanied the two women as they went off shopping. Catherine was unsure about all the contents of her cabin trunk but knew she needed cooking pots, beds and a crib for Kitty. She forbore to tell Mrs Burroughs that she actually needed two beds. She would leave Cameron to deal with that. Mrs Burroughs carried the list that Catherine had asked her to write when she had confessed that she couldn't read or write. She explained that she had a very good memory and that Miss Brodie had taught her her figures and how to manage money. Catherine was pushing Kitty in a very ornate baby-carriage, which had been unearthed from deep in the Burroughs's attic. This was another wonder for Catherine. She had been expecting to carry her baby in a shawl on her back. She hadn't known such a thing existed, and she wheeled it very proudly. Mrs Burroughs had even said she could borrow it until Kitty could walk.

'Miss Brodie said I am very good with figures and she can't understand how I can do it.'

Mrs Burroughs couldn't understand either, so she tested her as they walked along. She said it would astonish her husband when she told him about it. Catherine had asked Mrs Burroughs to show her where to find the shops and explained that what she needed first and foremost was cleaning materials and basic food. She would come back later after she had cleaned a space where she could open her trunk and check its contents. After that she had to work out where to put things after she had bought them.

They went to a shop called The Emporium. Catherine could not believe that so much variety existed in one shop, because 'shopping', except for that one clothing spree, had not figured in her education so far. Maggie had done all that for her. However, she proved to be a quick learner, and she decided to take only the cleaning materials to the cottage to begin with, as she thought that the place was just too dirty to put anything down. Quickly, she added up the cost of her purchases and paid for them, once again surprising Mrs Burroughs, who said that Miss Brodie would be proud of her. She would have been even prouder had she known that it was the first time Catherine had been in charge of her own money.

Then Mrs Burroughs happily took Kitty and told Catherine to come back when it was time to feed her and to have a bite herself. It wouldn't be right to take a wee baby into a dirty place, now would it? So with Freddy's cart loaded up, they went off to what would be Catherine's home for the next ten years.

As they walked, Freddy told Catherine that he wasn't doing very much today, so when he got there he would make sure the chimney was clean and rustle up some firewood. Then he would go and get some food from some people he knew who had hens and sold bits of meat cheaper than the Emporium. There were smaller shops, too, that were much cheaper.

'Only the nobs shop at the Emporium,' he said. He said there were also second-hand shops that sold good furniture. When she was ready he would show her. She thanked him profusely, asked how she much she owed him and told him to please put her purchases by the back door. While he was doing that, she went inside but came out quickly.

'Water,' she said. 'Do you know where the well is?' So he showed her the rusty looking tank and explained how it worked. Then he clambered onto the roof and cleared the guttering. After he finished he climbed down, then went off and got the food. When he got back he went round the back to where Cameron was gazing helplessly, hammer in hand, at a pile of timber.

'Hello, old man, how are you getting on?' he asked brightly, in an accent very similar to Cameron's own.

Cameron looked up in surprise and when he recognised Freddy he became angry. 'Don't you dare mock me.' He glared.

'Not mocking, old chap, I'm just letting you know that I'm on a remittance too. You need a few tips on how to survive and still manage to keep a little of your self-respect.'

'If what you're doing gives you self-respect, I don't think I want any of it.'

'Well, please yourself. Unless your family is much kinder than mine, a remittance won't support you. Sneer at me as much as you like, I am self-employed, which means that I can work when I like and even afford the odd drink.'

'Cap in hand and bullied by the likes of Miss Brodie?'

Freddy laughed. 'The Brodies and the Burroughs are the aristocracy here. And the Whelans and their like are the "would-be-if-they-could-bes" or "coming men". Next come the small business men, the smaller the business the lower in the pecking order. Then tradesmen, those employed by them and at the very bottom the casual labourers and the likes of us. So get rid of the accent and the straight back, get your hands dirty and learn to fit in.'

'Thanks for the sermon,' answered Cameron glumly. 'What about the landowners? Where do they fit in? Any horse breeders?'

'No. They are sheep men, all of them. It's not country for the sort of horses you are used to, more the sort of heavy hack your servants rode. The owners swan around playing at being aristocrats because they had the money to buy "stations" not farms. Some of these stations are nearly as big as an Irish county, but the men in their employ are the worst-off in the colony. They work from daylight to dark in all weathers, go out on foot to bring sheep off the mountains. For pay they get bed and board and a pittance. It's the nearest thing to slavery that I've ever heard of. At least for white men. Welcome to Otago!'

At that point Catherine came round the corner carrying two tin mugs of tea. Immediately Freddy fell right back into character.

'Ta very much, Mrs Cameron,' he smiled. 'I'm just hanging 'round to give your old man a bit of a hand.' Catherine looked puzzled.

'What old man?' she asked.

Freddy laughed. 'That's what you call your husband here in New Zealand.'

Still puzzled, she asked, 'Why? He's not that old! He's not nearly as old as you are.'

Both men laughed. Freddy said he was blessed if he knew.

Catherine said there was some bread and cheese on the table and she was now going to the Burroughs's to collect baby Kitty. 'Could someone cut some kindling and light a fire?' She looked directly at Cameron.

Freddy helped Cameron for a while, showing him how to do the repairs. Then he got tired of it and took Cameron off to get some furniture. He asked no questions when told that they wanted two beds but took them down and packed them onto the handcart. They were simple stretchers made from wood with hessian stretched as a mattress. When Cameron eyed them disdainfully, Freddy told him that they were all he could afford and they were suitable to his present station.

When they got back Freddy put the beds back together and then announced that he was going for a drink but that Cameron had better not come until he was seen to be working. Catherine had come back and was building up the fire. She thanked Freddy for being such a help, then she commented that her father was a drinking man and it made him hit people. Freddy laughed and said that he hadn't enough money for that much drink.

Cameron decided to walk up the road a bit with Freddy. 'You'd be better off staying home and getting on with the repairs. If I don't find work tomorrow I'll come back and give you a hand, but I won't help with the wall. You can finish that and I'll get on with digging the garden, or perhaps I'll fix the henhouse. I can't stick at one thing for any length of time. I get bored quickly. Until you can be useful you'd better stay home looking virtuous. Practise your accent and try to stop walking like a soldier. If Miss Busybody asks me, I'll tell her you're settling in nicely.'

Cameron exploded. 'I'll never "settle in" here. There must be better places in this God-forsaken country!'

Freddy grinned. 'It would be a lot more fun if God did forsake it for a bit. There's fun enough if you know where to look and if you stop comparing it to "home", wherever that may be. Remember, you got yourself here so now put up with it. I'm not asking where you come from and why you are here, and you aren't asking me,' and, pushing his cart, he went whistling down the road.

It was difficult enough for Cameron to take advice at the best of times, but he did try. Freddy found him a little work now and then helping him shift loads he couldn't do on his own, and he joked about getting another cart and starting a business.

For a little more than a year life went on relatively smoothly. People were starting to comment that Kitty, now a sturdy little girl who was walking easily, looked very like her father.

This did not please Cameron, but Catherine quickly answered that, yes she did take after her father's family and was the spitting image of one of his nephews.

Then came the day that Cameron rushed, white-faced, back into the house. 'Catherine, I've just seen two men I knew in the army. I can't stay here. Have you got any money? I have to get away.'

'Did they see you? Did they ever see you with a beard? I haven't got any money left, but it's remittance day tomorrow so you can pick it up then.'

'I'll stay inside. I'll stay in bed. I'll write a letter to Burroughs telling him I'm sick with an ague and could he give my money to you. I'm not going out. You go out and also find Freddy and tell him I'm sick and I can't help him tomorrow.'

While she was out he packed what he could into a sugar bag and tied a bit of rope to the bottom corners so he could sling it over his back, then he tried to work out where he could go. His mind was in turmoil, and he had realised that he couldn't plan ahead. He simply had to wait and see what happened. When Catherine came back she had a loaf of bread and some cheese, which he added to his pack. He could hardly eat the hearty meal she served him.

In the morning Catherine went to collect their money, and as usual she took Kitty to see Mrs Burroughs and have a cup of tea. Mrs Burroughs loved Kitty and treated her as the granddaughter that she never had. Catherine had no problem picking up Cameron's remittance, and Mrs Burroughs gave advice on how to dose the poor invalid. As she was leaving Mr Burroughs was showing two military men out. She heard him say, 'I'm sorry, gentlemen I can truly say that there is no one of that name in Dunedin. I can only suggest you go upcountry and try the sheep stations. That would be the most likely place to find him.'

Catherine went home and reported this to Cameron. He was steady now, almost seeming to relish the excitement. Darkness fell. They looked at each other. 'Well at least I know where not to go. You're a good woman, Catherine. I have been a right bastard to you, haven't I? But you've been good to me. In a queer sort of way I'll miss you.'

'In a queer sort of way I'll miss you too. It was awful to begin with, but we did learn to rub along together didn't we? I did learn to talk a bit better just listening to you. Goodbye, Jack. I hope you find somewhere safe.'

And for the first and last time ever they kissed each other awkwardly on the cheeks.

Then Cameron slipped silently into the darkness and out of Catherine's life.

Chapter Three

Catherine had settled comfortably into the life of a deserted wife and, with a peasant's practicality, had made the best of what she had. Her garden flourished and her hens thrived. She had a very small but steady income from both and was getting a few customers for the feather pillows she made. Nothing was wasted.

Of course, she still had her remittance. Mr Burroughs had explained that it would finish after ten years, so she still had about three years to go. She had confided to him at the very beginning that she didn't want to keep money in the house, and so he taught her about banking. Her innate frugality quickly grasped the meaning of 'interest', so her savings grew apace. Twice after Cameron left Burroughs had paid his remittance to her. Now, after seven years, she had accumulated what Burroughs called 'a tidy sum', which she seldom had to draw on, the garden and the hens supplying almost all of their needs, and she was able to sell her surplus.

Catherine knew to the last penny how much was in the bank and had dreams of one day being able to buy a little bit of land. Gold had been discovered in the hinterland, and Dunedin had rapidly grown into a city around her, so she and Kitty had to walk further and further to enjoy green fields. The people were changing too. New migrants, who had not been selected by the Free Church, were arriving by the hundreds every day. A great number of them were gold miners, and as they disappeared into the hinterland, more and more arrived. The merchants who had thrown up temporary shops to supply the miners' every need had prospered and they were now building more substantial buildings. The Free Church was slowly losing its stranglehold. Not entirely, however. Other churches were being built, but now that Dunedin was the most prosperous city in New Zealand its appearance was changing rapidly. Streets were being paved, and although it had lost most of its pioneer character, it was still a staunchly Scottish city and the Free Church was still a force to be reckoned with.

The Brodies were still in charge of the school system, and Kitty was a regular pupil though no longer a favourite with Miss Brodie. She asked too many questions. Miss Brodie had soon lost interest in Catherine apart from checking on her attendance at kirk. Freddy still dropped in to help with a few odd jobs and to enjoy a cup of tea. Sometimes he even brought a piece of meat and announced that he would be back for dinner. When Miss Brodie told him that she didn't approve of him calling on a married woman, he replied that he was making sure that she stayed on the straight and narrow, and didn't our Lord approve of acts of charity? Freddy loved Kitty and often brought her little treats. Apart from her continuing friendship with Mrs Burroughs, Catherine didn't socialise and had become quiet and withdrawn. She and Kitty regularly attended Miss Brodie's kirk, really wishing that they didn't have to. Catherine still secretly clung to her Catholic beliefs, although she knew they had no place in staunchly Protestant Dunedin. Kitty was speaking with her mother's brogue and picking up some of her expressions and some of her religion.

Early one Saturday morning an excited Kitty jumped on her mother before she was even out of bed. Catherine groaned. She wasn't properly awake, and she didn't want to be.

'Ma, get up quick! We've got a cow!'

'A cow? What do you mean "we've got a cow"? Are you dreaming or something?'

'Get up! Come and look! She's in the garden, eating the cabbages! She's really beautiful!'

She was indeed beautiful. When Catherine finally got outside to meet the cow who was destroying her garden, Kitty was sitting on her back while the Jersey munched contentedly on the remains of the cabbage patch. Noting her full udder, Catherine quickly tethered her, dragged a reluctant Kitty off her back and sent her inside for all the containers she could find, while she hurriedly washed the udder, pulled up something to sit on and with a happy sigh leaned her head against the warm flank and began to milk. This was what had been missing from her life! Soon almost every pot and jug was full and Kitty had enjoyed the very first drink of warm milk that she ever had in her whole life. When the milking was over and mother and daughter were happily grooming the cow, a stocky red-headed man leaned over the fence and said angrily, 'What do you think you are doing with my cow?'

'She broke down my fence, and ate my cabbages, and what are you going to be doing about that?'

'Oops, sorry. I'll have to come back and fix it. She's a devil, that cow. Worst I've got. Hates being milked, breaks out all the time. Doesn't like people.'

'I've had no trouble with her. I've just milked her and I'm keeping the milk to pay for my cabbages. It's not that she doesn't like people, she just doesn't like men. Didn't you know that some cows just won't put up with men? Put a dress on and she might behave better.' She and Kitty, who had climbed back on the cow's back, both laughed. The man smiled reluctantly and reached out to take the rope that was around the cow's neck.

'Well I'll be going. I said that I'll be back later to repair your fence.' Unfortunately for him, the cow had other ideas. She dug her heels in and pulled back. When he slacked off the rope, she presented a pretty little pair of sharp horns to him. From the cow's back Kitty shrieked with laughter. She slid down, took the rope from his hand and the cow amicably accompanied her.

'It looks as if we'd better come too, or perhaps I should lend you a dress?' Catherine smiled.

'If you wouldn't mind. Coming, I mean. Not the dress. She gets worse if I take a stick to her. Nothing on this earth would persuade me to wear a dress. Are you sure you don't mind coming? It's quite a step, about two miles.' He extended his hand. 'By the way, I'm George Kirk.'

'And I'm Mrs Cameron. Two miles is nothing is nothing to us. We're both good walkers' replied Catherine, and she went inside to take off her apron and change her shoes.

'My name's Kitty and I'm going to ride,' said Kitty, as she clambered aboard. 'Please, Mr Kirk, what's your cow's name?'

'Cow,' replied Kirk laconically 'Mustn't use bad language in front of ladies.'

'That's terrible. She must have a name. All cows have names,' Kitty said. 'Everything and everybody has a name. Your name's Mr Kirk, my name's Kitty and I'm nearly eight and Ma's name is Catherine. I'm going to name this cow,' Kitty said bossily. 'I'm going to call her "Surprise" because that's what she came and gave us this morning.' Catherine, who had just rejoined them, was annoyed with her daughter.

'Kitty, she's not your cow, she's Mr Kirk's cow. It's not for you to be giving her a name. Don't be cheeky or it's the back of my hand to you.'

'She's as feisty as the cow, your Kitty, but you've taught her good manners. It really doesn't matter what you call the cow because I won't be keeping her. She's just too much trouble. Wear a dress!' He snorted. 'Not likely!'

'Where will she go?' Catherine asked.

'I'll sell her to whoever offers me the best price. I haven't had her long enough to get fond of her. Doesn't like men, indeed! She's only a cow, and a cow of a cow at that. Here we are.' He opened a gate and Kitty rode proudly in.

Catherine looked around. 'It's a real dairy. Run down and dirty, but everything's here, two more cows, separator, everything. The other cows need milking. Can I help? The Jersey is very young. It's probably her first milking and she was very good for me this morning. Don't sell her. I wouldn't mind helping with her, her milk is so rich.'

Kirk looked at her in amazement. 'Do you actually like milking cows? It was my life back in the old country, so I just do it. I much prefer droving. What are you going to do with all that milk you took this morning? There's more there than the two of you can use.'

'We've milk to drink, cream for our porridge, and the skim milk I'll make into cheese. Don't worry, we'll use every drop. Being a dairymaid is the only thing I really know anything about.'

'Thank you. Because of that sorry bitch, I'm running late. I'd appreciate your help.' He was surprised to see that Kitty had brought the other cows in, and they were in their bails. Catherine found a bucket of water and showed Kitty how to wash the udders. Kirk leg-roped one of the cows and Catherine said sharply, 'Don't do that to mine. And I like milking outside better but I'll do it here now that she's bailed.' She set to work and finished before Kirk.

'If I came and cleaned this place up then helped with the milking every morning, what would you pay me? And you wouldn't have to sell Surprise. She's the best milker of the three.'

After a bit of haggling, a deal was struck. Catherine asked for cleaning materials and Kitty demanded grooming brushes. George agreed to provide both, muttering something about being hag-ridden and how women started being bossy at a very young age. But he was very pleasantly surprised when he arrived the next morning to find the cows already bailed and washed and Catherine teaching Kitty to milk Surprise. All the bails were labelled in very childish printing with the cows' names, *Supprise*, *Magie* and *Moley*. George didn't bother commenting.

The routine was quickly established, and as Kitty became more proficient, George was able to leave earlier on his delivery rounds and leave Catherine in charge while he attended to his other business, buying animals, which he drove to the goldfields to supply butchers there. This was very profitable, and the dairy was a sideline. Now that he had help, things might change, especially now that he didn't even have to do the milking.

Catherine had persuaded him to buy another Jersey heifer. She was named Maisie and had the same attitude to men as Surprise did. The two Jerseys provided the milk for cream and cottage cheese, and the business was thriving. George sold his old horse and cart and replaced them with a better rig. Kitty loved the new horse, whose name was 'Bronze', and she groomed the animals while Catherine was separating the cream. Catherine had never used a separator before but had seen one used and had always wanted one. Back in her old life they had left the milk to settle then skimmed the cream off the top.

Catherine learned to drive and with Kitty's help was able to manage the deliveries when George went droving. She asked for an increase in wages, which was very willingly given. Their relationship was strictly business and remained so for more than two years.

Kitty had amazing rapport with all animals. This gained praise from everyone who knew her, but unfortunately she had deservedly earned herself the reputation of being a bit of a cheeky brat.

The first sour note came when Miss Brodie came to see Catherine. She wanted to know why Kitty's attendance at school had become sporadic. She also told Catherine that it was improper for her to spend so much time with another man while she was still a married woman. Catherine tried to explain that she and he were still on very formal terms, calling each other Mrs Cameron and Mr Kirk and that their arrangement was strictly business. Miss Brodie wouldn't listen and stormed off, calling down the wrath of God upon Catherine who was naturally very upset. She ran off crying to tell George. George was very angry and had some choice things to say about Miss Busybody. To comfort Catherine he took her in his arms, and immediately their whole relationship changed. They kissed hungrily and fell onto a pile of hay. It had been a long drought for each of them, and it was ironic that it was

Miss Brodie who had brought them together.

After that they couldn't get enough of each other, and their attachment showed. Catherine bloomed, and the normally taciturn Kirk became quite jovial. Miss Brodie paid another even more acrimonious visit. Her influence was still powerful enough for her to spread enough gossip to make the faithful stay away, and produce sales dropped off.

Kirk begged Catherine to marry him, and she had to explain that it was impossible. Everyone knew her husband had decamped and hadn't been seen for years. Freddy still came to visit, in spite of Miss Brodie's warning, and tried to assure them that it was only the old-biddy churchgoers who would be bothered about them, but sadly most of their best customers fitted into that category. Although the power of the Wee Free Church was waning, the Brodies still had a very long arm.

Catherine went to see Mr Burroughs but without Kitty this time. With no pretence, she told him about everything that had happened. To her great surprise he was very sympathetic and said some very nasty things about the Brodies. The world would be a better place if people were to mind their own business, he said angrily. 'Unfortunately your remittance stops if you marry again, and it's not your fault that you can't marry again. That bounder Cameron left you in an invidious position, but your new relationship simply can't be ignored. Also your tenancy of the cottage ceases soon, so my best advice to you is to leave town and go where no one knows you. Go quietly, tell no one where you are going and arrive there as "Mrs Kirk".'

Catherine sighed. She didn't ask him about the long words – she got the gist of his message only too well. She asked for his advice and he taught her how to transfer her money to a bank in another town. Because she was illiterate, it could cause some problems. Of course if George were believed to be her husband, there would be no difficulty. He would give her a covering letter. So her account was transferred to the Bank of New Zealand in Queenstown, where Mr G. Ross, the manager, was a friend of his.

'You must carry this letter with you at all times,' he said. 'You probably won't see me again, my dear. I am too old to carry on here and Violet wants us to spend the rest of our lives near our daughter. That, unfortunately, means Australia. She has heard about your problems thanks to Miss Brodie who came to tell her what an immoral woman she considered you to be. Violet told her that Miss Busybody Brodie should mind her own business for a change and showed her the door with a few more very well chosen words. Violet has never had any time for the "Wee Frees", and she really enjoyed herself. You had better pop up and see her now while I write your letter and finish settling your affairs.'

Catherine went upstairs to find Violet in the midst of packing. They cried in each other's arms until common sense ruled, and then they discussed Catherine's problems over the inevitable cup of tea. When Violet suggested that she would ask Kitty to come and help her pack Catherine accepted gratefully.

'Nobody's speaking to me now, because of the way I spoke to Miss Busybody,' Violet said. 'I've been wanting to put her in her place for years, and you should have seen the look on her face! It was worth all the nastiness. I don't care because we'll be at sea in two weeks.'

'I never thought Miss Brodie would be like that,' answered Catherine. 'Now She's told Kitty she's to stop going to school.'

Later, when the two women arrived at the bottom of the stairs, Mr Burroughs said to Catherine, 'I suppose I shouldn't be doing this, but you aren't out of Dunedin yet and you aren't married, so we'll call it legal. I'm giving you your last remittance. It should help you well on your way, considering what a manager you are. Kirk is a lucky man. My final bit of advice: get out of Dunedin, and don't let anyone know where you are going. Lie if you have to, and above all, don't tell Kitty yet, or the whole world will know.'

'Nobody's talking to Kitty, so she isn't talking to anyone either. It breaks my heart to see her so unhappy. She's blaming us for all her troubles.'

Catherine arrived home after dark with an armful of stuff that Violet had given her. She found George waiting for her. He had given Kitty a meal and she was ready for bed. The fire was blazing and the cottage had never looked more comfortable. After Kitty had gone to bed the adults settled down to do some serious talking. Catherine outlined her conversation with Burroughs.

'We just have to go. It was so good here but it's not good now. We did well here, didn't we? But now, thanks to Busybody, we no longer can. The wrath of God works well for her, doesn't it. I got evicted today, too. The story that he told me is that the land is now inside the city boundary and is too valuable for farming. He's selling it for business or housing. Poor Charlie couldn't look me in the eye when he was telling me. He didn't mention the fact that it would make him a very rich man. But he thanked me for looking after the place so well. He said we could take the separator and anything else we can carry.

'And I have some better news. I was asked to drive some pedigree cattle upcountry to Queenstown for Mr Rees. You know about him. I've worked for him before – it was him that sold me my piece of land. I mean our piece of land.' He smiled fondly at Catherine. 'We can camp there and work for him until it's paid off. The cattle are coming in two weeks so we've that long to get rid of stuff. And get packed.'

That night they did some forward-planning. Foremost was the question of whether they should keep it from Kitty. They decided that there was no point. She should be pleased to leave Dunedin, especially as she would get away from the endless harassment of her old schoolmates.

George said they would have to sell the cows, but Catherine insisted that they keep the two young Jerseys because, as she pointed out, if they were to be drovers, what difference would two more cows make? And perhaps they could be the start of a business.

George explained that they weren't just going for a walk in the countryside. It would be easy at first, but later it was a long hard trek through tough country, and dairy cattle weren't as strong as beef cattle. Catherine was unwavering. She had time to dry them out, and they could sell them on the way if they had to. The others could go. He worried about how they would afford the move, and only then did she show him the cash she had received that day. She had managed their business; now she would manage their money, but he would have to do the necessary writing and signing. They talked until nearly daylight, then they had a comedy interlude when Catherine gave George Jack Cameron's trunks. The clothes were too tight in the top, too long in the leg, too posh. There were too many clothes, too many books, altogether too much useless stuff, but the trunks soon emptied and were great. George wanted to keep some of the books, but when Catherine said they were a waste of time and space he gave in. She said Kitty could already read, so why should she want to read books? They would give them to Freddy and get him to sell Cameron's belongings for them. Catherine doubted that Freddy would want the books, but George forbore to comment.

Catherine's trunks were much more use to them. One of them had bedding and other useful things that she had brought from Ireland, but they still had room in them. She had been very frugal and careful with her belongings. Clothes, food, tools, the separator; there was so much to sort and pack. There was no point in her and George staying in separate lodgings to try to keep up the pretence. Miss Brodie had seen to that.

They slept until Kitty woke them, and she showed little surprise at seeing them together. Over the last few weeks she had changed from a happy boisterous child to a sullen one, thanks to Miss Brodie, who had told her that because of her mother's behaviour she was no longer welcome at school. Of course the school bullies had quickly taken up the case and had made her life miserable. George and Catherine had decided that there was no need to keep the preparations for their move secret from her, besides which they would need her help.

'Why don't you just get married?' she asked. 'Then everything would be all right?'

Catherine started to cry. 'We can't. I'm still married to Jack Cameron.'

George swallowed and thought quickly. 'Listen, Kitty, you can't wipe out the past. You must remember that for your whole life. Everybody does things that they wish they could wipe out. You probably will too. You can try to forget, but the past is always with you. You can only try not to make the same mistakes again. We can't get married here because there are people who would remember Cameron, and people who get married when they are already married get put in prison. But I promise you that once we are clear of Dunedin your mother will be called Mrs Kirk for as long as she lives, and you will be my beloved daughter Kitty Kirk. You will have lots of brothers and sisters and we'll even let you name the first one. But you mustn't tell anybody we're going so they can't boo us out of town.'

'Nobody except Mrs Burroughs is talking to me anyway, but she is enjoying having nobody talking to her. She says it saves her time trying to think of something to say. She says that all they talk about is other people or nothing at all. She says, "Don't grow up to be like them. Learn to be yourself and to like yourself." How can I, when nobody likes me?' asked Kitty glumly.

George said, 'Don't bother about the people here, Kitty. We're leaving those people behind us. Once we are away try to forget them. Just remember there are two people who will love you no matter what you do. Catherine, please stop crying. We'll be all right, won't we Kitty? We'll be strong for one another. Now come on girls, we have work to do.'

So the secret packing began. With the help of Freddy, who had remained their loyal friend throughout, their belongings were smuggled along to the dairy each night until the cottage was empty. Catherine looked sadly around her.

'My first home of my own,' she said. 'I was so happy here.'

George, with his arm around her shoulders, said, 'Yes, and we'll be even happier when we're on our farm because it will be ours. No one will be able to make us leave. It will be hard work to begin with, because nobody has farmed there before. There will be a house and a barn to build, fences to put up – all before we buy any stock. I'm well known in the district and will always be able to get casual work and a bit of droving, but we'll have to get the buildings up and buy feed for our animals before the winter. So there won't be any money coming in, and we'll have to manage with what we've got, and it won't be easy. Are you sure you won't sell the Jerseys?'

'Quite sure,' Catherine said. She hadn't yet told George about her financial status, apart from her secret hoard. She would have her own home, and she would be happy.

The Third Life
On the Road 1866

Chapter Four

Their stealthy departure from Dunedin was successfully accomplished in darkness. George accompanied Catherine, Kitty and the Jerseys for a mile or so out of Dunedin then sneaked back to pick up the Durhams. Durhams, later to be known as 'Shorthorns' were all-purpose cattle, exceptionally hardy. They could be milked and provided good beef, but their milk was not as rich as milk from the recognised dairy breeds. Unusually, George was delighted to find that there were only five of them, three having died en route. On most droves he was paid per head of stock delivered, but this time he wanted the easiest trip possible. Many people along the way were used to seeing him picking up stock for droving to the inland farms, and they sold him feed when he needed it, so no one took any notice when he passed through Dunedin, except for the odd comment about there being so few of them.

Freddy had decided to walk along with him because his farewell present to Kitty was a pair of young well-trained heelers, and he wanted to make sure that George could handle them and would be able to teach her how to work them. It was an absolutely magnificent present, as a well-trained working dog could cost more than a horse. When George remonstrated, Freddy laughed and said that he was an old man with nothing to spend his money on, and he just might come and live with them when they got settled. Meanwhile, he would just walk along with George until they caught up with the others, because he wanted to enjoy the look on Kitty's face when she saw her dogs, and he wanted to be able to say goodbye properly. A last cup of tea together, then he would head back to town to start spreading lies about where they had gone in case there was anyone who was interested enough to ask. 'Middlemarch' sounded good, he thought. It was far enough in the wrong direction.

Kitty was ecstatic when she was given her new dogs and saw the Durhams. Of course there had been floods of tears when she found that Maggie and Molly had been be sold, but she lost some of her moroseness and became something like the old bouncy Kitty when she found out that George had swapped them for a seven-month-old Jersey bull. He didn't tell her or Catherine how much he had paid for the bull on top of swapping the two cows.

'Kitty, my dear,' said Freddy, ' let's have a little walk and find some sticks to make a cup of tea before I turn around and go home. Mr and Mrs Kirk can manage without us for a while, and I want us to have a wee chat before we say goodbye.'

Kitty frowned. 'Freddy, you can't call them "Mr and Mrs Kirk" when they're not married. Ma is still married to Jack. So she's still Mrs Cameron.'

'She and Jack were never properly married. If she could find him she could get it annulled because they… well…'

'I know, they never slept in the same bed. Mrs Burroughs told me a lot of stuff. She said people like Miss Brodie said that once you got married in Church you had to stay married for life whether you liked it or not. Mrs Burroughs didn't believe it. Ma and George sleep in the same bed, but if you aren't married that's a sin.'

'Now listen, Kitty, some people may think that it's a sin but I don't think God does. I think that in His eyes a real marriage is more important than a paper one and that's what your mother's marriage to George is, a real marriage, even if the Miss Brodies of this world don't think so. And George is the only father you'll ever have. He'll be a good one even if he has to say "No!" sometimes. Listen, Kitty, now that you're away from all the nasty people, don't make the mistake of thinking everyone you meet is going to be another Miss Brodie. They won't be, unless you are nasty to them first. In this life we all meet people who like us, as well as the ones that don't, so learn to enjoy meeting new people, and don't judge them too soon. But don't forget your old friends. I've talked too much. Let's go and have that cup of tea.'

'What about the sticks we are supposed to get?' asked Kitty.

Freddy laughed. 'I'm sure they'll have managed without our help.' They had. The tea was made and Freddy produced some expensive bought biscuits for a treat. After many hugs and goodbyes Catherine and Kitty smiled through their tears as they watched the old upright figure of their only friend walk away from them down the road. George coughed and surreptitiously wiped his eyes.

'I forgot to tell him that I'd called the calf "Frederick",' wailed Kitty.

'The calf's already got a name,' said George proudly, 'He's got papers. It's a very long name but the papers are packed away. You'll have to wait until we unpack to see them.' Then he whistled up the dogs, who also had 'papers' and as he walked with Kitty he explained what 'having papers' meant. Kitty wailed that he had to have a name if she was to train him so she'd just have to call him Bully. Catherine gathered up the reins and they headed towards their new lives.

Although the roads were good they travelled slowly at first so that the heifers could improve their condition after months at sea and become accustomed to grazing. Fortunately the Durhams were very docile and they accepted the Jerseys into their little herd without fuss. After their months at sea they loved the freedom of movement and the lush green grass of the eastern Otago and Southland roadsides.

As expected, the Durhams loved Kitty. The dogs were well trained and took up their positions, one in front of the little herd and one trotting along behind. Kitty, who had quickly mastered the art of working with them, walked with either and wished that she could have named them herself, but they already answered to 'Toss' and 'Ted'. By now the Durhams all had names of her choosing. She was also learning to drive so that she could relieve Catherine, who sometimes liked to walk with George.

With all these animals to care for, Kitty became less interested in the adults' affairs and became happily absorbed in the animals instead. After about a fortnight they were able to pick up the pace and make very good time, because all their animals were young and fit, and so were they. They were really enjoying life on the road. The grazing was good and they were able to restock at the little villages they passed through. They were passed by wheeled traffic carrying supplies south or heavily loaded with men who were full of optimism and heading for the goldfields. There were others who were dejectedly returning. George would greet them with a cheery 'Hello', but they seldom stopped to chat even when offered a cup of tea. George said that a man could walk twenty-five miles in a day and that was about the distance between the hotels along the road. Strangely enough that was the also the distance a horse could cover if it was on a long journey. A lot of the hotels had livery stables where travellers could change horses if they were in a hurry, and most had better facilities for horses than they had for humans. The Kirks had no need of hotels as they camped along the road.

Whenever she walked beside George, Kitty was full of questions, usually about animal welfare, feeding, pasturage and, as they moved along, fencing, shelter and detailed questions about their future home. Most important to her was when could she have a horse? Sometimes she surprised him by the depth of her questions, such as why did Mr Rees want to bring Durhams all the way from England when that was the only breed of cattle that they saw in passing? Why couldn't he get them here? This led to a lengthy explanation about herd improvement. If Durhams were for beef but could be milked, why had George bought dairy cows? Because a mate leaving for the goldfields had sold them to him very cheaply. He was happy about that because if it wasn't for Surprise he would never have met Catherine. He and Surprise had never become friends, but to a certain extent they had learned to tolerate one another. If ever he stopped to ask Kitty if she understood, she answered impatiently 'Of course!' and proved it by reciting the salient facts back to him.

From the time they left Dunedin, George had been giving his girls geography lessons. The stock had become accustomed to river crossings on foot or by ferry. By the time they had reached Balclutha and started inland away from the lush coastal pastures they knew that the going would be harder. Up until then they had made good time but from then on, although the roads were still fairly good, there was less feed along the verges, so they would have to start buying hay. Other things would be different too. Catherine would have to try to conquer her shyness and suspicion of people, because they would be accepting hospitality when it was offered. George was well known by most of the station holders along the route because he had frequently passed through their properties, and they all welcomed him because he brought news from the outside world. They extended hospitality, sold him hay if he needed it and let him camp in the shearers' quarters, but now that he was accompanied by a totally unexpected wife, they might be offered hospitality in the house. They would still stay in the shearers' quarters but would almost certainly be invited in for a meal.

The day before they came to the first really big station, they were sitting around the fire after their evening meal when George said, 'Kitty, from now on your mother and me, we're Mr and Mrs Kirk. Do you think you'll be able to remember that?'

'Of course I can. Freddy explained everything to me. Does this mean I'm Kitty Kirk? It sounds good.'

'No, these people have known me for years as a grumpy old single man. They'll understand a brand new wife, especially one as pretty as mine, but not a great, grown, eleven-year-old daughter.'

'Well, who am I then? I have to have a name and I really don't want to be Kitty Cameron any more. Kitty Smith? No. Kitty Burroughs? No. Kitty Brodie?' They all collapsed laughing.

'How would you like to be Kitty Lyons?' Catherine asked.

'Sounds all right.' She let out a few experimental roars, increasing in volume until the dogs came to see what was the matter. 'What made you think of that?'

'It was my name before I got married,' Catherine said baldly. She didn't tell Kitty that it was her own legal name.

'Why haven't you told me anything about when you were a little girl? Do I have a Grandma or Grandad? Uncles or Aunties?'

Catherine started to cry softly. 'Please, not now. I had a horrible childhood and I don't want to be made to think about it specially now when I'm really happy for the first time in my whole life. I promise I will tell you one day when you are older and you've learnt not to ask so many questions.'

'But I really want to know! If I never ask any questions I will never learn anything. Freddy said I must never stop asking questions.'

'Enough now, Kitty. I want to know, too, but we don't want to upset your Ma anymore do we? We have a big day tomorrow, meeting a lot of new people, and you girls will have to act as if you are used to your names. You specially, Kitty. So, bedtime.'

'What if someone asks me about my father?' Kitty asked.

'Just say that he was a soldier and you don't remember him. After all, that's the truth. If they start to ask too many questions, just change the subject. Start talking about animals, or better still, start asking them questions. Come on now, get to bed.'

The next day when they came to the station they were warmly welcomed. George always carried bundles of the latest fashion papers from England and some books that he knew the women would like. There was considerable regular traffic on the road, but copies of the *Otago Daily Times* were always welcome, although they now lived in the new breakaway province of Southland. Newspapers were read until they were almost in pieces, then they were cut into small squares and put on a spike in the long drop.

Any paper was a valuable commodity,

The women were delighted to meet Catherine. They got almost no new female company, so they immediately rushed her into the kitchen for a cup of tea and some home baking while the men inspected the cattle. They were amused at the idea of a stud farm in Central Otago; they thought it was an idea ahead of its time. All the same they wished Rees good luck. Who knows, perhaps one day they themselves might be ready for pedigree stock, they laughed as they joined the women for the ubiquitous cup of tea and scones.

Kitty, meanwhile, had joined the children: two boys a little older than her and a girl, slightly younger. Or rather they had joined her. The boys, who clearly had fixed ideas about what girls liked, were surprised to find out that she was more interested in animals than dolls, that in fact she didn't even have a doll! When she said that the dogs were hers, they didn't believe her until Peter, the younger boy, had rushed inside to ask George.

'It's true,' he yelled, and Kitty worked the dogs a little to show them that she really did know how.

'Would you like to see my dolls?' asked Elizabeth.

'Would you like to see our ponies?' asked big brother Sam.

'Ponies!' shrieked Kitty. The ponies were a clear winner. This was the first time that she had met children who treated her as an equal and the first time that they had met a child who had been to school. They had a governess. They found it astonishing that she could drive but not ride and swore that she would be able to ride before they left. Lessons would start straight after dinner. Elizabeth ran inside to complain that Kitty wouldn't play with her and wouldn't even look at her dolls. The boys were clearly charmed by her and, thinking he was complimenting her, one of them said she was nearly as good as a boy.

'Better, perhaps?' she asked. They all laughed and after a bit they conceded that she just *might* be as good as a boy but very definitely not better. The boys' father, overhearing, suggested that they should agree on 'different but equal'. They all agreed except for Elizabeth who had come out to call them in for dinner. She said that Kitty wasn't much of a girl, even if she did have long hair and wear a skirt. To avoid embarrassment the adults hastily rushed them into dinner when Kitty started to explain biology to Elizabeth rather more graphically than necessary.

As soon as they had eaten, the children reluctantly cleared the table and helped with the dishes, and then they all ran outside so that Kitty's equestrian education could begin. Before she was allowed to mount they told her that she had to learn to brush the pony (as if she didn't already know) but to pay special attention to the girth and saddle areas. Then she had to learn how to tack up. The boys explained that ladies rode on sidesaddles, but most farm women wore trousers under hoicked up skirts and rode astride. Kitty hoicked up her skirt and showed them that she dressed the same way but that she wore the skirt over her pants only for visiting and that she dispensed with it when they were on the trail.

The boys laughed at her when she threw her arms around the fat little grey pony's neck and kissed her lovingly on the nose. They said that Kitty was a bit of a girl after all. Elizabeth said that Silver was *her* pony and she kissed her too and girls' ponies really liked being kissed. The boys retorted that Elizabeth never rode her and that's why the pony was so fat. Elizabeth said she was far too busy helping Mama and that Silver wasn't very fat. At this stage Kitty stopped the battle before it got fully underway by asking if they could stop arguing long enough for her to have that promised riding lesson.

Elizabeth went angrily inside 'to help Mama', so they were able to get down to business. Kitty proved to be such an apt pupil that before long the boys caught their own ponies and hopped on bareback, and they all went for a short ride so she could try a gallop. When they got back Kitty wanted to try riding bareback, so Peter legged her up onto his own pony. And, like all boys, he couldn't resist putting in that little bit extra effort so that she landed on the ground on the other side. She laughed as hard as the boys did, picked herself up and got on safely the next time. Soon she was trotting a bit bumpily around the yard and managed a slow canter before they were called inside. When George asked how she had got on, Peter said, 'She did great, she's a real good sport. I think I might marry her when we grow up.'

When everyone had finished laughing Sam said gravely 'That would be daft. You want a wife that stays home and does all the cooking and stuff and doesn't want to muck around with animals all day. You'd starve.'

'If cooking and cleaning and mending is all that wives do I won't ever get married. I thought they...'

Never mind what you thought, Kitty.' George interrupted hastily, afraid of what Kitty might say next. 'Say "Thank you and goodnight" to everybody. We've a very long day ahead of us tomorrow.'

Kitty explained, 'I was just going to say that I thought they milked cows and made cheese.'

The next morning everyone turned out to wave them goodbye. Kitty was proudly at the reins. George and Catherine were walking at the rear of the small, gleaming herd. Without a word of instruction the dogs took up their appointed places. The boys had their father's permission to ride along with them for an hour or two. Earlier on, the boys had laughed at Kitty when she was grooming the Durhams, saying that you can't train cattle, but she surprised them by calling the Jerseys by name and having them come to her one at a time. These were the first dairy cows that the boys had seen, and they had watched the station women go mad for them.

'Those are Jerseys. They're used to being handled. But you can't train Durhams. They're just plain dumb.'

Kitty was indignant, 'Of course they're not dumb. People milk them. Of course it's smart women who train them not big dumb men. No animals are dumb. Dumb people just think they are. I reckon I could train nearly any animal if I could get it away from its mates for a while, but it does take an awful long time. I've started on a Durham but only one. Watch. "Nellie!" she yelled. One head in the little herd lifted, and a few tentative steps were taken in Kitty's direction. Kitty took two steps, Nellie took a few more, Kitty took one more, Nellie took another, and the further she got from the herd the faster she came. Kitty told the boys to come slowly up, saying Nellie's name as they came. She was plainly nervous of them but stood trembling under Kitty's hand and let them pat her.

'Good', said Kitty, 'She's not man-shy,' and then she had to explain George's problem with the Jerseys. 'No, they don't go for him, they just don't let him milk them. No, taking a stick to them makes them worse. They do what they want and they do what women want them to do, because they just don't like men.' The boys thought that the idea of a man putting on a dress before a cow would let him milk her was the funniest thing they had ever heard.

'What about bulls?' Peter asked.

'Don't be silly Peter. You live on a farm; you know what bulls are for don't you?'

Just then, probably fortunately, they were called in for breakfast, the three of them howling with laughter.

Sam received a scolding for not having done his chores, and when he was asked what on earth had he been doing Peter had answered for him, 'Just learning to talk to cows,' and the three of them erupted again.

Their mother looked annoyed and said, 'You boys usually don't get on with girls.'

The answer came: 'Kitty's different. She knows an awful lot about animals and she makes us laugh.'

As the little cavalcade left, the father remarked, 'She's a hard case girl, that Kitty, and isn't she great with animals?'

'She may be, but I'm picking she'll be a peck of trouble for somebody some day. The mother is a bit strange too. She's painfully shy even though she's been out here for a few years. I don't think she's mixed very much. She's still very Irish, and she's still a peasant. I think she's probably illiterate and she doesn't seem to know much about anything but dairy. I think she was widowed a time ago. That's probably why her daughter's such a hooligan, and I hope George can straighten her out. I couldn't get much out of the mother, she really is stupidly shy. I don't care if they are going to be landowners, she will always be a peasant.'

'If you can't get it out of her, nobody can. You're such a nosy parker. George said they'd had a dairy for a year or two. She ran it while he was away on the road. She's a great little businesswoman evidently, but it was just business until recently when he got up courage to ask her to marry him. He's saved nearly enough money to buy a farm, but not freehold it. The bloke who owned the land the dairy was on sold up because land prices in Dunedin are sky high. The gold's brought in so many businesses and so many people that the city has spilled out into the country and swallowed up so much of the best farmland that George decided to get married and go. He's always wanted a farm and he decided that the time had come. He reckoned that a farmer needs a wife, and what could be better than a woman who can run a dairy and make butter and cheese.'

'Goodness me! And you call me a nosy parker! Her being beautiful wouldn't have anything to do with it, would it, in spite of her being handicapped with that brat?'

'Come on, Kitty's not that bad! She's only ten or eleven years old, just a child. George says he can leave all the animal care to her except the heavy stuff. She's a great little worker. She's an asset, not a handicap.'

'Just you wait and see. She ignored Elizabeth and sent her inside in tears because she took over her pony. She turned our boys into strutting little men and look at the age of her! The boys are beyond the governess's control, so we just have to find the money to send them to school.'

'Don't start that again. We can't afford school fees unless you sell something. End of story. Don't bring it up again, understand. As for Kitty, she's just a child and she isn't even pretty. Elizabeth doesn't give a damn about that pony and won't even spend enough time with it to learn to ride properly. The boys just treated Kitty as if she were another boy. They behaved just as they would have if it had been a boy visiting. We males always strut our stuff no matter what our species and how old we are. All we need is a new audience. Male or female doesn't have a lot to do with it to begin with.

'One thing though, have you ever wondered what will become of us if there's a gold rush here or worse, if they decide to start sluicing? I don't want to think about it, and I try not to. Forget about school once and for all. Now, how about a cup of tea? Pax?'

'I don't like that Kitty either. She won't talk about anything but animals, but she doesn't pull hair like boys do,' Elizabeth piped up. 'But she made Silver shine and showed me how to plait her tail. I don't like her, but she's better than the boys.'

'All I can say is, just you wait and see. Men like her, women don't, and that's the end of it. She's trouble waiting to happen. She is bound to come to a bad end.' With that the three of them went inside for that cup of tea.

For the next few days the Kirks were back in their old routine. Then one morning Catherine was sick. Kitty panicked. She had never seen her mother in anything but robust health.

'George!' called Catherine, 'Come and tell Kitty our news.' And she bent over and retched again. George came up wearing the broadest smile that Kitty had ever seen on him. 'We're going to have a baby,' he said proudly.

'Having a baby makes you sick?' she asked incredulously. 'Other animals just get healthier and look better too. I wondered when you would be having a baby. It seemed to take a long time.'

George could hardly stop laughing but Catherine wasn't amused.

'Oh Kitty, Kitty, why must you always tie everything to animals? I'm not an animal! I'll soon stop being sick and in about a month I'll be looking really good too.'

'You always look good,' purred George fondly.

'Of course we're animals. Everything on us is the same and works the same way. You aren't the only ones. Toss and Ted have been at it too, and she's in pup as well. And two of the Durhams and Surprise are nearly ready for the bull.'

'Kitty, you'll be the death of me! Soon we'll have to put a gag on you before we take you into company! Now, Catherine's back on the cart, so let's get going. If there's anything else you want to know we'll talk while we walk.'

'Yes, how long before Ma drops it, and why do people keep going at it for so long when animals only have to do it once, except of course for dogs?'

Poor George was nearly speechless. 'For the first question: about nine months. The second question will have to wait because people find it a bit more complicated. You really do need to be a bit older to understand all that. I'm just not ready to try explaining everything yet.' Kitty wondered why he was wiping his eyes.

Next morning as they breakfasted, George announced it was Christmas Eve and that tomorrow they would be spending Christmas with some of his best friends. It was too much for Catherine who burst into tears and into her broadest brogue. 'Christmas!' she cried, 'Christmas, and I haven't made any presents and no special food, and here we are miles from anywhere. Oh George, when will we have a roof over our heads again?'

Kitty was looking at her mother in absolute horror. George, with his arms around Catherine, looked at her over Catherine's head. 'It's all right Kitty, I've been told that pregnant women take on like this, but I've never been this close to one before. They say they get over it after a bit.'

'I'm not worrying because she's crying. She cries all the time. I thought that having a baby would make her happy, but she cries even more, and you say she'll get over it. I'd have thought the only way to get over it would be when she drops the baby.'

Catherine shrieked. 'You little miss bloody know all, you know bloody nothing! You don't drop a baby, you *have* a baby. Or you give birth to a baby. Get back to your animals where you belong and get out of my sight!'

Now it was Kitty's turn to cry. She had never heard her mother swear before, let alone at her. Poor George. He'd never heard Catherine swear either and he'd never seen Kitty cry. He tried to push the phrase 'Kilkenny cats' out of his mind as Kitty scuttled back to her dogs. She threw her arms around Toss's black neck and sobbed into the coarse hair while Ted busied himself licking up the tears. Poor George was beside himself. He had so little experience of women, and now Catherine was sobbing, 'I'm sorry, I'm sorry I didn't mean it, I really didn't mean it.' George did what one always does in this situation. He gave her a loving hug, then he went and made a cup of tea.

They were barely on the way again, all tears dried, all apologies accepted, when they were overtaken by a man on horseback leading two packhorses. 'Good morning George. They told me you'd be on the road ahead and with a pretty new wife, too. And good morning to you, Mrs Kirk, you're looking bonny. And this must be Kitty. Good morning to you too, Miss Kitty.'

'You know all about us,' exclaimed Kitty, 'You *are* a nice man. What are your dogs' names?'

'Whoa there, miss. Let me chat with my old mate George for a bit. When l passed your campsite the ashes were warm, so I knew you weren't that far ahead. Kitty, would you like to hop on Brady, the bay packhorse. You can take the reins. He doesn't much like being on a lead. It's his first time under the pack.'

'That was smart, Dougal, you've made a friend for life. I must introduce you to my wife. Catherine, this is Dougal Storey. He's the manager of the next station we come to.'

'Good morning, Mr Storey. I thought that farms in New Zealand were managed by their owners.'

'Irish, eh? We have absentee English owners here too, but we don't have tenant farmers being evicted and turned out. We employ, pay and house our workers and supply them with flour, meat and potatoes. My wife will be delighted to meet you. She has the brogue herself – that's how she charmed me. She can tell you how it all works.'

Catherine was a bit alarmed at that, she didn't want to meet up with anyone from her home county, but she breathed a sigh of relief when she heard that Mrs Eily Storey was from County Down. That was such a very long way from Antrim. Catherine knew almost nothing about her own 'old country', but that was something she did know.

Kitty, on Brady, stationed herself beside the cart where she could chat with Catherine, while Dougal dismounted and walked beside George at the rear with Ted. Toss was in her usual position in the lead. After a few miles the loquacious Dougal retrieved his packhorse, not without a minor protest from both Kitty and Brady, and with a wave and a 'see you at Christmas dinner', he was on his way.

Catherine said, 'I do hope Eily is a bit more friendly than Mrs Clawson. I felt that she was looking down on me all the time. She didn't really want to have us in the house, but her husband had asked us in. When he introduced us he said, 'Mr and Mrs Kirk and Kitty will be coming in for dinner.' Her little daughter was snotty too. Mrs Clawson was ever so nosy. The questions never stopped, and sometimes I didn't even know what she was talking about.'

'Well, my dear, 'class' wasn't left behind in the old country. It may be a lot more watered down here, but the difference is that it's money that counts more than birth. Landowners will always look down on those they employ, even if the workers know more about farming than their employers. But Eily is one of us, and she'll be wanting a calf from our Jerseys.'

'We won't be like that when we're landowners will we, George?'

He laughed, 'Of course not, silly. We will be small farmers, not runholders. We'll only be able to afford a few acres and have our dairy. The Jerseys are the start of our herd. And we won't be able to employ help. We'll have to breed some strong sons and the heifers will have to breed lots of daughters. I wouldn't mind a few daughters, too, if they are all hard little workers like our Kitty here.'

'Well, I hope our cows have all heifers and I have all boys. Though I would like one daughter who is all girl and happy to be one.'

'I'll just have to do my best, won't I? And I don't mind telling you that I'll really enjoy doing it.'

'George! That's so rude! I don't like Kitty hearing you talk like that!' George almost doubled up with laughter. Kitty grinned.

'You're calling me rude! And worrying about Kitty hearing! You'd do better worrying about me hearing what she comes out with!'

'I do worry about what Kitty will say in company. She can't seem to understand what it's all right to say in front of other people. What will she be like when she grows up? Will she ever be a normal woman and get married and have babies?'

'Let's leave that to Kitty, shall we? She's still only a baby herself. Left to me, I'd be very happy for her to be an old maid and run the farm for us when we get old.'

'I think all those boys we are going to have would have a bit to say about that! I'll try to stop worrying about Kitty and start worrying about where we can find a bull for our girls. I don't want to use a Durham unless we have to. Next year Bully will be old enough.'

'Not a Durham. What a snob you are!' George teased. 'I heard that someone at Kingston has a Friesian bull and two cows. We could get one of ours in calf now, and the other can wait until our young fellow is up for it.'

'George!' shrieked a horrified Catherine. George winked at Kitty who couldn't stop laughing.

'George, don't talk like that in front of Kitty. She's bad enough already. She's only ten and she's a girl.'

'I'm very nearly eleven, and I'm sure you knew about cows and bulls when you were my age. Farm girls have to know about these things. And about birthing calves.'

'Yes, but not about *people*. That's for grown-ups.'

'Oh Catherine, my Catherine, what a prude you are, even after all you have been through! That's why I love you...'

At this point Kitty joined in. She snorted. 'Soppy stuff. I heard you say that people aren't like animals. That's stupid. People *are* just like animals and I reckon that if you can birth a cow you can birth a person. I just hope I never have to.' Catherine shrieked again as Kitty stalked off to find sticks for the fire.

'Christmas dinner will be good,' she muttered. 'I'm sick of beans and bacon.'

The next day they arrived at the Storey's. The wind was blowing in the right direction, so they could smell the mutton roasting on the spit before they actually arrived. They were given a warm welcome, especially Catherine who, as she was hugged enthusiastically by Eily, muttered apologies for having brought no presents.

'The company of another Irishwoman is the best present I could ever have!' Eily said delightedly as she dragged her away from the men. 'Leave the boys to settle the stock. Where's the famous Kitty?'

Catherine asked unhappily, 'Famous, what do you mean, famous? She's just a little girl.'

'Oh my dear, I've upset you. I'm not meaning to be unkind. My Dougal was so full of praise for her and so were some of the men who passed you on the road. He said she was as good as a man at managing stock.' She rubbed her stomach. 'He said he hoped if I can't give him a boy this time, could I please give him a girl as useful as your Kitty.'

'I would so like Kitty to be like other girls, just a bit. All she cares about is animals.' Abruptly changing the subject, she said, 'It's a very long time since I had a woman to talk to. Not properly, not since I left the old country. I'm carrying too.'

Eily delightedly exclaimed, "I thought you might be. As for talking to other women, I haven't been able to talk properly to any since I got here. I'm not classy enough for station owners' wives. They don't know where I belong. I'm not a servant and I'm not one of them. The likes of me bother them. They just don't know how to talk to me. All they can talk about is how hard it is to get good help, and they can't talk like that in front of me. I have such fun. I drop into my thickest brogue and they can't understand a word I say, but they can't talk about me because they know that I can understand them. And they can't be rude to me because their men sometimes need my Dougal's help. Like your George, he knows more about farming in New Zealand than any of them. And shepherds' wives are stand-offish, too, because I'm the boss's wife.'

Then it spilled over into woman's talk, mostly about pregnancy, babies and the weirdness of men. Of course they talked a bit about Ireland, but each spoke little about her own personal history. Each divulged that she had a brutal, bullying father, that she was glad to get away and that she would never go back. Then back to babies and what Queenstown might be like. Eily had never been there, but she had heard a lot about it. It was a proper town. She had been to Kingston, where she had seen the lake, and it was just plain beautiful. But since the miners came, it had become just another shanty town with pubs and shopkeepers selling basic food supplies. Quieter now though, since the miners were leaving. Eily had only been there once about four years ago.

Mr Rees had come past their station with a whale boat which he had bought in Bluff. It was on a big sort of sledge thing pulled by two bullocks. It was not the first boat to have been brought up that way but it was certainly the biggest. Mr Rees's family had travelled from Invercargill to go to their new home for the first time. Six months earlier the men who built Mr Rees's house had brought a much smaller boat with them, but it was on a cart. There were four men and the wife of one of them who had sailed in that one. The men came back regularly to take building materials and other stuff up to the Rees's place. Eily drew breath.

'Lucky Mrs Rees,' she went on. 'Fancy coming to a house all finished! She's lovely, no side at all. They had stopped at our place overnight and after tea she even helped with the dishes. She is a lovely lady, even if she is rich. We had no kids then so we rode along with them to watch the boat being launched. We saw Mr Rees coax the bullocks on board, then the luggage, and finally the family got in. It was a very big boat. Dougal told me it was nearly thirty feet long. It took two men to push it out from the shore, and it had two masts and two big sails and even a little sail in front. We stayed and watched them get the sails up and kept on watching until it was well under way. It was that lovely. Now Mr Rees has got another boat. It's a big schooner called the *Lady of the Lake,* and it comes up and down the lake all the time with wool and gold to Kingston, then it takes flour and sugar and gold miners and stuff back to Queenstown. There are lots of other boats now, too.'

'They must be very rich,' Catherine commented.

'The Reeses have got thousands and thousands of sheep. Sheep used to be driven from Dunedin, up the Clutha River, through Central Otago and then up the Kawarau River to the Lake. I've never been that way but they say it's horrible. I don't think the Reeses have got that many cattle though. They drove a lot up past here, but they all died when they were being driven from Kingston round the side of the lake. They fell off a really nasty part of the track called the Devil's Staircase. I've just heard about this stuff from the men, but your George knows more about it than anybody.'

Before Catherine (who really wanted to know) could ask more about this, several more women, shepherds' wives from neighbouring stations, came in, and after they had been introduced they all started carrying food out to the big tables that the men had set up near where they were turning the spits. As well as the sheep, they had roasted rabbits and ducks. Catherine had exclaimed at the number of rabbits, saying that back in the old country you could be evicted for killing them, transported or even hanged. She had worried when George had trapped them all the way from Dunedin once they were on the road. This caused a great deal of amusement and started the men on a round of stories about the times they had nearly been caught poaching 'back home'. One shepherd remarked wryly that he had actually been caught and had come to New Zealand via Australia, so in a way it had probably been a good thing as he could never have got here otherwise. He said it had all been a mite uncomfortable and he lifted his shirt to show scars from the lash criss-crossing his back. 'And I was only a boy,' he said. 'If I'd been a man I wouldn't have been let off so "leniently".'

To Catherine it was the best meal she had ever eaten, but it was spoiled a bit when a very dirty Kitty arrived and said she had groomed all the horses as a Christmas present.

'For us? Thank you!' asked one of the men in surprise.

'No,' said Kitty, equally surprised. 'For the horses. It's my Christmas present for them. They probably won't get anything else.'

'Hang on a minute, Girly. They are all getting a bucket of chaff for Christmas dinner.' Before she could say anything more she was sent inside to clean up, and when she was clean, to help the women.

After the meal was over those families who had a distance to travel went on their merry way – the men were very merry, the women not so. A very reluctant Kitty was made to stay inside to help with the dishes. When she met the baby, Chrissie, who was eighteen months old, it was love at first sight. She was allowed to bath her, then she fed her and played with her, talking softly to her all the time. Catherine and Eily were astonished at how moderate her language was, and while she was reluctantly putting her to bed Eily commented, 'Aren't you lucky. She'll be such a help to you when yours is born. What a woman she'll be! Will there be anything she can't do?'

'I can't believe it!' said Catherine, equally flabbergasted. 'Wait until I tell George. He will be as surprised as I am. I still can't believe it.' When the men came in Kitty had finished reading to Chrissie and was now singing lullabies to her.

'Well,' said Eily laughing, 'one thing she can't do: she can't sing!' When George was told about Kitty's behaviour, he wasn't at all surprised.

'Kitty keeps telling you that we are all animals and you keep telling her she's wrong. She's just treating Chrissie like she would treat any other baby animal,' he said.

Both the women were horrified. 'Babies are different! People aren't animals! You treat babies differently. You dress them. You teach them stuff. You have to do everything for them. You don't have to teach animals to eat,' Catherine said.

Eily added: 'and you don't have to have your animals baptised. Where was Kitty baptised?'

'Just before we left the old country. I didn't know what we were coming to, and her godparents organised it for me.'

'Kitty treats every baby the way it should be treated. She treats a pup differently from a calf and a chicken differently from a duckling, so why not a human baby differently from any other sort of baby?'

Kitty came out announcing that Chrissie was asleep and then asked when they were getting their own baby. She was satisfied when George told her that it took as long as it took for a cow. She was pleased with that, and except for querying the difference in size between women and cows, she took his answer on board. She then commented that Toss would have her pups a lot sooner. She asked could they come next Christmas – they could bring their own baby. Chrissie wouldn't be a baby any more; she would give her one of Toss's pups for Christmas and Eily would have another baby and…

'Who told you about that?' Eily shrieked.

'Nobody told me. I could tell. You look just like Mama but a bit more round. It's easy to tell. But can we come next Christmas, please? This has been the best day of my whole life.'

Both women burst into tears and hugged Kitty who struggled to get away.

'I hope this means "yes" ' said Kitty as she stumped off to bed.

'What a character!' said Dougal, also wiping away tears, but tears of laughter. 'She's so right. This has been my best Christmas since I left the old country. First time that I've felt that we're among friends.' They all agreed, and after hugs and handshakes they went to bed.

Next day, when they were on the road with Kitty driving and Catherine walking with George, she seemed very quiet, almost withdrawn, so George asked what was on her mind.

'Well,' she answered 'I heard a lot I didn't understand and Eily told me lots of stuff that I didn't understand either. I didn't know that Mr Rees's place that you have always called "The Camp" is a real town called Queenstown with pubs and banks and shops and all that. One of the men said that Mr Rees had to give up his land. Eily said that getting there was very dangerous because we had to climb over a Devil's Staircase where cattle fell off into the lake.' She was crying now. 'I thought we were going to have our own farm, not go to a town full of nasty rough drunken miners, and she said miners are ruining all the good land, like we saw at Nokomai. She said that Kingston was rough and horrible and full of drunks. What else haven't you told me?'

George stopped and put his arms around her. 'I'm sorry

Sweetheart, but when you overhear people talking you only get parts of the story, and a lot of those parts are wrong. We don't have to go over the Devil's Staircase, and if we did, the track has been made safer since that accident. Anyhow, I'm sure Mr Rees will take us in one of his boats. He's got two big ones. I'm sorry if I haven't told you enough about where we're going, but we will have our own farm, you'll see. But I think there a few things that you haven't told me too, aren't there? We have to find time and a place to talk about things away from little Big-Ears. We need to know everything about each other, and I mean *everything* . Let's stop and have a cup of tea.' So they did. A cup of tea was the answer to everything – for now.

A few days later they arrived at Kingston. Those last days had been the hardest of all, especially for poor Bronze. Although there was a good road, which was well defined and well travelled, it passed through a series of steep dips between terminal moraines left by the glacier that had carved out Lake Wakatipu. The brake had to be kept on all the way down, and then after a little pause at the bottom, the cart had to be pulled up an equally steep hill to the top of the next one. Progress was slow, and there was not much for the animals to eat, except for Bronze. George had provided for him, but for the cattle the grazing was very sparse.

When they arrived at Kingston, they found it still a busy place, although the main gold rushes were over. As well as being the busy feeder port for Queenstown, it was the junction for the Nevis Valley, another gold mining area. It was very much as Eily had described it. While George went to find grazing for the stock and a good camp site away from the noisy pubs in town, Catherine and Kitty started putting their meal together. They were a bit overwhelmed by the lowering mountains, which Kitty thought were spooky.

While they were doing this they were approached by a large man who asked if these were Rees's cattle. Catherine replied that they were. He walked around them then said they were his now. Rees had sold them to him, but hadn't mentioned the Jerseys. He'd take them even though he had no use for them. They'd do for beef, but Rees needn't expect any more money for them. Catherine tried to tell him that they were her property, but he wouldn't listen. As usual she burst into tears, and Kitty became very belligerent. For the first time ever both dogs became aggressive and came to stand beside Kitty. The man became angry with her, swore at her and was about to bash her, in spite of her snarling dogs, when fortunately, George came back.

He told George his story. George, never a man to lose his temper, came close to it when he was told, among other things, that he had better learn to keep his women under control and to start right now with that (expletive) brat who needed a real good leathering. He said he was taking his cattle right now, all of them, and if the mongrels gave him trouble he'd shoot them. George heard him out then asked him calmly if he would show him the bill of sale. If it couldn't be produced, then they would have to wait until Mr Rees confirmed the sale. Until then George could not hand the cattle over, and they would be in the usual grazing where George and his family would be camped right beside them. If any sale had been arranged it certainly did not include the two Jerseys, which belonged to his wife. There was no bill of sale, and the bully blustered off when George finished by saying that if anything happened to his registered, pedigreed dogs, he would find out what trouble really was. In any case, George would be talking to his friend Sergeant Bracken as soon as he got to Queenstown.

'Now,' said George, 'Let's get sorted because after that I really need a good cup of tea.'

When they woke to a fine cloudless morning, Catherine and Kitty were blown away by the beauty of their surroundings. The mountains still loomed, but the bright spring sunlight made all the difference. There was a little snow on the tops and the Wakatipu was almost flat calm.

George was already up. He had the fire going and the billy boiling. To make the day even better, he had bought a loaf of fresh bread, some eggs and a billy of milk. Such luxury after days of beans! And now they were starting the day with eggs, bread and milk! When they asked George about yesterday's encounter he told them that no one knew anything about that man except that he had been hanging around for days trying to buy stock. He probably thought a woman would be easy to fool, but he didn't expect trouble from a mere child. There were comments that while there were plenty of stock thieves around, no one had ever heard of one as brazen as that. There was no sign of him that morning.

After breakfast when Kitty went to tend to the animals, George told Catherine that now was the time to get things sorted out. Unless a wind came up there was little chance of Mr Rees coming today, but when he arrived they would find out what had happened in Queenstown since George was there with his last drove about a year ago. George was quite sure his land would be secure, but there were some wild rumours flying around, and he wouldn't be completely happy until he had talked to Mr Rees himself. He hadn't yet told Catherine about the boat trip because he wanted to surprise her. He wanted her to realise what a life they would have in a place as beautiful as this.

He had told her his life story, of the small farm that had no place for a third son so that when he heard that free passages to New Zealand were available to working men of good character, he gathered references from his pastor, his old teacher and their landlord and was on the next available boat. Yes, he did leave behind a childhood sweetheart, but he was young and had no future in the old country and she said she would never leave home. He made no promises to come back. She came with his family to say goodbye and he left with hardly a backward glance. His mother, his sisters and his sweetheart cried, of course, but he was a young man with adventure in his heart, and his only other choice would have been to join the English army. Catherine knew all about his life in Dunedin, and now he wanted her to be equally honest with him. She said it was important to her that Kitty should never know about her family connections in Ireland and swore him to secrecy. She explained why Kitty was born out of wedlock; it was so that she could never make claims on the family. They weren't unkind; they were very generous to her, but they had to protect their heritage. She told him the sorry story of 'Jack Cameron', how they saved his life, got him out of the country and gave him a remittance. She told George about the money she had in the bank and that she thought it might be enough for them to start off mortgage-free, but they would talk about that later, after she had seen the land and after they had talked with Mr Rees.

Finally she told him what was really worrying her about Kitty. She was afraid that she might have inherited what she described as 'bad blood'. The tears flowed as she told him that most members of the family couldn't 'control themselves.' She struggled to find the words. She told him that the only ones who didn't 'make babies all over the place' were George and Padraig who managed to stick with the one woman. She told him about Jack Cameron, whose preference was for his own sex. Finally, when he said mildly that Jack was a man and many men were like that, she told him about Maggie who had run away at age fifteen and had ended up the owner of a house for women who made their living like that. When he asked her when she had learned all this, since she had been bundled away so quickly, she replied that before Jack left he broke down in tears of self-pity. He could not help himself. They shouldn't have treated him that way; they should have let him keep his title. One of his nephews would have inherited and he himself would still be enjoying the life he was born into and had every right to because he was the oldest son. As George took her in his arms to comfort her, Kitty came rushing up full of excitement

'Crying again! Stop, because there's a boat coming and they say it's Mr Rees's whale boat and it will be full of wool and gold and miners going somewhere else, and if there's nothing to go back on it and nothing else turns up it will fit all of us, but they aren't sure about the stock. Mr Rees will be coming tomorrow in the *Lady of the Lake,* so we'll just have to wait for him to get here to find out. We still have to take the cart to pieces, and if we can do we should be able to go tomorrow, and I can't find Surprise. So please come and help me look for her. She broke the fence but the others didn't bother getting out.' Finally she drew breath.

'Whoa,' laughed George. 'That's all good news. And I'm pretty sure I know where Surprise is. But first we have some fences to mend. Catherine, love, we'll take the cart down to the edge of the lake, then could you start taking things out of the cart? Nothing heavy, mind. When we get back with Surprise I can start taking the cart to bits, but before I do that I need to check up on all the news that Kitty brought us and find out for sure whether they can take us. I want some news about what's happening in Queenstown, too. Please stop worrying about the boat trip; there's nothing to be frightened of. It's quite beautiful and I know you'll enjoy it.'

Kitty had gathered up the fencing tools and a halter for Surprise and was impatiently waiting. Catherine said she hated Kingston; it was so rowdy. Kitty and George walked off together, Kitty still chattering about what she had seen and heard.

'I do wish Ma didn't cry so much,' Kitty commented. 'She cries when she's sad and sometimes when she's really, really happy. I just don't understand it. I only cry when an animal dies, except when it's one we're going to eat, and I cry when I get really, really angry, like when that man tried to take our animals. I'm glad I kicked his shins so hard when he grabbed me!'

'Kitty, your Ma had a horrible life when she was young and she got into the habit of crying. Even when things are going well, it's a hard habit for her to break. I'd like you to be a bit kinder to her. But now I want to talk about you. We are going to a place where nobody knows you, so I want you to think about how to behave and I want you to think before you speak. Remember that your mother is my wife and you'll soon have a baby brother. Try not to say anything out of place, and don't tell anybody anything about us except that we are going to have a dairy. If they ask about your father just look sad and say you don't remember him. Say he was a soldier and went to war when you were just a baby. After all, that's the truth.'

'Yes, Pa, you've told me that before. Several times. I just wish

Ma would tell me something about him. And how do you know the baby will be a boy? It might be a dear little girl just like me,' said Kitty with her cheekiest grin. George laughed and said, 'Heaven forbid!' He hugged her in a burst of love. It was the first time she had called him 'Pa'.

'I wish I could talk to Ma like I can talk to you. You treat me like a grown-up, and she treats me like a – I suppose she treats me like a daughter – like a little girl. She hasn't noticed that I'm a big girl. Everyone says I can do a man's work. I wish I was a boy.'

'Kitty, I wouldn't exchange you for all the boys in the world,' George said.

'And you're the best father a girl could have,' Kitty answered with a hug.

While George fixed the fence Kitty, bursting with impatience, kept pestering him about Surprise. He wouldn't tell her. He teased her by taking his time over the repair, asking her to pass the staples one by one. When he had finished the job to his satisfaction he led her off in a different direction from where she had been looking earlier. Then a short walk, another broken fence, and there was Surprise lying down placidly chewing her cud. In the paddock with her were two black and white cows and a black and white bull. Kitty called to her. Calmly she got up and strolled over, stepping gracefully through the downed fence.

'Got what you wanted then,' said Kitty, scratching between the little horns as she slipped the halter on. 'That's good isn't it, Pa.'

George, fixing the fence, nearly choked on the staples he held in his mouth when Kitty continued conversationally, 'I told you days ago that she was bulling but you couldn't have heard me. I didn't think she'd be able to do anything about it but she's a clever girl, isn't she? And a dairy bull, too. Ma will be pleased, won't she?'

George took the last of the staples from his mouth. 'You're the one that should be called "Surprise", Kitty. You never fail to surprise me. How do you know all these things?'

Now it was Kitty's turn to look surprised. 'Freddy told me to look, listen and learn, and that's what I do all the time. Sometimes people don't notice that I'm there, and you tell me lots when we're walking together, and if I ask questions, sometimes you forget that I asked, but I remember. It's just as well you got that fence fixed. The bull has just noticed that we're taking his girlfriend away. Surprise doesn't seem to care. I suppose that's because she got what she wanted.'

George said 'Yes, some women are like that.' They both laughed.

'I shouldn't have said that. Sometimes, Kitty, I forget you're still a child. I very likely say lots of things you shouldn't really hear. I know that your Ma thinks so. Don't tell her that I said that.'

'I can't be the sort of girl Ma wants me to be. I just can't. I can't help getting dirty. I want to be able to cook and mend things, and I can already milk, and I know nearly everything she knows about cows, even stuff she thinks I shouldn't, but why should I have to pretend I don't know? Is it just because I'm young? Sometimes she says I'll have to wait until I'm married. How silly is that?'

'Don't be in too much of a hurry to grow up, Kitty. Come on, the boat's just coming in and we can watch them unloading. If we can get away tomorrow we've a lot to do. I think it would be good to start by having a cup of tea while we tell your Ma about Surprise's little surprise. It would be a good idea if you took Bronze for a bit of a canter later on. He hasn't had much fun lately. Not too much though – the last few days have been very hard on him.'

Their days on the road were now over. Kitty would always look back on them as some of the happiest days of her life. She would remember the secret exit from Dunedin, the easy and the hard days on the road. She would remember that she had enjoyed the routine they kept and how they had worked so well as a team. Above all she treasured the way she and George had bonded and felt that after nearly eleven years of needing one, she had found a father. And he was always going to be there for her.

They watched as the whale boat came in and was unloaded, but when George asked about loading his stock, he was told that they wouldn't be able to take all of them in the whale boat. Anyhow, Rees would be coming later with one of his other boats, and he would sort it, and they wouldn't be leaving until tomorrow. Another night in Kingston didn't appeal to the Kirks, but they could do nothing until they spoke to Rees. Fortunately it wasn't long before another sail appeared in the distance. It would be an hour or so before it arrived, so what did they do? They put the billy on. Some of the boatmen joined them, because they felt that they had better not go to the pub before they had talked to Rees. He was a good boss for a Christian, they said. He knew that a working man needed a drink outside of working hours, but he couldn't abide drunkenness. If they weren't sailing until tomorrow they'd go to the pub after they had spoken to him. If they turned up worse for wear in the morning, they wouldn't have a job.

The boat arrived after several cups of tea, and it was the schooner. After George had had a long talk with Rees the men joined Catherine and Kitty at the fire and Rees accepted a cup of tea.

'We have a bit of a problem,' George said. 'Mr Rees thinks we can fit all the cattle in, but not Bronze. However, he has an interesting possible solution. I'll let him tell you.'

'There's a party of horsemen coming from the south, and they will be arriving late this evening. There are some young people among them on their first long ride. I think you know the Clawson boys, Kitty. George thought that perhaps you might like to ride along with them.'

'Yes!' shrieked Kitty.

'No!' shrieked Catherine.

'It seems we have a difference of opinion,' smiled Rees. 'Mrs Kirk, it will be perfectly safe. They won't be going fast, the track is good and the weather is good. I hope you'll change your mind.'

'No,' said Catherine. 'Kitty and I have never been parted since the day she was born. She is still only a child, and I have to know what she's up to. She'll stay with me until the day she is safely married.'

Kitty, furiously angry, appealed to George. 'I can work as hard as she does, and I have to. But as soon as she doesn't want me to do anything, she calls me a child. Pa, I really want to go.'

Rees interrupted 'I think I'd better leave you to it. I'd like to invite you all to join me for a meal at my hotel this evening at six. You can let me know your decision then. But one thing before I go: Mrs Clawson has taken her daughter for a long holiday in Christchurch, and it's likely that she wants the family to join her there. If they do, poor Charles will be looking for a manager. You might consider the position.'

'No,' moaned Catherine, 'Never. That woman…'

Rees laughed. 'I see you've met the delightful Mrs Clawson. I'll see you at six,' and as he walked away the family squabble continued.

'Kitty, you are not going on any silly ride. We need your help with the cows. Your place is with me, and that's the end of it. Horses aren't for dairymaids. Remember I'm your mother, and you always have to do what you're told.'

Before Kitty managed to reach full voice, George cut in. 'Stop right now, both of you. Hear me, stop. I won't put up with this nonsense. Kitty, go to the cart. Bring that big heavy canvas bag here. NOW! Jump to it!' The astonished Kitty went.

'Now Catherine, you stop that. You be quiet and listen to me for once. I've had enough of you two fighting. I've put up with it for too long, but enough is enough and I won't tolerate it any longer. You have to let Kitty grow up at her own pace and be her own person. Besides, I have never had my wife to myself and I think it's about time that I did. We have business to do about our land and with the bank in Queenstown, and I don't want you to be bothering about what Kitty's up to. So, not another word. She'll be perfectly all right, so for goodness' sake forget about her for the next few days. It will be good for the pair of you.'

Kitty came back lugging the bag. She angrily dumped it in front of George. When he told her to open it, she told him to open it himself.

'It's yours,' he said. 'If you don't want it you can take it back. It was to be your birthday present, but I think you will need it a bit sooner.' He handed her his knife. 'Don't damage the bag. You'll need that again, too.'

Kitty got the bag open. 'A saddle!' she gasped, 'a bridle! A saddle cloth and saddle bags – does this mean I can go?' She launched herself at him. 'You're the best father a girl could have.'

'There's a price. No more fighting. Both of you. Now, kiss and make up.' Very reluctantly, they did. George laughed. 'You're like prize-fighters shaking hands. Still, I suppose that's better than nothing. Kitty, we'll need you in the morning to get all the beasties loaded before you go, so you'll have to get up really early. Get your stuff packed in your saddle bags tonight. Now, let's get cleaned up. It's nearly six.' Still snivelling, Catherine did as she had been told.

Neither Catherine nor Kitty had ever eaten out before and although Catherine had been careful to teach Kitty the table manners she had learned from Maggie, they were overwhelmed by the linen tablecloth, the table napkins and the menu. George, understanding Catherine's problem, offered to order for her. Kitty wanted to order for herself, and with sparkling eyes she bombarded Rees with questions about the food and told him that she was used to just one knife, one fork, one spoon. George and Catherine tried to hide their embarrassment, but Rees was delighted with her and said he thought that was a very good idea. It would save a lot of washing up. After they had finished their meal and were leaving, he said he would be down early in the morning to supervise the loading. Catherine was happy that Rees had said Grace before they ate.

When they got back to the yards they discovered that the riding party was camped nearby, but all was silent. The horses were in an adjacent paddock.

In the morning they were all busy. Kitty fitted head-collars and lead-ropes on all the cattle, looped the ropes around their necks and led them down to the landing. Toss and Ted were in attendance. Rees was already there as were a number of men with stock whips. Kitty was horrified. 'You can't use them. You'll frighten them. Let me load them.'

'Get out of the way Girlie. We know what we are doing.'

'Please, Mr Rees. Let me do it. I'll put them in cross ties.'

Rees said, 'Let her try first, and if that doesn't work it's business as usual. I've never before seen cattle in halters.'

They stood back and watched in disbelief as Kitty called the cattle on one by one by name. She secured their cross ties as she loaded them closely together. Four of the Durhams went in the whale boat, and the Jerseys together with Nellie went in the schooner.

'This will give us a good story to tell at the pub, but no one will believe us,' said one of them.

'Hey, Girlie, do you want a job?' asked another.

'Careful, you'll have us all out of a job and all of us looking very silly.'

The riders waved them goodbye as the boats got under way. Then the riding party started off, and the Kirk family was on its way to a whole new life.

The Fourth Life
Wakatipu Basin 1867

Chapter Five

Queenstown was not at all what any of the Kirks expected. George's last visit had been more than two years ago when the town was still a shanty town dedicated to the needs of gold miners and prospectors. Now that the easy placer gold had largely been washed from the rivers and the gold in the steep and rocky streams was much harder to get, there were no more bonanzas, just a lot of hard work for little return. Now sluicing, dredging and mining were getting off the ground, and as these were corporate enterprises that needed elaborate machinery, money was needed to set them up.

It was 1867. A new era was beginning and it was time for a change. In Queenstown permanent buildings were largely replacing canvas and corrugated iron, and the town was rapidly becoming increasingly prosperous and increasingly respectable. A gold mining shanty town is no place for a family, so Rees had moved his to a station near Kawarau Falls. He had applied to freehold 80 acres of land before the gold was discovered in the Wakatipu basin and had been confident that this would be granted. The application was not heard by the Waste Lands Board until February 1863, and Rees was appalled to learn that the government had decided it would never sell the freehold of any land likely to be proved auriferous. His protesting that he had helped the miners in every possibly way when he could have ordered them off his land made absolutely no difference. Even worse, his pastoral lease of 100,000 acres was also cancelled. When he was awarded £10,000 compensation, which barely covered his expenditure let alone the loss of his run, he protested that no money could possibly compensate him for the loss of everything he had worked for, and for the loss of his future. They soon began to consider the property at Kawarau Falls, as a temporary measure, because it simply didn't feel like the home they had loved and it was too close to the place where his dream had begun. He continued to be a conspicuous figure in the district's public life, especially in sporting activities, and remained a respected member of the community until he left in 1867 to take up a position as manager at Galloway Station near Alexandra. Ironically, the government did very well out of Rees, recovering the compensation Rees had been paid in just one day when the town of Queenstown was surveyed and the sections were sold as freehold. Rees was never to own another station after he left the Wakatipu.

George was amazed at the number and variety of boats on the lake. When he commented on this, Rees laughed and told him that there were so many that the *Lake Wakatip Mail,* a bi-weekly newspaper first published in May 1863, ran advertisements and timetables. 'We could have got there earlier had we taken a steamer,' he said, 'but they're fiendishly expensive. Anyway we aren't in a hurry, are we? I'm not going to be able to stay here much longer now that I'm virtually landless. I'm only glad I'm able to help you get settled and to avoid some of the pitfalls around freeholding land. At the moment you can only lease with first right of freehold, and as you know, I secured that for you when you first saw it. I've made appointments with a lawyer and a banker in Queenstown tomorrow. We'll offload the cattle at Frankton today. You'll stay with us tonight and until the riding party arrives. Mrs Rees is expecting you.'

So far Catherine had been very quiet. George thought she was still sulking about his overruling her about Kitty. When she spoke it became plain that she had other things on her mind.

'Mr Rees, I don't understand "leasehold". Does that mean we could buy the land and lose it? Is that what happened to you? If we get "leasehold", could we end up with no money and no land? If that could happen we would be better to keep our money and go somewhere else.'

Rees was surprised. 'My word, Mrs Kirk, you're quite the businesswoman aren't you? When we go to the bank all will be made plain. I put in your deposit as soon as it was possible, and I assure you that you won't lose your land or your money. There is a new government plan coming into law fairly soon. It's called deferred payment. You can ask the lawyer all about it tomorrow.'

'Is it the Bank of New Zealand?' asked Catherine, 'Our money was transferred here from the Bank of New Zealand in Dunedin. And why do we need to see a lawyer? Don't they cost a lot of money?'

Before Rees could answer, George cut in: 'I can see you're surprised, Mr Rees. Before we were married Catherine set up our dairy business and managed all our finances. But the land we were using was leasehold, and when the lease ran out we were out. Then the lease on Catherine's cottage ran out. We realised that we were meant to be together for life, so I decided that it was time for me to come and claim my farm. Because Catherine is a born and bred dairy-woman it made sense for us to turn it into a dairy farm. Besides we already had the Jerseys and quite a bit of dairy equipment.'

'Mr Rees, there's one thing I've got to tell you, I can't read nor write, so George will have to sign everything for me. I've tried, but squiggles on paper just look all the same. I can make a cross but that's all. Please don't tell anybody.'

'I understand. A cousin of mine has word blindness too. Poor chap – they tried to beat it out of him at school. He is a brilliant cricketer so it doesn't really matter.'

By now they had turned into the Frankton Arm of the lake and soon pulled up at the Frankton wharf. They almost immediately started unloading. Catherine took charge of the cattle and led them to a holding pen, while George and the men unloaded their belongings. They had the cart assembled and partly loaded by the time the whale boat arrived with the rest of the stock. Once again Catherine took charge of the cattle. She was directed to a different pen where a handsome Durham bull was waiting with his new harem. Then she separated Nellie from the Jerseys and put her in with her own kind. Of course, she had to listen to some good-natured banter from the onlookers about leading cows around like dogs.

George, with help from Rees's men, had been able to get the cart reassembled and man-handled out of the way so that the Kirk's belongings could be stowed ready for the journey to their final destination. Then they joined Rees in his cart, which had been loaded with the goods that were to be transported to his home. Toss rode in the cart. Ted trotted behind. After the cart was unloaded and most of the goods were stored in a large shed, the rest were stowed into a large dory. They climbed in and then were rowed across the narrow strip of water to the homestead.

Mrs Rees and little Mary Rose greeted them at the door of a simple homestead, which was not nearly as large as Catherine and George had expected. Rees had told them that he was leaving the Wakatipu district as soon as he could find a suitable position. When George protested, Rees said that both he and his wife Frances were broken-hearted at losing all that they had worked for after they had enjoyed only two years of undisturbed paradise in a place they had believed to be theirs for life.

Mrs Rees said it was teatime, and she led them into the homely kitchen. Rees said Grace, then they enjoyed the meal, which was already laid out – cold meat and salad, fresh bread and a selection of pickles were followed by stewed fruit with custard and scones. Catherine was intrigued with the little cast iron stove on which a kettle was boiling and a teapot stood warming on the hob. When she exclaimed that she wanted one, George laughed and said that he had to build a house first and after that he had to get a barn built before the winter. One day, perhaps.

Had Kitty been there she would have been delighted with five-year-old Mary Rose because of the way she looked after Toss and Ted. She showed them to their kennels, chained them up and made them happy with a large shin bone each.

Catherine was charmed by Mrs Rees's friendliness, and after the dishes were done the women left the men to their pipes and Mrs Rees showed Catherine where she and George were to sleep: a bed in the lean-to for which she apologised, saying that it was all they could manage – they were not going to be there much longer. To Catherine it was luxury and she soon confided to her hostess that she was pregnant. After a lot of baby talk, and after Mary Rose had put herself to bed, they rejoined their men and listened to the story of the first flock of sheep that was brought to the Lake.

From the beginning George had been on that momentous drove in 1860 when Rees had been detained awaiting the arrival of his partner, Colonel Grant. It was a horrendous journey with many river crossings. In charge was Alfred Duncan, who had been one of the first white men to sight Lake Wakatipu and now worked for Rees as a cadet. Rees and his partner were able to join them just before the worst of it. On Christmas Day, 1860, they made their way across the mighty Kawarau just before its junction with the Clutha. Mrs Rees had heard the story many times before, but Catherine was horrified. Mother of God, what sort of country had she come to? Sheep being made to swim dangerous rivers? Three thousand sheep? Were there that many in the whole world? How did you teach them to swim? Her head was swimming, but her questions would have to wait. Now it was time for bed.

They had another early start in the morning, as they were to sail to Queenstown, calling at Frankton on the way to check on the cattle. The Kirks would camp at Frankton for the night as the riding party was due sometime in the afternoon and would also be camping at Frankton. Besides, Bronze would need a good night's rest before he pulled the heavy cart to Millers Flat.

Catherine was very nervous when she saw the little sailing dinghy pulled up on the beach in front of the house. 'Are we going in that?' she asked. 'It's so tiny!'

Rees laughed. 'It may be small, but it's the quickest way to get to Queenstown, and I so enjoy sailing it. Come on, hop in.'

'I'll just go and say goodbye to Mrs Rees. She's been so good to me, giving me baby clothes and that.' After a tearful farewell she fearfully got into the dinghy with the dogs, and the men pushed off.

'This is the life!' said George as the little boat sped along. Rees laughed. 'It will be a lot slower and a bit rougher coming back, unless the wind changes, I can tell you. We're lucky the lake's so calm, but as you know it can change very quickly. Don't worry, I've sailed this little thing in all weathers. George, do you remember that trip in the whale boat when she was a bit overloaded...?' And they were off reminiscing again while a miserable Catherine clung to the gunwale. After their initial unease the dogs looked as if they were thoroughly enjoying themselves.

They called in at Frankton to leave the dogs and throw some hay to the cattle, and then they were off again. By the time they got to Queenstown Catherine was much more relaxed but very happy to be on shore and much happier when they had completed their business at the bank. The bank manager, Mr Ross, had pointed out that it would be a good idea if they were to build their house before they paid the final payment on their land. He thought that, with good management, they should be able to do both, but they had to take into consideration the fact that it would be a while before they had an income. He also explained to Catherine why they needed a lawyer and gave them some papers to give him. Catherine was uncomfortable when she had to explain that she had to give George legal access to her money because they couldn't actually marry. If they had been married, of course, it would have been his. That didn't bother him in the least; it was all in the letter from Mr Burroughs, and their secret was safe with him. Catherine thought he was too young to be a bank manager but didn't say so. Rees was waiting for them when they had finished their business.

'Lunch time?' he asked.

'Our shout,' said George. Catherine looked wonderingly at George who quickly explained, 'We buy Mr Rees lunch as a little thank-you for all he has done for us. There aren't many employers like him.'

'Come on, George,' laughed Rees. 'I'd like to think that we are friends who have been through a lot together, and unfortunately for me, my station in life has recently changed for the worse while yours will change for the better. You'll have to do some very hard work to begin with, but you are good at that. I'm hungry, and thank you, I accept your offer of lunch now that you are the landowner and I am looking for employment.' Both men laughed and shook hands and then they went to lunch. Before they ate, Rees said Grace.

Before they started on their return journey, Rees walked them round the township and introduced them to various tradesmen and shop-keepers who would be part of the Kirks's future. He also introduced them to his lawyer, and they had a satisfactory meeting with him. They came away knowing that they would not lose their land. The next to be introduced was the Rev. Coffey, the vicar, who seemed to be more interested in George's cricketing ability than anything else. Only then did they start off back.

Catherine hated the little boat. She had been warned that the journey home would take longer than their outward trip but that didn't help at all. When they left Queenstown Bay, as they turned into the Frankton Arm, they felt the full force of the wind. Her fear overcame her. She gave up and started whimpering quietly as, white-knuckled, she gripped the gunwale with all her strength. Nothing either of the men said could comfort her as she prayed, and both of them were appalled when her prayers were addressed to 'Holy Mary, Mother of God.'

'I thought you were Anglican.' said Rees, sternly. He was a devout Christian and a lay-reader of his church.

'You know that I am and I certainly thought she was,' said George wretchedly. 'She showed me the lines from her first marriage, and she was married in an Anglican Church, so she must have been a baptised Anglican. Kitty was baptised in the same church, so I thought no more about it. Well, you wouldn't, would you?'

'No, you wouldn't. I would like to forget about this. I can only suggest you get it sorted as soon as you can. Of course there is a service every Sunday in Queenstown, but I hold a service in Frankton for those who can't get to Queenstown easily. In view of your wife's condition it would be a good idea if you were to attend at Frankton, but you still must get yourselves to Queenstown on the first Sunday of each month so that you can partake of Holy Communion. There is still a lot of ill feeling against Catholics everywhere in Otago, and it's very strong here. When you lived in Dunedin you must have been aware of this. There, the members of the Free Church of Scotland don't like the Church of England either, or any church but their own if it comes to that. They still have far too much influence right through Otago. I also think that you should never take your wife in a small boat again, or anywhere she might become afraid.'

George nodded. 'I'm so sorry, Mr Rees, I had no idea. It'll take me a while to get over it, but I'll make jolly sure that she understands there'll be no more papist nonsense. I'm right with you all the way on this, and I just hope she hasn't infected Kitty. It has to be stamped out right now.'

'Good. Now we'll forget that this conversation ever took place. And I hope I'll see both of you on Sunday?'

'Of course, all three of us will be there. And thank you for all you have done for us.' They were now at the Frankton wharf and pulled the dinghy up on to the stony beach. George helped a silent and troubled Catherine out of the dinghy. They could hear laughing and cheering from the riding party who were camped some distance away, so the three of them wandered across to see what was going on.

The people were standing around in a large ring watching a little boy riding a pony. There were some small jumps set up, and he cleared most of them but fell off at the last. He was roundly applauded. Then the jumps were quickly removed and a young man rode out. He bowed then threw a handkerchief on the ground. He rode around the ring a few times to pick up speed, then he leant from the saddle and retrieved his handkerchief. He acknowledged his applause with graceful waves and beaming smiles.

'Show off,' Catherine muttered, and then she gasped as Kitty entered riding bareback on a plump grey pony with its reins knotted loosely around its chubby neck. She cantered once around the ring, and then she stood up on the broad back and did one more circuit bowing to the applause. It was too much for Catherine. 'Kitty!' she screamed, "Get off that horse! Now!'

'Pa!' Kitty called, and as if they had rehearsed George stepped forward and caught her as she jumped straight into his arms. The applause was tumultuous as, hand in hand, they stepped forward and bowed. Catherine was furious. 'How could you make such fools of yourselves, showing off like that!'

'Catherine,' said George angrily 'You were the one who made a fool of yourself. We saved you embarrassment by making it look as if your outcry was part of the show.'

'George, you're angry with me. You just don't understand. Kitty's...'

'You're damn right I'm angry. I'm angry because I thought you had told me everything and now I find that you have kept something very important from me. It seems to me that there's still a lot I don't understand. But now is not the time and place to talk. Now stop snivelling and start smiling and act as if you are proud of your talented daughter.'

Kitty had wandered off to rejoin her friends but now returned leading Bronze. 'Is it all right if I camp with my mates tonight?' she asked.

'No,' said Catherine.

'Of course,' said George simultaneously 'Just take Bronze over to the yards. There's a feed waiting for him there. We'll be over in a minute, and you can take us to meet your new friends.'

Kitty had been gone barely a minute when she rushed back

crying "Where are the Durhams? I can't see them anywhere.'

Rees, who had seen and heard all this and had probably been wishing he was somewhere else, said, 'I'm sorry, Kitty, I no longer have the sort of land I need to run them. My dream of starting a stud is no longer possible. They will be very well treated by my friend who bought them. His wife, who was with him, was so taken by the fact that they were halter and lead-broken that she claimed them as hers. She so loved that they had names written on their halters that she gave me a whole guinea for the halters and told me to give it to you. She wants you to visit her sometime, if it can be arranged, so she can learn from you. She spent ages petting them and learning their names. Her husband is delighted because although she is a keen horsewoman, this is the first time she has ever taken an interest in the farm animals. And by the way, that was a great bit of riding. Had you and George practised?'

Kitty looked a little happier and said that no, they never had, but she knew that she could count on George. She just wished she had been able to say goodbye to the heifers. She thanked Rees for the money then went back to tend to Bronze.

George and Catherine walked back with Rees to the dinghy. George started to thank him for everything he had done for them, but he brushed it aside. 'I shan't see you tomorrow,' he said but Eddie will be here to help you. My cart will be here with some things I no longer need, and Eddie will come with you. He'll camp with you for a day or two to help you get started. You don't have to pay him, just feed him. Mrs Rees has packed enough food for you for a few days to help you get started. We'll see you on Sunday, won't we? Kitty's a great girl but I can't help thinking it's a shame she wasn't born a boy.'

I wish she was a boy, too, Catherine thought. *I just don't know how to make her into a proper woman.*

Chapter Six

In the morning they packed up their camp and were having an early breakfast with Eddie when Kitty joined them. The riding party had already left. She was in high spirits, but Catherine was not, because George was uncharacteristically short with her. They were soon on their way to Millers Flat.

For a while Kitty and Ted walked with the Jerseys, who had seemed pleased to see her, then she hopped up on Eddie's cart, which was pulled by a heavy dun called Tubby. Toss rode in the cart with George and Catherine. After an hour or so, George pulled to a stop.

'Here we are,' he said happily.

'Where's the farm?' asked a bewildered Catherine. 'Is this our land?'

'It certainly is' said George proudly. 'I've already told you, this is a new country and nobody else has ever lived on this beautiful land. We have eighty acres of it, and we'll make it into a farm you'll be proud of.'

Catherine burst into tears. 'It's not a farm. It's just empty land, and it's not even green,' she sobbed.

Eddie pulled up. 'Where do we camp?' he asked.

'Over by the creek where I've levelled off a house site. I did that as soon as I put down my deposit, and every time I've come here I've done a bit more and brought in a bit more corrugated iron and timber. It's been over a year since I was here, but there's no gold in this creek so I'm sure that no one will have taken it. It should all still be here. Let's walk over and check it out. Come on, girls.' Kitty told the dogs to watch the cows while she and an unhappy Catherine went with the men as they walked over to look at the site of their future home.

'What a great site,' said Eddie enthusiastically. 'It's sheltered, it's got water and of course a great view of the mountains all around. That big range over there is called the "Crosscuts", like the saw, but there's a fight going on over the name. Some people don't think it's pretty enough. Let's go and get the carts.'

'It's wonderful. I love it already, but where will we put the animals?' asked Kitty. 'The dogs can't be expected to watch them all night.'

'First some fencing, then we start on the house,' answered George.

'Hang on a minute, mate,' said Eddie, 'First we bring the stuff over here and…'

'Have a cup of tea,' they said in unison. And so they did.

Kitty unharnessed the horses, tethered them, brushed them and fed them, while the others started on the well-practised routine of setting up camp. Catherine, still surly, became more so when George said that tomorrow they would need to make it more permanent, and without basing it on the cart, which would, of course, be needed as transport.

Eddie decided that his first job was, with Kitty's help, to rig up some fencing for the cattle. There was fencing material on the Rees's cart, so they walked off to find a likely spot. The summer days were very long, and they didn't stop working until twilight. At teatime Kitty told them proudly that Eddie had let her hammer in staples and she had got quite good at it. She was happy that the cattle were secure. She said they had made a very big 'paddock' as Eddie had called it. It was big because they had just used trees and stapled the wire directly on to them. It ran down to the creek in one corner, so water wasn't going to be a problem. They would be able to stay out there for a long time. And even better, she had made a little hut for herself and the dogs out there so they could watch the over the cattle until they settled in. She had learnt to make her own sleeping place when she was on the ride, she said, explaining that that sort of sleeping shelter was called a 'bivvy'. She gathered up her bed-roll and asked if she could please have something to eat because she was tired and wanted to go to bed. She grabbed some bread and a piece of cheese, whistled up the dogs and left.

'What a great little worker your daughter is, but so full of questions! I told her that if the cattle were to be in there for any length of time she'd have to clean up after them, and she told me all about how you had carted manure from your dairy to your vegetable garden in Dunedin. So we established a place where it would be put,' He yawned. 'That's it for me. Goodnight. I'll be over early in the morning.'

As soon as he left, Catherine made ready to start on George, but he shut her up abruptly.

'Look,' he said, 'I know there is a lot to be talked about, but it's still not the time. I've a lot more thinking to do first. We'll go for a walk after breakfast and you'll answer all my questions, and I mean all. You're disappointed in our land, and I thought I had told you all about it. If I hadn't, I'm sorry. What we have to hold on to is that we love each other and we are together for better or worse for the rest of our lives, even if no parson or priest has waved his fairy wand over us. We have to hang on to that and work it out from there. Bed now, and after our walk we will get on with the unloading and sorting. Thanks to Mrs Rees we don't have to worry about food for a day or so.'

It was late in the day before they went for their walk, and George got straight down to business. 'Now, just listen please, Catherine, you must be honest with me. If we can't trust each other, who can we trust? You must have realised how shocked Mr Rees and I were when you came out with that Catholic stuff. You never told me that you had been a Catholic and it sounded as if you still are.'

Catherine was sobbing. 'I'm afraid for my immortal soul and for Kitty's if we can't go to confession. I'm afraid we'll burn in Hell when we die. When I got married they told me that being an Anglican was just the same except that Mass was said in English, but they lied. It's not the same at all, and I miss it so. And I worry for Kitty if she doesn't learn God's truths.'

George shook his head sadly and took her in his arms. 'I really don't know what to say except that your God's truths are not my God's truths. You can't carry on in this community and be a practising Catholic. I love you but I can't make you into an Anglican. I know that some vicars hear confession, but we have a very different idea of religion. I don't believe anyone should be frightened of God, and I think that anyone should be able to do what they like about their beliefs.

'Unfortunately, most other people don't think the same way. I'm sorry, my dear, you must make up your own mind about this. You must pretend to be Anglican or destroy our chance of living happily here. And *do not* infect Kitty with this. When my child is born he will be christened into the Anglican faith no matter what you think. And nothing will persuade me ever to go into a Catholic church. Let's just get on with our day and you can tell me tonight what you have decided. Sometime we have to talk about your attitude to Kitty and why you seem bent on driving her away from you. But no more talking. I seem to have done all the talking so next time it will have to be your turn.'

When they got back to camp Eddie and Kitty were having a cup of tea. 'We've had several very long days and there are more to come' said George. 'Come on, my dear, it's been specially hard for you so you'd better have an easy day. And thanks, Eddie, for all your help. But just watch Kitty – she's inclined to get bossy.'

Eddie and Kitty laughed. 'I already found that out and we got it sorted, didn't we, Kitty? She's going to teach me about animals and she can be as bossy as she likes. In return I will teach her about fencing and I can be as bossy as I like, and I'll make her into a good little hammer-hand.'

'Smart man,' said George, laughing. 'That sounds like a good way out. Come on, we'd best get to bed.'

The next morning Kitty arrived late for breakfast. 'Sorry,' she said. 'It took me a while to find the girls. I called them and called them but they were having such a good time. They were running around like calves. They've never been in such a big field, I mean "paddock", before.'

George smiled. 'So you like our farm, do you?'

'Of course I do. I love it and it's ours. It's just beautiful. The mountains are beautiful, and when we get the ground cleared up and some proper fences put in it will be perfect. Eddie showed me where we could grow hay and oats next year, and he knows where we can borrow a chaff cutter. Don't you think Eddie looks a bit like Freddy?'

'Kitty, stop talking and eat your breakfast. Then you can help me get our boxes sorted out. I'll need your help for most of the day.' Catherine was red-eyed and clearly unhappy.

'I thought I was needed to hold the measuring tape when you were marking out where the house was going to be,' Kitty said to George.

'I will,' he answered 'but first you can help your mother until we get the other cart unloaded so that we can see what Mr Rees has given us. We should have everything properly stacked by dinner time, and after dinner you can help us load up stones from the creek for the chimney. Your Ma is not very well and she needs an afternoon sleep, so you must use the mornings to help her. In the afternoons you can help me.'

'That's fine,' answered Kitty, 'but I need me-time to do my own work with the animals. Bronze will need extra feed when he's working, but the girls have enough grass until the frosts come. I need time to make the compost heap. Can we possibly get a wheelbarrow from somewhere? I want to bring the manure to where the vegetable garden is going to be.'

Catherine snapped. 'Kitty, you have to understand that when you grow up you'll be a woman, and you had better start behaving like one. And don't talk so much.'

Kitty laughed. 'You keep telling me I'm just a child because I'm only eleven, but now you tell me that I have to behave like a woman. What say I do women's work in the mornings and go back to being a child in the afternoons?'

Catherine was furious. 'Enough of your nonsense. You're a girl and one day you'll be a woman and until then you'll do as I say or feel the back of my hand.'

Kitty was about to answer back, but she saw George shake his head slightly so she turned away to start on the boxes. Catherine told her to clean up the breakfast things, and she did so without a word. She had labelled all the boxes and bundles with their contents before they left Dunedin.

'Would you like me to make some shelves to put things on?' she asked.

'That's men's work,' snapped Catherine. 'We need to open everything so that we can see where things are.'

'But I labelled them. I can read the labels out to you so you can see which ones we need now and which ones we don't need until the house is ready. Wouldn't that be easier?'

Reluctantly, Catherine conceded. So they started sorting the 'now' packages and putting aside the others. They worked well together and had almost finished the sorting when the men came back with a large flat stone on the cart. 'This is our hearthstone,' said George. 'Eddie and I have decided that the best thing to do first is to measure up for the house and build the fireplace so we can start using it right away. So we want our dinner right now, please. And we'll need Kitty's help this afternoon while you have your rest.'

The afternoon went well. The house was designed and measured up, two small rooms with a passage between them that ran from the front door and opened into a large kitchen, which would take up half the house. Eddie was a huge help. He proved to be a well-educated man with a knowledge of mathematics. He scratched a plan in the dirt. The basic three rooms could be built before the winter and allowed for future additions as the family grew. George was delighted that he had been prevented from making too many mistakes. The next step was to measure up the yard and plan for future outhouses so that everything would be organized from the very beginning. The first building to be built had to be the long-drop and they would start on it immediately.

Straight after they had eaten the men started digging. Kitty was sent with the cart to the creek to fill up every empty container they had with water and bring them up to the house. Then she had to unharness Tubby and let him go with the others. None of them would need a feed, so she had some time left to clean up the paddock.

When she got back it was nearly dark and the others had eaten. She dropped down beside the fire and grabbed her plate.

'The days are very long,' she said. 'I don't know what I want to do first: eat or sleep.'

'You wouldn't be so tired if you spent your time helping me' said Catherine.

'And we wouldn't have got as much done if we hadn't had Kitty. We'll finish the long drop tomorrow and we'll need Kitty's help with water. The next day is Sunday and it's a day of rest. We go to Frankton for the service and stay for a shared meal with the congregation. It's a good chance for us to meet people. We can't take anything for lunch this time, but we will next week.'

'Do I really have to come? I don't really feel like meeting people,' Catherine said plaintively.

'You know why you have to come,' said George firmly.

'I love meeting new people. Some of them can be such fun and some aren't, and I enjoy finding out who is who,' Kitty put in.

Eddie, who had been taking all this in now intervened. 'I know just how you feel, Mrs K,' he said. 'But in a place like this, sometimes you need other people and other people need you. You don't have to love your neighbours, but you do have to know who they are. When we have the walls up all the men will come to help put the roof on. No money changes hands, but there has to be food provided, and some of the wives will help you with that. And you will need help when your baby comes. It is hard coming in to a new place and the first time is the worst time. I know all about it myself, and it's best to get it over with. You really need to come or they'll start wondering why you aren't there. That would start them talking, and that's the very last thing you want. But goodnight, all. We've a lot of heavy digging to do tomorrow.'

'Thanks Eddie, for those words of wisdom,' George called to his departing back.

'He is like Freddy, isn't he?' remarked Kitty as she left for her bivvy.

Next day the new privy was finished by mid-afternoon. It was a very deep hole sheltered by a neat corrugated-iron shed whose wooden door had a crescent cut in it. Kitty was let off her 'women's work' early because there was a need for several loads of water to be brought up so they could scrub up for Sunday. She also needed time to tend to the animals and clean their paddock.

The next morning they were on their way bright and early, dressed in their best. The adults were very aware that their best wasn't very grand. Catherine had discovered that Kitty's dress was too short and too tight, but Kitty didn't seem bothered by it. She was more interested in whether any of her friends from the ride would be there, and she had groomed Bronze until he shone. He also boasted a beautifully plaited mane and tail. When George commented that Kitty had spent more time on getting the horse ready than she'd spent on herself, she laughed and said she'd noticed how long it had taken him to clean the cart.

Eddie had left early behind the plodding Tubby, who had also been groomed and plaited up. When a delighted Eddie had asked what time Kitty had got up, she looked surprised and said it had been at daylight, as usual. Eddie was going back to work for Mr Rees and wouldn't be seeing them for a few days. When George thanked him for all he had done to help, he just smiled and said, 'That's what neighbours do. I'll see you at the service,' and plodded off.

He was there to meet them when they arrived. He showed them where to leave the cart. After Kitty had tethered Bronze and put his nosebag on, she disappeared. George already knew quite a few men from his droving days. They called him a 'dark horse' because he had snared such a beautiful wife. As they gathered for the service, all the young people rejoined their families.

After the service, while the women and girls were carrying food outside to the tables, Mrs Rees introduced Catherine to the other women. They were very friendly and welcoming. When one of them asked if Catherine was carrying her first baby, another laughed and told her that Catherine was the mother of the famous Kitty. Catherine cringed, but another woman said that her little daughter had seen the circus act and said she wanted to grow up to be just like Kitty and it was very likely she'd do her best to do just that.

'That's her over there hanging 'round Kitty. She won't be talking about anything else for days, and it will be nag, nag, nag, "When are you going to get me my pony? Christmas is too far away and I just had my birthday. I can't wait much longer"'

The little girl came excitedly to her mother, pulling Kitty with her.

'Mummy, I'd like to introduce Miss Kitty Kirk. Kitty, I would like to introduce my mother, Mrs Jordan. Did I get that right Mummy? May I introduce Kitty to the other ladies?'

They laughed when Mrs Jordan said that Sarah had been practising her manners for weeks and Kitty was formally introduced all round. Then the whole congregation gathered together for the meal. Immediately after they had eaten, those who had come some distance said their goodbyes and left for home. Kitty had readied Bronze and came back excitedly, asking, 'Where's Eddie?'

'He's gone already. Did you want to say goodbye?' asked George.

'I wanted to thank him. There's a wheelbarrow and a piece of canvas in the cart.'

'That's great,' said George happily. 'You'll be able to get your chores done much more quickly now. A wheelbarrow will be great for firewood and I can always use canvas.'

'Wait a bit,' laughed Kitty. 'That canvas is mine. It's a proper roof for my bivvy, so hands off.'

'We're going to have to talk about this,' Catherine cut in. 'I don't like you sleeping away from us. It's not proper.'

'Well, I do. I really like having my wife to myself,' George smirked.

'I bet you do!' said Kitty.

'Stop it, you two! I hate it when you're talking rude!' said Catherine.

They both laughed and started planning the next day's work. George and Eddie had previously spent some time making a kōneke, a sort of rough sledge that would be easier to load and unload than the cart. It wouldn't carry as much as the cart but would be easier on Bronze. Kitty commented that Tubby would be perfect for the job of getting stones from the creek and it was a pity he wouldn't be there. George outlined Kitty's task for the day: taking the kōneke to the creek and loading it with all the stones that she could lift. When she got back he would help her unload. He would then stack them and sort them while she went back for more. Ted would just have to get his exercise following the koneke while Toss, who was very close to whelping, would stay with Catherine. It would be a long hard day. She reminded him that she hadn't done any of her own work today and had to clean up two days' manure. Now that she had the wheelbarrow she thought she could manage that before breakfast. Catherine reminded them that Kitty was supposed to help her in the morning. Kitty, for once, said nothing, but George pointed out that if they were to have a warm house for the winter, he would need all the help he could get. Catherine herself was not now able to help with the heavy work, but would she please spare Kitty so that she could help him? If Catherine herself felt all right, perhaps she could do a bit of the driving. George wanted a good selection of stones at the house site when Eddie came back.

By now they were back at the house site. Kitty realised that she couldn't easily take a hungry horse and a wheelbarrow back to the paddock at the same time, so George decided to help her. As he watched her, she asked, 'Pa, I know we aren't supposed to work on Sunday, but Bronze has to be brushed and fed, so is that work or not? Here, you do the other side.' And she tossed a brush to him.

'I think it's fine. If you only do what's necessary for his proper care, I'm sure God will approve. The manure and the bivvy had better wait until tomorrow.' As casually as he could, he asked, 'Has your Ma ever talked to you about God?'

'Oh, yes. She taught me to say my beads and how to say my prayers, and she told me that the Virgin Mary is the mother of Jesus who is the son of God, but that just doesn't make sense to me because I know that virgins can't have babies. Then she told me that girls have to stay virgins until they get married because their babies have to have fathers. When I said that none of that makes sense to me, she told me it's called a "mystery of faith" and you don't have to understand, you just have to believe. There's so much I can't understand about this religious stuff. Miss Brodie's church was different again. I've decided that I'm not going to think about it until I'm older.'

'Good idea. And just get that Mick stuff right out of your head if you can. You know how people go on about them here where we've chosen to live. I don't hold with judging people because of the church they go to, but I want to make my life and my family's as easy as possible, so I say as little as I can about religion. I do go to church on Sundays, because you can't live easily in a community without belonging to a church. I believe there is a God, but I usually don't think about Him except on Sundays.'

'I'll do the same. Thanks Pa. That makes it easier. But I'm still a bit afraid of hellfire.'

George was nonplussed and couldn't answer without a lot of thought, so he said, 'Don't be. I don't believe in it. If God loves people, He wouldn't hurt them like that, would He? Let's go back and have a cup of tea so you can say goodnight to Ma, then you can be off. We need an early night so we can be on the job early.'

The next day established their routine. Apart from organising meals there wasn't any 'women's work' to be done, so Kitty could start her day by tending the animals and cleaning up the paddock. The wheelbarrow had to be filled ready for George to wheel back later. He had dug a garden patch and started a compost heap. Kitty would then ride back to the house and harness Bronze to the cart to bring up the water.

While Kitty was attending to her chores George would collect the wood. If there was time before Kitty arrived he would work on the garden or on the fowl house. Then, and only then, would they all have breakfast together, and George would outline the jobs for the day.

The summer days were long and hot, and when dinner time came Bronze needed a break from hauling stones from the creek. After they had eaten, George, Kitty and Bronze enjoyed a rest. Kitty usually dropped off to sleep. Her work schedule was punishing for an eleven-year-old. Catherine sometimes did the driving, but she was starting to grow noticeably larger. George fussed around her, although she kept reminding him that she was only twenty-six and while it was George's first baby, it was her second, and she knew what she was doing.

They realised that she must have got pregnant a lot earlier than she thought, so luckily the baby would be born before the worst of the winter. George warned her that autumn would be colder than anything she had yet experienced, and he had to hurry to get a roof over their heads as soon as possible.

There was a small tragedy. Toss had just one pup and it was born dead. Kitty was remarkably sanguine about it. After shedding a few tears and organising a funeral, she commented that Toss was young and it was quite common for a bitch to lose her first litter and she would surely get in pup again fairly soon.

One Friday afternoon Eddie and Tubby plodded in with a loaded cart. Kitty had just come up from the creek with her usual load and said that Bronze had had enough for the day. Catherine was brewing tea while George unloaded the kōneke. Eddie unloaded the cart so that Kitty could take both horses to the paddock.

Tubby didn't need a feed, and Bronze had his head in his nosebag. When the unloading was done and the horses unharnessed, Eddie commented on the graded piles of stones on the site. They were sitting drinking their tea when he reminded them that Sunday was the first Sunday of the month and that they were all expected to go to church in Queenstown. Mr Rees took his whale boat from Frankton, so transport would not be a problem. Catherine paled. 'I won't go in a boat,' she wailed.

'You will,' said George firmly. 'Of course you will. It's a big boat, as big as the one we came in from Kingston. You know that we're expected to go and take Communion once a month, so we are going. All of us.'

'We don't have to go out of the Frankton Arm,' put in Eddie. 'The boat is pulled up on the beach on this side of the peninsula, and we walk over the hill. It's just a very short walk. Apart from attending worship, we've got to the stage where we need help here, and that's the place to find it. Not from the Lord, but from the congregation. We'll ask them to come. I've checked, there isn't a cricket match on that Saturday, so we'll get a good turnout. The vicar has been trying to find you, George. He's heard that you're a handy cricketer, so he's sure to turn out to your working bee. And the wives bring food.'

'Do we really have to do this?' asked Catherine miserably.

'Of course we do, if you want a house to live in,' snapped George. 'I'm not a stonemason or a builder. I don't know where to begin, so I'll have to learn. In this country friends and neighbours help each other. In time we'll be helping them.'

'I'm off to bed,' Eddie put in. 'We've a lot to do tomorrow, and we can't work on Sunday. I have to talk to the boss about whether I can help you next week. If not I'll be back as soon as I can. Poor Bronze looks as if needs a break.' He said his goodnights and wandered off.

'I could do with a bit of a break, too,' Kitty said yawning. 'I do look forward to Sundays. I'm making friends. The mothers here don't mind their kids talking to me. They all want to see our circus trick again, but I haven't got that sort of pony and wouldn't want a fat little thing like that.'

'Forget about ponies. You won't be getting one. Goodnight, Kitty. You can help me tomorrow. I've got a nice surprise for you,' said Catherine.

'I love surprises. Good night,' and off she went.

'What's the surprise?' asked George, himself surprised.

'I've made her a lovely new dress.'

'Oh,' said George. 'Time for bed.'

Not long after daybreak Eddie arrived while Kitty was attending to all her usual chores. When they all got together for breakfast, George and Eddie discussed their plans for the day. When Kitty asked when she should get the water, she was told that it was all done and that she was *really* having the day off, because the men would be bringing up big stones and there was really truly nothing she could do to help them. She started lining up minor chores like the garden, cutting kindling wood, putting finishing touches to the still-unfinished hen house and various other small time-consuming chores, when George told her firmly that she was to help Catherine because they were going to need a big dinner and a big tea. She could, however, prepare a good nosebag for Tubby. And she must do whatever Catherine instructed her to do. Without argument, he underlined firmly.

It wasn't until they had finished cleaning up and were having a cup of tea, peeling onions, potatoes and carrots while they did, that Kitty remembered. 'What about my surprise?' she asked. Catherine produced the dress she had made and fortunately didn't notice the expression on Kitty's face.

'Well, what do you think?' she asked.

Kitty had collected herself and, remembering George's words she said, 'Thanks Ma. You've gone to a lot of trouble, and it's very pretty. I suppose my old one was a bit tight.'

'Try it on and let me look at you.' So Kitty did just that.

'It's lovely, Ma, I really do like it,' she said, with her fingers crossed behind her back. She really did hate it. 'But isn't it a bit too loose in the top?'

Catherine braced herself. 'That's room for you to grow. I've noticed that your er–chest is starting to swell. You are starting to get a bosom.'

'What!' shrieked Kitty. 'Already! I'm not ready yet!'

'Of course you are. You're nearly twelve. That's normal. That's when girls usually start.'

'Start what?'

'Start becoming women. Now listen to me carefully. There's a lot more about women's problems that you're not going to like, but you're just going to have to put up with it like all women do.'

She was right, Kitty didn't like it. Strangely enough Catherine was enjoying herself. She hadn't had her daughter's full attention for a very long time.

'Why wasn't I born a boy!' Kitty moaned. 'I don't want to be a woman.'

'Being born a boy wasn't God's design for you. You can't stop growing into what you're meant to be, so it's time to stop fighting it.'

'Does Pa know all about this stuff?' Kitty asked, still hoping it was all a pack of lies.

'Of course he does. All married men do. Now have you any more questions before we get back to work?'

'Yes. Could you please make me something I can ride in?'

'Astride?'

'Of course. All the farm ladies ride astride except for at a show. It might be fun learning to ride sidesaddle one day when we can afford one and we can get the right horse, because I can't see Bronze in a sidesaddle.'

'Please, Kitty, try to be nicer to me. I'm only trying to teach you what you need to be a woman and to know your place. Knowing your place means knowing that you are a dairymaid not a horsewoman. Only fine ladies ride in shows, and you'll never be one of those unless you marry well, and you won't do that unless you're a proper woman.'

'Of course I won't "marry well". I'm not pretty enough. I'll be nice to you when you stop trying to make me stop doing things I really want to do, the things I'm really good at. And I am working hard to help get our farm going, aren't I?'

'I hate it when you show off. You're good at riding, but what good is that going to be for you? You have to stop showing off and making people look at you. It's not womanly.'

Kitty looked at her levelly. 'I think we'd better go back to getting dinner or we might start fighting again. Pa hates it when we fight. And what are those Kilkenny cats he keeps on talking about?'

Catherine smiled in spite of herself. 'You'd better ask him that. We'd better get on with dinner. I'm glad you like the dress.'

When the men arrived back up for dinner behind a sweating Tubby, it was mid-afternoon. They checked that there was enough water for the ritual Saturday clean-up, then George said that they were all done for the day, men and horse. There was a great pile of large stones for George to sort on Monday.

When dinner was over and the men were attending to their ablutions, Kitty took Tubby to the paddock. She no longer needed to lead him. She pushed the wheelbarrow and called him, and he followed her. Bronze came trotting up, no doubt pleased to see his old mate after a week of purely bovine company. They whinnied softly at each other, then Bronze stood quietly by while Kitty brushed Tubby. Then she took the wheelbarrow and cleaned the paddock. She needed time away from the others. She had a lot to think about.

When she got back the others had finished bathing and were sitting around relaxing. The men were smoking their pipes and Eddie had brought some beer, which they were enjoying, to Catherine's very obvious disapproval.

'Come on, Mrs K,' wheedled Eddie, trying to bring her round. 'After a hard week's work a man deserves a beer or two.'

'The drink makes men vicious. I know all about that,' answered Catherine angrily. 'I don't want to have it anywhere near my house. My own father…' She realised she had said more than she wanted to, so she shut her mouth into a tight line and was silent.

'Steady on, lass,' said George. 'This is my place too, and if I want a beer I'm jolly well going to have one. I won't be getting drunk, but if I want a beer or two, I reckon I'm entitled, so I'm afraid you're just going to have to get used to it.'

Eddie said, 'You are going to have to lay in a keg next week for your house-raising. It's the custom. I'll see to it for you, and I'll make sure we have a stonemason or two. I know a chap who hasn't got much work on at present, and I might be able to get him on Friday. He's a good worker, and he could teach us before the crowd is around. That way we could have the fireplace and chimney in before Saturday. You'd have to pay him for Friday, but it would be well worth it if you can afford it. He'd doss down for the night, and he'd expect his tucker as well.'

George looked at Catherine who said, 'We can afford it, but I hate the very thought of paying for the drink.'

'Sometimes we all have to do things we don't like, and if you want a house to live in before winter, you'll have to get used to the idea. Now, a cup of tea then bed. We have to be away early in the morning. And it's going to be a nice fine calm day.'

Chapter Seven

Sunday broke, a nice fine morning, and the mountains had never looked more breathtakingly beautiful. The 'Crosscuts' had recently been renamed the 'Remarkables', a name which pleased nearly everybody, although a few old residents preferred the old name, saying that the new name was too fancy, too long or too posh, and too hard to spell.

The Kirks, dressed in their Sunday best and with Kitty uncomfortable and self-conscious in her new dress, all climbed into their cart, and they were accompanied by Eddie, who had opted for a faster ride to Frankton. A small flotilla was leaving from Frankton, and the Kirks embarked with the Rees family while Eddie joined some of his mates. It was a windless day, the lake was calm and there was no drama from the tight-lipped Catherine.

On arriving at Queenstown the boats were pulled up on the south side of the peninsula, and everybody walked the short distance over the low brown hill to the small wooden church. Catherine was happy with the service. She was able to embrace the similarities with her own faith, and she tried to ignore the differences. George, who had been watching her very closely, was able to sit back, relax and take a short nap during the sermon.

After the service they gathered together outside on the vicarage lawn for a comfortable get-together and a bite to eat. While the men were organising the Kirks' working bee, the women talked to Catherine about the food. They quickly understood that she was embarrassed about being a complete newcomer to this sort of thing and took charge in a kindly way. Kitty was having to put up with being joshed by the kids about turning into a girl in a pretty dress.

Finally the vicar made an announcement. The church in Arrowtown would be consecrated on the third Sunday of the next month, so he hoped to see them all there. There were cheers from the members of the congregation who lived closer to Arrowtown than Queenstown, because it would make their Sundays so much easier. As the Kirks were leaving, the vicar laid a friendly hand on George's arm.

'Mr Kirk,' he said with a smile. 'Mr Rees says you're a fine bowler, and I need one badly. If I come to your working bee on Saturday, will you help us out the following week?'

A surprised George stuttered, "I'm sadly out of practice. I don't think I'd be much use."

'I thought you might say that. Here.' He handed George a cricket ball. "I'm sure you might be able to spare a few minutes in the next two weeks. I'm sure that you think I won't be much use to you at your working bee, but let's see if we can surprise each other.'

George laughed. 'Seeing you put it so nicely, I'm sure I can. Mind you work hard for me this Saturday though. I'll have my eye on you!' and they shook hands.

As they walked back to the boat, Catherine commented: 'I didn't know you were friends with the vicar.'

'I've only met him once before – you met him too. I told you that in a new country there are different ways. That's why you shouldn't be on at Kitty about knowing her place. Everyone here makes their own place.'

'I remember hearing Freddy tell Jack that in this country, Jack is as good as his master and often better, but I don't believe that.'

'Freddy always made a lot of sense.'

As they reached the boat a worried-looking Kitty, with little Sarah Jordan firmly attached to her, joined them.

'What's bothering my girl?' asked George.

'The kids are saying that we have to be confirmed and we have to go to classes and the girls have to wear *white* dresses! I've already got a dress and I don't want another one, specially a *white* one!'

Mrs Jordan, who had come to retrieve her daughter, laughed and said, 'Don't worry, Kitty, it's painless and I can lend you a Confirmation frock and veil. We have a family one, and it only gets trotted out every ten years or so.'

'But I don't know what it's all about,' wailed Kitty.

'Don't worry, there'll be classes. It won't happen for a few months, so there's plenty of time.'

'Oh, thank you so much, Mrs Jordan,' said a shiny-eyed Catherine. 'Kitty, say thank you to Mrs Jordan.'

'Thank you Mrs Jordan. I still wish I knew what I am letting myself in for.'

Mrs Jordan laughed. 'Your parents can tell you all about it, Kitty. They'll both have been confirmed. It's just a step towards being a grown-up. Come on, Sarah, let go of Kitty. You'll be with her all day on Saturday.'

Kitty was very quiet on the way home, while the usually quiet Catherine was comparatively chatty. Once they had said goodbye at Frankton and were all in the cart, Kitty burst out, 'What's a veil?'

When Catherine explained, Kitty groaned. 'It just gets worse and worse and worse. White dress, veil, and I still don't know why I have to do this.'

'It'll be that lovely, Kitty, all the girls will be in white dresses and veils, and the boys will be in their best clothes and so will all the parents and the Bishop…'

'What's a bishop?" asked Kitty who was getting more bothered by the minute, and why are you laughing your silly face off, Eddie?'

'That's enough, Kitty," said George firmly. 'There's no need to be rude. Leave it for now. I'll explain it tomorrow, and you can ask me all the questions you want to ask then. Don't bother Ma, she has other things to think about. Now we're home. Go and deal with the horse and we'll have a nice cup of tea while we talk about what we're all going to do tomorrow.'

'Change out of that dress first, and hang it up' ordered Catherine.

When George and Catherine were alone he asked her why she was suddenly so happy. She said it was because she had just learned that the Church of England was a real church after all, with a Bishop and Confirmation and that. George then explained that there were a lot of differences and she still had to be careful that she didn't make any mistakes. Then he said he wanted to go to sleep because he was sick to death of talking.

The next morning Kitty attended to all her chores as usual and arrived for breakfast, with Tubby pulling the kōneke loaded with two days' manure. They were well organised and worked as a team. Kitty didn't complain about working with Catherine, and Catherine didn't complain when George wanted Kitty to help the men. Eddie had been 'lent' to George for the week so that the working bee could accomplish as much as possible. George laughed when Eddie said he was sure the vicar would be a huge help. Later, the two men were amazed at how brawny the vicar was when out of his clerical vestments and at how strong he actually was. They agreed that it must be all that cricket.

Catherine wanted a well dug, but it was explained to her that it was impossible because they had dug a very deep long-drop without striking water. Kitty wanted some fencing because the paddock, large as it was, was getting badly over grazed. George promised that next Monday, after they had finished cleaning up after the working bee, he and she would walk over their whole property then sit down at home and plan where everything was going to go, including the barn and the dairy. The barn had to be first because Surprise wouldn't be calving until spring and they had to be able to store winter feed. Catherine could think about everything she wanted for the dairy, and in the long winter nights she could tell

Kitty so she could write it all down. She said that with only one cow in milk she would be happy to tie her up in the garden near the house. It would be nice and handy, and she could have the baby with her while she milked. Surprise didn't really need tying up, but she had to think about her cabbages because, doubtless, Surprise would be thinking about them too.

One morning George asked Kitty to harness Bronze to their cart, and he asked Catherine if he could borrow Kitty for the morning as he needed to go to Arrowtown. He would help Catherine make a list of things she wanted from the shops and Kitty could attend to it. Eddie said he would be busy finding a good place to put the spit to cook the sheep on Saturday.

When Kitty and George were finally in the cart, she turned to him and said, 'Now talk. Explain why I have to go through all this white dress and veil sh— stuff. This is the third sort of religion I've had pushed at me and it's all mixed up in my brain, so talk.'

'Well, I know it's hard for you to understand, but here goes. Reason one: you'll break your Ma's heart if you don't and we don't want to live with that, do we?

'Reason two: wherever you live you are expected to belong to a church, so it's easier to go along with it and the Church of England has a more kindly attitude than most. Being confirmed makes you a communicant member of that congregation and means you are eligible to take Communion.'

'Yuk. That wine stuff. Why can Ma take communion? Do you have to do this once you're confirmed?'

'Yes, if you possibly can, at least once a month. Your Ma was confirmed into the Catholic Church, and the rules about Confirmation are near enough to ours, so we decided just to keep quiet about it. The Anglican Church isn't such a bad bet, Kitty. It doesn't preach hellfire and damnation like the Catholics and the "Wee Frees". Please just go along with it. It's a bit ridiculous, I know, but it's only one day out of your life, and seeing that you're being lent the dress, you'll never have to wear it again, so please, for the sake of peace, grit your teeth and get on with it.'

'Oh, all right. And you'd better practise your cricket, or you might get kicked out.'

George laughed. 'That won't happen. It's a bit harder to get out than to get in. Eddie and I will be having a go after work, and you can play too. Women play cricket, too, you know.'

'Great. Life just got a whole lot better.'

After they had finished their shopping and a corrugated iron tank was loaded on to the cart, George told Kitty that they were going to have dinner with the Jordans shortly after they left Arrowtown. Kitty was, of course, delighted. While George had been buying the tank and its bits and pieces of plumbing she had learnt her way around the township and was surprised to see so many friendly faces. Later when she commented on this to Catherine, George told her that this was one of the benefits of being a member of a congregation. Dinner with the Jordans! What an unexpected treat! With a twinkle in his eye, George told her that there might be an even bigger surprise to come.

'I don't need an even bigger treat,' she sighed happily. 'The day's absolutely perfect, and Bronze's huge load is awkward but light. He'll be able to be turned out while we are at Jordan's, won't he?'

George smiled. *Typical Kitty*, he thought, *Always thinking of her animals first.*

When they arrived at the Jordan's, as soon as Kitty started to unharness Bronze, Sarah was on his back asking if she could ride him to the paddock. Kitty laughed and told her she could, it would be quicker having her on Bronze's broad back than on Kitty's own.

'Have you asked her yet?' Sarah was obviously in a state of high excitement.

'Asked me what?' wondered Kitty.

'Wait until we get there' Colin Jordan said. 'Sarah, be quiet for once in your little life. It will make the surprise even better. We need to let Bronze go, first.'

'Can I stand up on his back?' Sarah asked Kitty.

'Not yet, Chicken. You aren't ready. You need to be a good bit bigger first. Little birds have to learn to walk before they fly. Don't worry, I'll tell you when you can.'

When they arrived at a shady grassy yard and a happy Bronze was having a roll, Kitty turned her attention to the next yard. An attractive grey pony was watching them warily.

'Is that an Arab? He's really, really beautiful.' asked Kitty. 'I've read about them and seen pictures of them but never actually seen one.'

'He's half,' squealed Sarah 'He's mine and he's called Rascal because he's not nice yet and Mummy and Daddy think you can fix him.'

'What's wrong with him?'

'Just about everything,' said Colin Jordan. 'He's impossible to catch unless you corner him, and then you have to watch his feet and his teeth. He's been lent to Sarah until she's too big for him because the owner, my pesky brother, gave up on him. There's nobody light enough to ride him. Albert was sneaky and showed him to Sarah before he showed him to me. He is a great horseman and had this idea of dealing in children's ponies but he came a gutser on this one. It was sold to him as broken in, cheap because it had a few faults. A *few* faults – I think he's got the whole lot. I'd have told him what to do with it in no uncertain terms, but my women ganged up on me, both Daisy and Sarah.'

'You can't get rid of him. He's mine and I'll cry and cry if you talk about it anymore. Mummy said we should ask Kitty to have a go at him and see what she can do. Please say "Yes", Kitty. Please say "Yes". '

'There's money in it for you, Kitty, if you can pull it off,' Colin said. 'My brother offered to pay a sizeable amount if you can turn that beast into a show pony, or even a school pony. Daisy is convinced that you can. I talked to George before I asked you, and he said it was your decision. So, what about it?'

Kitty looked squarely at George. 'Did you talk about it with Ma?'

George turned an interesting shade of red. 'I didn't think so,' she laughed. 'What say I try to get a halter onto him and if I can, you can tie him to the back of the buggy and bring him over

113

on Saturday. If I can't we'll have time to work out something. I won't do it unless I'm sure he won't hurt a kiddie. And it gives Pa time to try to sort it out with Ma. And if you can't, Pa, I'll drop you further in it by saying that it was all your idea. Now where's that halter and no, Sarah, you can't come and watch. I have to be alone with him in silence and silence is something you just can't manage. And please stop that racket. I need to concentrate.'

In a little over half an hour she arrived ready for dinner. 'He's tied to the gate. I gave him two handfuls of feed. Mrs Jordan, could you please be the one who unties him. Go on your own. Stop it, Sarah, if you won't do it my way, I'll walk away right now, you understand?

'Now, where were we? Before you untie him, give him another handful in the bucket I used. Leave the halter on and slip the snib through the rails. That way you'll keep all your fingers. And please go to the yard as often as you can and offer him more feed. And always on your own and always from the same bucket. Understand, Sarah?'

'I hate it when people are bossy with me. Mummy, please can you make Kitty stop being bossy?'

'Listen, Chicken, if I can't be bossy there's no way I can teach you to ride, so get used to it and get used to doing what you are told or there won't be any riding lessons, okay?'

Colin Jordan laughed. 'That's telling you, Miss Sarah. Perhaps Kitty would like to live at our place as your governess! Now, I'm sure Kitty must be absolutely starving. And I need a—'

'Nice cup of tea,' came in the chorus, right on cue.

After dinner, when the Kirks had started on the short journey home, Kitty, who had been very quiet, suddenly asked George: 'What happens if I earn money? Is it mine or is it Ma's? She keeps asking me for the guinea I got for the halters, but I want to keep it so that I can buy leather to make some more. She says that everything a child has belongs to their parents.'

'It's yours,' George answered.

'And if I make more? Is that mine as well? Or do I have to hand it over to Ma?'

'We'll have to see about getting you a bank account. I don't want to make Catherine cross at this stage, but I can't always agree with her. I guess that legally she's right, but I don't agree. I don't want to go behind her back, because she accuses me of always siding with you. And then she cries. You know how badly I handle that.'

'Poor Pa. I looked to see if there is a bank in Arrowtown, but there's only a branch and it's only open on Wednesdays. And you'll have to come too, because of my age. I just hope that when the baby comes, Ma will leave me alone a bit, but she's already telling me what I'm going to have to do to look after it.'

'Kitty, you're only eleven, but you have a very adult head on you. I can't make you out sometimes. I often wonder if you've ever been a child!'

'Pa, I'm very nearly twelve, and more and more I have to think for myself. I don't like going behind Ma's back either. If I didn't have you I think I'd go mad. While Ma is too heavy to go to Queenstown, you could find a reason for us to go, and I can get a bank account. Then if I make any money, I can go to Arrowtown on a Wednesday. That's if I can break in Sarah's pony.'

'Do you think you can manage to do that?'

'I'm pretty sure I can. I think Mr Jordan's brother is playing tricks. That pony has never had a bit in its mouth and I think, just think, mind you, that he might have made it man-shy. When Surprise calves I want you with me when I handle the calf because no animal should be afraid of a man just because he is a man, not if both are trained properly.'

Both were laughing when they pulled into their yard and saw what a great job Eddie had done while they were away.

'I've just finished. Let's get the tank off, then there's just one thing I want and that's a—'

'Yes,' interrupted George, 'So do we!'

'Ma, I had a lovely day. I finished your shopping and did what you said. I went to all the shops and got the best bargains. I think you will be pleased with me. And then we went and had dinner at Sarah's—'

'Why on earth would you do that?'

'Because that's what people here do,' said George, shortly. 'They have meals at friends' houses. It's always been like that, and I enjoy it. It's called hospitality. Everyone eats with their friends at each other's houses.'

'Mr Jordan asked me to break in a pony for Sarah.'

'What! I hope you told him that you didn't have time for that sort of thing.'

'I'd better go and put Bronze away,' said Kitty.

For the next two days the sorting and stacking continued. The tank was sitting on a temporary stand, and Kitty had to spend every minute she could spare from her usual chores to bring water from the creek.

While George and Kitty had been in Arrowtown, Eddie had arranged what he called the 'kitchen and dining room' on a flat, shady area near the creek where he had benches and seats up, and he had even made a large enclosure to be a playpen for the small children. There was a temporary corral for the horses.

When he proudly showed his handiwork to the family, each one of them was amazed.

'Great work, Eddie,' said George. 'No wonder you wanted us out of the way!'

'Where did all this stuff come from?' asked Catherine.

'Can we keep it like this?' Kitty's eyes were shining. 'It's so lovely, Eddie. You've thought of everything!'

'I had help.' Eddie laughed. 'This stuff goes to all the working bees. It goes back to its various homes over the next week. The keg is already cooling in the creek and the mutton is hanging from a tree in the shade. I'm surprised you didn't hear all the comings and goings, Mrs K. We didn't come past the camp, but we did make a fair bit of noise.'

'Well, the vicar came on his fancy horse. He wanted to know if the working bee was still on, and he wanted to know if you had been practising cricket. Then he asked for a cup of tea, so I made him one. I was that embarrassed.'

'Oh, Catherine, my Catherine. Whenever anybody calls in, anybody at all, the very first thing you do after shaking hands is to offer them a cup of tea. There's no need to be embarrassed at the vicar coming. Part of his job is to visit on everybody in his parish.'

'But he's a toff. I didn't know how to talk to him. He did hold out his hand but I didn't shake it. I do everything wrong, don't I? I was brought up to know my place, and here I don't seem to have a place, so how can I teach Kitty?'

Eddie laughed. 'It's toffs that don't have a place here, Mrs K. I mean the idea that someone is a toff. People are judged by how well they fit into the community. Because we are all good at different things, we all need each other. How long it will last like this I don't know, but let's just enjoy it while we can. Don't worry about Kitty. She will make her own place.'

'My word, Eddie. You're quite the philosopher, aren't you? I think you went to a pretty posh school and might have been brought up to be a bit of a toff yourself. Were you?' asked George.

'You could say that, but don't hold it against me. I didn't learn anything that was of any use to me until I got here. I've tried hard to live it down. Anyway,' he laughed, 'you know you aren't supposed to ask those sort of questions.'

'Why did you come here?' asked Kitty who had come back from tending to the horse.

'If you want me to tell you, you'll have to pour me another cup of tea. Thank you. Well, I had an uncle who was a bad boy. I don't quite know what he did, but he kept being a nuisance to the family. I do know he kept running away from school and he wouldn't go to university and he wouldn't marry who he was supposed to. They gave up on him and sent him to the "colonies" and they paid him to stay out of England. I don't know where he went or what became of him.'

'I do!' shrieked Kitty. 'His name is Freddy and he lives in Dunedin. The first time I saw you I said you were like Freddy. Not so much how you look but the way you talk and the things you talk about. The way you move, too.'

Eddie hugged her. 'My God! Really, I can't believe it! He *is* called Frederick. Thank you, thank you, Kitty. You're a little wonder. I didn't have any idea where to start looking. Now I'm off to Dunedin next week to try to find my long lost uncle that I've never met.'

'You won't have to look too far.' Kitty looked guiltily at Catherine. 'I wrote his address in one of the books he gave me. I was going to write to him when I found a post office, and there's one in Arrowtown so...'

'So you write your letter, and I'll take it to him. What a surprise that will be for Uncle Freddy! What's the book that he gave you?'

'You won't believe it, but it's *Great Expectations*! He said that there were some others that he was keeping for me. A whole boxful.'

Until bedtime they sat round the fire telling a delighted Eddie stories about Freddy. He was happiest when he heard that Freddy had given Kitty her dogs. Catherine recounted Freddy's numerous acts of kindness and assistance when she was a woman on her own. Kitty said she couldn't remember a time without Freddy. She always thought of him as a member of her family. He'd always talked to her as if she were an adult. She missed him and that's why she had planned to write to him. Having found a post office, she had already started to write her letter.

'Perfect,' said Eddie, 'and I didn't believe in coincidence!'

'What are coincidents?' asked Catherine. 'And you know I don't hold with sitting around reading books when you can be doing something useful. One thing Kitty doesn't need is any more books. I didn't even know you had one,' she said accusingly.

Nobody commented on this. George started telling them about his boyhood and long winter nights when his family sat around the fire, the boys taking it in turns to read while his mother and sisters did the mending. He would like to be able to do that with his own family one day. He explained 'coincidence' and then announced it was bedtime.

Chapter Eight

The morning of the working bee was fine and hot, and a very excited Kitty arrived for breakfast to announce that Toss had had her pups.

'Please don't tell anybody,' she asked. 'I don't want people, specially kids, going over and disturbing her. I want a bowl of porridge for her, then we'll all leave her alone. If I can get loose from Sarah, I'll sneak over and have a look at dinner time. There are five of them, and they are suckling, so I'm pretty sure there'll be no problems. And, before you ask, I haven't picked them up.'

To Eddie, who was taking a break from his cooking duties, she said, 'I don't how many boys there are, but one of the boys is yours, Eddie. Shall we call him Fred? No, I didn't think so.'

The work on the house started when the workers began to arrive and it was fully under way by seven o'clock, so a good start was made before the heat of the day. Some of the women arrived early and showed Catherine how to make oatmeal water. They all brought jugs with them, and these had to be kept filled and within reach of the thirsty men. After Kitty had unharnessed all the horses and hitched them in their shady corral, she was constantly on the run, carrying jugs of water or bringing water from the creek. She began to think that the whole world revolved around water, and her next thought was, of course it did, she just hadn't had to think about it before.

The Jordans arrived late, with an angry Rascal tied to the back of the buggy. Colin Jordan apologised when he joined the workers, but not before he muttered to Kitty, 'Look out for the little bast's – oops, sorry Kitty – look out for the wee darling's heels.'

Daisy Jordan unharnessed their horse and led him to the corral with an indignant Sarah on his back. She wanted to be with Kitty, who was sitting on the back of the buggy, talking quietly to Rascal.

'Sarah, I don't want you anywhere near him, or near me while I'm working with him, not until I can tell you he's safe. I have to put him somewhere well away from people. I don't have time to do anything else with him today, but later on you can help me get water from the creek.'

'Can I?' She looked at her mother. 'I mean, *may* I drive?'

If you are a good girl and don't annoy people. Now go away and leave me with your pony'

A disgruntled Sarah had the last word. 'You should at least say please,' she said. Daisy grabbed her daughter very firmly by the hand. 'That's quite enough, Sarah.' To Kitty she said, 'I think you're right about him being "man-shy". Colin can't get near him without drama – from both of them, I might add. And I think the wee beast was a bit put out when I caught him this morning. I just did exactly what you said. I want to talk to you about giving me some ground lessons.'

Kitty laughed. 'If you teach me about show riding and sidesaddle and all that stuff… but not now – I'll get shot if they start running out of water.'

The day was going very well. Catherine was learning to become part of a group of women, in spite of her earlier worries and her ingrown belief that she had to 'know her place'. The friendliness that was being shown to her by other women was instilling into her the beginnings of a sense that perhaps she did actually belong somewhere, that she was part of this community; and the friendship shown to her by the vicar and other men that she had thought of as 'High-Ups', and the way the working men ribbed them for their lack of ability and pretended clumsiness with tools left her more than a little confused.

The midday meal break went well. Eddie had cooked the mutton to perfection and proved he had great skill with the carving knife as well. The Rees family arrived at dinner time, apologising for being late and explaining that they had nearly finished packing and would need Eddie and Tubby on Monday. Eddie said that he was sorry, he had an urgent errand in Dunedin and was leaving on Sunday after church. Then he told the story of his long lost uncle and his connection to the Kirk family. However, he would leave his rig with the Reeses after church, and they could provide their own driver.

Now the vicar pretended to become very angry. He expected them both to be there on Saturday for his all-important cricket match, and knowing very well that Eddie wouldn't be there, threatened to excommunicate him. Eddie said that would be great, he wouldn't have to go to church anymore and could stay in bed all day. Catherine was visibly upset at this, and when it was explained to her that it was a joke, she muttered that that it was a very poor sort of joke. The vicar produced a spotless, large white handkerchief with which he dried her tears and said he was sorry, he didn't realise that church meant so much to her. She was left with very mixed feelings and wondering what queer sort of church she now belonged to. Was she now a heretic? Was there anyone she could ask?

She became more confused when Eddie said that George was a better bowler than he was and what's more he would lend George his whites. Everyone burst out laughing at the thought of stocky, broad-shouldered George in the tall, slender Eddie's gear. Poor Catherine hadn't the slightest idea what they were talking, much less laughing, about.

George told Mr Rees that he wanted him to be there for what might be his last cricket match in the Wakatipu district. In fact, he so much wanted to see him there that he was prepared to bribe him by asking him and Mrs Rees to be godparents to his forthcoming baby.

There were hoots of laughter at this, especially when Rees said that they would be honoured, but if the baby was a girl he wouldn't want her to be called 'Williamina'. There was more laughter when Mary Rose Rees asked if she could please be godsister and would that make her Kitty's godsister, too? Kitty, who had been promised that she could name the baby and had already been calling it Billy, said that she thought 'Frances', was a very nice name, but that 'Mary Rose' was even nicer. Mary Rose clapped her hands and Mrs Rees said that she had never liked the name 'Frances' but of course she thought that 'Mary Rose' was a lovely name. And they would be back for the christening if they possibly could. They were sorry that they had to go home so soon, but they had so much to do before they left. They would see everybody at church tomorrow. They would, except for the Presbyterians, who had another destination on Sundays. Working bees were interdenominational. Sometimes, they said, even the odd Mick turned up.

Two of the men, who happened to be Catholics, laughed at this and asked if they should go home. They were told they could stay until the very end when the keg ran dry if they really, really wanted to.

The dinner break was now over and everyone got back to work. The fireplace and the thick stone walls had been built, and the keg had been set in place but not yet broached. The remains of the meal were sorted and organised so they could be eaten when the men knocked off. When Catherine asked what 'knocked off' meant, the women were happy to explain it to her. She began to realise that there was a big difference between being 'laughed at' and being 'laughed with'. Life started to be a lot easier, and she was able to begin to make friends.

The women with smaller children had packed up their plates

and other belongings and had already arranged shared transport to get home. When Catherine commented on how well-organised everything was, they laughed.

'We do this so often,' one of them explained to her. 'You'll be part of it once your baby comes and your kitchen is in order. Don't worry about it. Everybody does what they do best.'

Another woman laughed. 'I'm a dreadful cook so that's why I'm always the queen of the dishes.'

'Only the washing-up. Betsy does the drying and Susan has a fantastic memory, so she sorts out everything into piles ready for the owners to take home. All those laundry baskets with labels on them. That's Susan's job.'

'I can't read nor write but I make the best sponge cakes because my hens lay the very best eggs in the whole Wakatipu Basin.'

'And, Flo, you are the biggest skite, too. And have the strongest kids and the whitest sheets and do the fanciest knitting, and you're the best dancer. We know all this because you keep telling us.'

Catherine joined the laughter without quite knowing why but feeling a whole lot better. 'I can't read nor write either,' she confessed, 'but I can make very good butter and cheese. And I have two Jersey cows. The first doesn't come in 'til September so I can't prove it until then.'

'Wonderful!' said Daisy Jordan. 'Catherine won't be able to remember all our names, so to begin with let's tell her what we're called each time we speak to her, until she knows us. There's a lot of noise coming from the creek, so we'd better go down and see what our men are up to before we get ourselves home and leave them to it.'

When they arrived the women were offered seats and glasses of sherry, which most of them refused. They seemed to have walked into the middle of a conversation.

'Women. They seem to think that Kitty can break him in,' said Colin Jordan.

'Or perhaps he'll kill her,' said someone else.

'Well, I was afraid, too, I can tell you, but it only took her about half an hour to get a halter on him and to teach Daisy how to catch him. I'm not allowed to go near him. And my dear respected brother Albert couldn't do that without roping and throwing him.'

'Well, she's a little wonder, that Kitty,' said Bill James. 'Mrs Kirk, you being Irish, are there any horse whisperers in your family?'

'No,' said Catherine, embarrassed by being the centre of attention, 'We are all dairy people.'

'Well, they must just pop up, I guess. Your Kitty sure seems to be one. I will be watching with great interest, because I have the same problem as Colin. I have a bas…excuse me, ladies, nasty horse that Albert sold me, and my women cry when I threaten to shoot him. And to make it worse Albert conned me into taking a bet that I couldn't handle him. And he did that to you, too, didn't he, Colin?'

This was answered with a red face and a shame-faced nod.

Daisy Jordan said, 'Well I don't believe in betting, but if I did, I would be betting on Kitty. She'll have that pony under control, and she'll be riding him to school when school opens.'

Catherine said, surprised, 'Kitty won't be going to school. She can already read and write and figure, so she doesn't need to. She went in Dunedin, and she hated it.'

Daisy Jordan, said in a horrified tone, 'Mrs Kirk, all our children go to school; it's compulsory.'

George said, 'Of course she'll be going to school. Whether she walks or rides Rascal is up to her. There's a lot more to be learnt at school than reading and writing, and the schools here aren't run by any church. They are run by the government. Education is supposed to be "free, compulsory and secular", but I've noticed that some prayers have crept in.'

'Relax, George. Hop down off your soap-box. You sound as if you are addressing a public meeting,' said one of the Presbyterians. 'We don't hold with the Wee Free type of education either. Most Presbyterians aren't Wee Free, you know.'

'Speaking of Kitty,' Daisy asked, 'Does anyone know where she is? It's time for us ladies to leave you little boys to your bad behaviour, and I can't find my daughter. Wherever Kitty is, Sarah is.'

'I can see Sarah over there by the big paddock, sitting up in a tree. Kitty has probably put her up there out of the way. Your daughter really does tend to get underfoot, doesn't she?' someone said.

'Kitty may well be working the pony or cleaning the paddock, and she likes to work alone. She'll be making a start on her Sunday chores. I'll call her.' George let out a loud 'cooee' followed by a piercing whistle and was answered in the same way. A ladder was put up to the tree and, hand in hand, the girls arrived.

'It's time to say "goodbye" to the ladies. What were you up to, perching Sarah in a tree like that? Were you working that pony?' Catherine asked.

'No, just putting her out of the way while I was cleaning up. And I wanted to show her something I didn't want her to touch. Tell them, Sarah.'

'Puppies. Toss has had the ugliest puppies you've ever seen. Kitty says there are three dogs and two bitches. Kitty says you're allowed to say bitches as long as you are talking about dogs, not ladies who aren't there. Why are you all laughing at me?'

'George, I'd like to buy a bitch when they're ready,' said Sam Fletcher, and he was followed by several other would-be purchasers.

'Sorry chaps, you'll have to deal with Kitty. They're her dogs, not mine.'

'Ouch. I was hoping to get one for a good price, but there's no chance of that now. In six or eight weeks, please Kitty?'

'Sorry, Mr Fletcher. I'm going to train them before I sell them. I'll let you know. I'm probably going to keep the bitches and breed them if I can borrow a stud for them.'

Sam Fletcher shook his head ruefully. 'The price is going up by the minute,' he said. 'Just keep me top of the list. It's a new experience for me. I've never had to bargain with an eleven-year-old, and a girl at that.'

'Would you feel better about it if I told you that you will be bargaining with a twelve-year-old?' And with that Kitty said a hurried goodbye to everyone and ran off towards the paddock.

She spent time with Rascal, and when she was satisfied that he was actually responding to her and had learnt his name, she went back to her paddock-cleaning and getting Bronze ready for Church. She went back to the camp for the porridge that she had put aside for Toss, who was very happy to have her puppies admired again. By the time she went back again there was very little noise coming from the creek, and Eddie and Catherine were enjoying a cup of tea. It wasn't long before George joined them, saying that there were only three men left, and they were all asleep.

Kitty sighed happily and said it was her best day ever. First, the safe arrival of the puppies, then a nice day with nice people and finally, time spent with Rascal. Also, the cart was clean for tomorrow, and Bronze would just need a brush-up and plaiting. Then she said, 'I have three questions, one for each of you. You first, Ma. Did you have a good day? You seemed to be having a good time with the ladies. You were all laughing a lot.'

Catherine answered: 'They were all very nice to me, specially Mrs Jordan. She said I am to call her Daisy. And there's one called Flo who can't read or write and actually makes a joke of it. So I told them that I can't either. It's good not to be hiding it. Flo told me after that nobody looks down on you because of it as long as you can make a joke of it. So that was nice.'

Kitty said: 'Eddie, can I ask you one question? When Mr Rees said he wanted you to work next week, you said that he could have Tubby and the cart but you were going to Dunedin. Isn't he your boss?'

'Not exactly,' Eddie answered. 'I own the rig and I work for Rees some of the time. Other times he hires the horse and cart, and I work somewhere else. He provides feed for Tubby and I have my independence. I'm not going to Galloway, because I like it too much here. It all depends on what happens in Dunedin. I'm going to have to sort things out. I was going to ask you if I could leave my stuff here until I get back. You can use Tubby of course, when Mr Rees is finished with him. I'll definitely be back as soon as possible to get the roof on and the barn built. Does that answer your question, Kitty?'

'More than. Almost too much. There's just one more thing—'

'You said only one question, Kitty, and that's all I am telling you. I'm leaving at first light, so I'm off to bed now. Good night.'

As he was gathering his things together, Kitty said, 'Naughty Eddie. Missing church! Won't the vicar ex-whatever you?'

'Not if I'm back on Saturday for cricket. Goodnight, all.'

George said, 'Well, what a surprise! Now, you said you had a question for me, Kitty? I hope it's short because I'm dead beat.'

'Does walking right round our farm count as work? You said that straight after the working bee we would plan properly where we were going to put things. You haven't even had time to look at the paddock lately, and if we don't get the stock out tomorrow, we're going to have to buy feed. As it is, I'm going to tether Surprise over here so Ma can spoil her a bit. I think she's missing you, Ma. I'd like to get them built up before the winter.'

'We'll do it as soon as we get home from church. That's not work, that's pleasure. And after that we'll admire the pups and bring Surprise over, then you and I will sit down and draw up a map. That's not work, that's education. Now, off to bed.'

They didn't stay for the meal at the church but as soon as they arrived home, they changed out of their Sunday clothes and, grabbing some bread, they set off. Neither of them had had any idea of how big eighty acres actually was, and by the time they reached the back boundary peg, they realised that they would have to finish it another day. Their block consisted of roughly flat-to-rolling land to where it was intersected by a road, on the other side of which the rest of their farm was moderately steep tussock country, which George said was good land for sheep. They hurried down to peg out another rough space for the stock so they could turn them out straight away.

It was twilight when they returned for their tea to find Catherine frantic with worry. When they told her that they had only managed to get to the back boundary and not right round their farm, her eyes widened.

'So big,' she gasped.

George laughed. 'Remember that we only started in the middle of the afternoon. It's large compared with the size of holdings in the old country, but very small by comparison with some of the big sheep stations here. Some of them are larger than a whole county in Ireland. Our farm is just a tiny part of what used to be Mr Rees's property. Apart from this valley and the Queenstown holding, he had stations at the head of the lake and all along the west side.'

'Can we start off by fencing off some paddocks? The one we have is too big. We need four smaller ones so that we can shift our stock into a clean paddock once a week. Sunday mornings would be good – then I wouldn't have to clean up that day. I wouldn't have to scrape up every day, but the used paddock could be done properly by the end of the week.'

'Good on you, girl. You've remembered the lectures I gave you about stock management when we were on the drove?'

'Every word. And, Ma, it would be good if you could think about what you want in the house yard and where you would like them put. You can tell us, and I can write it down while Pa measures it up. Think about everything you could ever want, even if it might take years before you get it all.'

'I feel better about not being able to read and write now I know I'm not the only one. Can we do this tomorrow?'

George yawned. 'We'd better finish what we started first. We'd better walk the boundary tomorrow morning, because we need the daylight, and the first thing we need is to fence our four paddocks and get stock management underway. You can walk around our house yard and dream about what you want. So, early breakfast, off to bed now.'

'Do you both have to go? I hate being left alone'

'Yes, we do both have to go. You won't be on your own. Surprise will be here, and I think Kitty might be persuaded to bring Toss and the pups over.'

'For sure. And I think you've both forgotten something very important to me.' She stood up and started running. 'Today happens to be my twelfth birthday!' and she was gone.

George came to call Kitty really early for breakfast and found her lunging Rascal. 'Already?' he said, surprised. At the sound of his voice the pony started and tried to pull the rope out of Kitty's hands.

'We're not ready for visitors yet; he's one very frightened little horse. Please just stand still and quiet until I settle him enough to let him go with Bronze.'

As they walked back to the camp, carrying the pups while Toss and Surprise followed, George told Kitty that Catherine was very upset that they had forgotten her birthday. Kitty laughed and said that she was the one who should be upset, and she wasn't because she had forgotten too. There had been so much happening that was much more important. And Toss had given her the best birthday present ever.

Next morning the sun had barely risen when they left the camp, and when they had reached the second survey peg, they sat down to have lunch. Kitty sighed happily. 'Just look at that view. They picked the right name for the Remarkables, didn't they? It's much nicer than giving mountains people's names or naming something so beautiful after an ugly old saw.'

'They did. And Mr Rees picked the right piece of land for us, didn't he? Now eat up quickly. From now on it's all downhill, and it would be good to have a bit of a walk around on this side of the road, because that's where I think our first fence should go. We should get as much fencing done as we can before Eddie gets back and he and I get on with the house. And I want to make the doors and arrange for the windows to be made. The nights are drawing in and the frosts could start any time.'

'And a drink of water is no substitute for a nice cup of tea, is it? Why does everyone always say "a nice cup of tea"? I've had some pretty nasty cups of tea.'

'I expect it's because people hope that their next cup of tea is going to be a nice one. One more thing: I notice you are learning a lot of long words, and I've been wondering where you are hearing them.'

'Mostly from Mr Dickens and quite a lot from Eddie. Some from you, and if anyone uses a word I don't understand, I ask what it means. Ma does that too. She doesn't like to see me reading, so I have to be sneaky about it. Eddie's going to bring me back some books, and I have to work out where I'm going to hide them.'

They arrived back mid-afternoon and had their nice cup of tea. They told Catherine what they had discovered, and then George settled down to use the remaining daylight to draw a rough outline of the property. Kitty found another piece of paper and persuaded Catherine to start to list all the things she wanted in the house yard: wash-house, fowl house and yard, garden plots, compost heap and a safe place for children to play while she was working. She wanted to visit her friend Flo to see what her place was like. This was a surprise. Except for Eily, neither of them had ever heard Catherine refer to anyone as her friend before. And she even knew where Flo lived.

'That's not far away, and it's on the same road as us. We won't be using Bronze tomorrow, so why don't we harness him up for you, and you can go over this afternoon?' George suggested.

She surprised them both. 'Yes, I'd like that. I'm sick of sitting 'round here on my own. One day when we can afford it I'd like a lighter cart. When we have the dairy up and running we'll need one.' George was happy with this small victory, although he wasn't all that keen on Flo. After dinner they saw Catherine off and went back to their fencing. To George's surprise Kitty had Rascal carrying a small pack saddle that she had fashioned from some sacks. She was packing some extra tools and staples into it.

'Will he be all right?' asked George anxiously.

'He has to get used to you being around. Just don't touch him and steer clear of both ends. When he gets easy with you, I'll introduce you, but we mustn't try to hurry him.'

George completely ignored the pony, who, after putting his ears back a few times, returned the favour.

At the end of the day's work Kitty held Rascal and told George to pack the tools into the saddle bags. Kitty talked soothingly while he did so, then George walked beside her as she led him back home.

'Good,' said Kitty. 'Tomorrow you can lead him. We'll see if you come out of that alive. We won't try his other end yet, though.'

'Good,' said George.

They got home to find a happy Catherine had unharnessed Bronze and hitched him to a stump. The billy was nearly boiling. She told them that she'd had a great time, Flo was a great character and they'd had a lot of laughs. Flo was going to Arrowtown the next afternoon and would pick Catherine up. She wanted Kitty to write her a list, and Flo wanted Kitty to write one for her, too. Dinner would have to be early. George agreed to everything. Catherine was happy for once and actually seemed to be settling in as a pioneering wife.

For the rest of the week the fencing went well. They fenced off the tussock land from the road. A gate in the back fence would provide a shorter route to Arrowtown. They were able to finish one of the paddocks and turn the stock into it. They also demolished the temporary paddock that Kitty and Eddie had put up. When they sat around the fire on Friday night, George bewailed the fact that the next two days would be spent away from the farm, at church on Sunday and cricket on Saturday. Catherine suddenly remembered that one of Mr Rees's men had left a parcel for George. When it was opened they found that it contained a white shirt, some very nearly white moleskins and a cricket cap.

'Do you mean to say that you have to dress up in good white clothes just to throw a ball around?' asked an astonished Catherine.

'Yes, and you'll have to dress up a bit, too, just to come and watch.'

'What about Kitty?'

'Don't worry about me, Ma. I have to be early because I've been asked to try out for the girls' team.'

'A girls' team! You'll be telling me next there's a ladies' team!'

'There is!' laughed the other two. 'But it's only the men and boys who take it seriously,' added George.

'What about clothes for Kitty? Does she have to have anything special to wear?'

'Not unless she turns out to be very good. She's not bad at bowling, but she's never had a shot at bat. We'll just have to wait and see. Come on, it's time to get some beauty sleep.'

'Beauty sleep has never done me any good,' said Kitty as she left.

The next morning they left for Frankton in a spotless cart behind a gleaming horse and arrived to find a good number of people already there. Sarah appeared from nowhere, grabbed Kitty and dragged her off, for once leaving George to attend to the horse.

Flo came and collected Catherine, and they walked off together to get good seats. The vicar came and asked George anxiously whether Eddie was back yet. When George said that he could hardly be expected to go to Dunedin, attend to business and get back in a week, the vicar said that he hoped George was as good a bowler as Eddie. This was a very important match.

George replied: 'I don't even know who we are playing. Eddie and I have been practising most evenings, but I'm rusty, and I didn't go to the sort of school that you and Eddie went to. I only played village cricket, so please don't expect too much of me.'

'We're playing Macetown. They're absolute fanatics up there, and their batsmen are dynamite. I don't think they have much else to do after work. They all live in the township and that means that they can spend a lot more time practising than we can. Come on.'

'Thanks for inspiring me with so much confidence. I am now terrified of facing a bunch of brawny miners, probably all younger than me by ten years or so. Thank you so much, Vicar.'

'Eddie gave you a good report. And if you can't bring yourself to call me by my Christian name, just make it "Vic", except on Sundays.'

Catherine and Flo had done their duty, taking and displaying Flo's beautiful baking in the refreshment tent, and when they had claimed their seats, Kitty and Sarah joined them.

'Guess what!' said an excited Sarah. 'Kitty's been picked for the ladies' team. Mummy told me to tell you that she's got some whites that we can lend her. Isn't she lucky?'

'I don't really want to do it. I've got a pony to break in, but Daisy said seeing that George would be coming anyway, I might as well come too.'

'Sometimes I don't understand you, Kitty. You make a great fuss about wearing a white dress and being confirmed, but you seem to be happy to dress up in white to play a stupid game. And it's cheeky to call Mrs Jordan by her first name.'

'My Mummy told her to so she's not being cheeky,' said Sarah indignantly.

'And don't let anyone hear you calling it a silly game,' Flo explained. 'It's more like a religion, except they let anyone play if they're good enough, even Micks. There's a young visiting priest who turns up sometimes, and his boss comes too. And our vicar is quite pally with him. It's not just a game, Catherine, it's a sacred game.'

Catherine sighed. 'I don't think I'll ever understand. It just seems to me like a terrible waste of time.'

Flo laughed. 'I gave up trying to understand the game years ago, so I just clap when everyone else does and say "ooh" and clap extra hard if any of the men watching yells out "Well played". Once or twice they stop playing, and the ones who were batting start walking about a bit, and two of the bowlers go and pick up bats, and the boys run around giving them all oranges. After this happens a few times we can get away and pretend to be very busy in the tea tent. I think that's all I actually know about cricket, and I've gotten by on that for years. What are you laughing about, Kitty?'

The men had started playing. Catherine, guided by Flo, watched, trying to hide her bewilderment. She took more interest while George was bowling, especially when he was given a short round of applause. He didn't last long at bat, and it would be nice to report that he had saved the day, but although he acquitted himself reasonably well, the mountain men had won.

After tea they went home, and as Kitty went to let Bronze go, Catherine called out to her to change her clothes. She checked the puppies and called back that she would be late because she was going to work Rascal. George followed her and was finally persuaded to put his hands on him. Then, with Kitty holding the pony's head, he picked up the forefeet and scraped the hooves. Kitty was pleased.

Sunday followed its usual pattern. Catherine was no longer reluctant to go out, and when they got home and the three of them walked round the house yard, measuring and marking, she queried the size of the barn until George told her that with the winter coming it would be needed to store stuff that they hadn't even bought yet, and also it would have to be a good size when the dairy was up and running.

Kitty clapped her hands to her mouth. 'I completely forgot to tell you that this morning when I went to get Bronze, our young Bully and Maisie were at it. Pa, we need a calendar to mark things like that on.'

'Until we find out how good his first calf is, we can't sell his services, but I'd like to let Flo have him for one of her cows. If she gets a nice Jersey-cross, it would be good,' Catherine said.

'We're going to have to get you your own transport before long, or you might have to go and live at Flo's,' joked George. 'I wonder when Eddie will be back. You girls go and make lists while I make mine.'

'Ma, why don't you come, too? I can show you where the shops are and tell you where the bank is and everything. You need to know where the doctor is and all. So far you've only seen the church.' It was agreed, and with their lists made, they went to bed.

Before they left in the morning Kitty asked George to come with her to the paddock and bring a hammer. Then they went through what became their routine of George catching Rascal and Kitty holding his head while George picked up his feet, even the hind ones, and got on with the business of cleaning and then hammering, so the pony could be prepared for the business of getting shod.

It was Catherine who drove them to Arrowtown, and while George went about his business, she and Kitty went round the shops. When they went to the grocer's Kitty introduced her mother and then told her just to hand over her list. Catherine was beginning to see the value of the written word, and while she watched her purchases being wrapped, Kitty ranged around the shop looking at all the things they couldn't yet afford. They still had money in the bank, and George would be able to take a few droving jobs after the house was finished and the baby was born. Until then they weren't wasting any cash on things that weren't absolutely necessary. After the groceries were bought, paid for and left for them to be picked up, they went for a walk around the little town so that Catherine could see where everything was. When they weren't shopping Kitty introduced Catherine to everyone. Catherine was now getting tired from walking, so they went back to the cart. Kitty looked at her suspiciously and then asked her if she might be having the baby sooner than they thought. Catherine snapped and said she didn't feel like talking about babies just now, thank you. So they sat and waited for George. When he got back they collected their purchases and George took the reins.

'Where are we going?' Catherine asked as they turned onto a road that was unfamiliar to her.

'To see the Jordans,' George answered. 'We can have a cup of tea, and Kitty wants to have a talk to Colin.'

'On first names now, are we? And what would she want to talk to him about?'

'Colin and I have always been on first names. Most men are. And Kitty no doubt wants to talk about pony business. You can ask her yourself when she wakes up. She's made a little nest back there and is having herself forty winks. She's good at that, isn't she?'

Catherine said nothing. She hadn't noticed this habit of her daughter's. She wondered what else she didn't know about her. She was quiet until they turned into the Jordan's gate.

'My goodness,' she gasped. 'This is so lovely. Everything painted the same colours, and look at the flowers!'

'Don't worry!' Daisy said as she and Sarah came to meet them. 'Like you, we lived on a building site and in a mess for a year or two. You will have everything nice sooner than you think. Cup of tea?'

Sarah was yelling, 'Kitty, Kitty, Kitty,' as her mother rolled her eyes.

'I can't wait until they get a teacher and school can start again. Hop along, girls. Find Colin and tell him there's a cup of tea going.'

When they went inside Catherine gasped again. 'It's all so lovely. It must have cost a lot.'

Daisy laughed. 'Mostly time. When your man has got your paddocks sorted and your farm up and running, he'll have time to work on the house. Don't forget we got started a long time before you did. We were on leasehold then, and you won't have that hanging over your head. And with a farmhand like Kitty, you'll have help we didn't have.'

'But I'll need her in the house, what with the baby and all.'

'Surely not! Not with only one baby and not your first! She'll be much more useful outside. George can safely leave all the stock work to her while he gets on with the out-buildings. I just hope our Sarah turns out like Kitty. Then we can put our feet up when we get old. Unlike you, we can't have any more children so it will be up to Sarah to marry someone useful.'

Just then the others arrived back. 'Go and wash up. I'm just about to put dinner on the table.'

'Gee, thanks. We'll give you a hand, won't we, Chicken?' Sarah pouted but nodded agreement.

Colin laughed. 'I wish we could hire Kitty as a governess. Sarah does what she says without argument.'

'Kitty's so mean,' put in Sarah. 'If I don't do what she says, she won't break my pony in and she won't give me riding lessons. I hate her.'

'We've noticed that. If you feel like that you don't have to put up with her anymore. Is that what you want?' teased Colin.

'No!' wailed his daughter.

'Stop it, you two', ordered Daisy. 'Let's have our meal in peace.'

Kitty couldn't resist it. 'Lovely, thank you, Daisy. And afterwards, what say Sarah and I do the washing up?'

While the girls were cleaning up and Colin and George were talking men's business, Daisy took Catherine on a tour of the yard and flower garden. 'Plan yours carefully, Catherine. Colin and I made heaps of mistakes that took time and money to fix. Most of your neighbours will give you plants next spring, and there are some you could get in before frost. But, of course, George will be flat out getting the house finished before the baby comes. We started off like you and everyone else, with three rooms, and later we built on at the back. It's taken us years, but it wouldn't have taken so long if we had listened to others.'

'I was unhappy when I first got here, because I expected a ready-made farm,' said Catherine, 'and I didn't know how to make friends. I've always lived apart from other people. I can't believe how nice people are to me here. But Kitty is just running wild, more like a boy than a girl. And I can't make her understand that she has to know her place.'

'Your place is easy to find. You're a farmer's wife like the rest of us. And don't you worry about Kitty. She's out on her own. She is accepted by everyone because of her talent. Well, nearly everyone. There's still brother Albert. I'd love to see his face when Kitty comes riding up on Rascal.'

The girls came out followed by the men. When Catherine had been helped into the cart, Daisy told everyone to wait a bit – there was something else – and disappeared. Kitty popped Sarah up on Bronze's back and said she needed to talk to her father for a bit. Daisy came back carrying a box, which she carefully put on the back of the cart.

Sarah saw the box and wailed: 'You're not giving Bossy away! I won't let you!'

'Of course not. She's just going for a little holiday. George, when you get home, you're going to have start building your fowl house because that's our brooder box, and in it is our best brooder, Bossy the bantam. She's sitting on a clutch of eggs. She's too old to lay eggs and drives the other hens mad because she takes over a nest and won't let them in. She's yours until she's raised them, so make sure they all have a good home.'

'I've a problem with Jordan females, George,' laughed Colin, 'but you don't have to, because you don't have to live with them. There's only one called "Bossy", and she's the least bossy of the three of them. Albert says it's my fault because I'm not bossy enough. He says I'm too soft with my horses, too, but I think we get along very well.'

'I detest that man. He can't tell the difference between being bossy and being a bully, and a bully is what he is,' Daisy exclaimed. 'I just hope Kitty can sort the pony out, so I can watch his horrible face, especially if there are other people there.'

'Rascal's coming along just fine, Daisy. But I would like to get along home and do some work with him. Thank you for a lovely dinner.'

After all the goodbyes and thank-yous were out of the way they left, and as soon as they arrived, Catherine started telling George exactly where and how she wanted her fowl house. Kitty left them happily arguing and went off to attend to the horses.

Two days later, at breakfast, she announced that Colin Jordan would be coming for dinner.

Catherine brightened and said she would enjoy seeing Daisy again now that George had nearly finished the hen house.

'Hen palace, you mean,' muttered George.

'Sorry, Ma. Daisy and Sarah aren't coming. Colin's coming on horse business. Rascal's accepting Pa, but he has to learn that other men aren't like Albert Jordan.'

'Well, I think you're spending far too much time with that wretched animal, and I don't think you should call the Jordans by their first names. It's not fitting for a child like you.'

Kitty flared up, then, with difficulty, managed to control herself. 'I do all my other jobs and manage to do some of Pa's so he can get on with things here. And for your information I am now a woman. Pa, please explain that there could be money in it, and then, maybe, she'll leave me alone. She's been on at me about money ever since she found out that the pups are worth money. And could you please bring Colin over to the paddock as soon as he arrives.' With that she stalked out, leaving a furiously angry Catherine and a very discomforted George.

When Colin Jordan arrived he was riding a thoroughbred and leading a sturdy saddled cob named Chocolate. They got straight down to business getting Rascal used to being handled by Colin and hopefully accepting of the fact that being a man didn't necessarily mean being cruel. Kitty left the men to it while she searched among the gear that Colin had brought, to fix a bridle for Rascal. Then she asked them to go back to the camp so she could introduce the pony to being bridled. Within a short space of time she arrived back, leading him, and tied him up next to the cob.

This was the first time Catherine had seen him and she gasped. 'He's beautiful. I don't like horses, but I've never seen one so pretty.'

Kitty smiled. She grabbed her cup of tea and suggested Catherine might like to come and pat him. It was a cease-fire but not an armistice.

During dinner Colin asked Kitty how many horses she had broken in, and when she laughed and told him that Rascal was the first, he couldn't believe it. How on earth did she know what she was doing? She told him that she didn't know how she knew, she just did. And that she thought it was mostly just common sense.

'You're Irish, aren't you? I think you must be a genuine whisperer.' And then he turned to Catherine and asked her if there were any whisperers in her family. She looked very uncomfortable and, as usual, answered that her people were all dairy as far back as she could remember. She didn't look any happier when Kitty broke in indignantly, saying that she wasn't Irish – she was a New Zealander. George and Colin laughingly applauded.

'What's next?' asked Colin as he finished his third cup of tea.

'Road training,' said Kitty. 'I want to have him really quiet by the time I start taking him out on his own. That's why I asked if I could borrow a horse suitable for Pa. I've started backing him, and I won't have Pa's help after Eddie gets back. It would be great if you could spare me an hour or two next week.'

'Of course I can, but what's the hurry?'

'I think you'd better ask your bossy wife. She's entered him in the show, and she's coming over as soon as he's under saddle, to teach me to ride. And she told me that you would be looking after Sarah while she was here.'

Colin groaned. 'I had better get on home. It's been a pleasure seeing you work, Kitty. Oops, I nearly forgot. I had a letter from Eddie. He'll be back by the weekend. The good news is that he's decided to stay in the Wakatipu and wants to buy a cottage in Arrowtown. He would like one of you to go over to Rees's place and bring his rig back here, if possible. He said he'd see you at church on Sunday.'

'I could do that, or Pa could. Ride Chocker over and drive back. We'd need to leave by first light, because it will be a very, very slow trip, even with an empty cart. You choose, Pa. we both have tons of stuff to do at home.'

'You, I think. I don't think my old backside would stand up to it. I'll be sore enough from the little riding I did today. It must be done – we owe Eddie so much. If you are sure you can handle it.'

'I'm sure you can, girl. I must be off or I'll be getting my ears boxed. I'll see you all on Sunday.' And mounted on his thoroughbred, Colin cantered off.

As he left George commented: 'That's a toff's horse, that one. There's a fellow in Dunedin who imports them direct from Ireland. They cost the earth but Colin must be able to afford it.'

Catherine questioned if it was proper for a young girl to be out on her own like that and was told that Colin obviously thought it was and George still had a lot to do before the roof went on next week, apart from putting the final touches on the fowl palace.

Kitty left them to it and was well away before they were up in the morning. She was very happy. She was enjoying a freedom she had never experienced before, and with a good keen willing horse under her, she was in absolute heaven. The Shotover River was low, so she knew she would have no trouble crossing on the way back. When she arrived at the Reeses she saw that the cart was standing loaded and covered with canvas, so she knew she was in for a very slow trip home. Mrs Rees and Mary Rose greeted her warmly and told her Mr Rees was away from home. After she had caught and harnessed the ever-reluctant Tubby, Mrs Rees insisted that she should have a cup of tea and a big fat sandwich before she left.

As expected, they were a very long time getting home. Tubby was a plodder on the road, trying to snatch a mouthful of grass whenever he could. If Kitty's concentration wavered for a second, his head went down, so she started talking to him. That worked for a while. He was a good plough horse and he was good at very hard work, so he had worked well taking stones from the creek, but long walks along roads were not his style at all. He had been trained to obey voice commands, so he listened to Kitty for a while, but he soon realised that what she was saying made no sense to him, so he slowed right down again. Exasperated, she finally tried singing. Singing was not one of her talents, but there was nobody to hear, so she belted out some songs, flat and out of tune, hoping that Tubby would try to get away from the noise. The first yell did jolt him out of his complacency and make him move faster for a few hundred yards, then he dropped back to his own pace, one foot after the other, as slowly as was equinely possible. Kitty thought she would walk and lead him, but Tubby had other ideas. He let her walk and drag him, so she decided she would have to let him take his own pace and just hope they got home before dark. Luckily, when they were only a mile from home his ears pricked up. Realising that he could stop this nonsense and get a feed, he actually began to hurry – by his standards.

Her parents came to greet her, George saying, 'I told you she'd be all right,' and Catherine saying, 'What on earth have you been doing all this time, you naughty girl?'

Kitty climbed down, saying, 'I'm tired, I'm starving and I will never drive that bloody horse anywhere again.'

George said, 'You did very well, my dear. I'll tend to the horses while you have a nice cup of tea and something to eat. Spare a thought for poor Chocolate having to trudge along behind Tubby all that way. Then get yourself to bed and don't get up early in the morning.'

Catherine pushed a cup of tea at her. 'Don't tell me you took all that time getting back from the Rees's place. I've been there and it doesn't take that long. Have you been getting up to mischief?'

'Ma, you were behind Bronze. Bronze trots. Bloody Tubby doesn't trot, Tubby walks. Tubby walks very slowly. Please let me eat and get to bed.'

'There's no need to swear. If the horse was that bad, Eddie wouldn't keep him. Tell me the truth: where have you been?'

'Bloody Hell,' Kitty swallowed her tea, grabbed a heel of bread and some cheese and ran out crying. On the way to her bivvy she met George, who grabbed her in a fatherly hug.

'You need more to eat than that. Come on back. You did so well. I can't think of another twelve-year-old who can do what you can do. Your Ma was a bit hasty, but that's because she was worried about you.'

'She wasn't worried about *me*. She was worried about me getting into mischief. Sometimes I think she's trying to make me hate her. Please, Pa, I have to get some sleep. Don't say anything to her – it'll only make it worse.'

When he got back, George said, 'I'm so proud of our girl. Sometimes I think we ask too much of her. After all, she's only twelve.'

'She's getting deceitful. She wouldn't tell me where she's been all this time. She's old enough to get into trouble, and she swore at me when I asked her.'

'Come on, Catherine, I couldn't have done it any quicker my-self, not behind Tubby. That horse has a mind of his own. Come on, drop it and let's get to bed.'

In the morning George went across to see if Kitty had managed to sleep in. He found her lunging a sweating Rascal. 'Great,' she said. 'I was just about to come and get you. I want to saddle him up and ride him today, and I want you to lead him for a bit.' She saw the look on George's face.

'No,' she said hastily, 'I've already ridden him bareback and this is the next step.'

'Come and have some breakfast. There won't be a word spoken about yesterday, I promise you.'

As they walked back, she asked, 'Please can I have as much time as you can spare before Eddie gets back? School starts in two weeks, and if I don't ride him to school, all bets are off, and if I can't prove I can make money, it will be very hard for me to go on handling horses, and there's nothing else I want to do. Anyway, you can get used to riding again. We can have Chocolate for as long as we want him, and he comes with winter feed.'

'We must get that roof on and the house comfortable as soon as possible, then we must get our barn built. I wonder how much time Eddie will be able to spare us when he gets back. There's a lot of work to be done and a lot of questions to be asked.'

During breakfast Kitty asked, 'Ma, when exactly is the baby due? You look awfully big for May. Could you be having twins?'

Catherine answered, plainly embarrassed, 'Not twins. It could happen any time.' George cut in: 'She didn't tell me for a long time, and she didn't want to tell you until she started showing. You know how shy she is about that sort of thing.'

'She probably didn't want me to know what you two had been up to!' said Kitty as, bread in hand, she ran out with Catherine's indignant screech ringing in her ears.

In about half an hour George joined her at the paddock, still laughing. 'You really dropped me in it that time, didn't you? I don't quite understand how your Ma can't understand why you aren't a sweet little innocent, when she's taught you all you need to know about dairying.'

'That's easy, Pa. She says that people aren't animals.'

Rascal seemed to be happy under saddle, and after an hour or so, Kitty told George to hop on Chocolate so they could see how they went. They rode back to the camp for dinner. After that they went riding round the farm without incident except George complaining about his sore bottom.

Next morning Kitty arrived for breakfast riding Rascal and with Chocolate all ready to go. George groaned but climbed aboard and off they went out along the road. Again Rascal went quietly, and after they had come back and had dinner, Kitty asked her mother if there was anything she wanted in Arrowtown, because she needed to expose the pony to traffic. Catherine thought the trip might be too hard on George, which he indignantly denied. When the pair of them were out on the road, George told Kitty that he would like to find out where the midwife and the doctor were located and persuade Catherine to visit them, rather than relying solely on Flo. While he did so Kitty went to make the acquaintance of the farrier, who knew about the bet between the Jordan brothers and told her that there were side bets being taken. Most people were betting on Albert. Kitty brought the pony in and explained Rascal's attitude to men. She half expected him to tell her that he knew his job and no little girl should try to tell him what to do, but he didn't. He allowed himself to be introduced to Rascal and went through the drill of picking up the feet and hammering them. He said that Colin Jordan had told him that smart-arse Albert was more than likely to be brought down a peg. They agreed to keep Rascal's shoeing a secret by pretending that she was delivering a message from Colin. George arrived, having completed his errand, and they had a fast trip home.

The next day, Saturday, was spent doing chores around the camp and cleaning up the paddock. Kitty cooked dinner and Catherine was delighted when Flo arrived to share it with them. The women talked babies non-stop, Flo exclaiming that she was pleased that the roof would be on next week, saying that she had been afraid that it might have been a race between the baby and the roof. She, too, had heard of the bet between the brothers and said she was sorry about it because people in the know said that Albert was a nasty piece of work and Colin couldn't possibly win, betting on a twelve-year-old girl against a very experienced horseman. Catherine said that it was very embarrassing for her – the bet should never have happened. She didn't like Kitty getting involved in men's business, and perhaps this would teach her and George a lesson. The two conspirators made eye contact and left hastily, leaving Catherine to vent her grievances and knowing that Flo would spread it all over the district before very long. George commented that the good thing about that was it would increase the odds in Colin's favour, although some people who had seen Rascal at the farrier's might talk. Kitty said that was why she had dismounted and led him the last half-mile. She was absolutely sure that she could ride a newly-shod Rascal to school on opening day. The only thing she was afraid of was what might happen if Albert tried to lay a hand on him.

Chapter Nine

They were at church early the next morning and standing outside chatting to some early arrivals when the Jordans arrived. Sarah tumbled out of their buggy and raced up to Kitty. She was followed by her mother, who was followed by Eddie and – Freddy! There was a unanimous gasp of delight from all the Kirks. Kitty rushed to hug Freddy fiercely, tears streaming down her face, but there was no time to talk. It was time to go in. Kitty didn't take her usual place among her young friends at the back but sat squashed into the Jordan's pew between Sarah and Freddy, whose hand she was clasping throughout the service, except when he went up to take Communion. At the end of the service the vicar announced that the next service would be taken by a lay-reader, Mr W.G. Rees, who had done so much for the church and for the whole Wakatipu district. The service would be followed by a farewell meal and informal get-together, and the vicar said that non-members of the congregation were welcome to join them.

As soon as they were out of the church, and before Kitty could get more than two words in, Mr and Mrs Rees came up, looking hard at Freddy. Eddie arrived and stood rather protectively at Freddy's side.

'Frederick? What brings you here? We thought you had gone to Australia,' said Rees coldly.

Mrs Rees stepped forward and looked hard from Eddie to Freddy and back again.

'Of course! I should have noticed the likeness! And the name,' she said delightedly. 'I must be stupid.'

'Cousin Frances,' said Freddy awkwardly, and kissed her chastely on the cheek. 'William,' he said, holding out his hand.

Rees was not so delighted and reluctantly shook hands with Freddy.

'Does the family know you are here? Have you communicated with them recently?'

'No, William,' answered Freddy, 'and I'll thank you not to tell them. Young Edward and I haven't decided quite what to do about it yet. He's not a remittance man and he's in touch with them all the time.' He noticed the interested audience standing around them. 'Our family isn't the slightest bit aristocratic, in fact they are in trade, so if any of your daughters fancy Eddie, he's a good lad but he doesn't come with a title.'

'Come on,' said the blushing Eddie. 'I think we've provided you with enough entertainment, so let's move on.' They separated themselves a little from the interested spectators. He turned to George. 'Uncle Fred and I have bought a house in Arrowtown, so let's go over there and talk as soon as we can get away from here.'

As the Reeses walked away Eddie said to George, 'Later we have a business proposition to put to you. It's pretty nebulous as yet, and there's all the rest to talk about too.' He started to laugh. 'Look over there!' Kitty was holding on to Freddy's arm while Sarah was clinging to Kitty's other arm. 'Shall we go over and hang onto some arms too?'

During lunch most of the attention centred on Freddy. In a small town a newcomer always attracts attention, and one previously known to a prominent citizen attracts more than most, along with a lot of wild surmises.

As soon as they politely could, they walked over to Eddie's new house where Freddy put the kettle on and Catherine oohed and aahed as she looked around, especially at the little Dover stove, which came to life and quickly had the kettle boiling.

Over tea Eddie explained they had decided to live in the Wakatipu district permanently. Freddy wanted to because, he said, the Kirks were the nearest thing to a family he had, and Eddie liked the idea of being a carter. Kitty burst out laughing. 'With Tubby?' She recounted their trip back from the Reeses and had everyone laughing. Eddie said that Tubby would be hired out to do what he did willingly, and he had already worked for several farmers in the district. He then explained that he was planning to buy at least two more horses – would Kitty please come and help him choose? She would love to, but not if he planned to buy them from Albert Jordan.

Freddy would be looking after the paperwork. Where did the Kirks come in? Eddie had organised stabling in Arrowtown but needed to find some grazing, and he had hopes that the Kirks would lease out their high ground. Catherine was tired and needed to get home, so it was agreed in principle that they would go ahead. Because the Kirks' house was the highest priority, Eddie would come home with them so they could get an early start, and Freddy would visit the next day.

'How will you get over?' asked Catherine.

Freddy smiled. 'On a horse, of course. My nephew here insisted that I should get a bit of practice in before we left Dunedin. That made the locals stare! Now I'll walk you over to your rig. Tomorrow I'll come and see you at about dinner time. I've business to attend to and I don't know whether it's to be done here or in Queenstown.'

In the morning work started at daylight. Kitty made breakfast in the fireplace that Eddie had built for the working bee and made a place where Catherine could be comfortable and out of the way but could supply cups of tea when required. Then she disappeared to attend to the animals, promising to come back in time to help with the dinner.

When she got back she found that Flo had arrived with scones and cakes and lots of questions. Kitty escaped, ostensibly to see if the men wanted anything.

'You'd better intercept Uncle before he gets here and tell him to keep his lip tightly buttoned in front of that woman,' Eddie warned. 'She's good-hearted, but she's not known as the "town crier" for nothing.'

'I worry about how much of our business Ma tells her, but I won't waste my time asking her to be careful what she says to her. She sees Flo as her best friend, so I just don't tell her anything about my work with horses. Now I'll leave you old gossips and go and meet Freddy. I'll tell the cooks that Chock needs exercise.'

Kitty let the horse have a good run, but it was a short one because she met Freddy sooner than she expected. She wheeled around and pulled up beside him.

'I bet you wouldn't have thought I could do that,' she told Freddy.

'You're quite wrong. Remember that lovely long letter you wrote and that Eddie brought me? He and I have been talking solidly for a week, so I think he's filled in nearly all the gaps. We still find it hard to believe how everything fitted together. I always meant to come and find you, but in less than a year...'

'Isn't it amazing how our lives have changed?'

'Yours was predictable, but mine! To go from a lonely life to being a family man in just over a week! Your meeting Eddie and Eddie finding me. You wouldn't believe it if you read it in a novel!'

As they neared home Kitty warned Freddy about Flo's loose tongue and that Catherine was inclined to confide in her. Freddy thought that when Catherine had her baby she might enjoy the company of other mothers with young children, but Kitty said Flo, who seemed to have installed herself as a sort of honorary grandmother, was knitting furiously. She chose to ignore the fact that Catherine had already had a child.

When they arrived Kitty said she would attend to Chock and

that thing faintly resembling a horse that Freddy was on. He could join the men while she helped with dinner. He was to tell them they could come down from the roof when they were ready.

Kitty went to fetch more water, then noted that the meal was all laid out and ready. The billy was boiling and the hot food sat on the hobs. Flo had helped with dinner. As expected, she was full of questions about Freddy as she helped Kitty carry the water buckets from the kōneke. Kitty was sure that Catherine had told her absolutely everything. Flo switched subjects to the lovely horse Kitty was riding. Was that the horse that the bet was all about? She was told no, it was another one belonging to the Jordans that they had lent to George. They had been so helpful to the Kirks. As soon as they got back with the water and rejoined Catherine, Flo said, 'With all this horse stuff going on, I hope you can find time to help your mother.'

'Mrs Parker, of course I can. I do what either of my parents needs me to do the most. We work together as a family, and how they organise my time is our family business. I'll thank you to know that I'm not answerable to you. If you want to know any more about us, I think you should ask Pa.'

Both women gasped. Poor Catherine didn't know which way to turn and stuttered out, 'Kitty, how could you be so rude to my friend. Say you're sorry right now, or go without your dinner!' The men had arrived to eat and had heard the last exchange. George, pretending that he hadn't heard, winked at Kitty and started asking her a barrage of questions about what she had been doing, then asked her to pour the tea. Freddy helped by asking Catherine to introduce her friend, so that attention was diverted from Kitty – for the moment.

Eddie also thought it was time for a diversion, so he began discussing the new business that he was starting, knowing that soon the whole district would know about it. It occurred to him that it might possibly save him the price of an advertisement in the *Lake Wakatip Mail* and would be around the district more quickly. Unfortunately, or perhaps fortunately, the whole district would also know that Kitty had rudely called Flo 'Mrs Parker' when her name was 'Porter'.

Flo asked him lots of questions about his business and then started on Freddy, who told her absolutely nothing, in his very best accent and with utmost courtesy. When she asked him about his relationship to the Reeses, saying that she had heard Mrs Rees call him cousin, he said frostily that she must have misheard. He quickly rose to his feet and asked Kitty if she could please show him the pony that everyone was talking about. When she said she would love to, but she would clean up first, he turned to Catherine and said that he wanted to see the pony. Afterwards he and Kitty would clean up together, just like they used to, but he wanted to see the pony first. Then after they had finished the chores, he would appreciate it if Kitty would ride a little of the way back to Arrowtown with him. Of course Catherine had to agree.

As soon as they had gone, Flo demanded: 'Just who is that man?'

'He happens to be my grandmother's brother,' Eddy answered, using the same accent as Freddy had. 'Come on, George, let's get back to work. Kitty told us before that we haven't time to sit around gossiping like a couple of old women.'

Freddy and Kitty came back and finished cleaning up before they set out for Arrowtown. Kitty told Catherine that she had fed Bossy and that some of the chickens had hatched, whereupon Flo said stridently that she had been going to give Catherine some hens. Kitty very politely answered that Daisy had given them a clutch, and it would be great if Mrs Porter were to give them some too, as some of Daisy's were bound to be roosters. George had built this enormous hen house and there was plenty of room for many more. And she thanked her very much for being such a good friend to Ma. Then she and Freddy mounted and left, exploding with laughter as soon as they were out of earshot.

Flo looked at Catherine and said that for all his poshness, Freddy was a very rude old man and that if Kitty spent too much time with him and Eddie and the likes of those Jordans – and as for calling Mrs Jordan by her first name, Flo herself had never been asked to do that. Kitty would get ideas beyond her station. Poor Catherine. She valued Flo's friendship and didn't want to lose it. She stuttered weakly that George had said that this was a new country, where everyone made their own station and what was important was how hard you worked and how well you did it. She felt that she had to obey her husband, although it sometimes felt uncomfortable to do so. Now that Kitty was a woman, and once the baby came, and when George didn't need her to help with the farm work, she would insist that Kitty worked with her in the house.

Flo sniffed as she gathered up her belongings. 'I think things may have gone too far for that. Next thing you know, your Kitty will be dressed like a toff and riding in the show.' Catherine burst into tears. Flo, who was basically a very kind-hearted woman, and not wanting to lose such a good source of information, gathered her into a hug and soothed her, saying that she would never let her down. Did she still want those chooks? Then she would bring them in a day or so, and they would be layers, not chickens. She was ready to leave when the men came back. She asked how they had got on, and George insisted on showing her their progress. She said it was going to be lovely, and when she wanted to see their fancy hen house, he showed her that, too. When she said she'd be back in a few days with some laying hens, he managed not to shudder and very politely bid her goodbye. Kitty arrived back as she was leaving and called out, 'Goodbye, Mrs Porter. We'll see you again soon?'

They were sitting around having a cup of tea when Kitty remarked to Eddie, 'There's a lot of your stuff still on the back of your cart. Do you want to unload it, or will you be leaving it there until you get sorted? It's covered with a canvas.'

'The canvas is mine, but I didn't leave anything else there. I've no idea what it can be. Let's have a look while there's still enough light. We can eat later.'

As soon as they started to uncover the load, they found that they had a load of shingles and a note reading, 'Dear George, Just some things we no longer need but that may be useful to you. I will be back for the christening if it is humanly possible. Keep in touch. Wm. Rees, Galloway Station.'

Eddie and George looked at each other in disbelief. 'You lucky bugger. But this changes everything. Neither you nor I know how to lay these things, but I know someone who does. Can you afford to pay him?'

They went and asked Catherine. She thought for a moment while George fetched paper and pencil, then she began dictating to him. She thought for a moment more, then said to George, 'Yes, I think we can, don't you?'

Eddie was gobsmacked. 'I've never seen anything like it,' he said. Catherine had finished the calculations before George had, despite his pencil and paper.

Kitty smiled. 'She does it all the time. It doesn't matter whether it's me, Pa or the bank manager, she always knows the answer before we do. Get used to it. Try her out for yourself. I know she'd be happy to help you with your business the way she got ours started in Dunedin. Just don't tell anybody.'

'As if I would tell you-know-who what day it is,' Eddie snorted. He said he had better start walking if he was to find the roofer and get him there early.

Kitty had a better idea. 'I want to give Rascal a really fast workout, and Chock needs a run. What say we leave at first light and belt across to Jordan's by the back road, and you can leave me and the horses there while you borrow another horse from Colin. By the time you get the business finished, we'll be spent and ready to come home. I need to know how long it takes to get to Arrowtown, because school starts next week.' So that's what they did, and arrived at the Jordans' for breakfast.

After Eddie had left for town the delighted Sarah was told that she was going to have a ride on Rascal. Colin swallowed and asked if Kitty was sure. She explained that there would be a parent on either side, and she herself would be at the head. The pony was still a bit tired, as he had never been so far so fast before, so it was a good time to see how he would react to someone who wasn't Kitty on his back.

'When can I ride by myself?' demanded Sarah.

'Not for a while, Kitty answered. 'He'll have to have the sting taken out of him first. What I had in mind was to ride him to school for the first term and get him used to the other kids and ponies, then in the holidays, he can come back and live here, and your Ma can take over and lunge him before you ride. If you don't argue with her, you and she can go for some lovely rides together when she thinks you're ready. If you work really hard you might be able to ride him to school in the spring, but only if you don't argue, okay?'

Sarah jumped up and down. 'Can we start now?'

Kitty winked at Colin. 'Not until you finish the dishes.'

Sarah opened her mouth to argue, thought about it, then closed her mouth again. She finished her task, then they went outside. Everything went well, but by the time Eddie got back, both Sarah and the pony were exhausted. Daisy elected to keep Rascal for the night, lunge him in the morning and bring him over to the Kirks' tomorrow. Meanwhile Eddie could ride back on the horse Colin had lent him. Kitty and Eddie had a very fast ride home, arriving, just in time for a late tea, to find that Rob the roofer had arrived not long before them, and he and George were sitting having a cup of tea, having finished their meal. Half the shingles had been unloaded, and they were set to go. Catherine had gone to lie down.

The exhilaration of the fast ride soon wore off. Kitty cleaned up after the meal, and since the horses had finished theirs, she took them back to the paddock to give them a good grooming before she turned them loose. Then, unusually for her, she went and had a short rest. Then she came and started taking shingles out of the cart and stacking them by the house. It was then nearly dark, so she went to eat. Catherine asked testily where she had been and what had she been doing instead of coming to help her set the food out and make the tea. Eddie answered for her, explaining that Kitty's help was really necessary, because it spared one of the men to work on the house.

Rob, the roofer, joined them. He owned a small gypsy caravan so he could live on his jobs. All materials were supplied by the owners, so all Rob carried with him were his tools and some spares in case his helpers weren't properly equipped. He couldn't find his horse.

'He's fed, groomed and turned out,' said Kitty. 'Do you want to go and see him? When you want him, I'll bring him in and get him ready for you. What's his name?'

'Thank you, Miss Kitty. He's never been so well treated. His name's Geeyup, because that's what I say to him, more than anything else. He's a good old chap.'

In the morning when Kitty came for breakfast, she went back to unloading the shingles. After she had a good pile out of the cart, she squealed, 'Ma, you just have to come and look at this!'

'Just bring it over here, whatever it is,' said Catherine crossly.

'I can't, Ma, it's too heavy. Here, I'll help you. It's something you just must see. I promise it will make you very happy.'

'What would make me very happy is if you would help me a bit more instead of wasting time gallivanting around the countryside.' But she lumbered across to the cart.

'Look,' Kitty said, quivering with excitement. 'A stove!'

'Holy Mary!' gasped Catherine. 'I can't believe it!'

George, who had just come down the ladder, came angrily across. 'You know you are never to say that!'

Kitty lifted the canvas. 'Holy Frances is more like it!'

'Holy Frances it is,' agreed George. He heard Catherine muttering something about 'blasphemy' and with one of his very rare bursts of anger, told her to shut up, show a bit of gratitude to the people who deserved it and go and get breakfast, and he'd deal with her and her bloody religion later. She stamped sulkily back and started to make tea. 'Eddie, come and give us a hand here, please.'

Kitty, who was silently packing shingles, had been horrified at George's outburst and was determined to find out what was wrong with saying 'Holy Mary'. It wasn't bad language, and Catherine said it all the time but, she realised, never when George was around. And why would it make George so angry? A mystery indeed! She continued loading shingles, then it struck her that the wheelbarrow would be needed to take the stove over to the house. It would have to wait until after breakfast. It was too heavy for her to push, and she'd be damned if she was going to unload again.

Breakfast was a strange meal. Catherine had retired, and the men were engrossed in talking about modifications to chimneys and future lean-tos, whatever they were. They had brought the wheelbarrow over, so Kitty sandwiched loading and unloading shingles with preparing the next meal. Fortunately, the bread was already baking in the camp-oven, so she peeled potatoes and onions and cut up the meat for the stew. When the men came down for the mid-morning cuppa, she apologised that the meal would be a bit late, or would she stop loading shingles? There weren't many left in the cart, but there seemed to be a lot of other stuff underneath that she would leave to be sorted when the shingles were off. No one commented about Catherine's non-appearance at dinner, but Kitty was praised for the excellence of her stew. She thanked them and said that Ma had been a good teacher.

Eddie insisted on helping her clean up. He said it was because they wanted her free to bring stuff up the ladder when they needed it, so please don't go running off to the horses. Kitty laughed and said he was starting to sound just like Ma. And then she realised that she hadn't taken Catherine as much as a cup of tea. The tea was still hot, so she poured a cup and took it over. Catherine's face was tear-stained. She took the cup and said she thought everyone had forgotten that she existed. Kitty tried to reassure her and asked her if she wasn't feeling well. She said that she was all right, just unhappy that George had lost his temper with her. Kitty said that she would go and get her something to eat. She would report to George that Catherine was just sulking. Of course, she didn't tell Catherine that.

When she got back, George was a little short with her because he had had to come down the ladder to get something. She explained where she had been. He replied that when they were hurrying to get the house finished, now that the first frosts were upon them, all hands were needed. At that moment, who should arrive but Flo, armed with her usual goodies and a squirming sack of indignant clucks. George rolled his eyes and, saying that was all he needed, scuttled back up the ladder.

'It's lovely to see you, Mrs Porter,' said Kitty, actually meaning it. 'Ma's having a bit of a lie-down. I was just going to take her a bite to eat, but before we do that, I would like to show you something, and perhaps we could let the hens out in their new home. I need you to tell me how to look after them, please. And I'll have to make the nesting boxes, because Pa is busy on the roof. We have to try to get the house finished before the baby comes.'

'You'll have to be quick about it, because your Mummy is very close to her time. But I'll help you with the hens and look at whatever it you want to show me, as long as it isn't a horse.'

Poor woman, she couldn't understand Kitty's sudden change of attitude and was proceeding carefully, so they saw the hens housed and fed, and Kitty assured her that, yes, she could do simple carpentry and was quite capable of building boxes. Now please come and look at the surprise, and then would she please pop in and see Catherine with something for her to eat and a cuppa. Flo was absolutely staggered when she saw the stove and demanded to know how much it cost. When she was told that it was a gift from Mrs Rees, she wouldn't believe it. Kitty said she had better just ask Catherine about it, because Mrs Rees had also written her a very nice letter, the very first Catherine had had in her whole life, and Kitty had to get back to work. She knew it would be all around the district in no time but calculated that Flo wouldn't give Catherine a chance to talk about anything else. She was wrong.

Flo went in to Catherine with a cup of tea, a buttered scone and a piece of cake. She stayed for a while then came out and told Kitty that seeing that Catherine was so close to her time, she would take her home to her place. This was more than Kitty could handle. She called: 'Pa, come down here now!' She heard George mutter something, but he didn't stop hammering. She called again. 'Pa, it's urgent, please come down.'

George caught the panic in her voice and came down quickly.

He told Kitty that it better be urgent, and Flo said it wasn't all that urgent just yet, but Catherine was very close to her time, and she was taking her home with her.

'No,' said George firmly. 'My wife will be having our baby in Arrowtown near to a midwife and the doctor. All the arrangements are made. Thank you all the same, Mrs Porter.'

Catherine had come out with a bag in her hand. 'No, I'm not going to do that. I want to have my baby at Flo's, and I want her to deliver it. She's the first friend I ever had in my life, and she's delivered lots of babies.'

George was keeping himself under control, but with difficulty. Flo started to butt in and George told her to be quiet – this was between him and his wife. He said he would appreciate it if she just went home and let them have this conversation in private. Catherine definitely would not be going with her. Of course, Catherine burst into tears, but for once, George wasn't moved.

'Catherine, you keep saying "my baby". You seem to forget that it's my baby as well. Surely I have some say in the matter.'

She said, 'But it's me that's having the baby, and I'm going to have it at Flo's.'

Now George lost it. 'Listen to me, woman, I would never have thought I would have to speak to you like this, but you have driven me to it. I am your husband, and there will be no more arguments about it, and for once you will do as I say. This is my first child, and I will decide where it is going to be born. No further argument, understand? You are my wife, and I love you dearly. I want the best for all of us. I know that Flo is your friend, but she is not a midwife, and you are going to have the best of care. Flo means well but she is not "the best of care". You are starting to let her rule your life and I won't have it. Kitty, put Bronze in the cart.'

Kitty said that Chock would be better, because he was faster and could certainly pull an unloaded cart. Eddie, who had heard it all and wished he hadn't, suggested that George and Catherine could stay at his place – there were plenty of beds, and Freddy would be delighted. Kitty would stay at home to feed Eddie and

Rob the roofer and pass stuff up to them as they worked. On the way to Arrowtown George explained his reasoning. First, Flo was not a midwife. Secondly, Mrs O'Leary, the midwife was a practising Catholic and understood very well the problem. Should Catherine come out with 'Holy Mary' or 'Mother of God' or any other Doolan crap, the midwife, knew how to keep quiet about it, as Flo certainly wouldn't. She might not even want to stay friends. Mrs O'Leary said that converts all had the same problem – they reverted when they were in pain or under pressure. No one could forget their early childhood learning and get it right out of their system. The only time she had broken confidence was once, when the worst came to the worst and the mother called for a priest. He had come, and the poor woman had died happy. Even her husband never knew, and she was able to be buried in the Anglican part of the cemetery. It was a long time ago, and he now lay beside her.

Catherine still snivelled quietly and said that she thought George hated Catholics. George said he really didn't hate anybody and named some of his Catholic friends, and he loved her, didn't he? He hated superstition in any form, and he hated any religion that bullied its followers and made them afraid by threatening them with hellfire if they didn't obey their man-made rules. He didn't really approve of the attitude to religion in the place where they had chosen to live, but settlers needed to be part of a community if they wanted to belong. He was an Anglican because it was tolerant and didn't preach hellfire for breaking its rules and he had been born into it. He hadn't gone to any church in New Zealand until he met up with Mr Rees.

They pulled up at Eddie's house where Freddy was delighted to see them. Of course they could stay until Catherine went into labour. He asked Catherine to put the kettle on while he showed George where to leave Chocolate. He actually had a small stable/shed at the back of his section. The cart would stay on the street. While George rubbed the horse down and fed him, he told Freddy what had happened with Flo. He wasn't sure how long it would be, but he would talk to the midwife in the morning. If it wasn't immediate, he would go home, because they had to get the house finished as much as possible before the frosts got heavy.

Freddy said he was very happy to help. He knew where the midwife lived. He thought it might be a good idea if Catherine stayed on with the baby until the house could be kept warm. They went back inside. Catherine had the kettle boiling and was studying the stove with great interest. Freddy said it was past his bedtime and they must be tired too. He would show Catherine how to use the stove in the morning.

George and Catherine went to see the midwife and were assured that she probably had at least a day or two, but it was a good idea to stay in town. Catherine said her friend Flo had said … and she was rebuked by Mrs O'Leary, who said firmly that Flo was not a midwife. She had assisted at a few births, but to the best of her knowledge, Flo had never actually delivered a baby.

When they got back to Freddy's, he was delighted to have his old friend staying for as long as she liked, and by the time she left she would have mastered the use of the oven. George said he had better get along home where there was still so much to be done. He would see them at church on Sunday. He would leave the cart as he had to call on the Jordans to find out if his use of Chock was okay. Monday was Kitty's big day. It was the first day of school, and all bets about Rascal would be settled. They would be in after school to tell her all about it. As George left, Freddy told George quietly that he didn't want Flo visiting and wouldn't be letting her in.

George arrived at Jordan's right on dinner time and told them all that had passed. Daisy reported that Rascal was going well. She was following Kitty's instructions, and now Colin could catch him and handle him, but it would be a long time before Sarah would be ready to ride on her own. She thought it would be a good idea if Kitty were to stay over on Sunday night. It was fine for George to use Chock, and she would saddle up another horse for him to take with him, because they would need two horses on Sunday and Monday. George protested that he had Bronze, but Colin laughed and insisted, saying that one thing George was short of was time, but that he was not to ride Smith, the other horse – it had better be left to Kitty.

Daisy said she would pop in to see Catherine tomorrow, as she was going to Arrowtown. Colin had just killed this morning, so she would take meat, eggs and vegetables to Freddy. She had promised to teach him how to handle his oven. George mentioned that the timing was great and told her about the Reeses' generosity. He'd already told them about the Flo saga. Daisy said that she and Freddy had become great mates. She was helping him to plan his garden, and he had talked to her and Colin about the plans for the cartage business. She went in frequently and would let George know if there was anything Catherine needed. She would come over to the farm and teach Kitty about the use of the oven. When she started talking about managing the dampers, George hastily took his leave, saying that he had to get home.

On Sunday they went to church as usual, leaving home early because Eddie was riding Bronze and Bronze could not keep up with the others. When they arrived Catherine was already there, talking animatedly to Flo. She looked at the horse her daughter had ridden in on and commented that he was too big for her. Kitty laughed and said he was not as big as Tubby. She said that Smith was lovely to ride but had one or two bad habits. Flo was startled and said she had heard of Smith. Fortunately, at that stage, they all went into church, Catherine sitting between Freddy and George.

Because now all members of the congregation lived within an easy ride from the church and the vicar had to rush to take a service in one of the neighbouring villages, the communal lunch was no longer a feature of the day. Freddy took one of Catherine's arms, saying, 'Come on, my dear, say goodbye to your friend. There's a lovely roast in the oven, and we'll have a nice family dinner before the others go home. Bring Smith with you, so you can keep an eye on him. The others will be fine here.'

The vicar rode past, calling out to Kitty, 'I see that I'm not the only one riding a thoroughbred, Kitty. I promise I won't ever be challenging you to a race, but I'd like us to go for a ride together some time.'

'Thank you, Vicar, that would be great, but it's early days yet.'

They enjoyed a lovely lunch and Catherine was proud of her very first roast dinner, especially since she had followed it with a steamed pudding. She said that Daisy was an excellent teacher. She had brought Catherine a recipe book and was embarrassed when reminded that she couldn't read. Catherine actually laughed about it and said she would give it to Kitty and explained that she could memorise anything if it was repeated a few times. Catherine told her family that she had had such a good time with Daisy, learning nursery rhymes and songs and singing together. She said she loved singing with others and since George brayed like a donkey and Kitty mooed like a calving cow, she was going to join the choir after Daisy had taught her all the words of the hymns.

A happy Catherine made for a happy George and a happy Kitty, so it was a happy group that made its way home. Kitty left the others to take Smith back, while they branched off to go home.

It was to be a momentous day. If everything went as well as hoped, Colin stood to make a lot of money, but his relationship with his older brother, who had always bullied him, would be even worse. Albert had always been a very bad loser who liked to bet on a sure thing. Daisy didn't realise just how many side-bets her husband had taken and how much they could lose. They got to the school early only to find what looked like the entire male population of the district waiting, including the vicar and the local policeman. The puzzled headmaster, who was new to the district, simply couldn't understand it. His lady assistant explained the situation and told him firmly that he wouldn't get a single enrolment until the schemozzle was over. There were cheers and groans when Kitty rode in on Rascal.

Albert was furious. He blustered and said that Sarah had to be riding him. Colin, who had insisted that the original bet be recorded and signed with a copy held by each of the brothers, now held his copy up for those who wanted to could come and scrutinise it.

Someone in the crowd started yelling, 'Pay up, Al! Pay up, Al!' and it became a chant. In a break in the chanting, Sarah's piping voice could be heard saying, 'I can ride him, Uncle Al. I can too!' Rascal had been very thoroughly lunged that morning, so Kitty shortened the stirrups and popped Sarah into the saddle, and the crowd moved back to let her proudly ride the pony around the improvised ring. Daisy had just lifted Sarah down when an enraged Albert came charging up. 'All right, you bastard, you win. But he's still my pony and I'll just take him back a bit earlier.' Rascal had other ideas. His ears had gone back when he saw Albert approaching, and Daisy's attention had been wholly on her daughter. As Albert went to grab the reins, Rascal got in first. He lunged forward and grabbed Albert's upper arm in his teeth. He shook his head a few times leaving a bloody wound, let go and then spun around to give Albert both barrels.

Fortunately for him, Albert had slipped to the ground when the pony had let go, and the hooves whistled over his head. Even more fortunately, Colin was at hand to grab the bridle and lead the pony away. Daisy grabbed Sarah and rushed her into the schoolroom, where she became the first enrolment of the year. Then they joined the assistant at the window.

Albert was now on his feet, cradling his bleeding arm. Kitty had taken Rascal to the horse paddock to wipe the sweat off him and calm him down before she let him loose with the other horses. Albert was screaming: 'Bring me my bloody gun. You can see that animal's dangerous. And it's my horse – I can do what I bloody well like with it. I can cut its bloody head off if I want.'

The mood of the crowd had changed. Instead of being festive it was becoming angry, and the losers had turned against Albert. The policeman stepped forward and took him by his uninjured arm and said formally, 'Mr Jordan, we'd better get you to the doctor. Think about this; you are a betting man, and if you bet on horses you know you have wins and losses. I've never heard of you welshing on a bet, and I don't think you'll have many friends left if you welsh on this one, so pay up and come and get that arm seen to.' Colin came up to make an offer.

'Al, I don't want there to be even worse bad feeling between us. I know how much Rascal cost you, and I would like to buy him from you for the same amount.'

Albert screamed: 'I told you, I'm going to shoot the dangerous little bastard. I should have done it instead of making the bet, and I'm going to do it before he kills someone. Besides, he's worth a lot more now than he was then.'

That did it. Someone yelled, 'Now I've heard everything!' The constable, afraid he was going to have a riot on his hands, looked around, and several of the little town's leading citizens stepped up beside him.

'Come on, Jordan, take the money and forget about the little pony. You've been beaten fair and square. Pay your debts like a gentleman or you'll probably get yourself run out of town.' Albert, in spite of his pain, reluctantly managed to start paying. He had to pay his brother in winnings nearly twice as much as Colin had paid him for the pony. Because he hadn't expected to lose, he didn't have much cash with him, but the doctor who had just arrived, stepped out of the crowd and insisted that Albert should come to the surgery. Assisted by the doctor on one side and the policeman on the other, Albert went. Those few bettors who had bet on Kitty followed behind and waited outside. They included Freddy, Eddie, Sam Fletcher, George and one or two men who had seen Kitty riding Rascal on the back roads. And, surprisingly, Flo's husband, Sandy Porter. Albert was going to have to sell something to pay his debts. Eddie seemed excessively jubilant.

Meanwhile, enrolments at the little school had finished, and the few pupils were being settled into classes. There were only two rooms, and the assistant teacher, otherwise known as the Infant Mistress, taught all pupils under the age of ten (which was most of them). The headmaster took the rest. At twelve Kitty was one of the oldest, and although she was reading way ahead of her age and was competent at writing and arithmetic, she was behind in history (kings and queens of England), geography (the colonies comprise the glorious British Empire) and general knowledge (whatever the headmaster had in mind at the moment). She was a little surprised to find that the day started with a short prayer and the singing of the national anthem. She had always wondered why the King needed God to save him. After the first time it was sung, Kitty was excused singing for the rest of the time she was at school.

Two days later, at ten in the morning, Billy Kirk decided to be born after only five hours' labour. Kitty was at school when Mrs O'Leary sent someone to tell the news to an anxious Freddy, who had been awake half the night. He was on his way to hire a horse when, fortunately, he ran into Daisy who had escorted Sarah to school and was about to return home. She persuaded Freddy that she could get the message to George a great deal more quickly than he could, and the best thing he could do was to meet Kitty and give her the news after school. She could go and see her mother and her new brother. Then Daisy took off.

When George arrived he found Kitty and Freddy talking to Catherine. Kitty was holding the baby with a bemused and doting look on her face. The bond she formed then was to last for both their lifetimes. She and Freddy went off to Freddy's, leaving the three Kirks together. Kitty stayed the night with Freddy and the beaming George.

Because there was now even more urgency to get the house finished, it was decided that George and Kitty should go back immediately and Catherine and Billy would stay on with Freddy until Mrs O'Leary deemed it fit for them to go home. They would come home when the place could be kept warm. The days were rapidly getting shorter, and the nights frostier. Rob the roofer had finished his work and gone. The windows and outside doors were fitted, but there was still a lot to do to make the place draught-proof and warm enough for a newborn.

Kitty made brief calls after school, but there was still all her work to be done at home. Besides, she had homework to do. George had bought two very good mantle lamps, a number of candlesticks and a good supply of candles. The stove was in place and working well, but there was still a lot to be done. George had measured the windows for curtains so that Kitty could go with Catherine to choose the material, have them cut to size and then hem them. Daisy had given Catherine a pram, so she was able to take her baby for walks around the little township. One morning she bumped into Flo, and they made arrangements to meet frequently. Flo's saying that she wouldn't come to the 'horrible man's house' saved Catherine the embarrassment of having to tell her that she wouldn't be let in anyway. Catherine asked her to come when she and Kitty bought the curtain material, and Flo, being Flo, had tried to take charge. She started to tell Catherine that she must buy a bolt or half a bolt of material and hold it up against the windows to cut it. Kitty, trying to be tactful, explained that George had a better way of doing it, and Flo snorted that it was women's business and what would a man know?

The shopkeeper saved the day. 'Good morning, Mrs Kirk. Good morning, Mrs Porter, and of course, Miss Kitty. What can I do for you?'

Before Flo could speak Kitty handed him the detailed measurements that she and George had worked on. 'All my mother needs to do is choose the material and an assortment of needles and spools of cotton, and two pair of scissors – they must be really good ones, Pa says.'

'In short, you want a complete sewing kit with everything in it that you could possibly want. I have the very thing right here.' He lifted a large sewing basket on to the counter and opened it. Laughing, he said, 'I may be a mere man, but may I point out that you had forgotten pins, thimbles, oh, several other things and most importantly something to keep everything in. The scissors are the very best quality, and there are three pair: a pair of shears and two pair of different sizes.'

Catherine gazed on this treasure chest with shining eyes. 'It's absolutely beautiful,' she gasped, 'but we can't possibly afford it.'

'I can,' said Kitty shortly. 'It's my present to you for giving me such a lovely little brother.'

The shopkeeper clapped his hands in applause. 'I should have congratulated you both, you for your new arrival, Mrs Kirk and you, Miss Kitty, for doing so well with that pony. You must be quite a rich little lady, and you are spending it well. I am not a betting man myself, but, ladies, I heard that both your husbands did very well indeed.'

Before the astonished ladies could speak, Kitty rushed in. 'Thank you, Mr Burton. Ma, could you two please go and look at curtaining while I sort out some other stuff. I have to write out Freddy's address so that everything can be delivered. Pa said you were to buy the best so it would last, and before you ask, yes he can afford it. And please don't take too long because I have work to do at home.' As soon as they were out of earshot she told the shopkeeper that George wanted to open an account but to keep it to himself. It was only to be used if George or Kitty was there and, even then, not if Flo was present. He said he understood perfectly and apologised for letting the cat out of the bag. He thought that Flo's husband would be in for it when she got home, but a lot of his money would have gone down the drain at the pub already. Kitty told him that she was too young to bet, and a female as well, in case he hadn't noticed. Mr Jordan had paid her well for breaking in the pony, and she had wanted to buy her mother a present.

She called to the others to please hurry – she had to get home. The shopkeeper told her that she had done the town a favour. Albert Jordan had had to sell his business to settle his bets. There had been nasty rumours of tar and feathers or even a lynch party, and she probably had heard that the nice young chap that was helping George and his uncle had bought it lock, stock and barrel and that they were forming a company with Colin Jordan. They wouldn't have had to pay much, as they had all backed Kitty heavily, as had George. He shut up promptly when he saw Catherine and Flo arriving back with what was probably Flo's choice. Kitty was anxious to finish the business and get home. As a present for being such good customers, Catherine was given a complete set of knitting needles and crochet hooks.

Chapter Ten

With her mind buzzing Kitty had what was probably her fastest ride home ever, and when she arrived, she saw Colin Jordan's horse but she curbed her impatience and attended to her horse. Her other chores would have to wait. She went inside to find the three men sitting at the table with papers strewn all over the place. She was about to deliver an angry little speech that she had been preparing all the way home, but George completely took the wind out of her sails.

'Ah, Kitty. Thank goodness you're here. Where have you been? We needed you.'

'Buying curtains. Flo turned up to help.' The three men groaned in unison. She continued: 'I suppose you're going to tell me about this partnership you are cooking up.'

'Flo already? My God, she doesn't miss a trick!'

'No, for once you can't blame her. I feel sorry for her poor husband. You should have seen her face and Ma's when Mr Burton commented that both you and he must have done very well from your bets. Luckily she didn't hear him talking about your business, but she'll probably pick up all the details very soon. And Eddie, remember you sort of talked about your plans for settling here in front of her. You said it would be good advertising.'

'Burton. That man has ears and a mouth like Flo but without the malice. It must be good for trade – drop in to buy some pins and the latest gossip.'

'Okay, I have work still to do, I'm thirsty and I would like a cup of tea.'

Eddie had forestalled her. 'Here's your tea. And I've done all your chores, so all there is to do is let Chock go. We'll tell you all about it while you eat. Colin is happy to ride home in the moonlight.'

Colin, Eddie and Freddy had indeed bought Albert out, because he had taken bets directly with them and with George and the few other brave souls who had believed in Kitty. Those who had bet that Albert would win had lost their money to bookmakers. They were angry with Albert, because he had bragged all over town and beyond that he was going to teach his smart-arse little brother the lesson of his life.

Kitty listened as she ate, but she said she was wondering why Freddy and Catherine weren't there, and she said she thought they should be included in any business discussions. George explained that he had chosen not to be involved in the company as he was a dairyman at heart and wanted to spend his winnings on setting up the dairy business so he and Catherine could work together. He was trying to find some more Jerseys, but he still expected to get a real good telling-off from Catherine when she found how much he had wagered, as well as a whole lot of 'What if you'd lost?'

George would be contracted on a casual basis when needed. Kitty would be employed fully in the next school holidays and whenever she had the time, to help choose and train horses. Bronze, who was now practically unemployed, would work for the company or would be exchanged for a lighter horse and trap that Catherine could manage easily. There was a very nice little vehicle that had been lying unused and dirty in Albert's yard, but it could be cleaned up, and Kitty could look for the right animal to pull it. The transport was to be organised and hopefully running in time to bring Catherine and Billy home when the house was ready for them.

'Anyone would think we were scared of her,' Kitty joked.

'I am,' laughed George.

'So am I. Well, I'm the one who gets the rough side of her tongue the most often. When the dairy gets going you can bet she will want me to give up the horses and transfer my love for them to cows. I won't. I did love the cows, and still do, but that was before I found out what I could do with horses. And Freddy? What about Freddy?'

'He's busy remembering forgotten skills, wallowing in a sea of paper. He was a bookkeeper at some stage in his past, somewhere or other. He's voted himself in as General Manager, Despatch Clerk and doubtless a lot of other titles if he can think of them. Sometimes he runs numbers over with Catherine, because there's no one on earth who can add up as quickly as she can. She doesn't have a clue about what he's doing, and we can't let her in on it because of Flo. Once everything is set up and legal, of course, we'll tell her all about it.'

'Your house is the first priority, of course,' Colin put in. 'Daisy and I are starting to clear up some of Albert's mess, and Eddie will join us once Catherine is home and sorted. We'll get transport for you first. But I'm off home now. Kitty, one of us will come to the school at lunch time, because there's a lot more we need to talk about.'

Each day after school Kitty went to Freddy's to play with Billy and to pick up any curtains that Catherine had finished hemming. On Saturday they came over to exchange Bronze and the cart for a lighter rig and for George to spend some time with his wife and son. They brought Smith back too. Kitty reluctantly had decided to give up on him. She told Daisy that the horse hadn't a brain in his head, that he was now fine on the ground, but let him out on the open road you just couldn't stop him, because the corners of his mouth were a mess of scar tissue. She thought he would make a wonderful show horse for Daisy, provided he was only ridden in the ring. On the open road he was just plain dangerous. At seven he was too old and not fast enough to go back to the track, so… George and Kitty drove home together in a neat little trap pulled by a large roan pony called Ruby. Tied on behind was another patient for Kitty. Chocolate was still at home, having a day off, not that he needed it.

Next day, after church, when they were all at Freddy's for dinner, Catherine was very happy to be told that she could come home after church next week. She was even happier when, after dinner, the family drove around the streets of Arrowtown in the trap with Catherine proudly at the reins. Ruby was a very pretty pony and had been polished to perfection. At first sight of the rig Catherine had asked suspiciously how much it had cost, but was instantly mollified when it was explained that it had been exchanged for Bronze and the cart.

The following week was very busy for Eddie, George and Kitty. The house had to be cleaned, the curtains hung, and it was looking very cosy indeed. Flo had turned up with some beautiful crocheted rugs she had made, and having inspected the kitchen she pointed out that there were a few necessities that had been overlooked. At her dictation Kitty made a list and suggested that Flo should meet Catherine in town to buy them. She said she would love to. Furthermore, she would bring everything back, install it and help with any other bits and pieces. Kitty thanked her and said that she would go to the shop after school and settle up.

For the rest of the week Flo turned up daily and was amazingly helpful. Kitty was at school, and apart from saying that she thought that Kitty should be at home helping, she didn't mention her again. She called in each morning and brought scones and cakes. She fed the hens and brought in the eggs. The camp oven remained the bread cooker, and George had a routine for baking bread. He mixed and kneaded the dough at night and put it into the camp oven. In the morning it was nicely risen. The fire had been carefully banked for the night, and it was a matter of minutes to clear the ashes away and settle the oven into the hot embers. More embers were settled onto the lid and a little more wood piled around it. As soon as they'd finished breakfast the fire was banked again, and by dinner time the smell of fresh bread called them to eat. Often they tucked large potatoes into the ashes to be ready at the same time as the bread. Once or twice a week Flo drove into town to meet Catherine and keep her up to date with the progress on the house.

On Sunday Catherine was brought triumphantly home. They made her wait until after dinner at Freddy's so they could take the remains of the leg of mutton home. Catherine drove the trap with Kitty beside her, because the proud father insisted on sitting in the back, cuddling and talking to his son. When Billy tired of this and started complaining, and complaining very loudly at that, the trap was stopped and they changed places. The squirming Billy was quickly handed back to his mother. Kitty took the reins, and for the rest of the way home they went a lot faster.

Life settled down. Kitty went to school in the morning. Eddie had gone back to Arrowtown where he and Colin spent their days clearing and organising the yard. Freddy tirelessly worked on the legalities and details of registering the company. After much debate they had decided to call it, simply, Wakatip Transport Company. During the May school holidays Colin, Eddie and Kitty went looking at horses. Because it was now early winter, it was far too late to buy feed. There was not a lot of work expected. Tubby would come into his own for the spring ploughing, and she would have to get him fit.

When the frosts became really hard Kitty had to leave her bivvy and move inside into Billy's room. Catherine was very happy about this, but Kitty of course was not. Catherine wanted to get back to the early days in Dunedin when Kitty was her loving and obedient daughter. She blamed the big change on Kitty's discovery of her affinity with horses and not on the fact that her daughter was growing up. Nor did she take into consideration Kitty's last horrible year in Dunedin, when she was branded as the daughter of an adulteress.

When Kitty shifted inside, Catherine started to pile domestic duties on her, as well as what had been established as her main job, looking after the animals. One task, however, she relished. Billy was a fretful, difficult baby, and every time he cried in the night, she took him to his mother. When he had finished feeding she got up again, changed his nappy, burped him and put him back in his cot. At school she started showing signs of fatigue. Because the roads were frozen she could not ride so fast, so of course this meant that she had to leave earlier. When, one Sunday after church, the headmaster tried to talk to her parents, Catherine said that the answer was obvious. Kitty had to leave school. This made George quite angry. He would not countenance her leaving without her Proficiency Certificate. He, George, would take on some of Kitty's duties so she would not be so tired. The teacher said that Kitty had a brain and that it would be good if she could go to high school, but Kitty herself vetoed this, saying she had a job to go to at the end of the year. At this Catherine bridled and said she needed Kitty to help her with Billy because he was such a handful. George said this would be discussed at home and thanked the teacher for his help. The discussion became rancid when Billy's cradle was moved into his parent's room so that Kitty could get some more sleep.

The Confirmation ceremony passed without fuss from Kitty, and as Rees still had business in the Wakatipu, he combined his visit with that and the christening of William Frederick Kirk, to whom he presented a handsome silver christening mug. Frances, in absentia, was named godmother. Everyone was very happy, except Flo, who had expected to be godmother. The uncomfortable Catherine managed to explain that it had been settled by George before they had even met Flo, and she had to be happy with that.

Kitty remained at school but no longer had to get up in the night to attend to Billy. Catherine had to do that herself and was not at all pleased about it. When she said that she, too, needed her sleep, she was ignored. George did some of Kitty's chores, and when the roads were closed because of deep snow, sometimes the school was closed too. When the school remained open and the roads were bad, Kitty stayed with Freddy and Eddie. Eddie was very often quite late home because he was courting the young teacher.

Courting a respectable young woman who lived with her parents was a long process, as the suitor was expected to prove his suitability. Eddie had a business on the way to being established. The company was registered and was due to open for business in the spring. Because of this Eddie had a distinct advantage over other suitors. Besides, Jeannie said very firmly that he was her choice and she absolutely wouldn't look at anyone else. They would be getting engaged on her next birthday. Her mother breathed a sigh of relief. Her daughter was twenty-three and was considered by most people to be 'on the shelf'. Now she could start planning the wedding.

Freddy had become very popular in the township, and the paperwork was in good order. Eddie owned the cottage, but Freddy disclosed that in all his years in Dunedin he had spent very little of his remittance. There was a very nice but run-down house on five acres just outside town. He proposed that he should buy that for Eddie to live in when they were married. It was a large house, just the thing for a large family. Eddie nearly choked on his tea when told that Freddy expected the family name to be kept going. Freddy would keep the cottage in town and turn the spare bedroom into the company office. The balance would be Freddy's wedding present to the young couple.

A happy Eddie raced around to tell his future in-laws, who said that their wedding present would be to do up the house for the young couple. Eddie planned to move in almost immediately so that the company office could be set up forthwith, signage and all. Jeannie said they could get engaged now and advance the date of the wedding. She had to give three months notice to the school as the policy was not to employ married women, and that gave her mother time to plan the wedding and her father to get the house cleaned up and ready for them. It was now early June, so it could be a spring wedding.

Everyone was delighted that things had worked out so well. Kitty declined the request to be bridesmaid. She just couldn't bear the thought of wearing that sort of dress. This made her very unpopular with Catherine, who said once again that it was time she started being a girl. Kitty said that she was very happy the way she was, thank you very much. She was doing all her chores, and if Catherine would stop telling her to stop wasting time when she was doing her homework, she would get her certificate and leave school at the end of the year. If not she would have to go back next year.

The winter was a hard one. At the end of it everyone was happy. The wedding was celebrated but the honeymoon had to be put off for a while until the business got going. Jeannie would be busy all day sewing curtains and sorting out the huge old house.

Kitty loved Jeannie. She borrowed an old retired pony from Colin for lawn-mowing duties and compost-making. When Jeannie asked to be taught to ride, Kitty was surprised. 'Aren't you going to start having babies?' she asked. Jeannie laughed and said they had decided not to start a family for at least a year so that they could have some fun first. Kitty was baffled. 'I thought that when you get married you – you know – and you have babies.' An amused Jeannie laughed and said: 'There can be plenty of "you know" without having to have babies.'

Kitty was amazed. 'How?' she demanded.

'I'm not going to tell you that. When you get older and need to know, come and ask me then. I really shouldn't be talking to you about this sort of thing, so for heaven's sake don't tell anybody that we had this conversation or I'll be in trouble. My problem is that you've become my very good friend, and I constantly forget how young you are. Now, when can I learn to ride?'

Spring came and with it, Surprise's heifer calf, who, after some discussion, was named Patches. As Catherine said, she was sort of spotty and sort of blotchy. George favoured 'Dot' because, in his eyes, she was half-Jersey and therefore half-dotty anyway. Kitty wanted 'Polka', which Catherine dismissed as being too posh. Surprise and Patches settled nicely into Catherine's routine. They were together until Patches had had the beestings (colostrum), which took about two days. Then they were in adjacent yards until Patches learnt to drink out of a bucket. They were back together for a while after morning milking until Patches learned that there was more nourishment in a bucket than in her mother.

Catherine was now much happier. She was pregnant again, and apart from demanding more of Kitty's time and being told again that if her daughter failed Proficiency, George was adamant that she would repeat the year, Catherine got on with the business of looking after the house and the baby and largely left Kitty alone. If Catherine wanted to go out she had Ruby and the trap, which she could manage by herself, so she could call on Flo when Flo wasn't visiting her. Always a good cook on an open fire, her time at Freddy's, when Daisy came and gave both her and Freddy cooking lessons, had made her proficient in the use of the oven. The camp oven was still used for bread and had its own outdoor fireplace. This left the oven free for her baking, and she was soon turning out cakes and scones. Kitty, surprisingly, became very interested in baking, and she would read a recipe out to Catherine until it had been learnt by rote. Their repertoire increased. Flo became a little jealous until she, who had believed that you could learn nothing from books, now wanted recipes read out to her.

This period of near-harmony made George very happy, although he saw it as a truce rather a complete cessation of hostilities. Things flared up again when the weather became warm enough for Kitty to move back to her bivvy.

The cartage business was now up and running very nicely and very efficiently. Tubby and Eddie came to the Kirks' to do the spring ploughing. Freddy had found an advertisement in the paper about a dairy farm in northern Southland that was selling up, and George had persuaded a reluctant Catherine to travel with him to check it out, but she happily agreed when she learnt that they would stay for a night or two with Dougal and Eily. She asked Kitty if she would enjoy seeing Chrissie again, and their baby, Duncan, who was two months older than Billy. Kitty looked at her blankly and asked her who she expected to look after the farm and the animals if there was nobody here. Catherine hadn't thought of that and, screeching, said that a girl as young as Kitty couldn't possibly stay on her own. It wouldn't be proper. A furious argument followed, and Kitty was about to storm out when she had a bright idea.

'What say I stay at the Jordans' at night? I could get up early and ride over, check everything before school, come back after school and check again then ride back to stay the night.'

'Impossible.' said Catherine. 'What about Surprise? You wouldn't have time to milk her. It could only work if you didn't go to school.'

At this George decided to enter the fray. 'Be quiet a moment, you two. It could work. We could take Surprise and the calf over to the Jordans' the day before we leave and put everything else into one of the back paddocks. Then Kitty would only have to come over once a day to look around and tend to the hens. We take the dogs and she takes the pups, except the one she promised to the Scotts.'

'No. It's too far for Surprise to walk. She'll have to stay home from school, and that's the end of it.'

'It's far from the end of it. Kitty will not be missing school so close to the exams. It's not very far to the Jordans' when you go the back way.'

'What back way?' asked Catherine in surprise. 'I've never heard of any back way.'

They realised that she'd never walked over the farm further than the front pasture. When George explained, she was horrified.

'You mean that Kitty has been sneaking out that way all this time without my knowing!'

Kitty left to go to bed. She'd had enough.

George had had enough, too. 'Listen, Catherine, this is what is going to happen, and there won't be any argument. The stock is going into the back paddock, except for Surprise who is going to the Jordans' with Kitty.

'I'm sure your friend Flo would be happy to pop across every day to look after the hens, and then Kitty would have an easier time. And no more nonsense about her using the back way. It's a lot shorter than going by the road. We've already planned to make it fit for vehicles when we have Tubby here for the ploughing. Then you can use it too. It'll take half an hour off your trip to Arrowtown.'

He stood up, yawned and stretched. 'Bedtime. If you don't start trusting your daughter, you'll end up driving her away altogether.'

All went as planned. Catherine and George arrived back with two Jersey cows that were not young but still capable of producing calves, plus a butter churn and various other pieces of dairy equipment she had never thought she would be able to own. The dogs had had a good run, and Toss was in pup again. George had enjoyed a whole week of complete harmony, Billy had been good for once and George was happy that Catherine was pregnant again. His life and business were right on track.

Kitty had enjoyed being away from home. Eddie and Tubby had made a good start on ploughing the fields that the company was leasing from George. The back track was now suitable for vehicles, except if heavy rain made it muddy. The front thirty acres were reserved for the dairy, and the rest, which included the high country, was leased to the company. Materials were being assembled for a large barn, big enough to accommodate the needs of the dairy business and the cartage business. When Catherine wanted work started on the dairy straight away, George told her firmly that other things came first and that with only one cow in milk she could manage very well as she was until the winter feed was organised and her other cow calved. The new cows were turned out to enjoy Bully's attention, along with Flo's old Durham.

The end of the school year came, and Kitty graduated in about the middle of the class. She had her certificate. Catherine demanded more of Kitty's time and refused to understand that Kitty had a paid job, but when she realised that her daughter was actually earning money, she wanted her to hand it over. Once again George had to intervene and explain that Kitty was paying for various fittings in the barn and make it sound as if she were handing all her money to him. It was partly true. Kitty was fixing herself a tack room with a work bench where she could repair leather goods. She intended to put in a bunk for next winter. When asked why she chose the inconvenience of the attic, she replied tersely, 'For privacy.' When her mother wanted to know what was up there, Kitty just said it was horse stuff.

Kitty turned thirteen, and life went on pretty much as usual. Another row erupted when George and Catherine took Bully and Patches to the local show and stock market. Catherine wanted Kitty to prepare them and show them. Kitty said she was sorry but she hadn't time, she was showing some horses. George said that there was no problem, he could do it and Catherine just had to learn because showing was now to be part of their lives if they were to sell their pedigree bull calves. He would show Bully, and she would have to show the calf. He would be selling Bully's services.

The next eruption came when Catherine saw her daughter, resplendent in one of Daisy's riding habits, riding sidesaddle and showing horses in several classes. 'Just who does she think she is?' she hissed to George. 'This horse business has turned her head. She thinks she's a nob, and she's only a dairymaid.'

'Shut up and clap,' hissed George back. 'Be proud of your daughter. She's a horsewoman and never will be a dairymaid. Get used to it. Keep your spite under your hat at least until we get home, and for God's sake, smile.'

George proudly led Bully around the ring and introduced him by his three-worded polysyllabic pedigree name, and of course he won his class, being the only dairy bull in the district. Catherine was pleased to learn that only a child could show a calf, and she wanted to send for Kitty. George laughed and said that Kitty wasn't dressed for the job and that since she had qualified as a 'lady rider', she could no longer be considered to be a child. Before anything else could be said, Sarah arrived, fresh from winning 'Best School Pony' on Rascal, saying that Kitty had sent her over in case they wanted her to show Patches.

When it came time for the events, Kitty, riding several different horses came a consistent second or third in every event she entered. Daisy, on Smith, won every event she entered, including the high jump. This took some managing as the judges said it was unknown for a woman to compete against men. It was grudgingly agreed that she could compete, and they were horrified when she won on a horse that several of them had owned and sold on as being either useless or dangerous. Daisy didn't want to keep Smith, because apart from in the show ring or on the race track, he was useless. Several men came to her and offered to buy him. Colin overheard this and said that after the presentations they would be having an auction and selling not only Smith but also several of the other horses that Daisy and Kitty had shown and anything that anyone else wanted to sell.

Freddy had offered to be auctioneer, and he made it a hilarious event. All the horses the Jordans offered sold well above the price expected, and they had bought some replacements. Smith brought in a phenomenal price.

When they were ready to leave, the Jordans, accompanied by Kitty, came up leading Chocolate, who was still wearing a ribbon around his neck. Colin said, 'George, I understand that it just happens to be your fortieth birthday today. Well, Daisy, Kitty, Sarah and I just happen to have a present for you,' and he handed him Chock's reins. 'The horse is from Daisy, Sarah and me, and the bridle and saddle are from your talented daughter. Happy Birthday, old man.'

George did not know what to say. Kitty gave him a big kiss, and the men who were standing around sang 'Happy Birthday' and cheered. Catherine turned to Kitty and told her to come with them, as she didn't want her to be late home.

Daisy asked if Kitty could please come with them as they would need her to help them with their new horses, which included two that Kitty had chosen for the cartage company. There was a great deal to do, and they would be very late finishing. Jeannie said she and Eddie would very much like Kitty to stay the night as she might be too tired to ride home, and they would like the Kirks to come to dinner after church tomorrow. George quickly said that that would be splendid but now they'd better be off. Billy was starting to play up and needed to be home in bed. Jeannie wanted to get her mother, Catherine, Daisy and Freddy, who now fancied himself as a chef, to get together to plan for a company Christmas dinner. They could work out a date on Sunday.

The rest of the year passed in a rush. Christmas dinner was

a splendid affair, and Kitty had been extravagant with presents, especially for baby Billy, whom she adored. She had sold Sam Fletcher a pup and given one to the Scotts. The remaining three went to Colin, Eddie and Jeannie, and Freddy. The female Jordans received beautiful bridles that she had made herself.

A few days later Kitty came back from working a stock horse in the high country, and she was bursting with a new idea. She'd found a spot on their stream where there were some abandoned pipes and the remains of a water-race. She thought it might be possible to pipe water to some of the paddocks without drying up the stream. It was. The dairy paddocks were too large and were to have been reorganised anyway. George climbed onto Chock, and they rode around, looking into all the possibilities. When they were riding home George was happily looking into the future and including Kitty in his plans. Kitty told him unhappily that her future had to lie off the farm. Things were difficult enough now, but when she finally got through to Catherine that she would never, ever become a dairymaid and they would have to employ someone else that they would actually have to pay, it would be impossible for Kitty to live there. Now that they had four cows and a heifer calf, and three of those cows in calf, that time wasn't too far off.

George was upset. He thought about it, then conceded that his life would be better if he weren't always piggy-in-the-middle. He said that Kitty would always be his daughter, and he didn't want to lose her too soon. He and Catherine could manage four cows easily themselves, as they had in Dunedin, because they weren't going to sell milk, just cheese and butter, and they would have pigs. He would appreciate it if Kitty would stay for as long as she could. Their dairy would be better equipped and organised than the one in Dunedin and would be finished by the time the baby was born.

For the next eighteen months or so, life went on in the same pattern. Kitty was employed by the cartage company, which was prospering, Catherine had her new son, who they called Georgeboy, who was a big baby, the image of his father. Wee Billy was still impossible. Georgeboy was followed a year later by Catherine's long-desired daughter. The little girl was named Elizabeth, and she was the image of her mother. They called her Lizzie, and Catherine doted on her from the very beginning. Billy hated his siblings and had to be kept away from them, or they wore his tooth marks. Kitty was still the only person who could manage him.

After a few months a parcel containing an exquisite christening robe arrived from the happy grandmother. It was too late and too small for the robust Georgeboy but perfect for beautiful Lizzie. There was a sad letter telling George that his father had died, but also bringing good news in that one of his brothers wanted to come to New Zealand because there was no work for him at home. Another dairyman would be very welcome. Sadly it didn't make things any better between Catherine and Kitty.

Kitty had now passed her fourteenth birthday and was starting to feel interested in the opposite sex. Not in any particular person, but she talked to Jeannie, who still hadn't had any children. She explained that she sort of understood what cows felt when they were 'bulling'. It was just a feeling as yet, but did that feeling ever become uncontrollable? She was determined not to give in to it without being married, but now what? Jeannie said she really must talk to her mother. She said that she, Jeannie, would always be there for Kitty, no matter what happened.

One day Freddy arrived for dinner at the Kirks'. He walked into the middle of a row. Kitty had said it was now time for her to be told something about her father, and Catherine refused point-blank. When George said yes, it was time, she refused and burst into tears. Freddy, on hearing this, told her if she didn't tell Kitty, he would tell her. Eddie had inadvertently stumbled on it on his recent visit to Ireland. It was absolutely time for Kitty to know. He agreed it was not a good idea to tell her the family name, it wasn't a name to be proud of, but everything else she should be told, and she should be told the truth. George hoped that with this behind them, his women might get on better. Poor George was wrong.

Tearfully, Catherine stuttered a bit then started. The whole sorry saga came tumbling out. She had to be prompted to talk about what she called 'the urge'. Freddy took over. He explained that almost all in the family matured early and became uncontrollable. The whole district knew about this and tried to keep their daughters out of sight or marry them off young. Kitty's father had just turned fifteen, so his promise to marry Catherine had been well meant but nonetheless a lie.

Catherine said that she couldn't understand about Jack Cameron and why she had been rushed into marrying him straight after Kitty's birth or why he'd had to be sent out of the country in such a hurry. He had never even attempted to touch her. Freddy explained that Jack's vice had been boys. Catherine said that Kitty should not be hearing this – she was too young to understand. This made Kitty laugh.

'Oh Ma,' she said. 'There's quite a bit of that 'round here. If you really want to know, ask Flo.' Then she thought a bit, then asked, 'Does this mean that I am actually related to Jack Cameron?'

'I'm afraid it does,' said Freddy. 'He's your grandfather's brother. "Cameron" is his middle name. Eddie saw his name on a memorial in the local churchyard. Apparently he was lost at sea two years before you were born. Eddie learnt about this when he went to see about buying some thoroughbreds for a mate in Dunedin. Oh yes, Kitty, the whole family are horsemen, but the only "whisperer" was a woman some generations ago, before they developed this habit of marrying rich English women. Your Arthur has done just that and has a brood of children. He is now the heir. His older brother was killed in India in 1857. I think that covers everything, and I hope, Catherine, you will now feel free to answer any more questions that crop up.'

'I don't think this needed to be talked about yet,' said Catherine. 'Kitty's too young. I was going to tell her before she got married.'

'Ma, I'm only about three months younger than you were when you got pregnant. I'm much more likely to avoid that sort of trouble now than I was when you tried to keep me ignorant.'

'All I wanted to do was to keep you innocent and teach you to be a proper obedient girl and to know your place and not get ideas above your station. Was that so bad?'

'Ma, that time in Dunedin destroyed any "innocence" I ever had. I was called every dirty name those kids could think of. I had stones thrown at me, and I was chased out of school not because of anything I'd done but because you and Pa got together. That turned out to be the best thing that ever happened to both of us, but until I got to know Pa, the only person I could talk to was Freddy. And what did innocence get you? It got you pregnant with me when you were only fourteen.'

'I was in love, and he promised that we would get married.'

George intervened. 'There was no chance of that. He would have to have waited until he was twenty-one before he could get married without his father's permission. Anyway, I am very happy that it happened the way it did, because it gave me the love of my life and two sons and two daughters to adore. Now, I think it's time to stop talking and get on with our chores. And thank you, Freddy, for being here. You have always been a good friend to all of us.'

Kitty had a horse to exercise, so she rode along with Freddy as far as the back gate. They chatted about land usage and company business and made no reference to the previous conversation. When they said goodbye and Kitty leaned over and hugged Freddy, there were tears in her eyes.

'Thank you for everything, Freddy. I don't know what I would have done without you.'

For the next few months there was comparative peace in the Kirk home. Kitty's fifteenth birthday passed quietly, and Billy had grown into a little boy who was too lively for words. George had built a childproof yard beside the dairy, and Kitty had stocked it with a lot of expensive toys, but Billy, now three, was starting to fret about being contained. He had to be kept away from his siblings, so whenever possible Kitty started taking him up in front of her when exercising a quiet horse. After he started trying to fight her for control of the reins, she brought over Sarah's old pre-Rascal school pony and took him on a leading rein. George started to do the same thing, but Catherine didn't approve. She said he had to grow up knowing that he was born to be a dairyman, not a horseman. George laughed and said that everyone should learn to ride, whatever his job. George was born to be a dairyman, and he couldn't remember when he couldn't ride. How could anyone know what a three-year-old would want to be when he grew up? The idea that anyone could actually choose a job was utterly foreign to Catherine, and she said so. When she said that they were building up the dairy business for their children, or what was the point, George said that he hoped that was so, but he thought that they were enjoying building it up for themselves, and he hoped that at least one of their children would want to carry it on. Seeing that she was pregnant again, could she please give him another boy? Meanwhile, Kitty was strengthening the bond with Billy that would last all their lives.

After the autumn rains were over and all the tanks were full, George, Kitty and the company sat down to talk about the use of the stream. George wanted to subdivide the dairy paddocks, now four large ones, into eight small ones. That way he would need water piped to troughs. He also pointed out that the dairy and the house had to have clean water, so he planned to fence off the stream. He outlined Kitty's discovery of the old mine-workings and suggested that they should go and have a look so they could plan the best usage of the land he was leasing to the company.

After they'd explored the stream from beginning to end and had decided that the scheme was feasible, it was left to the farmers, George and Colin, to plan the subdivision. Freddy and Catherine would work out the finances, and Eddie would try to find a former goldminer to advise them about the hydraulics and work on building a dam for the house. Catherine took a bit of persuading because she was so naturally thrifty, but she came to see it as a good idea because they would be able to increase the size of the herd. Then Kitty would have to stay home and help her mother. She shouldn't be roaming all over the countryside the way she did.

The fencing went ahead as planned, and quickly, as it was agreed to employ a local fencing gang to do the work. Bully, who had done his work for the season, now looked a fearsome beast (which he wasn't) and had been retired to the high country along with Tubby (whose work was mostly seasonal) and any company horses who needed a break. Eddie came back from Queenstown, saying he had employed a man who had been a gold miner and a farmer. He was, Eddie said, a tall strong-looking man in his mid-twenties. He didn't ride but was a fast walker and was on his way. He wanted to stay on the farm on working days but would go back to Queenstown each Friday night and return each Sunday night. He went to church in Queenstown, and his life was there. His name was John Kregg.

Catherine said that now Kitty would have to move inside, and they could fix up the bivvy for him. She was furious to learn that Kitty hadn't been sleeping in the bivvy for ages – she'd made herself a very comfortable bunk in her tack room, and that's where she slept now. At the rate Catherine was breeding they needed every bit of room they had for the family. They would soon have to build on another room or two. Catherine was furious and demanded to see Kitty's room. She was even angrier when she saw that it was only accessible by ladder and that George had known about it, having built the bunk. George said he needed Kitty's help to fix up the bivvy for the man who was on his way, and then they both fled.

John Kregg arrived about an hour later, and after they had had a cup of tea, he wanted to see his accommodation, then he wanted to look at the job. Luckily he had brought a bed-roll. After making sure that the bivvy was waterproof, he could sort the rest out later. He wanted to get to work. It was now mid-afternoon, but when Kitty said she would bring up some horses, he refused, saying that he and horses had nothing to do with one another. They could ride if they wished, but he would walk, thank you very much. George said it was too late in the day to get to the back boundary, but they would go and look at the site for the dairy and plan the dam. Catherine was anxious to get that built as soon as possible, as more cows would be coming into milk in spring. When John wanted to know who was the boss here and who he had to answer to, George felt a bit affronted. He explained that he and Colin were the bosses, but the dairy was his and Catherine's. He managed the farm, but she was the butter and cheese maker and very skilled at it. She knew the dairy business and how best to progress it, so anything she suggested had to become a priority because the business would have to be the main support for the rapidly growing family. There was a steady income from the lease to the company, but Colin managed that land, and the company employed George on a casual basis. It also employed Kitty. George said that Catherine was actually easy to get on with in every respect except for her dealings with Kitty, which were volcanic, to say the least. He went on to explain the company structure and how that worked. John said he now understood, he just wanted to make it quite plain that he wouldn't take orders from a woman.

In the morning John, George and Colin walked the length of the stream, with Colin complaining that if God had meant him to climb hills He would have given him four legs. The back of the farm now had a boundary fence but had not yet been subdivided. Apart from the stream there was a small creek crossing the property, which could be useful if it was decided to put in more fences, but that could wait. When Tubby and Bully spotted them and wandered up, John seemed uncomfortable. When George said he thought John had been a farmer, he explained that yes, he had worked on farms, but that it had been agricultural work, mainly just labouring. While they were there, Kitty arrived on a sweating horse, and it was explained to John that if stones were to be moved, Kitty and Tubby would be on the job with the kōneke. He queried whether a slight young woman like Kitty would be able to manage a monster like Tubby, they all laughed, and Colin said that he didn't think a horse that Kitty couldn't manage had been born yet.

When John detailed the need to shift the miners' pipes and various other things and wanted to know if they had the manpower for the job, Kitty asked if they would bring Tubby down with them when they came back home and load what was wanted onto the kōneke so she could bring it up in the morning. On her way down she would work out the best route for Tubby and the koneke. Then she turned to Colin and said that because it looked as if she would be working with them on the waterworks, it would be best if, when Colin came back down to get his horse, he took 'this donkey' with him, because it was ready to go back to its owner. If a faster horse was needed, they would use Chock. She rode off. The men watched as she started taking a diagonal path across the hillside. When Tubby decided he would quite like to go too, Colin grabbed him and said that he had walked up but was damned if he was going to walk down and told Tubby to stand.

They spent time assessing the creek, and when John said they had to work out the best way to get things up there and was told that Kitty was doing just that, he queried it and was told that she and Colin would organise it, and they would probably be starting in the morning. He would be talking to Kitty, and because Tubby loved doing earthworks, he couldn't see that there would be any problems. If any more labour was needed it was Eddie's job to organise it. When John asked who the boss of the job was, they looked surprised and said that of course he was. If he wanted anything he just had to ask. The company wanted it done as soon as possible, as they wanted to turn some of their horses out. John said everything sounded good, but he wanted to make it plain that he wasn't taking any orders from any bossy little girl. He wasn't used to working with girls, he didn't think it right. Kitty was too bossy, and they seemed to take far too much notice of her. Colin said mildly that she could get more work out of a horse than anybody else. They worked as a team, and each member did what they did best. Then he hopped on Tubby and started off downhill, following the route that he had seen Kitty taking. John watched in amazement and asked how he could manage such a big horse when he didn't have a bridle on it. George said that Kitty had trained the horse to be ridden, and draught horses were trained for voice control. John looked at him as if he were speaking a foreign language.

When they got back down, Colin had been and gone. The kōneke stood waiting to be loaded. Kitty had been helping

Catherine lay out the evening meal, and Billy was clinging on her back. She asked them if they would load the kōneke before they ate so she could get an early start in the morning. She also asked George if they had anything that needed to be done in Arrowtown and to write her a list so she could see to it. If so, could he take Chock to the back paddock in the morning? She and Tubby had some work to do on the track to the workings, and she would like George to write down just what he or John wanted her to do apart from carting stuff.

John wasn't too happy about this, as he saw it as being ordered around by a female, especially a young one wearing a child-like backpack, but George assured him that both mother and daughter were brilliant organisers, and it was much quicker to tell them what was wanted and let them plan it. After tea he saw them in action. Catherine would take care of any Arrowtown business, freeing Kitty to work with the men. She'd take a list to Freddy, and he would sort it for her. When they were working at the top of the hill the women would fix food for them to take with them, and the main meal would be in the evening instead of at midday.

At breakfast John noted Kitty's absence and asked when she would be starting, because there was stuff he needed on the kōneke. George and Catherine laughed and told him that she was probably halfway up the hill by now. When he and George arrived at the site they found the kōneke unloaded and Kitty and Colin sitting, enjoying a cup of tea. The billy was simmering over hot coals and Colin's horse was grazing nearby. Tubby and the kōneke were turned around, ready to start off back down the hill as no stones needed to be shifted. The job mainly consisted of reorganising the old mining waterworks, and it was John who took charge of that.

The work went well. It turned out that John was not very literate but soon learned that if he told Kitty or George that he wanted anything, it arrived without question or delay. George and Colin were quick learners, and it was only a matter of days before they reached the spot where the stream crossed the road. John went to Queenstown on Friday evenings, so Saturdays became the day that odd jobs were done around the house and yard. When Kitty got tired of Billy being on her back or under everybody's feet, she popped him on the nearest horse or cow. As Catherine wanted to have the dairy up and running before spring, she largely left Kitty alone.

The company had decided that as a goodwill gesture to the community, stonemasons would be employed to build a low bridge where the stream crossed the road. With an eye to the future, it would be built two lanes wide. Kitty and Tubby carted stones for them, while Catherine grumbled that she didn't think that it was really necessary.

One day while John, George and Colin were working on the dam, Catherine decided to take the babies to visit an ailing Flo, leaving Billy with Kitty. When Kitty, who was as usual wearing Billy as a backpack, went to call the men to dinner, John was surprised to find a meal every bit as good as Catherine could produce. He asked Kitty if there was anything that she couldn't do. She grinned wickedly and replied that she didn't know; there were one or two very important things she hadn't tried yet. George laughed and Colin choked on his cup of tea. Billy joined in by banging his spoon on the tray of his highchair and throwing his plate on the floor.

John was shocked. He didn't think that sort of talk was suitable in female company, let alone for it to be such a young female who made the joke. The others hadn't noticed his discomfort and carried on joking until it was time to go back to work.

It was, luckily, a mild winter, and they were able to get the dam finished and the pipework done sooner than they had expected. The dairy was being set up under Catherine's direction. Another cow calved, a bull calf this time, and though Catherine was disappointed, George pointed out that with its pedigree, it would fetch a very good price, and it would be better to raise it than to eat it. He told John that he expected a good income from the pigs, which would be fed with the skim milk. He explained that they would not be selling milk, just cheese and butter and would be setting up a stall so they could sell from home. John said that it all seemed a lot of work, and Catherine said that Kitty would be giving up the horses and working with the dairy. That started the usual battle, and as usual Kitty walked out.

It was Friday afternoon and John was walking over to the bivvy to collect the things he wanted to take to Queenstown. He had about a week's work left to do at the Kirks' and had another job lined up. Kitty came running around the corner of the barn, still crying from another row with her mother. She cannoned into him and knocked the pair of them flying. He was on his feet first and put out a hand to help her up and she found herself in his arms. So she surprised herself by kissing him. He, equally surprised, kissed her back. They both must have decided that they liked it, so they exchanged a few more kisses and then broke apart.

'I don't think we should have done that,' he said. 'I've never kissed a girl before.'

'I've never wanted to kiss anyone either. I think that was a sort of an accident, but I really liked it. I'm just sort of scared of what happens when you want to find out what comes next.'

'Kitty, we shouldn't be talking about this. It embarrasses me. I'm going now. I've got a lot of thinking to do. How old are you?'

'I'm fifteen, sixteen early next year. It won't be long before I leave home. Ma just won't leave me alone about working in the dairy, and I won't do it. When I go, it will make George's life a lot easier. These rows just tear him apart. You don't have to worry about me. Accidents happen. When I go I'll leave the Wakatipu because otherwise the war will go on forever.'

'You've an old head on those fifteen-year-old shoulders. I've discovered that I like you very much, except you are bossy. I'm twelve years older than you and like I said, I've a lot of thinking to do. I'm not going to start anything I can't finish.' He shouldered his bag and walked off down the road.

When Kitty got back to the house, there was more drama. Catherine was folded up with pain and was afraid she was losing the baby. She wanted Flo. She screamed that it was all Kitty's fault for upsetting her, but Kitty had gone to put Chock in the trap for a fast trip to pick up Flo.

She took Billy with her. When they got back, George wanted to go for the doctor, but both women assured him that the doctor wouldn't be necessary – most women lost a baby or two and Flo could cope perfectly. It turned out to be so and next morning she took Catherine home with her so, that she could have a good rest. Flo's recently widowed daughter would come over and look after the Kirk children so that Kitty could get on with the dairying while George and John finished off the work in hand.

When Lucy, Flo's daughter, got into the trap with Kitty, she thanked God she was out of there. She told Kitty that she and Flo had hardly passed a day of their lives without some sort of argument. She had gone, pregnant, into a loveless marriage, mainly to get away from home. She lost the baby, and when her brutal husband was killed in a mining accident she was more relieved than sorry. Now she wanted to get away from Flo. She told Kitty not to worry. She hated gossip and tittle-tattle, and whatever happened at the Kirks' would go no further.

When Kitty started to tell Lucy about her own problems, Lucy laughed and reminded Kitty whose daughter she was. She had listened to Catherine and Flo discussing Kitty's bad behavior and ingratitude at great length and had always wanted to meet Kitty in person because she sounded like fun. Kitty was delighted with Lucy. She had just turned twenty, and she and Kitty exchanged stories about each other that they had heard from their respective mothers. Kitty had had to listen to Flo lamenting having a snivelling ungrateful daughter dumped back in her lap, and she wanted to get her out of her house by getting her married off again as soon as possible. They agreed that it was very hard to live with a mother who was determined to control them.

By the time they reached home, they had discussed how they would share the work. Lucy's brutal husband had stopped supporting her as soon as he realised there wasn't going to be a baby, so she'd worked for her keep on a neighbouring farm. She'd milked cows and enjoyed it so would do the dairy work while Kitty looked after the children and the house. Kitty hoped that Lucy would become indispensible so that when she finally bolted Lucy could fill her place and do the work that Kitty would never do. In her turn Lucy would get away from Flo and the endless stream of awful men that her mother dragged up to meet her. She'd had enough of marriage for a while, thank you very much.

George was pleased to see them. He held a crying Lizzie, and Billy was, as usual, making a nuisance of himself tormenting Georgeboy. Kitty took over the children and put them to bed while Lucy and George got to know each other. George had put on the kettle and put out some tea things, and they all sat down to work out the work schedule. Lucy told George that she would sooner milk a herd of cows than take care of one Billy. She said she wasn't good with children and much preferred the company of cows.

John arrived back for his final week's work, but he and Kitty didn't get much chance to talk. Lucy told Kitty that were she ever to marry again she would like a man just like John, but it was plain that he had eyes only for Kitty. George had noticed the same thing and quietly asked Kitty what she felt about John. Kitty blushed and stammered and said she didn't yet know. So George told John he had noticed what was going on and was happy with any outcome or none, and they left it at that and not a word to Catherine.

When Catherine arrived home after a week of being cosseted by Flo, George told her that things were working so well that he wanted to employ Lucy, so that he and Kitty could finish the fencing. He had realised that the fence around the dam had to be child-proof as well as stock-proof. When Catherine said Kitty should do the dairy and he should employ John, he told her that Lucy would cost half as much and that he was sick and tired of the continual fighting, By employing Lucy he would get some peace. Also Lucy knew a lot more about dairy than Kitty did. Better a willing worker than a reluctant, truculent one. The girls had happily agreed that another bunk would be erected in the tack shed, so what was Catherine's problem?

Catherine said that her problem was that Kitty should be doing her duty to her family, not gallivanting around the countryside.

George controlled himself with difficulty and tried to point out to her that Kitty always worked willingly with him and that the fencing could not be finished without her. Catherine said again that he should employ John and that Kitty should take her rightful place. George gave up trying to reason with her and told her that she was being one-eyed and ridiculous, he was exercising his husbandly privilege and the farm was going to be managed his way. He told her to belt up and start thinking about how much they had achieved in the few short years they'd been on the farm; she should think about where she'd be now if she'd stayed in Ireland. She ought to think about Kitty's generosity to her, beginning with her horse and trap and her expensive sewing basket and to think about how kind and generous and supportive their friends and community had always been to them. Then he stumped off to bed without his customary cup of tea, leaving her in tears.

After church on Sunday Lucy was included in dinner with Jeannie and Eddie, whose house was now completely finished and whose garden was a picture. Jeannie was bubbling with excitement.

'Guess what,' she said. 'We've decided that now is the time to start a family, so you can wait to hear some good news.'

After congratulations and well-wishing, Jeannie told them about a ball that was going to be held in Queenstown on New Year's Eve to celebrate the arrival of a new decade and how much the town had prospered in its few short years. The company was providing transport in the form of a hay-wagon ('Not pulled by Tubby I hope,' interjected Kitty) and most of the younger people were going. The road along the Frankton Arm was now passable for vehicles and had cut the distance between the towns considerably. Kitty and Lucy must come. Lucy said that she had nothing to wear except widow's weeds that she was trying to get out of, and they spent a pleasant half-hour with Lucy trying on Jeannie's dresses. They were both bigger than Kitty, who said she was sure Daisy would help her out. Lucy was riding in the trap with the family. Kitty, on one of the company's problem horses, shot off to call on the Jordans, who weren't very regular churchgoers.

Kitty told them that she had two problems: first, she had nothing to wear and second she couldn't dance. Sarah jumped up and down and said that dancing was easy; she could come over after work and get lessons. As for a dress, that was no problem. Daisy would see to it. Kitty rode off happy. The only reason she wanted to go was that she hoped to see John. She had chosen a bright red dress that Daisy had bought on a whim and now didn't fancy herself in, and if Kitty liked it she could keep it. Kitty did like it. She had never had anything bright and loved the colour. She had no idea whether it suited her or not, but she would wear it and love it.

Kitty had confided in Lucy that she was definitely leaving early next year. She had a place she could go to for a while. She could visit the woman who had bought the Durhams. She had been there a few times and knew she was always welcome, but she wanted to get somewhere permanent where she could support herself. She'd told Freddy, and he was looking out for her. Lucy had one thing to ask of Kitty. Before she left could Kitty teach her to ride. But Flo was not to know. Kitty said that of course she would, but weren't they a sorry pair, both afraid of their mothers! The situation was explained to Jeannie, who welcomed Lucy, who began getting herself over there on her afternoons off to have preliminary lessons on the lawn-mowing pony. She made such progress that she soon graduated to more interesting horses. Kitty took over the tuition, and soon Lucy was riding Chock around the back paddocks.

One day when Flo was visiting Catherine, she wanted to know when Lucy would get some days off to visit her mother. Catherine stared at her in surprise and told her that Lucy had had half-days off ever since she started and was treated as family at dinner after church on Sundays. Flo had seen her at church every week. Surely that counted as a day off. So they marched down to the dairy to confront Lucy, who was busy cleaning. Flo demanded to know what she had been doing on her days off, and she answered that she had been visiting friends. Flo said that she should be coming home to help her poor old mother, and she should be handing over her wages to that same poor old mother. She thought she would get

Catherine to pay Lucy's wages directly to her. Fearing an explosion, Catherine told her that because of her own illiteracy, George was the pay-clerk, and she knew he would not countenance it. Lucy said that she would drop by someday soon.

On her next afternoon off she rode over on Chock, and her mother was horrified. Who did she think she was, riding in here like Lady Muck? Why wasn't she wearing black when it hadn't been a year since her husband had died? Lucy said that she was now an independent woman, and as a widow she was legally permitted to make her own decisions. She didn't even get off her horse. She turned and cantered off.

At the company Christmas dinner, Lucy was included since she and Jeannie had become great friends. Catherine said she thought Lucy should be spending the day with her own folk, but no one agreed with her. The conversation turned to the New Year's Eve ball, and when Catherine heard this, she said firmly that Kitty wouldn't be going. It was not suitable for her to be unchaperoned, and they weren't the sort of people who went to balls. To her discomfort, everyone laughed. Daisy pointed out that she would be chaperoned by two respectable married women and a widow. George asked who said that they weren't the sort of people who went to balls, because they were landowners and business owners, and that made them as good as anybody else. They would be going, too, if they didn't have to stay home with the kids. Lucy asked why they didn't ask Flo, who, she was sure, would be happy to oblige. Jeannie said that she and Eddie were going because they had started a family and they wanted to have fun before they got bogged down. Freddy said he was going too. So that settled it; they were all going.

When the cart pulled up at the gate and Kitty and Lucy appeared wearing their borrowed finery, there was a gasp from their respective mothers. Kitty was told to take it off, she looked like a tart. Lucy was told to take it off, she should still be in deep mourning. George said that was enough of that and told them to get in the cart. He admired Kitty's shining black hair, so like her mother's, and so seldom loosed from its tight braids. So they all went to the ball.

They hadn't been there very long before John spotted them and came and asked Kitty to dance. He said he wasn't much of a dancer but would do his best, and she told him that she had just learnt to dance and she too would do her best. Touching him made Kitty deliriously happy. Kitty told John that things between her and Catherine had become absolutely impossible and she intended to leave home in the next week or so. When the dance ended, as he returned her to her family, he said that they must talk. Had her feelings changed? He stayed chatting to them until the next dance began and Colin claimed her. John asked for the Supper Waltz and she happily agreed. As Colin danced her off, he explained to her the significance of the Supper Waltz and the Last Waltz. If you danced them both with the same person you were, to all intents and purposes, announcing yourselves to be a couple. Kitty smiled and said he would have to wait and see, just as she would. He said it wouldn't be a bad thing, but she was young yet, although fifteen was the legal age for marriage. It would be a good idea if she were to talk to Daisy. Kitty agreed. George claimed her and said he had noticed that John had eyes only for her and what was she going to do about it? She said she didn't know yet, wait and see. Then it was Eddie's turn to comment and to tell her that she should talk to Jeannie. She told him she did, all the time. Finally Freddy who had been watching all this told her to follow her own heart and not to take advice from anyone.

At last the M.C. announced the Supper Waltz and said that before they went in for supper it would be midnight and a piper would pipe in the New Year. There would be three cheers and the singing of *Auld Lang Syne* followed by the national anthem. Then supper would begin with the royal toast and one or two speeches before they started eating. John rather clumsily waltzed Kitty off and held her close to him. He asked her for the Last Waltz, and she asked him if that was some sort of declaration. He said it was, they had to talk about it and he would meet her at the back gate tomorrow morning if she liked the idea, then he would talk to George. Kitty looked up at him with shining eyes that told him all he wanted to know.

After supper the piper and some of the men left to go first footing, the traditional Scottish Hogmanay celebration. The piper went from house to house followed by a dark man, who had to be the first across the threshold, carrying a piece of coal. This ensured good fortune for the household in the coming year. He exchanged the coal for a wee drappie (scotch) and pieces of cake for him, the piper and their followers, who had all crowded into the house. There was more than one piper and team, but it still often took until daylight before all the houses had been covered. In the southern latitudes the sun rose between four and five in the morning, and it was broad daylight before the Arrowtown party arrived home. Kitty, George and Lucy went and changed into working clothes and got straight into the dairy business. Catherine went inside to make breakfast and put the bread on for dinner. She had so much to tell Flo about their daughters' behaviour, none of it good. The children had slept through the night, so Flo was wide awake and had made some delicious pancakes for breakfast. She had brought several sorts of jam, and of course the Kirks always had cream. Kitty didn't come in for breakfast, and they assumed that she was too tired. Not so. She had had a good sleep lying in the hay in the cart as they drove home, and she was on her way to the back gate.

John was waiting for her. He had got a lift with the Jordans and was lying dozing in the sun. They fell into each other's arms then settled down to talk. John had got a job at the head of the lake. It was a permanent job for a married man in the timber mill, and it came with a small rent-free cottage. Would Kitty marry him and come to live with him at what he described as the ends of the earth? It wouldn't be an easy life, but they'd manage if they didn't have children too quickly. Kitty was a strong woman, so he thought they could make a go of it. She told him that Jeannie knew how not to have children until you wanted them. He was horrified and thought it was wrong but agreed to talk to Eddie. He now wanted to ask George for her hand in marriage. He absolutely refused to get on the horse, so Kitty let it go and walked alongside him.

When they got back to the house dinner was on the table, but

John told George that he wanted to talk to him privately, so they wandered outside for a smoke. When George heard the story he said he didn't think the wedding should be a hurried affair, but John explained that he had to be married and at the head of the lake by the first of March, and he wanted to go and settle affairs with his family, so as far as he was concerned the sooner the better. How about the end of January?

They went in to dinner and George broke the news to Catherine and Lucy. It went down badly with Catherine. Lucy hugged Kitty and shook hands with John, congratulating him. Then she left them to it and went back to the dairy for some peace and quiet. That was a wise choice.

Catherine came up with every argument she could think of and Kitty countered them. George did not intervene. Finally Kitty turned to John and said 'You may not even want to marry me when I tell you this. I am a bastard. I was conceived when she was fourteen, born out of wedlock when she was younger than I am now, and she dares to me that I'm too young to marry.'

Catherine screeched that Kitty should not be telling family secrets to a stranger.

'The man I hope to marry isn't a stranger. I'll never keep any secrets from my own family if I have one. Now John knows, he may not want to marry a bastard.' Kitty turned back to John. 'She won't even tell me my father's name, except that his Christian name was Arthur. His family must have plenty of money, because they got her married off as soon as I was born and shipped her and her husband off to New Zealand. They gave her a remittance until she and George got together.' To Catherine and George, she said.

'I'm moving out of here right now. I'll go and stay with Jeannie until John makes up his mind, and one way or the other, I'll move right out of the Wakatipu.' She left.

John turned to George and asked 'Is this true?'

'Unfortunately it is.'

John looked miserable. He said, 'I'll have to go away and think about this. Kitty is the only girl I've ever felt comfortable with, and I think she'd make a good wife. I promise you that I will never tell anyone what I learned today.' He turned and went to see Kitty. He found her in tears.

'Why didn't you tell me?' he demanded.

'I was going to,' she answered. 'I wouldn't have married you without telling you. There just hasn't been time.'

'I don't think any the less of you. I probably still want to marry you, but now I have to think. Your mother is an immoral woman and a hypocrite. Tomorrow I'm going to Waitati to see my family and sort myself out. I was going to tell them our good news, but it can wait. I have to get my head together because I can't get this job unless I'm a married man, so I must have a wife. Wait until I get sorted out and don't run away till I get back.' He hugged her briefly and left. Lucy came and joined them, and Kitty told her that something had come up and the marriage was postponed. Lucy helped her to pack her things, and she left for Jeannie's. She told Jeannie and Eddie that Catherine had gone too far, and she just couldn't possibly live with her one moment longer.

Three weeks later Freddy said he wanted to see George, Catherine and Kitty at the office because there was something legal to be discussed. Kitty arrived early because she wanted to avoid Catherine. She asked if any of the legal stuff concerned her. Some of it did. The family in Ireland had had their eldest son declared dead, and according to his memorial stone he had died two years before Kitty was born. The agent had also sent a copy of Kitty's christening record and Catherine's marriage lines from the parish register. Kitty laughed. 'How could she marry a man who had been dead for two years?'

'Miracles happen,' said Freddy. 'It's pointless worrying about this stuff. It isn't going to affect you here. What does affect you is that for some reason or other you've lost a year of your age. The date of your birth shows that you were born in 1855, not 1854, so your coming birthday will be your fifteenth, not your sixteenth. The thing that does affect you is that, legally, you are now the legitimate daughter of a non-existent man. That is, if you want to follow it up.'

Kitty laughed. 'Don't bother. The thing that matters is that I'm still only fourteen. That could have got me into trouble because I was planning to get married.'

'You said you were planning to get married? Is it off then?'

'I don't know. I want to have no secrets from John, but he took it badly when I told him I was a bastard. So he's gone away to have a think, and I don't know where I am. It's probably just as well I didn't have to tell him I'm only fourteen. Anyhow, my birthday's not that far off. Do you have to tell Ma that you've found out about this? It would give her an excuse to come after me again.'

'No, I don't suppose I do. I have some news for them that doesn't concern you, so if you want to dodge them you'd better skip.'

The news that concerned George and Catherine was that since Jack Cameron didn't exist and was now officially dead under his real name, Catherine had never been legally married. This meant that that she and George could marry. Catherine was pregnant again, and she said she didn't want to get married here, because 'What would people think?' They would go away and get married somewhere else after the baby was born. Besides, she needed to be here to keep an eye on Kitty. Freddy caught George's eye, but they said nothing. George asked if he could get his family legitimated. Freddy was sure it could be done. Catherine then asked Freddy why he had wanted Kitty to come to the meeting. His answer was that she had come and gone before they got there, so he'd sorted out her business first. It was the wrong answer. Catherine said that as a mother, she had every right to know what her daughter's business was. Freddy shrugged and said that she had better ask her daughter herself. George thanked Freddy and rushed Catherine out of the office. He was aglow at the thought of making his family legitimate and told Catherine that it was about time she concentrated more on being his wife and less on being Kitty's mother.

On Sunday Catherine looked for Kitty at church, but she wasn't there nor was she at dinner. When she asked she was told that Kitty was now attending church in Queenstown. Any questions she had were answered by telling her that if she wanted to know about Kitty, she should ask her herself. Catherine asked how she could ask her when she never saw her. When George was asked how business was, he replied that it was going very well. Lucy and Catherine were working well together while he looked after the pasture. Bully's services were much in demand, and it was very peaceful at home. Furthermore, a younger brother, who had been in nappies when George left home, was somewhere at sea on his way to New Zealand and could possibly work on the farm.

Kitty's fifteenth birthday passed quietly with no celebration. There had been no word from John, and she hid her unhappiness by working harder than she ever had. She became as thin as whipcord but found satisfaction in what she was doing. As well as handling horses for Colin, she was filling in as a driver if a regular driver was sick. One thing that delighted her was a beautiful chestnut filly that the company had given her for her birthday. She managed to avoid her mother. The only information Catherine got about Kitty came from Flo, who passed on anything she heard.

On Easter Sunday John turned up at church. After the service he asked George where Kitty was and was told that she now attended church in Queenstown and was no longer living at home. He swore and said that he would now take off for Queenstown and meet her on the road, and George had to point out that there were two roads and she was just as likely to ride cross-country as take either of them. George asked if he could take it that John had made up his mind about Kitty and, if so, why hadn't he written? John said that he had never written a letter in his life and wasn't really capable of it. He would have been back sooner, but his father had died and he'd had to stay longer than he had planned. George told him that there was an Easter dinner at the church and they were all going, but he advised John to stay well out of Catherine's way. Kitty would be staying with either Daisy or Jeannie, so he would be able to catch up with her later on. He had to be content with that.

He caught up with her at the Jordans'. She was working with her new, as yet un-named, horse in their round pen, watched by

Sarah. He saw her face light up but was a little hurt that she didn't run to him.

'Shush,' said Sarah importantly. 'She can't stop right now. It's a green horse that doesn't know anything, and she's in the middle of something. We just have to wait and be quiet until she finishes. She won't be long.' Kitty finished what she was doing, and before greeting John, she told Sarah that she could brush the filly and get her ready to be turned out. Kitty would watch her while she stood here and talked to John. Then and only then, she said, 'I hope you've come to tell me what you've decided.'

He held out his arms to her. 'I've come back to claim you. The job is for a married man. I need a wife, but I won't play second fiddle to a horse.' She pulled away from him.

'I've been so unhappy. Not a word from you. When it got past the day we were to be married and past the day we were to have been at the head of the lake, I thought you'd decided that you couldn't marry a bastard, so I've been getting ready to leave. Why didn't you write?'

He told her about what he'd been doing and told her he was incapable of writing a letter. He could read reasonably well and could write his name and occupation, but that was about all.

Sarah had finished. Kitty inspected her work and told her she could let the horse go. As they walked back towards the house Kitty asked, 'What about the job? We'd be three months late getting there. Will they have kept it open for you?'

'I went to their agent in Dunedin to tell him why I hadn't showed up. He said that was lucky because there had been a hold up in some machinery arriving, and I wasn't wanted until the first Monday in October. He gave me a list of things we'd need for the house. It's apparently very primitive, just one bedroom and one other room. He suggested that we go and look at it before we move in. What do you think?'

'I think we should go and have tea and tell them that the wedding's on again. Before it can happen we have to get Ma's permission. You'll have to do that on your own because if I go near her it will end in a screaming match, and Pa has been a happy man since I left. I see him most days but I haven't seen her since the day you left. I'm not going to face her until everything is settled and she knows it's out of her control.'

The Jordans welcomed John back and congratulated them when they heard that the wedding was on again. Sarah got all excited and started asking how many bridesmaids would there be and could she be the chief one. John looked pained but not as pained as Kitty. She quickly told Sarah that she wanted a very quiet wedding, no bridesmaids, no white dress, just two attendants, who had to be adult to sign the register. When Sarah started to fuss Kitty told her firmly that it was her wedding, not Sarah's.

The next day John walked across to the Kirks' to talk to George and Catherine. As expected Catherine threw a tantrum. Billy had always been a right handful and was now becoming worse because he was missing Kitty. Kitty was an ungrateful brat; the oldest daughter's job was to stay home and look after her parents. John had had enough. He stood up and looking Catherine straight in the eye and said, 'That's it, Mrs Kirk. I am a moral man, but you leave me no alternative. I need a wife to get this job, so I will get her pregnant, and when she starts to show, I'll parade her around the district so everyone will see. You didn't practise what you are preaching. You'd better make up your mind right now, because I can't wait any longer if I want the job. I know that George isn't Kitty's father, but he's the head of the household, and what he says goes.'

George called, 'Stop, John. Catherine, stop crying and say yes. Say "yes" right now and we can get on with our lives. Kitty has said she will never live in this house again, and if you oppose her you'll very likely never see her again.' He prodded her, and she reluctantly mumbled, 'All right then, but I still don't like it.'

John sat down again. 'This job in a timber mill is at the head of the lake. It starts at the beginning of October, and it's for a married man, so we'll get married in September. It won't be a fancy wedding, just a very quiet one. We will announce our engagement immediately. That gives everybody time to get used to the idea and for us to get ourselves organised. Kitty needs to get to know me better and understand that I am the boss, and we need to go up to the head to check on the house.'

Catherine made one last bid. 'We could build you a house here and you could both work on the farm. Then we could stay together as a family, as we should.'

'No!' said George and John firmly, and in unison.

John left after making arrangements for them all to meet at Jeannie's because Kitty wouldn't set foot in the family home ever again. Over the months she had watched for Catherine to go out in the trap and had taken advantage of her absence to remove all her own belongings including her dogs and her leather-working tools and hides.

Freddy was invited to the meeting as well, and it went comparatively amicably. A date for the wedding was set in September, and although Catherine protested, John was adamant that the wedding would be in Queenstown. Over a cup of tea and a slice of cake that Freddy had made, it was agreed that to keep everything proper, John would stay with Freddy while Kitty would continue to live with Jeannie and Eddie.

John and Kitty took a day trip in the little paddle steamer to look at the house. John was horrified. It wasn't even lined and would be freezing in the winter. There was only a small open fire for both cooking and heating. Kitty said that she could manage very well but reminded John that they would have to have that talk with Jeannie and Eddie about how to delay a family. They decided that he would come back whenever he could and work on the house. As soon as they were married they would move in. There were two weeks after the wedding before John had to start work, and they would make good use of them.

Everything went as planned. Kitty went and introduced herself to the Bryants, whose tourist business was in its infancy. Work had just begun on their accommodation house. Kitty was able to arrange grazing for her horse in return for helping in the house whenever Mrs Bryant needed a hand. They all got on very well.

When John heard this he said that he didn't know that Kitty had planned to bring a horse. She looked surprised and said she had to have a horse. He was surprised that she found the Bryants friendly as they had a reputation for not mixing with the timber workers. He surprised her by telling her not to get too friendly.

The day of the wedding was a real spring day, warm in the sun but still with a nip in the air. Daisy and Sarah had given up on trying to get Kitty into a white dress, but she had agreed Daisy could do her hair. Those present were Lucy, as her attendant and George's friend Pete as best man. Daisy, Colin and Sarah were there as were Freddy, Eddie and Jeannie. George and Catherine and the children were accompanied by Flo, who had Billy firmly by the collar. Catherine and Sarah cried all through the ceremony, which was performed by Rev. Coffey. George and Catherine signed as witnesses, Catherine making her usual cross and not being aware that George had supplied her and Kitty's legal names. Kitty was surprised to read that when John registered their intention to marry he had written his name as 'John Greigg, gold miner'. Two days later, in the church register, he was 'John Greig, labourer.' She never questioned him about it, although she did wonder. For the first time she signed her name as Catherine Greig.

After the ceremony they all went to lunch at Eichardt's Hotel, where the very happy couple were to spend the night before they left the next morning to begin their new life.

When they arrived to board, the steamer Kitty's horse and dogs were already on board and John remarked that he hadn't realised that he was marrying a zoo.

Kitty was delighted that her first experience of married life had lived up to her expectations and that a completely new life was about to begin. Like a fairy-tale princess, she knew that she was married and would live 'happily ever after' and they sailed away to begin their new life.

Book Two

Love And Loss

The Fifth Life
Kinloch 1870

Chapter One

In 1870 newly-weds John and Kitty arrived at the head of Lake Wakatipu after a three-hour journey in the paddle-steamer *Antrim*. This sturdy little ship was only two years old and had been built from timber milled locally at Mill Creek where John would be working. The ship had been built to ship timber to Queenstown and service the settlements at the head of the lake. It was not Kitty's first trip up the lake, but she would always be entranced by its beauty.

After a little while Kitty noticed Mrs Bryant, who was looking tired as she struggled with two little girls, so she went across to help her by playing with the children. When the two husbands had singly disappeared to chat with other men, as men do, Kitty took Josie and Minnie for a walk around the little ship with a small hand gripped firmly in each of hers. Then, still leaving their mother in peace, she entertained them for an hour or so until they neared Glenorchy, the only other port at the head of the lake.

Mrs Bryant was very thankful for the break and told Kitty that she'd even managed to doze a little, which was, for her, an unexpected luxury. She hoped that Kitty had managed to tire the little girls out so they'd be ready for a nap when they got home. The two women sat and chatted while the cargo and animals for Glenorchy were unloaded. Then, as the paddles started churning and the little steamer pulled out, Kitty remarked that it was strange to be going to live at a place that still didn't have a name.

'I feel very strongly about that,' answered Mary Bryant. 'There are some people with no imagination who want to call it "Dartmoor" just because it's on the banks of the river Dart, but I certainly don't want to spend the rest of my life in a place with the same name as an English prison! Imagine writing home and telling them I was in Dartmoor! Anyway, I've written to the appropriate authorities suggesting "Kinloch", which, like "Glenorchy", is a Gaelic word meaning "head of the loch". What do you think, Mrs Greig?' Kitty, who was a bit startled at being called 'Mrs Greig', answered that she thought it was a lovely name, much better than 'Dartmoor', and since people were already referring to the place as 'the Head of the Lake', it was perfect.

'Shall we just start calling it that?' Kitty suggested. 'Then perhaps other people will copy.'

'My husband hopes to start a tourist business, and we really don't think anyone honest would be attracted to a holiday in Dartmoor. Let's do it, and I shall pass on your suggestion to Richard.'

'Speaking of names,' Kitty said, 'I have a beautiful chestnut filly on board, and I've already spoken to your husband about grazing for her. I haven't had her long, and I was stuck for a really nice name for her. Your Josie solved my problem for me. She took one look at her and said her name was "Flame", so Flame she is. Do you like horses, Mrs Bryant?'

'I love them. I used to be quite a rider before I had children and had to turn my attention to other things. My husband, however, doesn't like horses at all, and he stubbornly insists on walking everywhere. You know, I've been wondering where I'd seen you before, but now I remember. You're Kitty Kirk, aren't you? I saw you riding at the show. They say you're a "whisperer" as well as able to break in problem horses. I didn't realise you were so young. It's a pity there won't be much call for your skills here in Kinloch.'

'My husband, like yours, insists on walking everywhere too. He doesn't like horses either, and he hasn't much time for any animals, come to that. I know a great deal about animals, but I think I have a lot to learn about being a wife.'

Mary Bryant laughed. 'I'm sorry, my dear young lady, but that's a never-ending lesson. Men turn into a different species as soon as they get married. I sometimes think they might be a little afraid of us and that's why they have to dominate us. They also have the firm belief that any work they do is vastly more important than anything we do. I have found that it's best to agree with anything they say and then go your own way. They almost never notice.'

Kitty raised her eyebrows. Smiling, Mary Bryant carried on. 'Never get into an argument unless you absolutely have to, and then make sure that you lose. Don't hesitate to deceive them if you feel you must and are sure that you can get away with it. Just remember we understand men better than they understand us, but they don't know that, and we just have to get along with them. I sometimes wonder if the Almighty got it right when He made humans, but then He's a male isn't He? My goodness, here we are. We have arrived in Kinloch. That does sound good, doesn't it?'

As soon as she was ashore Kitty let her dogs go to have a run while she watched Flame being lowered in a sling. Then she spent a little time soothing her indignant horse before she led her off to her new pasture. The only horses that could be seen were a team of Clydesdales similar to Tubby who were patiently waiting for goods to be unloaded. Kitty hoped that they weren't the only horses here.

John caught up with Kitty and walked beside her. 'I don't want you to spend too much time with Mrs Bryant,' he said.

'Why ever not? She's lovely and I so enjoyed playing with her children. It means I've made friends with someone here already. I thought you would be pleased for me.'

'Workers mix with workers; they stay with their own kind. People will think you're a snob if you spend time with snobs.'

Kitty laughed. 'You sound like Ma.'

'Don't you ever mock me, Kitty,' said John angrily. 'Don't forget that I'm your husband!'

'Oh, my dearest, I'm so sorry. I would never hurt you, and I'm so happy to be your wife.' She lowered her head and continued. 'But, John, I have to do some work for the Bryants to pay for grazing. That's being a worker isn't it? And I will make friends with workers' wives when they arrive, I promise.'

'I still don't know why you had to bring such a useless animal with you. I'd hoped it wouldn't cost us anything for feed, and now you tell me it costs us for the grazing. You'll have enough to do looking after me and the house and garden without having to pander to the Bryants.'

They had reached the grazing and Kitty let her horse go with a few reassuring pats, silently resolving to come back and brush her later. Remembering Mrs Bryant's advice, she wisely decided not to pursue the argument any further. John, unfortunately, had other ideas. 'And what about the dogs? I suppose you're going to tell me that they eat grass too?'

'John, please let's not argue. I can sell each of Toss's pups for as much as you earn in a week. They are booked up before they are even born, so please don't worry about money yet. I have enough to get us by until you start at the mill.'

John's eyes narrowed. 'Did I hear you say that you've got money? Where did you get money from?'

'I've been earning money since we arrived in the Wakatipu. Apart from the pups, I made and sold horse tack and belts and fancy saddle bags. People paid me good money to train their horses. I bought horses, and after I trained them I sold them for a lot more than I paid for them. I've always had money.'

'No wonder your mother didn't want to let you go. What does George think about this?'

'Pa wanted me to have my own money. He said it was best not to let Ma know how much I earned. I paid for things about the farm that he wanted, and I bought Ma her horse and trap. I bought lots of things for Billy and the girls. I *have* been taught to manage money. Even though Ma can't read or write she is brilliant with figures and she manages all the farm and dairy money. She and George have long discussions about what's needed on the farm before they buy anything. Anything I didn't learn from her I learnt from Freddy.'

'Well, I don't like it. Managing money is the man's job. By law everything a woman has belongs to her husband, and I don't want anybody thinking that I can't support my wife. So we'll have to talk about this later. I don't want you working. And you can hand that money over to me.'

'We're here. Let's go in and get a fire going so we can have a cup of tea before I make a meal. We've three weeks before you start work. I've brought seeds and potatoes that I want to get into the ground so that we can have vegetables as soon as possible.'

'Good idea, but Kitty, just remember that *I* am the man and that means that *I* am the boss. You and your Mum've been spoilt by George, but that doesn't mean that I'm going to spoil you. I'll decide how our money is to be spent, not you, understand?'

Kitty nodded miserably. She immediately resolved that she would not yet tell John about her Arrowtown bank account. She was fairly sure that a law had recently been passed allowing married women to own money and anything that they had owned before they got married. She'd heard Daisy and Jeannie laughing about it and now wished that she'd taken more notice of what they were saying. She hadn't realised that other men didn't have the same attitude about money as the men she knew best. She knew she could always write and ask Freddy about it, and John didn't need to know. She would give him the cash she'd brought with her and play the game. She thought again about Mrs Bryant's advice and wondered if it was as light-hearted as she'd thought. It now struck her that it had probably been the voice of experience.

She set about getting the meal while John started unpacking. She had to point out to him that all the bags and boxes had been carefully labelled, and he praised her for that. Kitty resolved to put the argument behind her, but she worried about having an argument on the very day after they had married. She loved him, and she had married him. Soon they would go to bed, everything would come right and they would live happily ever after. Love would conquer all their differences.

They made good use of the weeks they had before John started work. Both of them were hard workers. The garden was planned, dug and sown. It was also fenced off from wandering stock. None of the other mill cottages were occupied until the week before work started, and during that week the men were expected to get familiarised with their future jobs.

As the other millers moved in Kitty introduced herself to their wives and played with their children. There were envious mutters about the Greigs having the best house, and even a garden, until Kitty explained that they had come early so that they could spend some time fixing the place up. One woman asked why you would bother when the house belonged to the mill. Kitty, surprised at this attitude, said they liked to be comfortable and warm and if you didn't fix it yourselves, no one would fix it for you. And if you wanted to eat vegetables, you had to grow them. Most of the other women were getting on with home improvements as best they could, but none of them was as good with a hammer as Kitty, who was happy to lend a helping hand wherever it was needed.

When the men started work they had to leave home early to walk the two miles to the mill. Kitty, always an early riser, was up before her husband and had his breakfast ready for him. The bread was on to bake and his lunch, which had been packed the night before, was also ready. It consisted of cold meat and pickle sandwiches and griddle cakes with jam. She had brought the jam and pickles with her and wondered where she would be able to find berries for jam when the bottles became empty. She wished she had some cheese.

When John came home after his first day's work he made Kitty very happy by saying that she had done him proud; he had the best lunch of any of the hands. Even the boss had commented on it.

Kitty didn't tell John that she had had a great day on her first day at home alone. After doing her domestic chores she was walking with Flame when she met Richard Bryant, who was clearly annoyed about something, and he asked her if she'd seen any of his cows. She hadn't but she whistled up her dogs and sent them out while they walked on together for a bit. It seemed to be no time at all before the dogs were back behind three cows and one rather surprised-looking sheep. The owner looked even more surprised than the sheep. 'Amazing,' he said. 'Did you train them yourself? My wife tells me you are a wizard with animals.'

'No,' Kitty explained. 'They taught me how to train them. It's not difficult. It's in their nature, and you just have to go along with them and learn their ways. Then you adapt their instincts to get them doing what you want them to do. It's basically the same with other animals, too.' When Bryant thanked her and said he'd been held up and was running late, she offered to help him with the milking. He accepted gratefully and was a bit embarrassed to find that she had finished two of the cows and was starting to clean up before he had finished one. When he thanked her, she asked him if she brought the cows in every morning except Sunday, would it pay for Flame's grazing? He said it would be more than enough, she could take some milk as well, and he produced a billy. She thanked him and said he wouldn't be left in the lurch on Sundays because it would take only three or four days to get Ted to work for him.

When he asked whether the dogs could work sheep as well, she said that yes, they could, but they were heelers and controlled cattle by nipping at their heels. That was not a good idea with sheep because it might give the dogs wrong ideas and they might start worrying the sheep. If they were kept working cattle they would be fine. They made an arrangement that Kitty would come over in the morning before she worked her horse so she could start giving lessons to man and dogs on how to work together.

When John came home that night the evening meal was waiting for him. After he had finished his plate of stew, Kitty produced a rice pudding. He looked at it and stiffened. He asked where she had got the milk from. When she told him he became very angry and said that he had told her to keep away from the Bryants. She said that she was just paying for the grazing, and did he want to go without butter and cheese when nobody needed to know they had it? She had made friends with the other wives, except the one who could get on with nobody and was jealous of everybody. He was interested in the gossip and said the woman's husband was a no-hoper and probably wouldn't be kept on for long. He ate his pudding with relish, and Kitty hoped he had got over her helping Richard Bryant.

Life went on fairly smoothly. Kitty had plenty of time to manage all her household duties and her outside interests. In the morning Ted disappeared to bring in the cows on his own and came back to collect her to help with the milking. Occasionally, when he got bored because Kitty was working around the house and Toss was busy with her pups, Ted would join Mr Bryant on one of his walks.

This remarkable man was a qualified ship's captain who'd left seafaring and joined the Water Police in Victoria in 1858. He was a member of a detachment that was sent to New Zealand in 1861. In 1862 he joined the Water Police in Port Chalmers, and in 1864 Sergeant Bryant became the Harbour Master at Queenstown. There he married soon after he arrived.

His bride, Mary Anne, now twenty-five-years-old to his forty-one, had left home in Ireland when she was fourteen as a companion-governess to a young girl. The family had treated her well and had even sent her with their daughter to a 'finishing school' in Melbourne. When she was no longer needed because her charge had grown up, they found her a similar position with the Beetham family who were to leave for New Zealand. In 1863 Mr Beetham became the Resident Magistrate in Queenstown, and from their house Mary married Richard Bryant in 1864. At twenty-five she would have been considered to be an 'old maid' or, less elegantly, 'on the shelf', but they had a long and very successful marriage. In spite of her rather genteel upbringing, she adapted brilliantly to the hardships of being a pioneering wife in a remote locality. They were an exceptionally hard-working couple.

Unfortunately, Richard, a stern Wesleyan, lacked the common touch and never become popular in the district. No matter what he did, no one could forget he had been a policeman nor could he. His wife, however, was a generous, good-humoured and compassionate woman who didn't share his faults.

Not long after they married, Richard, who was fond of money, was lured by stories of fortunes made by gold miners and decided to try the life for himself. The Bryants moved to Tucker Beach, about six miles from Queenstown, where they didn't make a fortune but came away with two daughters and invaluable experience about living as frugally and self-sufficiently as pioneers must. When they bought land at the Head of the Lake, they had a very good idea of what to expect. An ambitious, hard-working and far-seeing couple, they saw the advantages the infant tourism business could have in what was called 'one of the most beautiful places on a most beautiful lake.' So they bought the land and Mary remained in Queenstown while Richard contracted Messrs Luckie and Fletcher to build a substantial four-roomed house, which was where the family was living when Mary Bryant, pregnant with her third child, met Kitty Greig in September 1870.

The tourism business immediately boomed. Mary Bryant was an extraordinary woman. She managed a growing business, a growing family and a growing garden, and in her leisure moments, she lovingly tended a fernery, which Richard had built her in a sheltered position. Mary collected ferns while she was out picking blackberries and gooseberries, which, with briar roses, were probably a legacy of long-gone prospectors and now grew like weeds. As the business, now rather grandly named 'Glacier Hotel' grew, mountaineering guests carefully brought back samples from as high as they could be found and Mary's little hobby brought its own customers.

Mary bought books and learnt about ferns, and with what she learnt from her distinguished visitors, she herself became well known as an expert on the ferns of the district. Over the years many new or rare species found their way into her fernery.

Richard found other sources of income. He established a bar in their big front room, which he ran like the policeman he was, rather than a jovial host. He closed sharp at 10 p.m., and he alone decided when a man had had enough to drink and refused to sell him anymore. Drunkenness was not allowed in the bar. Offenders were quickly evicted. Richard must have been one of the most unpopular barmen in the history of the Wakatipu, or for that matter, anywhere.

He built a post office next to his house and personally appointed the Post Master, no less than one Richard Bryant, who also became the Census Taker. As he scorned horses, this meant he had to cover a huge district, stretching as far as the West Coast, on foot. It is not necessary to guess who looked after the post office in his absence.

Horses soon became an essential part of the tourist business, and Kitty was often asked to help out in the house or with the horses. John badly wanted to start their family (did he really want to keep Kitty at home even more?) and Kitty, who was feeling very secure in her life, was happy to go along with him. She was enjoying the intimate side of married life very much, sometimes to the consternation and bewilderment of John. It was, after all, the Victorian age, when women were still expected to be totally submissive rather than joyful or, even more disturbingly, inventive. And these things were not to be talked about. Men whose wives behaved differently often wondered if there should be a moral question to be asked but found themselves unable to voice it. This was difficult for John, who had been brought up as a strict member of his church and had always adhered to its principles, even though the church was totally silent on the subject of the marriage bed. He could never bring himself to discuss it with his wife.

Baby Catherine was born late in 1871. Kitty held her baby as all new mothers do and felt that this was what she had been born to do. This was true love as no one in the world had ever felt it before and Catherine was the prettiest, most perfect baby that had ever been born. She had her grandmother's violet eyes and perfect features, and already her black hair curled onto her shoulders. Kitty's friends, the other mill workers' wives who came to see her, bringing the customary small gifts, all exclaimed at the baby's beauty. John, who, as all men do, had hoped for a son, was a very proud father from the moment he saw her. This unfortunately didn't last long. The baby might be beautiful but she certainly was *not* a boy.

'It's a good thing that she looks like Ma instead of like me,' Kitty commented when she first saw her baby. John agreed and wandered off. Kitty wondered if her mother had felt the same about her when she was a newborn or if she was disappointed that she wasn't beautiful. Catherine always said that she had only wanted a girl. Kitty remembered happy days with her mother in Dunedin and wondered when and why things between them had gone so horribly wrong.

First daughters were almost always called after their mothers, and Kitty thought she was following in a long line of Catherines. She wondered why her mother wasn't delighted to hear her granddaughter being called 'Katie'. Kitty had never been told that her mother was baptised 'Kathleen' and known as 'Katy' until she was re-christened 'Catherine' on her marriage to Cameron. Kitty was actually the first of the Catherines.

Mrs Bryant called and presented Katie with a beautiful shawl and some baby clothes. She apologised for them not being new but hand-me-downs from her own girls. Kitty loved them, but she was a bit worried about how the other women, and for that matter John, would feel about it.

She didn't have long to wait to find out. The women said how lucky she was and showed no signs of jealousy. They understood Kitty's relationship with Mrs Bryant. They profited from it, as Kitty always brought home more milk than the Greigs could possibly use, and she shared it generously with her friends. She was generous in other ways, too. She wrote letters for those who wanted them written and had started teaching some of them to read. When one of the husbands objected to his wife being taught when he himself was illiterate and wanted Kitty to teach him instead, Kitty said she was happy to do so as long as she taught him 'as well as' rather than 'instead of'. Surprisingly, he agreed, and the pair happily learned together.

John wasn't very happy about all this. He realised that his marriage wasn't what he'd always thought marriage should be like. He couldn't reproach Kitty for the way she managed the household, and when he asked her how she could spend so much time on her other interests, she said she didn't sit around drinking tea and gossiping and she'd made a sling so that she could carry Katie around on her back while she did other things. There was always one of the other wives who was happy to mind the baby while Kitty worked her horse. Since she couldn't ride out just yet, she exercised Flame on a lunge and then spent some time teaching her to do tricks. When she did this she usually had an audience of mothers and their children. Flame was now happy to be led round with two or three children on her back. Kitty, who had been an only child until Billy was born, was anxious to have another child, and John, of course, wanted his son. In 1873 Anne Elizabeth, who was named for John's mother, arrived on the scene. John was bitterly disappointed. This baby, although not a beauty like her sister, was a very personable child. Blonde and big-boned like her father, she had a beaming smile that made everybody respond to her, and their life went on as before. John had always gone for a walk after tea, but now he started staying out later so that Kitty could get the children to bed and the bread made before she herself went to bed.

It had been decided that they would go back and spend a few days with friends and family for Christmas. Toss was past her breeding days, and Kitty wanted to go to Arrowtown to pick up another bitch to keep Ted happy. When he became past it, she would get another dog. Kitty borrowed Ruby and the trap and took John with her to see Sam Fletcher. Kitty selected a two-year-old bitch, and John was horrified when he heard what she was prepared to pay for it. When Sam pointed out that they would get their money back from the first litter, John realised that he hadn't seen any money from any of the dogs that they'd sold. Sam looked puzzled and said that, as always, he had paid the money directly into their bank account.

'Thanks, Sam. We'll be in touch. We're just going to see Freddy. We've left the girls with Grandma, and we don't want to wear her out.' Kitty hurried John off because she felt trouble brewing and didn't want any spectators if he was going to explode. He was. He gripped her viciously by her upper arm and said 'We're not going to Freddy's. We're going to this bank right now to get my money out. You have some explaining to do, my girl. Why are you keeping my money from me?'

'John, you're hurting me. The bank here is just an agency and it's closed today. I want to go to Freddy's and not have this out on the open street. I am not keeping money from you. It's invested and making more money. Please let go of my arm; you're hurting me.'

'I don't understand this nonsense. Money is for spending not for hiding away, and it's *me* that has the spending of it. We're not going back home without it. Do you not understand that?'

'I hear what you're saying. Now will you please let go of my arm!'

'If you don't listen to me, I might have to hurt more than your arm. Let's get inside and have this out. Freddy will understand that a man has his rights, and he'll help me make you see sense.' He gave a vicious twist to Kitty's arm.

When they got inside Freddy took one look at Kitty's tear-stained face, put a 'Closed' sign on the door and started to make a cup of tea. Before he could finish asking, 'What is all this about?' John burst out with his story about Kitty's deceptiveness in keeping his money from him.

Kitty said miserably that it was about their savings. John said that she had some cock and bull story about money making money and as the man he had a right to say where the money went, because it should go into his pocket, not into some bloody bank. He was making good money, and so why would they need savings? Kitty said that one day the timber would be cut out and they would need to buy a home somewhere, or maybe a small farm, because they wouldn't be able to live at Kinloch forever. John said there was no way he was ever going to live on a farm, not ever. He reached into sermons he had heard and quoted, 'Sufficient unto the day is the evil thereof.'

Freddy had been listening silently to all this. He turned to Kitty and said, 'My dear, I would like you to go for a walk because I really need to talk to John alone, man to man. Would you like to trot along to the baker's and buy some of those buns with the pink icing, the ones that they call "Sally Lunns" while I explain the whole banking system and how money can actually make money. Don't hurry.' Kitty looked silently at John, who put his hand into his pocket and pulled out some money, which he handed to her. She looked at Freddy and left.

When she got back Freddy had the kettle boiling and the teapot already warmed. He told Kitty she was in for a treat, not only the Sally Lunns but Darjeeling tea, which would be the best tea she had ever tasted. Kitty felt that she could cut the atmosphere with a knife. For the first time since she had known him, Freddy seemed a bit distracted. John sat in one of Freddy's most comfortable chairs looking anything but. Freddy burbled bits of trivia while he went about the mundane task of making tea, and John glared at Kitty. Finally he could no longer contain himself and burst out, 'Kitty, did you know about this nonsense about men not being in control of their money because of some stupid act of Parliament?'

'Not really, I seem to remember Daisy and Jeannie laughing about something of the sort, but it was when I was madly in love and all fired up about getting married. I didn't take any notice of what they were talking about, except that I heard them say it wasn't anything to worry about, it wasn't going to make any difference to them. Why do you ask?'

'It seems that whatever money you have or earn is yours and you don't have to hand it over to me. That gives you women too much power. It's not right. When we got married you promised to obey me and that's what you will bloody well do, understand?'

'Hey, steady on, man,' Freddy cut in. 'At that very same ceremony I heard you promise to endow Kitty with all your worldly goods. Have you done that?'

'That's just church words,' blustered John.

'If you think it's 'just Church words', why should they apply to Kitty and not to you?'

John was getting visibly angrier, if that was possible. 'Come on, Kitty, we're getting out of here. As far as I'm concerned, nothing has changed. You're going to get that money out of the bank and hand it over to me, understand? No bloody Act of Parliament is going to change my life.'

'Settle down, John. What you ask is just not possible. George had Kitty sign a contract with the bank when he opened her account. Legally she has to leave the money invested for at least ten years, letting it accrue interest. That can't be broken even if you spend a fortune in lawyer's fees. When she went into business with Sam Fletcher they also signed a water-tight contract settling all the details about sales and feed etc. and Sam has to account for the money every month. Kitty's half of the balance has to be paid into that same bank account, and the contract time was extended until Kitty turns twenty-five, so I'm afraid it's Kitty's until the account matures.' Or, he thought, until it rolls over. He was fussing with the teapot so that John couldn't see his crossed fingers.

Kitty broke in and said that their lives would go on as before. Whatever she earned at Kinloch would be spent at Kinloch if that's what he wanted.

John settled down enough to drink his tea and eat his bun, but he sat sulking while Kitty and Freddy sat gossiping about their mutual friends. When Kitty made a move to go and was saying goodbye to Freddy, John burst out and said that whatever the law said, he still didn't like it. It was totally unfair to husbands.

Freddy lost patience with him. He told him sharply that the law was the law and that it had actually been passed before they had married. If John had been spending money that Kitty had earned without her permission, he was, as a point of fact, breaking the law. Kitty broke in to say that of course he had her permission. She lied.

Freddy realised that she was lying and told John that he couldn't blame Kitty for things that been set in place long before she knew that John Greig even existed. Kitty looked at John pleadingly and said he should ask his fellow workers how many of them handed their pay envelopes unopened to their wives. She said he would find out that most of them did. She had never asked for that, and she never would. And furthermore, he seemed to enjoy the better lifestyle they had because of her work. He didn't answer her but said a sullen goodbye to Freddy, grabbed Kitty by the arm and marched her out.

As soon as they were out of the door she told him he was hurting her and tried to pull her arm away, but he kept a firm grip on it until they got back to the trap. Then he had to let go because she had to drive. The trip back was a silent one, interrupted only when Ruby went to turn into the Jordans' and John, hissing, 'No, you don't!' tried to grab the reins.

'John, please, you're frightening the pony and you're pulling her the wrong way.'

'Of course you have to be in charge, don't you,' he snarled.

'I'm only in charge of the trap because you won't let me teach you to drive.'

'It's not your job to teach me anything. Your job is to do as I tell you.' And they drove on in silence until they got back to the dairy. Kitty could no longer think of it as home, although her relations with her mother were better than they had ever been, because Catherine was happy that her daughter was now a 'proper woman' and knew 'her place.' And she loved her grandchildren.

When Kitty started to unharness the pony John said, 'For God's sake, can't you leave the damn thing until I've had a cup of tea.'

Kitty couldn't let it go. 'I'm sorry, John, she's not my pony, and at Pa's place I have to treat her the way he taught me.'

At that point George came out of the house saying, 'Hello, you two. Kitty, do you want a hand? John, there's already a cup of tea on the table with your name on it. I'm sure you must be ready for it, and I want to meet the new little bitch. I've got a kennel ready for her far enough away for us not to hear her whining all night. She'll settle down when you get her home.'

When John was safely out of earshot George turned to Kitty and asked, 'What's the matter, Lovey? What's going on?'

Kitty, brush in hand, buried her face in Ruby's warm flank and sobbed her heart out. George patiently waited with an arm around her until the storm had passed. When the worst was over and they were leading Ruby back to her paddock, Kitty poured out the whole story to George. She didn't know what to do. John refused to believe that she couldn't withdraw the money, even though Freddy had tried to explain what fixed deposit meant. She didn't know if he had registered that because of her age when the arrangement was made, George had to co-sign any withdrawals even after the deposit matured. It had been set up to protect Kitty from her mother, not some future husband.

When she told him that she thought the only way to heal the breach was to find a way to give John access to the money, George said firmly that that wasn't going to happen. He would make sure of that, and under the current agreement there was no way that it could. Kitty said she loved John and she didn't want this to destroy her marriage. George said that he thought John was a reasonable man and it would all blow over once he realised that Kitty was powerless and couldn't lay her hands on it either. He would try to talk to him tomorrow. They fed the pup and put her to bed and walked back to the house.

When they went in it was to an air of festivity, but it was obvious that John was still angry. Kitty hoped that it would come right when they went to bed. That seemed to be the answer to most of their problems.

Lucy and Will, George's young brother, were there, as were Flo and her long-suffering husband. Obviously romance was in the air. Catherine and Flo had fed all the children and put them to bed, but the irrepressible Billy kept popping out until his mother delivered a few belts to his bottom.

Then the announcement was made. Will and Lucy were

engaged. Kitty hugged Lucy and laughingly said, 'I thought you were so set against marriage that nothing would ever persuade you to try it again!'

'You've forgotten what I said. It was that I wouldn't ever marry again unless I could find another George, and I have. And what's more, he's younger and better looking.'

'Just a minute, Lucy,' spluttered George. 'I'm older, I grant you, but what's this "better looking" business?' and he pranced around the room, which was so crowded that as a prance it wasn't at all effective.

When everyone had stopped laughing, Lucy continued, 'George and Will are building us a house on the back road, and we are so happy that we don't have to move away from all of you. And, Kitty, please can we have one of your pups as a wedding present?'

'Of course you can,' Kitty laughed. 'But you might have to wait a while. Toss is getting old, and I want to train my new baby first. Then we can advertise what she's got.'

Kitty remembered that Lucy had said she wouldn't marry unless she found a man like John, not George, and wished that she, herself, had found a man like George. She was sure that Lucy would be happier than she was. Then she chided herself for disloyalty to John.

There was beer and sherry on a table already groaning with Flo's goodies, and after a while a trap drew up. The three Jordans plus Eddie, Freddy and Jeannie spilled into the room, and the party began. Kitty was happy because John stopped being the skeleton at the feast after he had a few more beers and actually began enjoying himself, but she also noticed that he was ignoring Freddy, and this upset her.

Chapter Two

Things remained strained between John and Kitty, although George's talk with John had softened his attitude a bit. He tried to be apologetic when he saw the bruises on Kitty's arm, but all he said was that he must have squeezed too hard. That was all he said, and it had to pass for an apology.

Later, when they were on the *Antrim* going home, he remarked that she shouldn't have agreed to giving Lucy and Will a pup that was evidently worth a lot of money without consulting him first. She thought for a minute, then she asked, 'John, why are you so worried about money? You have a good job and are paid very generous wages, and we live very well. Money seems to occupy your mind more than it used to. I hand everything I make over to you, and I don't know what you do with it, and I don't ask, so please tell me what your problem is so we can share it'.

He was looking down at her as she sat with Annie on her knee and Katie playing around her feet. 'Sometimes I wonder about you, Kitty. You still don't seem to understand what marriage is all about. I know that George has set a bad example and so have

Colin and Eddie, so I suppose I can't really blame you. Marriage means that a wife has to obey her husband, all the time, not just when she feels like it.'

'But I always do,' said Kitty looking perplexed. 'You just don't get it, do you?' he said, shaking his head. 'It also means that you should ask if you can do things before you do them instead of doing them and telling me about it afterwards. Now do you understand?'

'I'm sorry, John, I still don't quite understand. I thought marriage was a partnership between two people who love each other, and you know that I really love you, don't you?'

'In every partnership there is a junior partner, and you're it, get it? And that doesn't give you the right to question me. If you don't listen to me now I might sell that useless bloody horse and throw out all those books you waste so much time with.' And with that he walked away leaving Kitty drenched in misery.

She sat for a while wondering why things had gone so horribly wrong and why she hadn't seen this side of John's character. Then she started to remember. She remembered him asking George who was the boss of each job. She remembered him being annoyed about her being left to find the best track for a horse to take up to the back of the farm and the way he looked at her when she said that Tubby could always be counted on to find the easiest way to get anywhere. She also remembered his annoyance when he had asked George about picking up his pay or about buying something for the job and being told that Catherine would have his wages ready for him every Friday afternoon. George would be discussing costs, etc., with Catherine and would ask John to please give her a list of everything he needed for the next week's work before he left on Fridays. John said he had told George right at the beginning that he would never work for a woman, and he still meant it. George had replied mildly that John was working for him and so was Catherine. George always used her head for figures because she was better at it than him. Anyway, it was his business and now could they please get on with the job.

Kitty realised that she was still only nineteen, and although she was married with two children and possibly pregnant with another, she had never had anything to do with anyone in the sort of marriage that she herself had landed in. She just didn't know what to do. Since she had been recognised for her horse-handling abilities, she had always been treated as an adult, but now she felt like a frightened child who had no one in Kinloch that she could talk to. She still loved John, but did he love her? How could she stop him selling Flame?

When he found out about the arrangements for the pups, he had said he would take over and sell them himself. Freddy had explained that he had formed a company consisting of himself, Sam Fletcher and George, Kitty's legal guardian. Freddy was still legally the owner of the dogs because no paperwork had been done when he gave them to Kitty. Kitty was a junior member who was employed by the company. John said that as Kitty's husband he was now her legal guardian and would now take over. Freddy had laughed and declared that that was only possible if he, George and Sam agreed, and did John think that was remotely possible? Anyway he, Freddy, still owned the dogs. If John tried to interfere he and the company could have him in court and sue the socks off him. The new law said that married women and widows legally came of age at eighteen, so he wasn't Kitty's guardian. Kitty hadn't heard any of this conversation, because it had taken place while she had been out buying Sally Lunns.

Some time later Kitty found out that when George had tried to talk to John, he wasn't even prepared to listen. He was, in fact, quite rude. Poor Kitty didn't know what to do, and it didn't make for a happy atmosphere. She wasn't surprised when John cut short their visit, but she hoped that things would be better when they got home and John wasn't hemmed in by her family and friends.

As soon as the little family plus the new dog were on board the *Antrim,* John wandered off and didn't rejoin Kitty until the ship was approaching Kinloch. As they neared the wharf another man joined them. He nodded to John and held out his hand to Kitty.

'Mrs Greig? I've been wanting to meet you. I'm Allie's husband.

Our Betsy talks about you a lot. So, of course, does Allie. Has she spoken to you about the picnic?'

'You're Mr Hansen? I'm very pleased to meet you. We've been away for a few days and, no, she hasn't mentioned any picnic. What's she up to now? She's a bundle of energy, isn't she?'

'She sure is! Sometimes I simply can't keep up with her! Anyway, she and Mary Bryant have had their heads together, and they have decided it would be a good idea to have a picnic for all the kids in the village, to try to bring the community closer together. Don't you think that's a brilliant idea? They've drawn up a roster giving everyone a job, and I hope they ask everyone before they go ahead. But you know Allie. She says you're one of her dearest friends and she's organised quite a role for you, so I hope you'll come on board. She's given me a lot of jobs, and doubtless she'll be after you too, Greig.'

Kitty seized her opportunity. 'I'd love to, provided my husband doesn't mind.'

Hansen laughed. 'If your husband doesn't mind! Oh dear, what a laugh – you make him sound terribly bossy. Luckily that's not the John Greig I know. He's always most agreeable. I'm sure he will grant you his gracious permission, especially when my Alice gets after him. There she is, with Betsy. Both my girls are waiting for me.'

When they disembarked Betsy ran up in excitement. 'Auntie Kitty, Auntie Kitty, you've got a new pup! Daddy says I can have one of Toss's pups and some man in Arrowtown said I can choose it. When is she getting some, and how soon can I have it?'

Her father quickly interjected, stopping the ebullient Betsy in mid-speech. 'I'm sorry, Mrs Greig, I should have mentioned this earlier. I was doing business with Sam Fletcher when I was in town, and I was admiring Popeye. When I said that I wanted something similar for Betsy, he gave me a little lecture and told me that Popeye was an expensive pedigree working dog and not at all suitable as a child's pet. Then he told me about the arrangement that he had set up with you and the others. Before I had time to think he said that he would sell me one right now on one condition: that I got you to train it. What do you think of that?'

Kitty laughed. 'That sounds very like Sam. Always the wheeler and dealer.'

'Isn't he? And always so charming that he wins every time. Though he did say that you had the drop on him from the very beginning. He ended up taking back from me almost as much as he had paid me for a deal, and I thought that I'd just bettered him for once. But he wrote you a letter confirming the sale, and here it is. Let's shake hands on it,' he said, holding out his hand to Kitty. They shook hands, and after a final hug from Betsy they went their separate ways.

Kitty was worried about John's reaction. He had been silent for too long, taking no part in the conversation.

'I'm sorry, John. There was no time to ask you if all that was all right. And I didn't know about the picnic because they must have dreamed it up while we were away.'

'You should have told me you were *that* chummy with the boss's wife. I had a right to know about that.'

'I honestly didn't know Allie was the boss's wife. To the rest of us Allie is just one of the girls. Some of the others must have known, but we never talk about our husbands.'

'I suppose that's something to be thankful for, but I find the whole thing disrespectful. The boss is the boss.'

'John, I'm not arguing about it. If you don't want me to do whatever it is they want me to, you're going to have to tell them. And you're going to have to tell them why. I just can't bring myself to do that. And I've realised that I'm having another child.'

She went on: 'I love you, you know that, but I can't go on like this. You're earning a really good wage, and you take the money that I earn, but you won't let me have enough to dress the girls properly or to buy them any little treats. They have to wear other kids' hand-me-downs, and now they need shoes. It's embarrassing for me to see them going about shabby, and it makes you look bad. You never tell me what you do with our money.'

John looked at her. He blustered, 'How I spend my money is

no business of anybody else's, and you'd better not be blethering about it to that bunch of gossips. As for the clothes, you can stay home a bit more and mend them, can't you? I don't want you to be accepting charity from anybody. You've got plenty of money in that bloody bank, so you can find a way to get some from there. And don't go running to bloody Freddy, either. Now you're telling me you're having another baby already, and I'm telling you that it had better be a boy!'

Early that evening a knock came at the door. Kitty answered it, delighted to have an interruption. She ushered in the Hansens.

'Sorry to call on you unannounced like this. We want to talk to both of you about the picnic and let you know what we'd like you to do. Is that all right?' asked Allie.

John answered quickly 'I'm not much in favour of picnics and such. I think it wastes a lot of time that could be better used doing real work.'

Hansen looked at him levelly and said, 'You have every right to refuse, but you'll be the only man in the district who's not taking part, and that won't make you very popular. I hope you aren't speaking for your wife, because we need her. You will be available won't you, Mrs Greig? Alice has big plans for you and Flame.'

Kitty said, 'I would really like to help if John doesn't mind. What do you want me to do, and how long do I have to get ready?'

'We are having a women's meeting tomorrow afternoon and sorting out jobs. I think Mary has got you and Flame entertaining the kids, and she said something about doing something with your dogs. She's in charge of entertainment, so you work with her.'

'Alice has me organising the men putting up tents and such, and organising races and games for young and old. She's a hard boss but a fair one. She does all the accounts and correspondence for the mill, and on the whole she's a good boss. It saves me having to employ someone else, and it keeps her wages in the family.'

Alice pulled at his sleeve and said, 'It's time to go. We have other people to see. I'm sorry to come at an awkward time, but it has to be after work so I can talk to the men away from work. It would be interrupting the run of things if I had to call them away to the office one at a time. I hope you will change your mind, Mr. Greig. There's plenty for a strong man to do, and it will be fun. See you tomorrow, Kitty. Goodnight, Mr Greig.'

'Goodnight, Mr Hansen. Goodnight Allie.' Kitty closed the door and turned to face her husband.

Surprisingly, all John said was, 'Make me a cup of tea.' He drank it in silence then went out into the night. He usually went out for walks at night, and Kitty was usually asleep by the time he got home. In the early days of their marriage, she found this disturbing as she wanted him with her all the time, but now she was accustomed to it, and tonight it was a relief. She did a few chores then started making the bread. She always enjoyed kneading the bread. She found the steady, regular hands-on contact with the sweet-smelling dough very relaxing. She hoped she would be asleep when John got home, and she was.

At breakfast John announced that he had decided to take part in this picnic thing. He had met some of his mates when he was on his walk, and they were talking about it. They wanted him on their tug-of-war team as back stop; and he could hardly refuse his mates, could he? Then he picked up his lunch and went.

Kitty finished spooning porridge into Annie's mouth, gave her face a quick wash and popped her into a play pen. She was an easy, sweet-natured child, such a change from her wilful sisters. As Kitty cleaned porridge from the table, the floor and finally a squirming Katie, she wondered wistfully what the next one would be like. It was four years since Katie's birth, two since Annie's. She let her mind wander over the years of her marriage and thought of her belief that she was going to live happily ever after. Ted had finished his morning job of bringing in the cows and was scratching at the back door. He now had them in before Kitty or Bryant got there. Kitty sighed and with Annie on her back and Katie held tightly by the hand, she went out, let Toss off the chain and went to work her horse.

Kitty made Katie a little harness that fitted on her shoulders. A rein could be attached to the centre of the back, and it gave her mother security and the child more freedom of movement than being held by the hand. The other women thought it such a great idea that Kitty was besieged with orders for them. Kitty's only problem with it was getting the angry Katie into it before they went out. Katie was beautiful like her grandmother, but Kitty couldn't decide whether her wilful daughter was more like Catherine or John in temperament. She was probably a bit of both.

Time spent with Flame in the mornings was brief because her main workout was in the afternoons with her child audience. So she went down to the Bryants' because she felt she needed to talk to someone. Mary was older than the other women and had never been part of the gossip circle. She heard Kitty out and said John was very old fashioned and that Richard, for all his stern Wesleyanism, worked with her as a partner, not as a boss. She thought all Kitty could do was to try to get John to socialise a bit with couples and not spend so much of his leisure time in male company. Some men, she added, can be much more malicious gossips than women.

This surprised Kitty, because she hadn't realised that John had leisure time or where he spent it. Then the conversation shifted to the picnic and what Mary wanted Kitty to do. Mary had a playroom and a secure yard constructed for the children. Her Josie, who wanted to be a teacher, had become quite a responsible little mother. Mary had lost the baby she was expecting when Kitty first met her, but her third child, Harry, was just a few months older than Katie. It was a necessary arrangement for such a busy woman that Kitty should come to help whenever she was needed, and they arranged that any money she earned would, from now on, be kept at the Bryants' house until Kitty wanted it. She would still be paid in milk and eggs for any help she gave Richard.

The picnic day was a great success. All the men, farmers, fellers and millers, worked together, and it was taken for granted that John would play his part. When Allie bustled up and issued orders, they would all, including her husband, laugh and yell out, 'Yes, Your Majesty!' No one noticed that John wasn't joining in. He did, however, join in with the work.

The day couldn't have been better. The weather was brilliant, and the events all went just as planned. It started at 10 a.m. with running races for children of all ages, followed by a mothers' race and a fathers' race, then Kitty and Flame did their tricks. There were too many children for Flame to give pony rides, much to the disappointment of her usual fans. Then came lunch, a sumptuous feast, which was provided by the women who had been bounteously supplied with meat, eggs, butter and milk by the farmers. Everything was cooked to perfection and everyone over ate. Exhausted children dropped off to sleep in the most unusual places, and a few adults were seen to be napping as well.

In the afternoon Kitty was first on with her dogs. They weren't given any cattle to herd, but they showed how easily and quickly they could be directed by voice or by gesture and how they obeyed instantly. After they had finished several farmers came wanting to buy pups from the very pregnant Toss's next litter. Kitty explained that they were all pre-sold and told them they had to talk to Sam Fletcher. She showed them the new little bitch, who rejoiced in the unlikely name of Moira, part of her very long pedigree name. Kitty showed them how quickly Moira had learnt how to obey basic commands and how she was now learning to work at a distance. Someone wondered how such a young woman could hold the attention of grizzled farmers and asked if she was the famous Kitty Kirk. She told them she was now Mrs John Greig. John, who had been watching unhappily from the sidelines, was congratulated and told he must be very proud of his talented wife. He wasn't, he was embarrassed and angry, but he managed to smile.

The day finished with a few horse events, but there were no ponies of Flame's size and class, so she and Kitty didn't compete but they gave a little dressage display, which was roundly applauded.

The day ended with a lolly scramble for the kids and a speech or two. When one of the speakers asked if the picnic should be made an annual event, there was a resounding shout of 'Yes!'

The Greigs' life returned to pretty much the same pattern after the picnic. John became aware that there wasn't much cash coming in, but he didn't seem to notice that his daughters were better dressed and had new shoes. He was anxiously awaiting the arrival of his son – when baby Maggie arrived he was furious. There were more boys than girls in his family, he said. His sister had four boys before she had a girl, so it must be Kitty's fault.

When Kitty tried to explain that Catherine was managing to produce boys and girls alternately, he said that since no one but Catherine knew about Kitty's father, the problem probably came from him. Then he said he was going for a walk, and as usual he stormed out into the night.

Kitty was happy with her daughters. Among the mill-women, child-minding was never a problem. When any one of them had a baby, their older children magically disappeared for a few days and came back when the mother was on her feet again. It was amazingly co-operative for such a large group of women. Of course there were small cliques among them and even some nasty gossip, but when it was called for, the whole group came together as a team. The picnic had become an annual event. As Mary Bryant and Alice Hansen had hoped, the whole village had become more of a community.

The next event of great importance in the Greig household was the birth of Georgie in 1876. John Greig had his son. The birth was not the easy time that Kitty had when the girls were born. It was a protracted birth, leaving Kitty weak and exhausted. Nor was wee George as robust as his sisters. Kitty's friends stepped in and helped in every way they could. John questioned the right of the women to come into his house and do the chores. This earned him the rough side of Alice Hansen's tongue. She had noticed that he was entirely besotted with his long-awaited boy and kept lifting the baby from his crib, picking him up and holding him. When the baby became tired and fretful he expected Kitty to feed him to quieten him. He didn't want to listen when he was told that lack of sleep could harm the child. Alice became short-tempered and told him that his behaviour was not that of a loving father but of someone who didn't give a toss for his child. He was treating wee George like a new toy, and his insistence on Kitty trying to feed him so often could stress her to the point where her milk dried up. When he said he was prepared to pay for a wet-nurse, Alice lost it completely and screamed at him that there wasn't such a person in the whole district and in this day and age wet-nursing was a thing of the past. These days babies were fed diluted cows' milk from a bottle. Some of these babies couldn't stomach cows' milk but did better on goats' milk, but none of them thrived as well as they did on their own mother's milk. If you wanted a healthy baby you had to look after the mother's health. John had started to protest that Kitty was a very strong woman when Kitty cried out from the bedroom that the baby was refusing to feed. He was too fretful. Alice rushed in, picked him up to change his nappy and put him in his crib. She called over her shoulder to John, 'Take your wife a cup of tea or soup. She must keep drinking.'

When she came out John had gone out without making tea. Alice went to the neighbours for help to carry Kitty and Georgie to the Hansens' house. When Kitty said weakly that John often went for walks at night, the man carrying Kitty said that he was probably down the road wetting the baby's head. Kitty didn't understand what he meant. She said that John would be very angry when he found them gone. Alice answered that she was sure her husband could deal with that. Kitty would be staying with them until she was stronger and the baby was feeding properly. Later Kitty learned that John had stormed around the village at about 11 p.m. looking for his son.

He came to the Hansens' before work in the morning. He was met at the door by his boss, who told him that Kitty and the baby were sleeping. He protested that a man had a right to see his son and he wanted to, right now. Hansen told him that a man certainly had a right to see his son, but he didn't have the right to make him ill.

'Your son isn't strong and is not guaranteed to survive unless he is properly cared for, and that's something you can't do or won't do. Your wife needs peace and quiet, bed rest and time to recover from that long hard labour, and she apparently won't be getting it living with you.'

'She's a very strong woman, and her place is at home with me.'

'Greig, I've had more than enough of this. You're one of my best and strongest workers. If you weren't you'd be down the road right now. I simply will not tolerate your attitude to women any longer, and you have to start by showing more respect to your wife – and mine. Leave the care of your family to the women. Do you understand me?'

John muttered something about the union.

'Don't be totally ridiculous, man, you've never joined the union and I'm not firing you. Talk to Ivan if you like, he's the union delegate, but you'll only make a fool of yourself. You can come and see your wife after work if you behave yourself. How many times do we have to keep telling you that if you want your baby to survive, your wife has to be healthy. I am warning you again that I am just about losing patience.' The two men walked on in silence.

When they arrived at the mill John muttered that he hadn't got any lunch. Hansen snorted and said that if he wasn't capable of making his own lunch, he had better start learning now. When John replied that he didn't do women's work his boss snorted and said, 'You can bloody well starve, then.'

Kitty stayed with the Hansens' for a fortnight. Her little girls came and visited her in the mornings. They were well cared for by her friends, but Katie said she didn't like baby Georgie because he was smelly, he cried, they couldn't play with him and she wanted to go home.

Kitty said, 'We'll all go home soon, Katie. It wasn't so long ago that you were a noisy, smelly, crying baby. Georgie will grow out of it, just like you did.'

'That's not true,' said Katie indignantly. 'I would member if I was. I have an eggslent memry, everyone says so.'

This made Kitty and Betsy Hansen laugh. Betsy was delighted with their visitors. Her own little brother was nearly as useless as baby George, although he didn't sleep all day. He could crawl around a bit but couldn't walk or talk. Katie, Maggie and Annie were happy. They all thought Betsy was wonderful, and when they came to visit their mother, they paid her scant attention and spent all their time with Betsy.

When the time came for Kitty and Georgie to go home, the women who went to the house to stock it up with food were disgusted with the state of it. Nothing had been cleaned since Kitty left. The table and the bench were covered with old food, and there wasn't a single clean dish in the house. Knowing what a meticulous housekeeper Kitty was, they worked in shifts to make it liveable, and what a story they had to tell their husbands! Small communities thrive on gossip, both friendly and malicious, and this made some of the men look at John Greig in a different way. If anyone mentioned it in his hearing, he glared and said real men didn't do women's work.

At home he was quieter than usual but openly adored his son. He now knew better than to pick him up from sleep but spent time sitting by his crib. Every minute Georgie was awake his father was watching him. He told Kitty that he thought the baby spent far too much time asleep, and when Kitty told him that that was what young babies did, he doubted her. He checked up with some of the men at work and was told the same thing. When he asked how long it was before they could walk, he was told he had three children and surely should have known that, he said dismissively that they were girls, and he didn't take all that much notice of them. And he didn't take much notice of the disbelieving or disapproving looks the men were wearing. Of course, they went home and told their wives, who of course told Kitty and Allie, who of course told her husband. John didn't notice how the atmosphere was cooling. He had his son. His fellow-workers still admired him for his strength, and his boss admired him for his dedication to hard physical work.

Chapter Three

The mill was constantly being modernised. New machinery had just been installed when tragedy struck. A new foreman had just been appointed and had made the mistake of climbing up onto the breaking-out bench. 'Let her rip, boys!' he yelled. There was a bit of a jolt as the motor started. He slipped and fell and was carried into the hungry maw of the huge saw. The machinery, being new and modern, could be stopped immediately. The foreman was alive but had sustained shocking injuries. Allie came rushing from the office, saw what had happened, wrote a note sending for help and dispatched the fastest runner.

Unfortunately, the *Antrim* had already left, so there was no option but to row. Women arrived with any material they could find that was suitable for staunching blood flow. Others arrived with food and bottles of water for the rowers, to sustain them for the marathon row, they had before them. The four strongest men in the village were chosen to row and the horrible journey began. The rowers worked two at a time in shifts. It was thirty-two back-breaking miles to Queenstown, which they accomplished in the remarkable time of five hours. Their patient died just as they pulled into Queenstown Bay.

Their ordeal was not yet over. Had their passenger survived they could have handed him over to a doctor and their job would have been finished, but they had to go to the police station and make separate statements. Hot food and drink was brought to them, when what they needed was to sleep. People doubted that they could have completed the distance from Kinloch in the time they claimed, but this was later verified. They were given beds, and after a few hours sleep they went to a pub where they became very, very drunk without having to buy a drink. They were still drunk when they boarded the steamer the next morning. They were even drunker when they disembarked at Kinloch having been treated onboard as the heroes that they undoubtedly were.

Of course the news reached Kinloch on the same ship, and by the time the news had circulated they were all home in their beds. Kitty was horrified to see her husband in the state he was in, and because he was such a heavy man she needed help to bring him home. As he was muttering that a man needed a drink after the time he'd had, one of his helpers said that he must have swallowed three or four times as much as he usually did to have achieved this state of drunkenness, not to say that he didn't deserve it. Kitty was angry and exclaimed, 'My husband is NOT a drinking man!' This made the men carrying him laugh.

'Where do you think he goes every night?' one asked. 'Same place as we all do. We all like a drop or two after work.'

'And Greig likes more than most of us. He sure can carry his grog,' he said with admiration.

'With the amount he can put away, he's just lucky he can afford it. You must be an excellent manager, Mrs G.'

Kitty muttered something. She simply had nothing to say. She felt as if she had been struck by lightning, and so much became clear to her. She walked on in silence while the men carried him home inside and helped him to bed. One thoughtfully asked her to bring in something to vomit into when he became conscious.

They turned down her offer of tea, saying that they had to get back to work.

The next hurdle Kitty faced was the celebration for the heroes. The band was playing and the people cheering as the four men climbed up beside Hansen, Bryant and representatives of the rest of the community. Speeches were made, and each man was presented with an illuminated address and a purse. Of course mention was made of the foreman, and the crowd stood in silence for two minutes. He had only been in Kinloch for a few days, and no one had had time to get to know him, so the mood of the gathering remained a celebration of the oarsmen and their marathon row.

The mood was such that nobody noticed how quiet Kitty was. She nodded, smiled and shook hands when she was congratulated on having such a hero for a husband, and she managed to make an appropriate answer. She kept reminding herself that she had married for better or worse and was trying to work out how to manage 'worse'.

'Worse' wasn't long in coming. John was becoming increasingly morose with everyone in the little household except Georgie. Katie loved Maggie. Annie felt left out and was always looking for her father's affection. His lack of response had never deterred her. She was only three when Georgie was born but seemed from the start to understand that Georgie was the key to her father's heart, but now she was four she played with the one-year-old Georgie whenever he was on the floor, and he had learnt that, apart from his mother, Annie was his best friend, and he cried when John took him away from her.

John was very concerned that his son wasn't walking yet and spent too much time trying to teach him. When Kitty tried to tell him that none of his strong healthy daughters had walked at the age of one, he told her that boys should be doing everything at a younger age than girls and Georgie was spending far too much time in bed just because she couldn't be bothered looking after him properly. If she spent as much time teaching him to walk as she spent training those damned pups, he would surely be walking by now.

Kitty knew better than to argue. Futilely, she had told him to talk to the fathers of sons among his workmates. Whether he did or not she would never know because he never told her. She was in this marriage for life, although she felt her love for John had flown. The only part of it that held any hope was the time they spent in bed. They had been told that Georgie's birth had left her unable to have any more children, but John disputed that. He wanted more sons.

Kitty confided in Allie. She really wanted to talk to Mary Bryant but hesitated because of what she now knew, that Richard Bryant was running a bar. She didn't know what Mary thought about that and didn't yet want to ask her. Knowing what a strict Wesleyan the man was, she couldn't quite see how it fitted in with his principles.

She talked about this with Allie. Allie said that she didn't know how Mary felt about it either, but she knew that although Richard Bryant didn't drink, he was very fond of money; he was a very enterprising man and sometimes stretched himself too thin chasing it. She also said that Wesleyans weren't such kill-joys as the Wee Frees. They loved singing and some of their best hymns had been adopted by the Anglicans, so they might be a tad more tolerant.

Allie told Kitty she just couldn't understand how Kitty didn't know about John's drinking habits, until she explained that John had always 'gone out for walks' at night while she went to bed exhausted and fell asleep as soon as she had finished her evening chores. And since baby Georgie had arrived, she had to get up to him several times a night as he, unlike his sisters, was a very poor sleeper.

John was only one of a number of heavy drinkers among the workmen at the mill, and many of those men were among the best workers. Allie had never understood how they could manage late nights, alcohol and hard work, but they did. She asked if John had the alcohol habit before they were married. Kitty thought a bit and said, 'He and Pa sometimes had a beer after they had finished, but Pa's not a drinking man. John always spent weekends in Queenstown, and I don't know what he did there. I suppose he probably did drink. I just don't know. There's so much that I just don't know. And the main thing I don't know is what I'm going to do next. I was only fifteen when I married, and I thought I would live happily ever after.'

'I think we all think that, and only some of us are as lucky as I have been.'

'All the couples I knew well back home were like you. They worked together like partners. I didn't know that John had other ideas until we got here. All I have decided is that he isn't going to get any more of my hard-earned money to hand over to Richard Bryant.'

'Richard isn't too bad. He won't sell liquor to anyone he thinks is drunk, but unfortunately hardened drinkers can hold a lot before it shows. And at least Richard does shut down every night at ten. The trouble is that there's a crew member on the steamer who brings in crates of rum and sells the locals however much they want. He's the biggest problem because what he does is legal. The men buy it and pay someone else for it, and the guy who delivers it says he's only the middle man. We can't do a thing about it. I'm sorry. Eric's told the hands that they are not permitted to turn the single men's quarters into a booze barn. I just don't know how we can help you, Kitty, but all of us are here for you.'

When John found out that all of Kitty's previous hiding places for money were always empty, he became annoyed. She said she wasn't earning any. She didn't have time. Then she told him she needed him to give her more for basic needs. There was still some work for her at Bryants, but she got food for that, not cash. They were living on charity because everyone now knew how John's money was spent. There were no boy's clothes forthcoming, and Georgie was still wearing clothes the daughters had outgrown. John furiously told her that she would just have to be a better manager, and where was the money she got from riding lessons? She replied that she exchanged riding lessons for clothes, soap and other necessities.

As she had expected, John exploded. How dare she tell all those women that he wasn't providing for his family? She responded that she didn't have to tell them. Everyone knew that John was a drunkard before she had found out for herself. She was told that after Georgie's birth, when she was so ill and the women had cleaned out their house, their men had carted away so many bottles that everyone in the village realised why Kitty and the girls were so shabby, and they pitied her.

Georgie had finally managed to struggle to his feet. One of John's workmates had told him if he kept on forcing the child on to his feet, he would make the boy bandy-legged, so John had reluctantly left him alone. He still doted on him, coming home from work and playing with him in a way he had never played with the girls. On Sundays he took the boy with him everywhere he went. Annie trailed along when she could keep up until, at last, John realised she could be useful and started getting her to mind Georgie when he got tired and scratchy. Annie trotted along behind John carrying Georgie's blanket and her own old grubby soft toy.

The women thought John was a lovely father to Georgie and Annie – pity about the other girls. The men thought he was daft and made jokes about him. Kitty carried on as she had. She made money from dog and horse training, and her hiding place for it was in the Bryants' cowshed or in Allie's care.

Since Billy Kirk had been about ten, he'd spent the school holidays at Kinloch. Always an impossible child, he was devoted to Kitty and behaved reasonably for her but for no one else, unless that person owned horses and was knowledgeable about them. He made himself useful around the horses that were used for the Bryants' fledgling horse tours. Richard soon realised that Billy could groom and tack up a horse quicker than he could himself, so he made good use of him. Richard still didn't like horses. He had started employing Kitty as a guide for some of the horse tours, and whenever a man didn't like the idea of being led by a woman, he told them, 'She's a slight, wiry woman, no oil painting but able to use her tongue in no uncertain terms, and she's a very fine horsewoman.' Kitty enjoyed the work. Richard Bryant paid her well, and she received generous tips, so she could dress the part and she kept her money and her riding habit at Bryants'. Richard was very good at seeing when people were useful to him, and you can be sure he made good use of Billy. And he didn't have to pay him. Billy was young enough to be happy when he was flipped the odd coin.

To begin with John found Billy detestable (most people did) but after he had delivered a few really hard wallops, Billy respected him and they rubbed along well enough. After Georgie was born John began to see Billy as another male in the house, somewhat like what he hoped his son would grow to be. Sometimes, before John went out for his evening walk, they used to rough-house a bit while the girls squealed delightedly. Kitty, of course, was delighted, too. She loved Billy, and the atmosphere in the house was so much better when Billy was there.

The Glenorchy races were an important event on the social calendar, and Billy was staying with them. John had carried Georgie off to see some friends and Billy had gone to look at the horses when Kitty was approached by an unhappy looking man. 'Are you Kitty Kirk?' he asked.

Kitty smiled, 'I was,' she answered. 'I'm Mrs Greig now. Why?'

'I need help,' he said. 'I've been looking after this horse that belongs to my boss, and I've got very fond of it. Now he tells me that if the horse doesn't place he's going to shoot him for dog tucker. I'm no rider and too heavy anyway. Would you ride him and save his life? Please?'

'I've lost my nerve for that sort of thing since I had children,' Kitty answered. As they walked towards the horse lines the man carried Maggie for Kitty, who had a little girl in each hand.

'Here he is,' the man who had introduced himself as Tom Cooper said.

Kitty took one look. 'It's Smith!' she exclaimed. Smith lifted his head and answered her with a whinny. 'He's in terrible shape!' she said 'What's happened to him?'

'He'll be in even worse shape next week if you can't help me save him,' Tom said miserably. 'None of the jockeys will go near him. They're already calling him dog tucker, and that's what he'll be.'

Kitty thought for a moment. 'Have you got silks? Small ones? I just might be able to find you a jockey. And we'll need a cap that comes well over his face.' Tom went to find the silks, then he looked after the girls while Kitty went to find her brother. It wasn't hard. When Kitty dragged him away from the favourite by whispering in his ear to tell him what she wanted from him, he couldn't get away quickly enough.

When Tom saw him he gasped. 'A child! What are you thinking about?'

'Do you have any better ideas? This is my brother, Billy Kirk. He's older than he looks. He may be small for his age, but he can ride. I rode in a race or two when I was his age. I can guarantee he won't fall off. He doesn't know anything about tactics, but Smith does, and they both like to win. What say you go and make sure he'll get paid if they run in a place. I'll get the pair of them tacked up. By the way, I don't trust that boss of yours to pay up when he discovers Billy's age, so you'd better get it in writing.'

'They'll all laugh at me and make a joke of it, but I'm used to that. He'll make a joke of it, too, and make a great show, but he'll do it for laughs, because he'll be that sure Smith won't do it.'

'I'll make him laugh on the other side of his face,' said Billy, with all the confidence of his age. And he did just that.

It would be nice to report that Smith won hands down, but he didn't. He pushed into a very close second behind the favourite. There was a roar from the crowd. There were very few bets on Smith, but fair-minded people love to see an underdog succeed. There was another roar when Billy took his over-large cap off. The owner took it well and shook hands with all those who congratulated him and asked Billy if he would like a job. Billy said he would, as soon as his father let him leave school. Could he work for him in the holidays? He said he'd had a great ride; he just had to sit there because Smith knew exactly what to do and he had taught Billy a lot.

The only person who wasn't pleased was John. While he was proud of Billy, he hissed to Kitty that she should have told him what she was up to, because he could have made a mint by betting on Smith. He handed Georgie over, saying that he wouldn't stay awake. Then he left Kitty with the four children, and walked away to rejoin his mates, who asked him if his wife had given him any tips for the next races. He looked quite angry and was about to reply when one of his mates, overhearing, called out and told John he was a lucky bugger getting hot tips from an expert.

John snorted and walked off. The man came back and asked Kitty for a tip. When she said she had to see the horses before she advised him, he went with her and Billy as they wandered over to the saddling paddock. Billy and the punter each had a little girl riding on their shoulders. Kitty carried Georgie and Katie trotted along behind them.

Kitty gave the man several tips, all but one of which was successful, and Billy was offered another ride, which he accepted with alacrity and came a creditable third. His future career was now set out for him. Kitty wondered what their parents would think, but Billy was wild and uncontrollable, and he had already caused them a lot of grief.

Smith had been saved, and Tom, his carer, had won enough money to feed the horse for quite some time. The owner, in a fit of very public generosity, had given Smith to Tom, earning huge applause from the crowd. The owner laughed, and it made sense because he couldn't afford to feed him.

It had been a good day, except that when they were on the boat going home, John's mate told him how much he had won from Kitty's tips. John demanded to know how much Kitty had been paid for the information. His mate laughed and said he'd offered her a percentage but she had turned it down, saying that her husband wouldn't have let her take money from a stranger. He said John should have hung 'round and done some betting himself. John was silent as he sat holding the sleeping Georgie.

In 1881 Georgie turned five. John had told Kitty he wanted his boy to have a birthday party. She protested that Georgie was not a sociable boy and didn't like the birthday parties he'd been to and had refused to go to any more. He was still very small for his age and not robust. He tried to avoid the rough and tumble that little boys went in for. He wouldn't even attempt to kick a rugby ball around after he had been pushed into a game and been tackled. He just sat on the ground and cried. His father was mortified and so was Georgie when the other boys laughed and jeered. He cried all the more when John chased them away.

John insisted on the party and gave Kitty enough money for a lavish feast. He took Georgie to Queenstown and brought him home the next day wearing new clothes and loaded with parcels. When Kitty asked what was in them, she was told that Georgie would open them at the party.

Georgie, who was utterly exhausted, burst into tears. 'Dada,' he cried, 'I told you and told you I don't want a party. I hate those kids and they hate me. Mummy, can I please go to bed right now? Don't make me have a party!'

As Kitty bundled him off to bed John muttered darkly, 'If I say there's going to be a party, there's going to be a bloody party.' When Kitty came out of the bedroom she was obviously nervous. 'John,' she said, 'I hate having to tell you this, but none of the little boys will come to the party. Georgie won't go to their parties and they won't come to his.'

'What!' John screamed. 'I'll go and sort it out with their bloody fathers. They can make them come. How dare they spoil my son's birthday!'

Katie said comfortingly, 'Never mind, Dada, we can still have the party. All the girls want to come.'

That was too much for John. He leapt to his feet, but before he could reach Katie the three girls had disappeared. He grabbed his coat and charged out into the dark. Kitty hoped against hope that he would be too drunk to hit Katie when he got home.

Kitty told the girls where she was going and went to talk to Allie. As she left Katie called out, 'Don't worry, Mummy, we've made a wee hut for ourselves under the bed, and we'll be as quiet as mice.'

Kitty couldn't help herself. She smiled, but she was wondering how all her romantic dreams of living happily ever after could have turned out as badly as this.

Both the Hansens were at home. She poured out all her problems and then apologised, saying she shouldn't be spilling all this stuff on to them, but she was at her wits' end. Allie put her arms around her, making comforting noises. She didn't quite know what to say to her. When Hansen told Kitty to call him 'Eric', she involuntarily looked over her shoulder. He laughed and told her that anything that was said in their house stayed in their house. Then he told her that he, too, was worried about John's behaviour. He was still one of the hardest workers, but he was starting to alienate himself from his fellows.

'He was always a bit of a loner, but now he can't seem to think or talk about anything but wee Georgie. I can't fault him for his dedication to the job, and he makes fewer mistakes than anyone, but the men are starting to talk about him. Frankly, they're sick of him. He can't seem to understand that giving the boy the best toys and the best clothes won't make him the best liked. Poor Georgie, when he turned up with a brand new football, he gave it to the best player and told him that he could keep it. All the other boy said was "Thanks, Georgie, I'm sorry but you're still useless and it won't get you on to the team," and he ran away with the ball. Later he relented and told Georgie to eat a lot, get bigger and heavier and learn how to play.'

'Georgie can't help it that he's not the sort of son that his father wanted. John wanted a carbon copy of himself and just can't accept the fact that Georgie is not physically strong. He seems to think it's my fault because I don't know who my father is. John says Georgie's inherited something he calls "bad blood" from him.'

Allie said that John should appreciate the fact that his son might not be sporty, but he was by far and away the cleverest child in the school, even though he was only five. He could read better than most of the boys who were older than him, and he could figure better than many adults. That didn't make the boys like him any better.

It was time for Kitty to go home. The Hansens said goodnight and said they would keep on thinking about her problem and see if they could come up with anything that might help. They would always be there for her, and they hoped they had helped by listening. They both hugged her and Kitty left with tears in her eyes.

John came home a bit earlier than usual and made Kitty get up and make some tea and a sandwich. This became his pattern. He would go out at the usual time but would come back earlier, usually in a foul mood. Often he insisted that they had to go and make another son, a better one next time. Kitty remembered what Mary Bryant had once said: 'Least said, soonest mended.' She bit her tongue and resolved to follow that advice.

One day John came home from work and announced, 'I've decided what you're going to do with all our money that's lying around in the bank. My son is going to boarding school, and he's going to be a lawyer or something. Mrs Hansen came into the smoko room at lunch time and congratulated me on having the cleverest boy at the Head of the Lake and possibly in the whole Wakatipu. That made those snot-noses sit up! One cheeky bastard said he must take after his mother, and they all laughed and said it would take more money than I could afford.'

Kitty said Georgie was far too young to go to boarding school yet. John carried on: 'I know that. Mrs H. said there were scholarships he could go in for, but when I told them we had money in the bank that we would use and didn't need charity, she said it wasn't charity, it was a sort of competition that even rich kids went in for to see who was the smartest. He's got to wait until he's thirteen.' Kitty said it still seemed a bit young, but John said he should be going to school now but Mrs Hansen said he could go with Betsy to the Bryant's place and get lessons with that woman that teaches their kids. She said that it wouldn't cost much, but if I wanted she would stop it from my wages. She told me to discuss it with you, and I said I was the boss in my own house, she could go ahead, thank you very much. And here are Betsy's old school books for Georgie.'

Kitty's eyes lit up. 'Oh thank you, John, I always knew you'd want to do the best for our boy.' She went to hug him, but he brushed her off. He rarely touched anybody except Georgie. Inwardly, she was thanking the Hansens.

Chapter Four

Life became a lot easier. John stayed home in the evenings until Georgie went to bed. Georgie told him about what he had been learning and read to him from his books. John wondered what use it was to know some of that stuff. Georgie told him it was fun finding out about far-away countries and how people had lived long ago. He liked to learn about old kings and their wars and especially about the winning of the great British Empire. He asked if he could have an atlas, and John, who didn't know what he was talking about, said of course he could and told Kitty to get him one. When it arrived he was a bit nonplussed but enjoyed poring over it with Georgie. When Georgie said wistfully that if he were stronger he would like to be a soldier, John glared at Kitty, who, wisely, said nothing.

The boy remained physically frail, but he loved going up to the dam with his father at the weekends to sail the little fleet of toy boats that John had bought for him. His favourite was made of tin, and if a stubby little candle was put in it, it puttered along on its own. It could have a string attached to it or its little rudder could be bent so it ran in circles. It was the envy of the other boys and even some of the fathers. Annie always tagged along.

Billy came to visit periodically. Immediately after his successful day at Glenorchy, he had managed to get himself expelled from school, had taken up his apprenticeship and had left home. His relationship with his brother George (no longer 'Georgeboy', just 'George') had gone beyond nasty to vicious. George was a tall, good-looking lad, fair-haired like his father, and he got on well with everyone except Billy. He had become a competent rider and was frequently hired as a jockey, much to Billy's disgust. Catherine was too absorbed with her beautiful daughter Lizzie to take much notice of what she called 'George's little hobby'. George senior got the companionship and respect from him that he had never been able to get from Billy.

Billy had learnt that it was a waste of time trying to fight George physically as Billy was five feet tall and George towered over him, but Billy had to win at all costs, by fair means or foul. Unfortunately, so did George. The place they fought most of their battles was on the race track where they were both adept at concealing foul play.

It came to a head at the Invercargill Races in 1880. Though George was only thirteen and a half, he looked older and had been told that he wouldn't be getting more rides because he was already nearly six feet tall and would soon be too heavy, except in the winter steeple-chases. Billy gloated. George threatened to wipe the stupid grin off Billy's stupid face, and a very public row was stopped by onlookers.

Halfway through the next race their horses crashed into each other and into the running rail, then fell to the ground in a tangle of equine and human bodies. Billy's foot, ankle and leg were smashed and George lay dead on the track. The big question: was the mishap caused by deliberate interference? There was an inquiry, which resulted in it being declared a foul but no decision as to whether it was accidental or deliberate could be reached. This matter was debated for years among racegoers.

Billy's shattered leg was patched up and, although withered, was made into what was known as a 'natural leg'. This was done by twisting the skin and flesh around the muscle and enclosing it in a hollow wooden leg. A bad-tempered Billy convalesced at Kinloch, where he bloody-mindedly stumbled about teaching himself to walk, after a fashion. Although he had trouble getting around, he was back on the track again in six months, winning to thunderous applause.

In 1884 tragedy struck the Greig family and disaster struck Billy. Georgie, who had been getting weaker and weaker began having seizures and was diagnosed with epilepsy. Epilepsy was known as the 'falling sickness' and was considered to be shameful. John was in complete denial and wanted to consult another doctor as well as the one in Queenstown, but Georgie was too sick to travel. During this period Kitty had received news that Freddy had died, but because of Georgie's health, she hadn't been able to go to his funeral. She had looked on him as a dearly loved grandfather, and he had cared very deeply for her. He left a huge hole in her heart. She hadn't been able to say goodbye to him, and she felt that she couldn't even mourn him properly because her whole heart and mind were taken up with Georgie. She couldn't talk about Freddy with John, because John hated him.

Georgie died. The whole Greig household was in chaos. John was furiously angry, firstly with Kitty because he believed it was caused by her 'bad blood', secondly with the doctor, who wasn't able to save him and finally with God, who had given him only one unhealthy boy instead of the bunch of strong sons he deserved. All he had now was a wife, who was a bastard with bad blood (and possibly barren into the bargain), who had given him a tribe of useless girls who wouldn't stop crying. And on top of that, Richard Bryant had told him that while he was sorry for his loss, he had to stay away from the bar until he could behave more rationally. Rational, John was not. What else could a man do but go home and trash the house? Kitty and the girls were terrified and ran out into the darkness. He simply could not believe that anyone else could feel the grief that he did.

He completely withdrew, leaving Kitty to manage all the funeral arrangements. Eric Hansen helped her, and Betsy took charge of the girls. Katie was twelve, Annie eleven and Maggie ten. They had all loved their brother, and it was their first experience of losing a loved one. Allie helped clean up the house and was there for Kitty, who was numb from her double tragedy.

Things slowly returned to something like normal. John went back to work and Kitty tried to get on with her normal life. One thing, however, bothered Kitty. Once she had asked John if he would like to go and see his family in Waitati to get a break from Kinloch. He told her brusquely that he had no family in New Zealand and would she please leave him alone. She knew better than to mention the story he had told her before they married, and she tried to get it out of her mind. He said he had been born in Tasmania, but now she wondered if there was any truth in that either. She didn't like being married to a mystery man who hadn't even been sure of how to spell his surname. This led her to wondering how much she actually liked being married at all. Hastily, she banished this thought by thinking about how much she loved her daughters and how supportive the community was.

In the winter Billy took on jobs breaking in horses or retraining some who were difficult to handle, and this nearly put paid to his career and even his life. He was not known for his kindness to horses, and this led to constant rows with Kitty. Billy was a 'flogger' when racing. Use of the whip was compulsory. A jockey could be fined for 'not riding the horse out' because the most important thing was to keep the punters happy, not the welfare of the horses.

In 1884 he had just finished grooming a horse he was breaking in for John Smith at Arthurs Point and had possibly been a bit too heavy-handed with it. When he went to mount, the horse managed to spin around and lash out, catching Billy on his bad leg and giving him another really bad break, this time in his thigh. Billy was rushed to Frankton Hospital.

Kitty got a message that she was wanted urgently at the steamer wharf, and she raced down to find Billy being unloaded onto a stretcher. He was accompanied by a distraught George, who said, 'The worst possible thing has happened.' He explained how Billy had got his accident and that the wound had become badly swollen and possibly infected. To avoid gangrene there been nothing for it but to amputate. All Billy's hopes to be a champion jockey had been lost with his leg. He kept crying that he wanted Kitty, and as it was impossible for him to convalesce at home, George had taken him straight from hospital to the Frankton wharf and brought him on the boat to Kinloch. George said he would book himself into the hotel for the night to save a row with John and would go back home on the morning boat.

Kitty took Billy home with her and set about nursing him. She was afraid of what John would say, but he was surprisingly sympathetic. He spent quite a bit of time in the evening sitting with Billy and telling him about what had happened at work and passing on good wishes from his workmates at the mill. Then he would go out for his usual evening walk.

Physically, Billy healed amazingly quickly. Kitty made him eat vegetables, which he hated. When she told him that it would make him heal more quickly, he told her that there wasn't much point in getting better if he couldn't ride. She told him that of course he would ride again but only if he really wanted to. She told him to pull himself together. Sure it was a terrible thing that he had lost his leg, but it was up to him to prove to himself that he wasn't finished. It was a hard line to take with such a young man, but she knew that sympathy simply would not work with Billy.

One Saturday they had a visit from one of John's workmates. He was an old man who had been a seaman. He started playing with the girls and amusing them by picking them up and dancing with them, then he turned a somersault and stood on his hands. When he did so his trouser-leg slipped up and revealed a wooden leg. Billy was gobsmacked and wanted to know if he would ever be able to do that. He was told that of course he could, if he really wanted to. It all depended on Billy himself. The old sailor said he had come to measure Billy and make him his very own wooden leg. The old man said that he was called Peggy because that's what one-legged sailors were called. At sea one-legged sailors were employed as cooks, but Peggy hadn't wanted to be in the galley, so he set about cooking the worst-tasting meals in the whole world. He used salt where he should have used sugar, sugar where he should have used salt. One day he had an inspiration and put Epsom Salts and molasses into the stew. And the bread didn't rise. Well it wouldn't, would it? Peggy had 'forgotten' to put any yeast in it. He was surprised to find himself on the wharf at the next port, because he had thought to find himself on a desert island where he had planned to find himself a beautiful dusky maiden.

The next day Kitty hoisted Billy onto Flame and taught him how women who rode sidesaddle used their crop on the side away from their legs and how horses could be taught to respond. She offered to get a sidesaddle so that he could learn the technique, but he snorted and said that he wasn't a bloody girl! He learned very quickly and soon got angry when Kitty wouldn't let him gallop Flame, and she watched him very closely whenever he was handling her.

It took Peggy a week or so to finish the leg, and although he warned Billy to go slowly or his stump would get sore, 'slowly' was just not in Billy's vocabulary, so he had to learn the hard way. After another week he declared that he was fit enough to go back and ride some proper horses. And, yes, he would keep on eating those bloody vegetables.

He went back to the racing stables and had to prove himself to get back into work. No one believed that he could, but they felt sorry for him and admired his guts, so they gave him a try. To begin with he was only allowed to ride training-gallops until he was given a ride on a "no-hoper", which he rode into a place and had his job back.

As before, he was constantly in trouble. He seemed unable to understand or obey riding instructions. He was popular with punters because he won much more often than he lost, but sometimes trainers didn't want to win. This was what Billy couldn't understand. Throughout his entire riding career he always rode to win. When he became an owner and a trainer it was the same. His horses were ridden to win. Less than a year after his amputation he was again riding winners.

John enjoyed Billy's visits and took him with him on his evening walks. Billy never stayed long; he never stayed anywhere for long, and wherever he went he managed to wear out his welcome. He was very good at offending people. In Kinloch he offended the Hansens. This made Kitty very angry, and she showed it. But he was her brother and she still loved him. She couldn't bring herself to tell him to stay away, but she did give him a good talking to. His nieces loved him, too.

Not long after their brother died the younger girls were able to go to the little school that had just opened at Mill Creek, where the last working sawmill in the district remained. Annie and Maggie got up early and walked to Mill Creek with John. Twelve was too old to start school, but Katie had been well taught by Kitty.

Kitty was worried about money because John seemed to have forgotten that he still had a family to support. She also worried about how long it would be before the mill closed. John refused to discuss the future except to say that they would never leave Kinloch. Unknown to Kitty, he had put her name down for a section in the hope of getting hold of the money lying in the bank. He knew he would always be able to get labouring work in the district. The Hansens were planning to leave when the mill closed, if not before. Although Kitty had no money of her own, she became an indefatigable money-raiser for the school.

Katie was working full-time in Kitty's old job with Mrs Bryant and already saving up so that she could leave Kinloch as soon as she was old enough. John demanded that she hand over any money she earned, but she refused and had to dodge his fists. Kitty was getting more and more guiding work from Richard, but that was largely off-season as the Bryant boys were now old enough to work during the long summer holidays.

Kitty needed something steady. She was out walking her dogs

one day when she stopped to talk to some old men who were splitting shingles. Beech shingles were the most common roofing material after corrugated iron and had the advantage of being a lot cheaper. A very heavy sharp knife was used to whack a pre-sawn beam, ten-inch by four inch into quarter-inch slices. It required great judgment and a steady hand as it had to be done with a single stroke. Kitty watched for a while, then asked if she could have a go. They laughed and said it wasn't women's work, she should stick to her horses. But one of them handed her his knife and she managed the single stroke, but the shingle was too thick. It didn't take long for her to get the knack, and after a bit of bargaining they allowed her to join the team.

After a few mornings of Kitty arriving with lunch for three and cheerfully making the tea, she picked up speed and sometimes even surpassed the tally. She had been using old Herbie's second knife, and she decided to get a pair of her own. She soon became very fast and very accurate, with less wastage than the old chaps. Great camaraderie developed between Kitty, Herbie and Jock. Now she had a steady income.

In 1887 disaster struck the settlement and the milling industry. Cattle rustling was rife and the meat was smuggled out of the district with the aid of some of the farmers. Times were hard as New Zealand's worst depression began to creep into the country. The law was catching up with the cattle thieves, and they attempted to cover their tracks by burning some hides that could be used in evidence against them. The wind changed and blew very strongly, and within a few minutes the whole valley was a sheet of flame. Men, women and the larger children formed bucket brigades, working for hours saturating blankets on the shingle roofs of the hotel and the houses. All the buildings were saved, but the fire virtually spelt ruin to the milling industry and temporarily damaged the tourist industry. However, some trees were still usable for posts or for firewood and shingles.

John still had his job and Kitty hers. The writing was on the wall, but John refused to read it. He was adamant that he would not leave Kinloch. Katie had fewer hours at Glacier Hotel but still saved every penny towards her departure. Maggie planned to become a school teacher and wanted further education. She had spent some of her school holidays in Arrowtown with Jeannie and could hardly wait to get away because so many of her friends had already left the Kinloch district. Kitty had decided to go with them, and she doubted whether John would even notice that she had gone, except that he was continually demanding money to pay for his section. Annie wanted to stay behind to be with her father. They all muddled along together for the next couple of years. When Annie told John about Kitty and the girls' planning to leave, He told her she was a good girl and not to worry. They were a family, and he would never allow Kitty to go, because she was his wife and she was keeping all his money away from him. Stiffly, he let her hug him.

Christmas dinner was a communal affair organised by Allie and cooked by the workers' wives. The men decorated the little hall and had a competition to choose Father Christmas. This was always won by Jock, the shingle cutter, who not only had a long beard but a beautiful white one. There was, as always, a doubting Thomas who didn't believe Father Christmas should have a Geordie accent, because he was a German like Prince Albert, who had brought Father Christmas to England along with Christmas trees.

In 1889 it was, as usual, a riotously happy occasion. Diners came from miles around, and because of the exceptionally heavy rain, which began about midday and didn't stop, many people decided to doss down in the hall. Fortunately, the rain began after the meal had been served and therefore didn't interrupt the festivities.

The speeches began after everyone had eaten. The last speaker was Eric Hansen. He began by welcoming everyone, and after a few more pleasantries he said, 'Last week we went to Dunedin to renew our management term for the next five years. We were successful.' Everyone cheered.

'Unfortunately, we were only given a renewal for three years, because there is no guarantee how long the timber will last. After three years the operation will probably start winding down and a manager experienced in closing operations will be employed. My Alice gave them a piece of her mind when they had the cheek to ask if she would stay on managing the office until the end. She said that as we hadn't signed yet, we reserved the right to leave when and if we got a better offer. So that's how we stand.

'Now, how do you chaps stand? Some of you will be kept on until the end. It would be a good idea to learn something about demolishing and salvaging machinery if you can. Otherwise you will probably be laid off in gangs. Talk to Ivan and join the union. Whatever you do, don't sign anything without asking Alice. We'll be here for a while yet because the timber isn't holding badly, but it didn't really recover from the fire. I'm sorry. We've built a good operation here, haven't we? But as they say, all good things come to an end. Goodnight.' And, quietly, the Hansens went out into the rain.

Kitty was more than ever determined to leave Kinloch as soon as she could. Kinloch had been good for her, but marriage had not.

The week between Christmas and New Year was a time of celebration for the residents at the Head of the Lake. Festivities began on Boxing Day with the Caledonian Games followed by a concert and ball. There were various activities throughout the week: a children's day and a picnic, wood chopping and shearing contests. Kitty took part in the shingle-cutting competition, much to John's disgust, but now Kitty had made up her mind to leave, she no longer feared his rages. The week culminated in a games day and a grand ball on New Year's Eve followed by a race meeting on New Year's Day.

In 1899 the weather was not kind. Boxing Day was miserable and the usual picnic didn't take place. The rivers were rising but not high enough to deter the Kinloch crowd from riding to Glenorchy. There were a few races but the wind was biting, so the usual Highland dancing and caber throwing were cancelled. However, the ball and the concert were a great success.

Katie, Annie and Maggie sang in the interval, and Katie also played her violin for some of the dances. The dancing went on until daylight, then the Kinloch people climbed on their horses for the weary ride home. It was a night Kitty was to remember for the rest of her life.

For the rest of the week the weather was bad and New Year's Eve was a cold showery day with the wind whistling down the valley. The lake wasn't particularly rough. A party of young people from Kinloch usually rode over to Glenorchy, but with the river running a banker, that was just not possible.

Katie had dipped into her savings and had bought herself a new, black shiny hat of which she was particularly proud. Maggie was very excited because it was the first time she was allowed to go, so they were both very disappointed. Many of the young men of the district were very interested in Katie, but all she wanted to do was to get out of Kinloch. She had no romantic ideas about marriage because, from what she'd seen of it, she thought it was something best avoided.

Because the lake was not too rough, Joe Oliver, aged twenty-eight, who was one of the most experienced and capable boatmen on the lake, offered to take a small party over to Glenorchy in his sturdy little boat. He must have made the trip scores if not hundreds of times. The party consisted of Katie and Maggie Greig, their friend Lily Forsythe and Lily's two brothers, who were also very skilled boatmen. Joe knew the lake and its moods very well indeed, and none of them considered the lake to be too rough.

Kitty and Joe Forsythe stood watching until the boat was just a speck against the Glenorchy shore. The waves were rising, but when Kitty voiced her concern Forsythe reassured her that Joe Oliver was one of the best boatmen on the lake. 'All the same,' he qualified, 'I'm glad they're staying for the night. You know my Joe has tickets on your Katie, don't you? I don't blame him. She's such a beauty, and a thoroughly nice girl into the bargain.'

Kitty laughed. 'She's lucky she doesn't take after me, isn't she? I agree, they'd make a lovely pair, but Katie's determined to get out of Kinloch and see a bit of a different life before she settles down.

Annie's the only one who wants to stay.' They'd lost sight of the boat so they turned and left.

At Glenorchy the fun went on. Lake Wakatipu had now blown up very rough and one of the spectators thought he heard someone shouting or crying, but he dismissed the thought because the bagpipes were very loud and competing with the screaming seagulls. Those who wondered why the Kinloch people hadn't come thought that since the rivers were too high to cross and the lake was so choppy they had decided against it. Their parents, who weren't expecting them home, were also unconcerned.

It was only when the steamer arrived on the following afternoon that the horrible truth was realised. A search was organised and some days later the boat was found washed up on Pigeon Island. Later again, Katie's pride, her new black shiny hat, was found on the beach at Twenty-Five Mile Creek. The bodies were never found. Lake Wakatipu seldom gives up its victims.

Kitty wanted to die. She had lost all the people she had loved most. She had lost her son, two of her daughters and Freddy. A week later Billy arrived bringing the news that when George Kirk heard about the girls he had a heart attack and died.

Billy stayed with Kitty and showed a caring sensitivity that seemed right out of character. He refused to go drinking with John, and stayed close to his sister. He told her that she was the only person that he'd ever cared for and he would stay with her until she was away from Kinloch. He helped her to pack and leave. She didn't want a farewell party, she just wanted to go. When she told John she was leaving, he blustered and forbade her to go. When he said he would sue her for restitution of conjugal rights, Billy said his lawyer was very good – how good was John's? When Kitty told John she was going anyway because she couldn't bear to stay in Kinloch one day longer, he threatened her and demanded money to pay for his section. Annie insisted that she was going to stay with John, so Kitty and Billy walked away and left them to it. Kitty never saw either of them again. They stayed with Allie and Eric until Billy was able to arrange to ship Kitty's animals.

As they sailed down the lake Kitty looked at the mountains she loved and vowed that she would never leave the Wakatipu but would never go back to the Head of the Lake. She reflected on the past twenty years. She remembered the young bride, madly in love and expecting to live happily ever after. How could a life go so horribly wrong? Whatever the future held for her, nothing would ever be as bad as this. She sighed and said to herself that at least she still had Billy.

The Sixth Life
Skippers 1890

Chapter Five

When Kitty and Billy arrived in Queenstown and were waiting for Flame to be unloaded, Kitty asked where they were going to spend the night. He told her they had a mile or so to walk, unless that old nag could still carry her. Kitty told him indignantly that Flame might be twenty-five but she was still fit and had worked on a guiding trip two days before Christmas. Billy's arm went around Kitty's shoulders as the tears, which were never far from the surface, ran down her face.

She stood with her face in Flame's warm flank while Billy saw to her meagre belongings. She had brought very little from Kinloch. She'd given her remaining dog to Richard Bryant and had been too numb to think about packing. Billy and Allie had done what they could, hampered as they were by John and Annie.

With Kitty's few bags and boxes safely in storage, they walked along the road towards Arthurs Point. On the way Billy explained that he had a friend who owned an old hotel with a few acres and a derelict stable. He had agreed that they could stay there, but as the place was up for sale, it could only be temporary. When they arrived there was a note on the table saying that the owner had been called away for some time but to make themselves at home. There was some mail for Billy, and while he attended to it, Kitty looked around. There was nothing to eat in the cupboard or the safe, but she found some tea and soon had a fire going. The place was meticulously tidy.

Billy looked up from his mail. 'I'm so sorry, Sis, I've got to go tomorrow. Some problems have cropped up, and I've been offered a ride I can't turn down. I want to be here with you, but I have to earn a living. I'll leave you all the money I have with me. Tell me you'll be all right?'

Billy, I can never thank you enough for all you have done for me. You don't need to give me money. I had money at the Bryants' that Allie picked up for me, and I had with some I kept at her place. I have some in the bank, and I hope there is enough there to buy me a place. I'll go in tomorrow and find out. Don't worry about me. I'll be all right.'

'You do need another horse, so I can at least bring you one,' Billy offered.

'No thanks. I do *not* need a clapped-out, beaten-up thoroughbred. I want something shorter and sturdier that hasn't been galloped or belted, so I think I had better find my own horse. But thanks for the offer.'

In the morning Kitty decided that the bank could wait. She would ride as far as Arrowtown with Billy. She needed to stock up with food and wanted to see how many, if any, of her old friends still lived there. She already knew that the Jordans had left. Sarah had gone to boarding school in Dunedin and had wanted to stay there so she could compete in a more extensive show circuit than the Wakatipu/Central Otago area. Daisy had liked the idea, too. She won almost every event she entered and had become bored with it. So they had sold up in Arrowtown and bought a property in Mosgiel, where Kitty had heard that they were doing well. Kitty resolved to write to Daisy and catch up.

After Freddy's death, when Eddie had received news that he had inherited a title and a considerable estate in England, he,

Jeannie and her widowed mother had packed up their family and left. Jeannie had been very nervous about the whole thing. She didn't like the idea of being a 'Lady'. Eddie laughed and told her she was already a lady in his eyes and she shouldn't be afraid of a capital L. She'd always wanted to travel, and Eddie had assured her that she would be just fine. He'd be there to hold her hand. They had sold Freddy's cottage but had leased out their farmlet 'just in case'. Kitty had had a letter from Jeannie after her girls were lost but hadn't yet written back.

That left only Lucy, Will, Catherine and Flossie still living in the Wakatipu. Billy had flatly refused to discuss the family, and Kitty was not surprised to hear that he had fallen out with all of them. She decided to go and see Lucy and Will first.

She had a pleasant ride over with Billy and said goodbye to him as she turned into the dairy. Will and Lucy were pleased to see her. They told her there had been unpleasantness about George's will, which had been written after Catherine's dementia became apparent and it was obvious that she would be unable to cope on her own. Since Flossie was the only unmarried daughter, she had been left the house at the back of the property and five acres of land, provided she cared for Catherine. Will, George's brother, had been left the original house and dairy, with the proviso that if they ever wished to sell, the proceeds would be shared among George's children. George had secretly put a share in Kitty's bank account some time before he died. None of Will and Lucy's own family wanted to have anything to do with the dairy, because they were all married, comfortably off and settled in their own lives and were all totally sick of a life with cows.

George had been scrupulously fair. Billy's siblings thought he had been disinherited (and he had thought so, too, because George had so often threatened it) and they thought he shouldn't have anything. Will and Lucy thought that Kitty might have come to claim her share too, and they were gob-smacked when she told them that she wasn't George's daughter and therefore was not entitled to anything and certainly wasn't there for trouble, she'd had more than enough of it already in her own life. She just wanted to catch up with some old friends, of which there didn't seem to be many left. She told them about the circumstances of her birth. She said she was sure there wouldn't be any problems with Billy because he'd be happy that George had remembered him at all. Billy had told Kitty he never wanted to see any of them again. She'd replied that she wouldn't be surprised if they weren't all that keen on seeing him either.

Kitty had only met Will once or twice, and she was happy to find that she really liked him. He was so like George; what was there not to like? She and Lucy were immediately back to being best friends. Lucy and Will were also sick and tired of cows, business and family squabbling. There was a further complication. Fifteen years before he died George had sold Will a half share in the dairy, and he had spent that money on modernising the equipment.

Now they wanted to sell up, and some of George's children were making problems. None of them wanted to buy Will out; they just wanted as much money as they could get and were prepared to pay lawyers to try to get it. Kitty now understood why Billy had called them a waste of time. She spent the night with Lucy and Will in her old home, in her old bedroom in the house she'd sworn she would never return to. Fortunately the memories that came flooding back were happy ones. She was able to push Catherine to the back of her mind because she intended to visit her in the morning. She was still struggling with the idea that, for the first time in more than twenty years, she could go where she wanted when she wanted and was responsible for no other living being except her horse. She knew she had to move forward and find a home and a way to make a living.

After a convivial breakfast Kitty washed the dishes while the others went to work in the dairy. They had sold most of the cows but had kept a few so they could sell the business as a going concern. It was a nostalgia trip for Kitty. So many things around the kitchen had been there for more than twenty years, and she cried over the copy of *Great Expectations* that Freddy had given her so long ago.

She saddled up her horse and rode the well-remembered track

to the back of the farm. She had to introduce herself to Florrie, who had been a toddler when Kitty left home. Since then they had had no contact at all. She was very standoffish to begin with as she thought that Kitty was another sibling looking for trouble. Kitty quickly reassured her that she wanted nothing, and since Catherine was still asleep the two women began to get to know each other over a cup of tea. It seemed that Florrie's siblings thought that since she had been left the house, she shouldn't have a share of the will as well. Florrie had to provide for Catherine for the rest of her life. Until the dairy was sold Will and Lucy were happy to help her out. Florrie was Catherine's true daughter in that she had a bountiful garden, one cow and hens, and she sold vegetables, eggs, milk and cream. It took Kitty back to her Dunedin days. Florrie wasn't an Irish beauty like Lizzie, but she was a very personable young woman, though not a happy one. She told Kitty that their sisters had married in their teens and Catherine had taunted her for being on the shelf. That was why George had provided so well for her future. Kitty commented that Florrie could still marry; at twenty-three she was hardly on the shelf. Florrie answered that Kitty hadn't seen their mother yet, and who would marry anyone who had to look after a mad woman? Although Catherine did have occasional days when she was quite lucid, those days were becoming further apart.

A call came from the bedroom and Florrie got to her feet. 'It would be better if you waited here,' she told Kitty. 'She probably won't know you, and she gets very hard to manage when she sees someone she doesn't know.'

As Kitty waited she listened to the sounds coming from the bedroom. She realised Catherine was still only in her early fifties, and it seemed most unfair that she could become demented at such a young age, unfair not only to Catherine but to all around her. Kitty wondered how George, who had worshipped his wife, had managed to cope. She wondered what she could do to help Florrie.

When Florrie and Catherine came in, Catherine took one look at Kitty and screamed, 'Arthur, I knew you'd come back and get me! Take me away with you! I hate all these people!' and she threw herself at Kitty. Kitty looked at Florrie in horror and didn't know what to do.

Florrie took charge. 'Come on, Ma, Mr Arthur needs a cup of tea after coming all this way. Sit down here and talk to him while I get your medicine. You both need a cup of tea before you go.'

'Make the tea and fix him some food too,' Catherine ordered. 'And I've told and told you not to call me Ma, you cheeky besom.'

Kitty managed to reach over and hold Catherine's hand but couldn't bring herself to speak. Catherine didn't appear to notice and just burbled on happily about people Kitty had never heard about. She said that now that she was going to have a baby they would have to run away and get married.

Florrie quickly put a plate containing two raw chops and a potato in front of Kitty, then put a hand on their mother's shoulder. 'Why don't you have a cup of tea and let Mr Arthur eat his breakfast? He's come such a long way. He probably needs a rest. And it's time for your medicine, too.' Catherine obediently opened her mouth for the medicine, then said she hoped that Florrie wouldn't try to stop them from running away. Florrie said that of course she wouldn't; she'd go and pack Catherine's bag, then she'd drive them to the coach. Catherine drank her tea, and when she started to become drowsy Florrie whispered to Kitty to go and harness the trap as quickly as she could. It was the same trap that Kitty had bought for Catherine all those years ago, and the same old pony was looking to be in good condition for her age.

Back inside, she helped Florrie carry Catherine out to the trap. When she seemed about to protest Florrie said loudly, 'Please, Mr Arthur, will you drive?' Catherine subsided when Kitty took the reins. Florrie went back and brought out a suitcase and whispered to Kitty to drive to Frankton Hospital.

Catherine, propped up between her daughters, was now peacefully dozing. Kitty asked how often Catherine was like this, and Florrie answered that it was irregular but happening more frequently than it used to. She asked who Arthur was, because she said, Catherine was asking after him all the time. Kitty explained that he was her own father, who had been a soldier, but apart from that Kitty knew nothing about him. Florrie was horrified and said she hadn't known George wasn't Kitty's father, because he'd always spoken fondly of Kitty as his daughter. Kitty said that George was the only father she had ever known, and he'd taught her so much. She couldn't have loved him more dearly.

When they arrived at the hospital Kitty stayed with Catherine while Florrie went in and got help. When Catherine was loaded onto a stretcher and carried inside, Kitty remarked at how quickly the admission had gone, without any delay or paperwork. Florrie said they were used to it, and she got back into the trap. They headed back via the dairy so they could tell Will and Lucy what had happened.

They stayed for dinner with Will and Lucy; they had so much to share and so much time to cover. They talked about George never telling his other children that Kitty was not their sister but their half-sister. They talked about the mysterious Arthur, and Kitty was finally able to talk to someone about her lost children.

When they drove back, Florrie pressed Kitty to stay the night, and Kitty was happy to accept. They did all the usual chores, brushed their horses, milked the cow and fed the hens. Florrie said it was wonderful to have someone in the house that she could talk to, and they wondered if Kitty would be able to come again without Catherine reacting the way she had. They decided to give it a try. Kitty said that it was lovely having a sister, a real sister at last. Neither of them mentioned Billy.

The next morning Kitty hitched Flame to the back of the trap, and they drove to the hospital to check on Catherine. They didn't see her, but the doctor talked to them. He told them that these episodes were becoming too frequent and their little hospital was ill-equipped to deal with her. When her condition became permanent she would have to be transferred to the Otago provincial mental institution. He said the current event seemed to have been triggered by someone called Arthur, who should be kept away from her. He asked who Arthur was. Kitty explained that he was Catherine's long dead first love and her own father. It was her physical appearance that had started Catherine off this time; she also explained that Catherine hadn't seen her for some years and Kitty must bear a strong resemblance to the father she had never known. The doctor now remembered who Kitty was and started expressing his sympathy for her double loss. When he also spoke of Georgie the tears poured down Kitty's cheeks, and the doctor sent for a cup of tea. He said he hoped that Kitty would be able to share Florrie's burden and commented that it was a pity that none of the rest of the family were prepared to help, but some families seemed to be like that.

There was one question he would like to have answered: Catherine kept asking for a priest and she was registered as an Anglican. Kitty was able to explain, and it was decided that at this stage of her life it wouldn't matter if she returned to her original faith, seeing that George was no longer there.

The sisters left and went their separate ways, but before they parted they arranged to meet again before Catherine was released. Catherine's future seemed inevitable, and Florrie had to think about what she wanted to do when it happened. Kitty also had to think about her future. How was she going to earn a living? They briefly considered pooling resources and living together but decided not to, mainly because they hardly knew each other yet and Kitty, though missing her daughters, was enjoying living alone.

Autumn was beautiful. Kitty was remembering her early years in the Wakatipu basin. Although Kinloch was less than thirty miles away to the northwest as the crow flies, the two places had a totally different climate. Queenstown was sunnier and had fewer rainy days. Kitty remembered the long cloudless days and hot summer sun of her childhood. And now she was remembering the beautiful colours of autumn and the English trees the first settlers had planted in Arrowtown. Although it was not yet autumn she would go to Arrowtown the next time she went to see Florrie. She thought of the wind and the rain at Kinloch and the damp winter cold that seemed to soak into her bones. She remembered the dark monochrome of the lowering beech forest but also remembered the sheer beauty of the mountains and her enjoyment of her guiding trips. Year-round it was green while Queenstown and Arrowtown were gold or brown. She had to stop thinking about her years at the Head of the Lake – remembering about the place led to thinking about the people. It was too soon for that to be bearable. She wondered if it ever could be bearable. She would always weep for her daughters and her long-lost son. Then she remembered her girlish dreams of being married and living happily ever after.

She collected herself, wiped away her tears and began planning. She had to find feed for her horse and start looking for permanent accommodation. She liked where she was. The sun shone in first thing in the morning. The old pub had more bedrooms than she needed, but it was snug and warm. She would like to rent it, at least for the winter or until she found her own place. Until then, she would start to repair the stable so that her horse could have shelter in the cold nights ahead. Having left everything but the barest basics behind her, she had to start making a list of immediate essentials and withdraw enough money to keep her and her horse for the coming winter.

She was working on the stable when a laden cart arrived at her door. Billy rode behind, leading two horses. Kitty was introduced to Barney, the owner of the place, then she went to tether the horses. She put the kettle on and began to make a meal while the men started to unload. She was understandably anxious to find out what this visit held for her.

During the meal she learned that Barney was getting married in three months' time and was going to live near Dunedin, at least for a while. He didn't want to sell Jack's Hotel just yet but would be happy to rent it to Kitty for the winter if she wanted it. He said the improvements Kitty had made to the stable would add to the overall value, and he would pay for whatever she needed to finish the job. He was amazed that a woman could do what she was doing and joked that he would marry her if he wasn't already spoken for.

She laughed and said that one thing she could be sure of was that his bride would be younger and prettier than she herself was. He smiled and said he had to agree. She added that the very last thing she needed was another husband.

Then Kitty asked Billy what the story was about the two horses he'd been leading. He laughed and said they were hers. Kitty got very angry and told him that she would choose her own horses, thank you very much, and he could jolly well take them back where they came from. He couldn't stop laughing and said he couldn't take them back. They were hers and that was that. They'd been given to her by an old lady who had known Kitty when Kitty was young. She'd bought a lot of animal halters from Kitty when the Kirks first came to the Wakatipu, and Kitty had gone to visit her once or twice. Now she was old and arthritic and was going to live with her family in Dunedin. Her family had tried to sell all her stuff, but there was no market for it so she got them to find Billy to ask him where Kitty was because she wanted to give all the gear to her. He and Barney were carting some feed to Kitty, and it didn't take long to throw the stuff on board. The cart belonged to Barney, and he was bringing it up empty to take some of his furniture back to Dunedin. It had all worked out very well for everybody, hadn't it?

Kitty said it was all very well for him to say that, but she was stuck with two horses she didn't want. Billy replied that the least she could do was look at them. The old lady had done all the groundwork herself for as long as she could, and no one else had touched them. They had never been bitted or backed, so Kitty could consider that a point in their favour. Whether she decided to keep them or to sell them for dog-tucker, she would have to turn them out for the night. Billy was far too busy helping Barney.

Reluctantly she went to attend to them, and she found that she couldn't fault them. They were part Arab, just the right size and beautifully conformed. She also liked the tack she had been given. It was old but very high quality, and the best of care had obviously been taken of it. There was everything that she could possibly need and all of it better quality than she had ever been able to afford. There were even leather-working tools and hides.

The horses responded to her when she brushed them and talked to them and when she read the names, which were worked into the halters, she liked them too. The chestnut gelding was 'Sauce' and the grey filly was 'Mouse'. She would soon find out whether they were named for colour or temperament. Back along memory lane she went, to her twelve-year-old self being given a guinea for the halters she had made. She remembered the two visits she had made to her benefactress to teach her how to do leatherwork and how best to handle her new heifers. She had intended to go to her when living with Catherine had become impossible, but she had met John Greig and married him. She started thinking about how different her life could have been. That led to her thinking about her daughters, and that memory was still far too fresh to bear. Now she was just 'Billy Kirk's sister' and, because of that, viewed with suspicion in some quarters. She had not only to find a way to make a living but also to find a new identity that was her own.

It was starting to get dark when Billy came to call her in. 'When will I go and get the knackers?' he asked with a broad grin on his face. 'Barney wants to get away at first light, so please can you do us an early breakfast and some lunch? His furniture is all packed and ready to go. You neglected his moke and mine, apart from a quick brush.'

'I did put them in the yard and chuck them a feed, but if you want more done, why don't you do it?' He didn't.

The next morning after Barney left, Kitty did some more work on the stable so that she could stow her new tack before she started working her horses. She liked the way they hung their heads over the fence and watched her. Billy busied himself splitting and stacking wood.

Around midday Florrie rolled up in her trap. Catherine was back in hospital for a few days, so she was free to visit. Kitty insisted that she stay for dinner and told her and Billy that they could at least be civil to each other for her sake. Over the meal they did manage to thaw out and talk to each other. Billy said that since Lizzie had been Catherine's run-away favourite child, she had been given so much more love and attention than any of the others. She was always better dressed than any of her sisters, so she should have been the one to look after Catherine. She turned out to be the most grasping. She had been the family beauty, so she was the daughter Catherine had always wanted. Lizzie had delighted Catherine by 'marrying well' at the age of eighteen, but after that nothing had been seen of her until she had turned up at George's funeral and begun proceedings to contest the will. After Kitty and Billy, Catherine was adamant that none of her younger children would ever learn to ride. Their life had to be centred around the dairy. George, in his turn, had insisted that they should go to school and be encouraged to read books and that Freddy should take a hand in their education.

'Lizzie even wants to grab my place, even though he settled Ma and me there and gave me the title deeds years before he wrote the will. Ma had to be got away from the dairy because she didn't know what she was doing anymore and she was making a right royal mess of things. Lizzie is still going to sue me, and her rich husband is backing her.'

Billy had listened to all of this and decided that Florrie wasn't a 'waste of time' after all.

'Well, Florrie, I'm sometimes rich, and I've sometimes been a wee bit naughty and needed a good lawyer. I'll talk to him about this. Often he doesn't charge much if the client is poor or he finds the case interesting. I keep him entertained and keep him in business by being naughty and by giving him good tips, and I'll help you when I can so long as you promise to pray for my horses to win!'

Kitty was happy that the three of them were melding into a family and were now enjoying one another's company. Florrie had brought eggs and vegetables with her. She had built up a little delivery round and was able to take Catherine with her. When she did, Catherine thought that she was back in Dunedin and that Flossie was Kitty, and she was very happy. She asked why people kept calling her 'Mrs Kirk' when everyone knew she was 'Mrs Cameron'.

Neither Florrie nor Billy had ever heard of her marriage to Jack Cameron, so Kitty had a lot of explaining to do. They talked into the small hours as she told them of Catherine's forced marriage and the couple's forced emigration. Kitty didn't know who Jack Cameron was, but she knew that he was her father's uncle. She knew that she must have looked like him as well as like Catherine's still-loved Arthur. Apart from that, she had absolutely no idea who they were except that they lived in Ireland and were horse breeders. Nor did she know why Cameron had fled in such secrecy and whether he was alive or dead.

The next day Billy left early, and flying visits became his usual practice. Barney came back again to remove the rest of his furniture. Kitty bought some from him so that she could keep on living there in some comfort, but he took all the quality stuff. When Kitty asked him how big his house in Dunedin was, he told her that it was big, but not that big, and he was taking all the good stuff away to sell so that he could buy brand new things because his bride didn't like antiques. He didn't mind, because although he liked his antiques, other people liked them better so he was getting a very good price for them at auction. His lady was young and wanted everything new and modern.

Shortly after Barney left Kitty was in Queenstown when a young man caught up with her and told her that there had been a grass fire on Gorge Road and Kitty's house had been in the way, however, he and a friend had managed to get the fire under control before too much damage had been done. Kitty thanked him and hurried home. She found that the boys had done a good job. They had beaten out the grass fire with sacks and had thrown water onto the side of the building.

Jack's Hotel was a part wooden, part stone structure, and the wooden part had become very dry. Kitty walked around to check up, and she decided that the grass fire had burnt itself into a very satisfactory fire-break around the stable and yards. One window of the house had burned, and the inside smelt chokingly strongly of smoke. The bedrooms, which were in the stone part, were undamaged but also smelt of smoke, so Kitty busied herself carrying all the bedding outside to air. She would bed herself down in the hay in the stable until she could scrub the whole place clean.

The cleaning had taken her almost a week when Billy arrived. He said that Barney had come with him as far as Cromwell and had decided to sell the house cheap because of the fire damage. He gave Billy first refusal, but he knew that Kitty wanted it more than he did and that she had the money. Billy thought he'd better come and let her know that Barney wanted his money in a hurry because his marriage had fallen through and he had decided to go and dry his tears in Australia. He was leaving in less than a month, so he was asking for a very reasonable price, so did she want it?

Of course she did. Billy would take her bank-draft to his lawyer when he went back to Cromwell, and he would handle the transaction. Billy did not entirely trust Barney, and he had learnt the hard way that you should never try to handle property transactions yourself – always go through a lawyer. He grumbled a bit about sleeping in the hay, but when he smelt the bedrooms he stopped grumbling.

A week later there was another fire that destroyed the entire wooden part of the building. Kitty was devastated. Billy had taken the bank-draft to the lawyer, but Kitty hadn't yet done anything about insurance, thinking that lightning didn't strike twice in the same place. She went to stay with Florrie, returning each day to work her horses. Until she heard from Billy she didn't know whether she owned the property or not. She started to clear away the wreckage, helped by the occasional passer-by. The fire had gone through quickly. The stove was relatively undamaged but otherwise almost none of the wooden part had survived.

She was doing this when Billy arrived. He told her that the property was hers and the lawyer was holding the title deeds for her. When he had heard of the fire he had withheld payment until he'd beaten the price down. Barney had been really anxious to catch his boat and had agreed to the reduced payment. The lawyer said he smelt an enormous rodent.

'It seems that our Barney was not the gentleman we took him for,' Billy said. 'He had me fooled completely, and that's something that doesn't happen very often. My lawyer found out that there had never been a young bride. Barney had been up to some mischief and wanted to get out of the country with as much money as possible. That was why he carted away and sold everything valuable as quickly as he could. He intended to sell the property to us from the very beginning, but he had the building insured and planned to burn it down so that he could collect the insurance before we took possession. He had it planned to the very last detail, and his timing had to be perfect so that he could get away with the money from the sale and the insurance. My lawyer found out that the police were after him as well. He had pulled the same trick in other places under other names and with other insurance companies. And he'd got away with it.'

'What a crook!' Kitty exclaimed. 'He seemed so nice! I thought he had forgotten to pay for the timber for the stable, but of course he never meant to!'

'Look on the bright side, Sis. You got a piece of land at a very good price, and the difference should mean you will have enough to put on a new kitchen and patch up some of the stonework. I told you it pays to have a good lawyer. Nobody loses. Barney got the money to get away, and you can bet that it isn't Australia he's gone to! The lawyer didn't dob him in case it meant that we ended up with no land and no money, and besides I think he rather admired Barney's nerve.'

Kitty now had a home and two useful horses, but she still had no steady income. There were still a few old people who remembered her and her uncanny ability to handle horses, but most people no longer had horses. Older people just wanted to talk about them. Those who still had horses had old horses. The only work she was getting was occasional guiding jobs. These paid very well, but they were infrequent and the days were drawing in, so she was busying herself making her home comfortable for the winter.

Billy had organised a working party to build a two-room lean-to against the remaining stone building, which was more damaged than they had thought. The mortar had suffered from the heat. One of his mates had recently worked for the railways, and purely by coincidence the finished wooden structure was painted hematite red, a paint that was used on railway buildings the length of New Zealand. Most of the building materials had been similarly 'donated'. Kitty had enough money to finish the house and make it snug for the winter. She had been given covers along with the horses, but she also wanted to finish the stable. She needed to do some fencing as well but also needed to hold on to enough money to support herself and her horses for the winter. She had decided that if nothing else was available she should be able to get domestic work in one of the hotels when the summer tourist season began. She could clean and she could cook, so it shouldn't be too hard. She briefly considered writing and asking Mrs Bryant for a reference, but even thinking about anything to do with Kinloch made the tears come, so she pushed that thought right out of her head.

Billy knew a friendly carter who came to Queenstown fairly regularly with an empty cart to pick up a load. He was happy to carry up horse feed and anything else Billy wanted delivered to Kitty. Sometimes it was only a letter. He always stayed for a meal or a cup of tea. He said he owed Billy because he was a keen follower of the horses, and Billy's tips often made him a small fortune. After Billy's visits started to become less frequent, the carter still brought odds and ends that Kitty might find useful. She knew better than to ask where anything had come from.

Kitty worked steadily through that first winter getting her house snug. She also needed to work her horses. Their names had been well chosen. Mouse was very gentle and biddable. She was happy to carry anybody and would have been a perfect school pony. Sauce lived up to his name. He wasn't at all vicious; he would accept a carrot from anyone and never kicked or bit, but he was a trickster. Kitty loved riding him because he was fun and kept her on her toes. He loved an audience and was a real show-off.

She visited Florrie when they were out for exercise. The sisters had devised a code; a cloth was tied on the gate when Catherine was at home and out of bed. Then Kitty would wear a widow's bonnet and veil so that she wouldn't be mistaken for Arthur. Kitty often wondered about Arthur. Apart from the fact that he had fathered her and was Jack Cameron's nephew, she knew absolutely nothing about him and, with Catherine the way she was, would never be able to learn anything more.

Kitty realised that winter she could happily live alone. Billy couldn't come when the days were so short, and during the long nights she worked at her leatherwork in her warm kitchen. She planned to have a good selection for sale at the local show. She had dreams of perhaps entering her horses, but earning a living had to come first. She sighed and bent to her work. The only problem about living alone was that it gave her too much time to think – and to remember. She knew she would never be able to forget her lost children, and she didn't want to. She could only hope that time would cushion her memories. She wondered about Annie. She had written to her, hoping that she and John were well. She wrote that she hoped Annie didn't think that she had to choose between her parents and she hoped that Annie would think about visiting her. She told Annie that she loved her very much and was missing her.

She received a terse answer: 'You were the one who CHOSE, not me. Do your duty and come home. Pa says he will forgive you. If you CHOOSE not to come home, don't write again,' Kitty didn't write again.

Spring crept into the valley, and Kitty started putting in her garden. She had built a fowl house, and Florrie had promised her a clutch of eggs. Kitty had put notices in shop windows advertising her services as a guide and also as a riding teacher. She had also spoken to hotel proprietors about work in the tourist season. She learned that their practice was to employ the same local staff each year. They signed on in November and were dismissed after Easter. She hoped for a lucky break, and she got one. One afternoon Hector McCleod arrived at her door and asked her if she would guide him to Skippers.

Chapter Six

Skippers was no longer the populous mining village that it had been when Kitty had been growing up at Millers Flat. The gold in the Shotover River and its tributary creeks that was easy to get by placer mining had largely gone.

This gold was gained by panning and the equipment, a shovel and a gold pan, could be carried by one man, but in addition to his tools a man had to carry all the basics for survival in a very harsh and remote environment. The summers were extremely hot and the winters viciously cold, but still men came in their thousands to 'the richest river in the world'. At the height of the rush the population of the area was estimated to be more than four thousand. Gold fever is not a disease so much as an addiction. There's a sort of hysteria about it. Men will take themselves from one end of the world to the other in pursuit of a fortune that mostly only those first on the spot actually find. Those who don't strike it rich are condemning themselves to a brutal nomadic life for very little reward, if any.

Those who do make money are the proprietors of the grog shops, which spring up like mushrooms immediately in the wake of a strike, and those shanties go on to the next strike as quickly as they had come.

All along the Shotover townships sprang up. There were banks, stores and numerous more or less respectable hotels, several of which were run by women. Many a miner would sell his gold and spend all his takings before he even got back to his claim.

However, this was in the 60s, and when Kitty arrived on the scene in the 90s things were very different. The days of men washing for gold were virtually over, although a few hearty souls still persisted, working alone along the length of the river and of Skippers Creek, a tributary of the Shotover River. These loners were known as 'hatters', and many of them built quite substantial dwellings complete with vegetable gardens.

Sluicing, a method of extracting gold by using high pressure hoses, was in full swing and destroying much of the countryside, including many of the fertile flat terraces that had provided homes and crops. These terraces were large; one that was almost sluiced away was the Race Course Terrace. A lot of the action had shifted to Skippers Creek. At the Skippers township sluicing had washed away ground perilously close to the hotel dining room and bakery and, a little further along, to the town hall and library.

The population was rapidly declining. In 1886 the district had 482 inhabitants: 387 men and 95 women. In 1896 when Kitty arrived, it had shrunk to 274 men and 87 women. This was for the whole district, not just the Skippers township. By now most of the men were working in the mines, of which there were several. The most profitable and longest lasting was the Phoenix mine at Bullendale. It was the most up-to-date. Electricity had been generated for the mine since 1886, and it had had telephone connection since 1896. At the zenith of the mine's prosperity the population of Bullendale in 1891 reached 236, but from then on it slowly declined. When Kitty arrived on the scene it had fallen to 189, and from then on it continued to dwindle until the mine closed in 1902.

Kitty took a long look at Hector McCleod. He was dressed for the city, down to his shiny shoes, and he carried a suitcase.

'Can you ride? I mean really ride, not just sit on a horse in a park?' she asked.

'Well, not really. I have been on a horse a few times, so I'm sure I can manage. I have to get there today.'

Kitty looked at him again. 'It can't be today. It will be dark in two hours, and no one in their right mind would try to ride up there in the dark. Go in the coach in the morning.'

'It's urgent. I have to go now.'

'You'd have to start walking. Against my better judgment, I'll take you, and it'll cost you. I'm good to go at first light. You have to go back to town, buy yourself some sensible clothes and boots, eat a really good meal, get some sleep and be back by four-thirty in the morning. Get the hotel to make you up a good substantial lunch.'

'For God's sake, how long is this going to take?' Hector asked fretfully.

'That depends how quickly you can learn to ride, but I would say at least six or seven hours. And you'll be in very bad shape when you get there. One other thing: if I decide to turn back, we turn back, and no argument.'

'Look, I'm young and fit, and I'm a man. If you can do it, I know I can.'

This made Kitty laugh. 'And I'm an old woman, right? And you're only here because someone in town told you that I'm the only person on God's earth crazy enough to try to take a useless townie who doesn't even know one end of a horse from the other to Skippers? And that describes you, does it not? Couldn't you see they were joking? Well, they're right, I am crazy, because I love a challenge, but it has to be on my terms, and you'll have to pay well if I get you there.'

Hector had the grace to blush, but he nodded his head. 'I don't seem to have a choice, do I? Money's no object. They said that you were pretty outspoken.'

'And skinny and no beauty. I've heard that one before. Now, run along, Sonny, and get yourself ready. I'll see you in the morning.

On second thoughts, get them to make you up two lunches. And tell those bar-flies that they can start taking bets, but I want a percentage.'

The road to Skippers was narrow and tortuous. It had been largely scraped out by Chinese labourers, but in places it had needed the expertise of the best engineers and workmen who could handle explosives. It went from river level up to three hundred feet. Pinchers Bluff, the most difficult section, had only been completed for vehicles in 1890. The road crawled around two cliff faces and down again to river level at Deep Creek. It was not a joy ride for nervous or beginner riders.

Hector arrived promptly in the morning, and Kitty had the horses ready. He was dressed as he had been instructed. When she made him sit down and eat breakfast before they left, he objected; he said he wanted to get going. She pointed out that he had just had a brisk walk, and furthermore, he had promised to do what he was told. Then she took him out and mounted him on Mouse, who was sporting a neck-strap. He was shown how to hold the reins and not to saw on them, and to grab the neck strap if he was nervous. Kitty told him that, with luck, if he was a good boy and listened carefully, he might to be able to ride by the time they got there.

She led him out onto the road and mounted Sauce, who decided that a small display of pyrotechnics was in order. When Hector asked why she made her horse do that, she nearly fell off laughing and told him her horse was a show-off in company and was just giving her a riding lesson.

The first few miles were easy going, and Hector was adapting well to his riding lesson. He had been calling her 'Mrs Greig' and was a bit uncomfortable when she said he was to call her 'Kitty'. He asked her if she would please stop calling him 'Sonny' and start calling him 'Hec'. When he blurted out that people in Queenstown had told him all about her, she replied that she wished that they would let her alone to forget her misery, and they rode along in silence for a while. Then the riding lesson continued. When they arrived at Skippers Saddle, Kitty called a halt. Hec questioned it.

She replied: 'See that big rock over there? Well, you're going to hold the horses while I go behind it, and then I'll hold the horses while you go behind it.'

When he came out from behind the rock, he was walking stiffly. Kitty made him walk around a bit and do some knee bends until he loosened up. She told him that although he was doing quite well, this was the beginning of the hard bit; he hadn't been riding yet, just sitting on the horse. The hard part was going to be really hard, and there were some places where they might have to get off and walk. He was not to question her. When he asked if she would be walking if he weren't with her, she snapped at him and said probably not, but she wasn't a raw beginner. She said that if he wasn't raw now, he would be when they got there, in spite of the sheepskin that she had thoughtfully tied onto his saddle. Then they began the long descent down the pack trail into Long Gully.

Hec struggled to remember his instructions: lean back a bit, feet a little forward, don't pull on the reins, if you want to hold onto anything hang onto the neck-strap. Kitty had told him that Mouse would follow closely behind Sauce, and she had to have her head free, so really all Hec had to do was sit there. She also told him that when they got to the bottom of the gully they would be stopping for a rest. When he protested that he didn't have time for rests she told him tersely that they would all need a break; horses weren't bicycles. She told him that he himself would be crying for a break. She didn't tell him the worst was yet to come. The people in Queenstown were right; you'd have to be crazy to attempt to take a new chum into Skippers, but she was now committed, and the lad wasn't doing too badly. So they continued picking their way down Long Gully in the spring sun.

Hec didn't complain when they crossed over and climbed up to Long Gully Hotel. When they had dismounted to climb up the hill he fell, got up, then struggled up and cast himself full-length on the hotel veranda. While Kitty attended to the horses, unsaddling them so that they could have a roll and a rest, Hec had a hot cup of tea thrust into his hand. Kitty was asked what on earth she thought she was doing bringing a beginner on such a trip so early in the season. She might be a tough old bird, but a beginner was a beginner and she ought to have more sense. Kitty just shrugged and told them to ask Hec what was so urgent and did he want to carry on. So they asked him, and he rather abruptly answered that he wasn't prepared to discuss his business. He did, however, disclose that he was a law clerk and was on his employer's business. He ate a scone and dozed off while Kitty asked about the state of the track ahead. She was told it was good, that riders had been in and out, but because of the late snowfall the coaches had, as yet, only come in as far as Long Gully. Hec must have been told this when he went to book his trip. Kitty was furious. She shook him awake and asked him why he hadn't told her.

He told her he didn't know where Long Gully was and explained that his job was on the line; this was a test. Kitty saddled up the horses. When she told him that they were turning back, he told her that if they did, she wouldn't be paid, because they had a verbal contract a great many people knew about, and that made it legally binding. She didn't know whether or not he was bluffing. Still angry, she said all right, she would get him there alive or dead, but nothing had been said about getting him back. They would carry on, she said, adding that so far it had been a picnic, and they would now see whether he was a man or a boy. And she threw him into the saddle.

They hadn't gone very far when they had the good fortune to meet two men who were on their way out. Kitty was able to find out from them what lay ahead, and she was happy to learn the river was still low because the spring thaw had hardly started. She also learned that the new road round Pinchers Bluff was clear but she would have to be careful at Blue Slip.

They asked her what time she had left Queenstown, and when they were told that Hec was a learner, they told her they were doing bloody well. They said that if he lived to get to Skippers, he'd be a champion, and they laughed, patted him on the leg and wished him well.

They pushed on. There were places where they dismounted and climbed. This wasn't really necessary; it was to stretch Hec's legs. Kitty walked in front, and she told Hec to hold onto Mouse's tail and let her pull him up. To Hec it seemed to last forever, and he mentally damned Kitty for being such a harridan and a slave driver. He didn't yet understand why he needed to stretch his legs. He was obsessed with getting there as soon as possible, but he did find out that remounting was very painful.

When they reached Deep Creek, Kitty called another halt and the horses had a drink while Hec and Kitty ate their lunch. Hec didn't like the idea of drinking creek water, but he was thirsty and, copying Kitty, he learned to kneel and cup his hands. He had to admit that the water tasted beautiful, and Kitty wondered how anyone could grow up so completely citified. They mounted up and rode on.

There were still a few hatters working the river bed, and at Māori Point Hec found the noise and smoke from the dredge disturbing. The horses weren't very enthusiastic about it either and fussed a little, but with a bit of coercion from Kitty they carried on. As they got closer to Skippers, Hec marvelled at the sluicing that was going on. He had heard of such a thing but was amazed at the noise and fury of the water and the damage it was doing to the landscape. The horses liked it less than they liked the dredging. They became fractious and had to be led past it. They arrived at their destination late in the afternoon when the sun had been off the township for some hours and the chill had well and truly set in. The first person they asked directed them to Hec's sister's house, but before Kitty could go in, she had to see to her horses.

Hec's brother-in-law walked along with her to the hotel to arrange for the horses to be fed and stabled for the night. He stayed with her and helped with the brushing. He asked her what on earth was going on. She said she didn't know but it must be very urgent for Hec to put himself through what he had. Hamish said he hadn't known young Hector could even ride. Kitty told him that Hec couldn't when they left Queenstown but she hoped he could now. She said that what he would now need more than anything else was a good hot bath.

Hec's sister Heather welcomed Kitty in. Hec was sitting uncomfortably at the table, clutching a cup of tea. Kitty clapped her hand on his shoulder and told him how well he had done. She apologised for being so tough on him but said he would never have got there if she had nurse-maided him. Now could they be friends? He nodded and smiled painfully. Kitty repeated that what he needed now was a hot bath. Heather told her that she had put the copper on and it would be hot very soon. Kitty said it should be uncomfortably hot and to throw in a good big handful of washing soda. She said he wouldn't be going anywhere tomorrow, so he would have plenty of time to attend to his urgent business, and he would need to do as much walking as possible.

He protested that he had to get back to Dunedin as soon as he could, so they would have to leave tomorrow. Kitty and Heather looked at each other, and Heather took over. 'No, Hector, my lad, you aren't going anywhere tomorrow. I'll write a letter explaining why you're not actually a day late, and you know the old man will listen to me. Now, into the bath with you and stay in as long as you like. We'll eat when you come out.'

When he had gone out, Kitty said, 'When you write that letter, tell the "old man" he's so frightened of that Hec's as game as they come, and the only time I had any problem was when I suggested we turn back. Then he got on his high horse so to speak and threatened to fire me if we didn't carry on. Why is he so afraid of this "old man"?'

Heather laughed. 'The "old man" is our father, and he is also the head of the law firm that poor Hector is articled to. He firmly believes he must not show any favouritism to his son, but that shouldn't make him come down so meanly on Hector and send him on this mad excursion when there are older clerks who can already ride.'

'That is mean, but maybe those older men knew what was involved and refused to take it on. Can't Hec stand up to him?

Not many young chaps could do what he's done. Is this mission so urgent?'

'Probably not, but it had better be. It's quite ridiculous. We have a telephone and a post office, but the old man persists in acting as if we live in Siberia. He wants my signature on something, but I've refused to even look at it until tomorrow, and I shall tell him so. The old man is an autocrat and a bully. He refused to let me marry Hamish, even though I was only six months short of twenty-one, so I stood up to him for the first time in my life and waited until I came of age. Then we didn't invite him to our wedding. We got married secretly in a Methodist church instead of the Wee Free. When he found out about it, he assumed I was pregnant. I wasn't, but he still threatened to disinherit me. Hamish told the old man he thought that was a very good idea, because perhaps he would finally understand that he had absolutely no right to interfere in our lives anymore.' Heather paused. 'You know, I think he probably plans to cross-examine Hector about us. He's pretty ruthless.'

'Will your letter about Hec help?'

'I think so. I'll take the blame for what he'll believe is a delay. I have a weapon now. I'm the mother of his grandchildren, and I make the rules about when he can see them and what school they go to. He doesn't want to see them grow up like "barbarians" – his exact words – and had booked them into a church school in Dunedin, the one Hector went to. I told him they were very happy running 'round in the wilds of Skippers and would stay here until the end of primary school. That brought him to heel very nicely. If he didn't like it, he could lump it.

'The old man doesn't rate happiness very highly, because he's probably never tried it. I can't imagine what is important enough to torture Hector so. The poor boy has to stay where he is for nearly four more years before he can get away from the firm, and the old man should understand that he'll lose him if he doesn't treat him better. And I shall tell him so. I'll threaten to put Hector into the mining company office as soon as he turns twenty-one. Or give him the money to go to Australia. That's in another three years, and it would mean Hector would never qualify as a lawyer, which would take the "and Son" out of the family business.'

Hamish arrived home just as Hec came out from the bath. He had fallen asleep in the tub, and the water had got quite cold, but he felt much better. They had a jovial meal. Hamish had a way with words, and Kitty had a way with repartee that kept them all laughing. Kitty asked Hamish if he was sure he was a Scot, because Scots were meant to be dour. Without a word he got up and left the room. Kitty was afraid she had offended him.

'Now you've done it,' Hec groaned.

Hamish reappeared with bagpipes and walked up and down playing them. They were extremely loud in the small room. Hec had his hands over his ears. The performance was brought to a halt mid-wail by a scream from the next room – 'Dad, Stop!'

Hamish grinned at Kitty. 'Now do you believe I'm a genuine Scot?' he asked.

'I think so,' she answered. 'I still have a wee few doubts. You aren't wearing the right clothes, and I can't tell whether you are playing well or badly.'

Hec had the last word. 'Is it possible to play the horrible things well?' he asked. 'Heather said she got to appreciate them when you went to Scotland, and they sound lovely over water. 'Well, Hamish,' said Hec, 'I'd really appreciate hearing you playing them under water. Quite deep water!'

Kitty really enjoyed having a free morning wandering around Skippers. In the afternoon, the family business having been concluded, Hamish took Hector to explain something about gold and what men had to do to get it. They walked the two miles from Skippers to the Nugget mine. Hec realised that he really liked being in Skippers and wondered aloud whether he could stand nearly four more years in Dunedin. Hamish told him he should do his best to do so, because sooner or later the gold would run out. Probably sooner. If he could hold out and qualify, he needn't stay in the family firm. He could take a year or two off, see a bit of life, try other occupations, and he would always have a job to go back to, not necessarily in Dunedin.

Heather had invited the local women to meet Kitty. Most of them had heard of her, and in a closed community any visitor is welcome. They all expressed surprise that a woman could cope with such a hard ride, but one grandmother said she had lived in Arrowtown and knew about Kitty's childhood exploits. She entertained the group with the story of Rascal. She was a good storyteller. Over the years the story had been embroidered so much that Kitty hardly recognised herself, and when she tried to correct it, they just thought that she was being overly modest.

Kitty and Hec left early the next morning. Heather and Hamish told Kitty they would be delighted to have her back any time, and please would she make it soon? The proprietor of the hotel had talked to her about bringing guests to his establishment, and they had come to an agreement that would benefit both parties. Kitty left on the homeward journey feeling that she might be able to make a living from her horses after all.

A much more confident Hec made the ride back easier, and it was uneventful. He was also much happier in himself and less afraid of his father. Heather had been good for him. When they reached Skippers Saddle and were able to ride two-abreast, Kitty gave him another riding lesson.

'Since you can't get away until tomorrow morning,' she said, 'when we get to my place we'll have something to eat and you can clean up. Then we'll ride into town. You've done something to be proud of, and now you'll be the toast of the town. Strut your stuff. Stand up for yourself with your father, too. Ask the horsemen in the office if any of them have ever ridden into Skippers. Would you lose your job if you moved out of home?'

'Now, there's a thought. Heather tells me he can't fire me. Thanks, Kitty, you and Heather have given me a lot to think about. And thanks for everything. You've helped me grow up.'

When they got back they found Billy chopping wood. Kitty hadn't seen him for months, and they had a lot to talk about. He was delighted to hear about their exploit and insisted that he would groom and tack up old Flame and his thoroughbred for the triumphal entry into town. He said he would clean Hec's boots and that Kitty was to wear her red dress.

They did as they were told. Hec was, of course, very tired, but he did manage to pull himself together and ride proudly down Ballarat Street to Eichardt's Hotel, where he found himself the hero of the hour.

'By God, Kitty,' one old-timer said, 'ye rode out with a boy and ye brought back a man! Good on ye. I reckon ye could teach a snake to ride.'

Kitty said goodbye to Hec, and after he passed her a folded cheque, she left him to enjoy the limelight. She rode back home to spend time with her brother. It wasn't until she got home that she looked at the cheque, which was signed by Hamish. She gasped and handed it to Billy. He looked at it and raising an eyebrow, whistled and asked her what else she had taught Hec besides teaching him to ride and nearly killing him in the process. This earned him a box on the ears.

Billy was restless. He had spent all his life, it seemed to him, riding horses, and he still loved them. Although he had done very well for himself, having first been hailed as Central Otago's leading jockey and trainer when he was still only twenty, the hard work and the long hours were telling on his spirit. He was sick and tired of being always spoken of as 'the one-legged jockey' as if he were some sort of freak and having only one leg was the most important thing about him. In short, he was bored and he wanted to try something else before he reached the ripe old age of thirty, which wasn't that long away. He had decided that he would go to Australia for a while. Or somewhere. Or anywhere. He had come to say goodbye and to get Kitty to bank some more money for him so he would have a bigger nest-egg when he came home.

He told Kitty that he had just been discharged from court following his appearance on a charge of selling a horse that didn't belong to him. 'I had broken the damn thing in and hadn't been paid for it. It wasn't a racehorse's arse and, sure, the damn donkey wasn't mine. The owner kept saying he'd pay me, and I wouldn't let him have it until he did. So I kept the bloody thing and fed it for months until I got sick of waiting for my money so I sold it. Then the bastard charged me with theft. I'd kept all the accounts, and when the magistrate looked them over, he threw the case out of court.'

'Well, at least it wasn't over a woman this time,' Kitty remarked wryly, referring to one of Billy's previous misdemeanours.

Billy grinned. 'At least she was worth it. This was just a waste of time over a piece of dog-tucker.'

'Just remember, Billy Boy, it was a 'piece of dog tucker' that got you started on your career!' Kitty reminded him.

A week after Billy left, Kitty rode into town to do the banking and to see if she could get some more business. She was doing some shopping in the chemist's when the doctor came in supporting a man who was clearly exhausted. He had walked all night to see if the doctor would try to make his way up to Skippers to visit a gravely ill child. Of course the doctor would go as soon as he could, but he had another life and death case that was waiting to be attended to. He would leave at first light, but did they know of any way to get a prescription up any earlier? There wasn't a pack train going until the next day. When Kitty said she would take it, the father asked, 'When?' and Kitty said 'Now!'

While the prescription was being made up, customers in the shop regaled the doctor with the story of Kitty's previous heroic ride. Kitty, who had been buying a few little luxuries for Heather, said she would only stop at home to change her clothes, grab something to eat and saddle up a faster horse. She didn't realise that she was embarking on a new career and establishing herself as a legend.

Kitty made good time taking the prescription to Skippers. Sauce was sure-footed and very keen. When she took a short break at Long Gully, she met Julien Bourdeau, the regular packer into Skippers. She told him about an idea she had. She wanted to be a packer too but only to carry fragile goods, pharmaceuticals, haberdashery and little luxuries that women like. And emergencies like prescriptions.

'And things they don't want their husbands to know about,' Bordeau said with a humorous gleam in his eye. 'Go for it, Lassie, I don't reckon you're going to put me out of business.' He laughed. 'It's not an easy life, and I know you're one tough lady, but even so, I think you'll get mighty sick of it after a while. Anyhow, come in for a cuppa any time you find me home.'

'Likewise,' said Kitty over her shoulder as she rode off. She continued to make good time, and a surprised Heather grabbed the medication and rushed it to the neighbour's. Kitty took her horse to his lodging at the stable. The hotel proprietor told her that even though they weren't in business yet, an errand of mercy deserved free lodging, and as long as the hotel remained in business, she was never charged.

It would be nice to say that the baby survived, because of Kitty's heroic effort, but he didn't. The doctor arrived late the next day, but he could do nothing. The little boy only lingered for a few days more. By then Kitty was back home at Jack's Hotel. Of course the whole exercise brought back vivid memories of her own wee Georgie, and again she wept for him and for her daughters. For several days they haunted her so much that she couldn't leave home. She tried to tell herself that she was lucky to have had so many good times with them. She realised that she would have to consider Annie as lost, too, because she doubted whether she would ever see or hear from her again.

When she rode back into town, it was again to a hero's welcome, and she found that the 'Kitty legend' had grown. She wasn't sure she wanted to be a legend, because she was still so unhappy, but she went to the chemist shop, loaded up with a list of small things that Heather had suggested and listed the prices for. The chemist's assistant offered further suggestions and called her boss. She explained that she was carrying things that were too small and fragile for 'Old Bidoo', who had said that he was very happy with it. She was charging purchasers a small percentage; was the chemist happy with that? He said he was very happy and made more suggestions, but she explained that this first time she only wanted to take what one horse could carry in its saddlebags. He also said he now knew where to come when there were prescriptions to be carried. He suggested that she should fill up any spare space with out-of-date women's magazines that could be given away.

Kitty went to the general store and bought some haberdashery items to use as packing for the fragile items. She went home, tried to get a good night's sleep and left on Mouse early the next morning. Since there was no urgency, she didn't hurry but gave herself over to enjoying the beautiful and fascinating landscape. She met various people who were on their way out and took time to chat with them. She was surprised to find that they all knew who she was, and she began to feel that she had come home. Her sadness seemed to lift a little. Skippers has always had that effect on people. Anyone who has been there a few times always wants to go back.

Heather was pleased to see her and exclaimed delightedly when she saw the merchandise. She said she would tell the other women about it. Shrewdly, she said that if they came together for afternoon tea they would be more likely to buy than if they came singly, because they would likely become a bit competitive. This proved to be right, and it wasn't long before everything had been sold. Kitty explained about her commission and having to make a living, and everyone was happy about that. One woman asked if she could match some knitting wool. She wanted four skeins and a bottle of witch-hazel, Kitty asked her to write it down, and several others also wrote down orders. When she was asked when she would be back, she said she'd come once a week depending on the weather, unless the chemist had an urgent prescription.

Her business grew from there. The first summer was a good one, and before she had made many trips she had to take a pack horse as well. When Flame died she bought two big strong chestnut ponies, so she always had a horse to ride and one to lead. With Billy away she had to arrange for winter feed, and worse, she had to pay for it. The ponies were suitable for riding lessons. Queenstown had a growing number of summer visitors from Dunedin and Invercargill who had holiday houses in the town, and some of their children wanted riding lessons or just to be taken for rides. Kitty became increasingly busy. She was supporting herself and her horses. She was getting by, but it was a struggle and the winters were hard.

She managed, but as she had known, it wasn't going to be easy. Twice there were urgent prescriptions that she managed to take through in bad weather, once even in a snowstorm. This added to the 'Kitty legend'. Years later it was said that 'Kitty could get through when no man could, always riding a chestnut horse and always wearing a red dress.' When Kitty heard this she would shrug her shoulders and say that in emergencies she took only one sure-footed horse and she walked a lot of the time. But still the legend grew and had her battling through blizzards all winter.

She sometimes stayed a few days with Heather and Hamish, and her love for Skippers grew. Once she heard her hosts discussing the mine at Bullendale. Kitty said she had heard about it but had never been there; what was it like? Hamish said he happened to be going up the following day. Kitty would be welcome to ride along with him if she wanted to. Of course she jumped at the chance to broaden her horizons, and they left at first light with Kitty mounted on one of the company horses.

The narrow, winding, steep road to Skippers was easy in comparison, and although it, too, called for careful riding, the Bullendale track was far worse. Both Hamish and Kitty were very capable riders, and Hamish said it was great – he had never had such a fast ride in, except on his own. He had never had a companion who could actually keep up with him. Next time she came he would show her the broad valley known as the Branches, where they and the horses could enjoy a good gallop.

When they arrived at the mine earlier than he was expected and he told the staff how long the ride had taken, it became, suitably exaggerated, another chapter in the Kitty legend.

Hamish told Kitty that she couldn't see the actual mine, only the office, because most miners were a superstitious lot and wouldn't tolerate women near the mine. He would leave her with the mine manager's wife. About a hundred men worked at the mine and a number of them were married, so there was quite a little village perched high on the side of the hill at Bullendale.

Elsie, the mine manager's wife, was delighted to have another woman to talk to, and she had heard from the women at Skippers about Kitty's packing business. Their husbands wondered why they found it necessary to use her when there was now a post office and postage was cheap. It had to be explained to them that wool and thread had to be matched, swatches of material had to be pored over because choices had to be made, catalogues of patterns and fashion magazines were a necessity of life and birthday presents for husbands had to be bought in secret. Men simply didn't understand women's need for some of the finer things of life.

Elsie herself was a keen horsewoman and proposed that she would put in orders for Kitty to bring to Skippers. Elsie would then collect them for delivery to Bullendale. When Kitty mentioned commission Elsie laughed and shrugged it off. She didn't want commission, she didn't need it, she wanted something to relieve the boredom. Because of her locality she couldn't put in a garden. Her children were in boarding school and the mine would eventually stop being productive.

When that happened her husband would probably be looking for another job. Perhaps not, though, as the isolation here had meant that there was little to spend money on, so they had been able to save a nice little nest egg. Her husband was a very moderate drinker, and her only extravagance was her horse. She had loved her time here, but now she was over it. They talked horses for a while, as horsewomen do. Elsie lamented the fact that she had no one to ride with.

When the men came back and Hamish said they had better get a wriggle on, Elsie invited Kitty to come back any time and please stay for a few days as she would then have someone to ride with. Kitty enthusiastically agreed.

Hamish had the horses saddled and ready to go, so they were off. It was slower going than their morning ride had been because in the shady places it had iced up and although their horses had shoes with heels (small protuberances that made them grip better in winter conditions) caution was still necessary. Hamish said they were still making very good time. He hoped young Hec would continue with riding lessons, but like most boys his age, he probably thought he now knew everything. When Kitty said sadly that she had never had a boy that age, Hamish gruffly said, 'Sorry', and for a while they rode on in silence.

When they got back to Skippers, by the time they had finished with grooming and feeding the horses and had walked home, they were greeted by a house smelling of the most welcoming smell ever, the smell of fresh bread. To go with the bread, Heather served them big bowls of delicious steaming soup. When Heather asked after Elsie, Kitty told her about her growing discontent with her home and her readiness to move. Heather and Hamish explained to Kitty that with the mining industry, the only thing permanent was its very impermanence.

'What do you mean?' asked Kitty aghast. 'Do you mean you will have to leave here, too?'

'Well,' said Hamish, 'I'm employed as a mine inspector. My job is basically to keep the mine owners and managers honest, which means making sure that they are telling the truth about their mines' production. The powers that be must get the most they can from taxes and levies. If there are no longer any mines to inspect, of course there won't be any work for me.'

'We just love it here, and ideally we would stay here until the children finish primary school,' put in Heather. 'It would be hard to find anywhere else where they could run so free and the teachers were so brilliant. But they are both smart enough for high school, and we would sooner have them at home than at boarding school. Hamish hates the airs and graces and clubbiness that some boarding schools seem to engender. We don't know where we will go or even if Hamish will stay in the mining business. We are very fortunate that money isn't a problem. The only thing we are sure about is that as long as the old man is alive, we won't be anywhere near Dunedin.'

'I hate it when people that I have come to know and love move out of my life,' said Kitty miserably. 'But it seems to be the story of my life. I'll still have my brother Billy and my sister Florrie, thank goodness.'

Heather and Hamish had, of course, heard of Billy Kirk, and Kitty was able to entertain them with his latest exploits. His letters were always amusing, but unfortunately, they didn't come very often and twice she had had her letters to him returned, marked *Gone, no address.*

When she told them about Florrie and Catherine, they were shocked and sympathetic. They all agreed that the sooner that Catherine could be admitted to Seacliff, Otago's mental asylum, the better it would be for Florrie. Kitty, who always did her best to find humour, if any could be found, in any situation, had them laughing when she told them of her experience of being mistaken for Arthur, the father she had never known.

Kitty, though always short of money, was happy with her life. Her ponies, who had been named Adam and Eve before she bought them, were proving to be very docile and were adapting well as learner's ponies so, with Mouse, she could now take three pupils at a time. She still got occasional guiding trips. In summer, she had increasing numbers of tourists who wanted to ride to Skippers, so she could honour her original arrangement with the hotel proprietor. The odd tall customer who was put off by the small size of his steed had it explained to him that they weren't that small; one inch taller and they would be classified as horses, small horses but definitely horses. She explained that they were more sure-footed than larger animals. Because no one else was providing riding trips, they usually came round.

Kitty went to visit Florrie and found her in a bit of a state. Catherine was becoming increasingly out of control and was trashing the house. Kitty heard the racket from outside and decided to assume her 'Arthur' persona. She marched into the house and shouted, 'Catherine, what on earth do you think you are doing? I thought we were getting ready to run away!'

Catherine stopped and said, 'Arthur, why do you call me "Catherine" when you know my name is Kathleen? I'm your own Katy. Why are you wearing a dress?'

Kitty thought quickly. 'Shsh, Katy dear, I'm in disguise. I can't let them see me here or they'll send me away. Let's get this woman here to clean up the mess and pack up your bag. First get her to make us a nice cup of tea. You, whatever your name is, did you hear what I said? Jump to it! A cup of tea and a biscuit and your mistress's medicine, and don't waste time. I'm in a hurry!'

'Yes sir, Mr Arthur,' answered Florrie obsequiously.

'Good girl,' said Kitty condescendingly, winking at Florrie.

'Oh, Arthur, I've been waiting so long. I don't know where I am, and I don't know why people keep calling me Catherine.' Arms outstretched, she moved towards Kitty who adroitly avoided her.

'Darling Katy,' she said. 'I've come such a long way, and I'm very tired and thirsty. Could you please get that maid to hurry with the tea and some bread and cheese. Then we'll be on our way.'

Florrie hurried up. 'Will that be all, sir?' she asked.

'Pack a bag for your mistress and one for yourself, too, and I believe she needs medicine, so don't forget that. Jump to it!'

'Why is she coming?' asked Catherine. 'I don't like her. She swans around here as if she owns the place.'

'No unmarried lady travels without a maid. You know that. We'll find you another when we get there. Now, you don't seem to have a groom, so I shall go and harness the horse. Drink your tea and take your medicine, then we'll be on our way. Tell that maid to hurry up. You stay here and send her out with the bags.'

Kitty put her own horse in the trap. When Florrie came out with the bags, she was struggling to control her laughter. She whispered to Kitty that she should be on stage. She also said Catherine was giving her trouble about her medication. Kitty strode back into the kitchen.

'Katy darling, please stop wasting time. Do you want them to catch us? Take your medicine and let's get going.' Catherine took her medicine.

They drove out past the dairy, waving to Lucy as they passed. Lucy or Will helped on the hospital run when Kitty wasn't available.

At the hospital the well-practised routine was in place. When Catherine was taken away by the nurses, Kitty and Florrie talked to the doctor. Kitty told him what she had walked into that morning. Florrie said that she now had no control when Catherine had one of her rages. She said that after this morning's episode she didn't think there would be an unbroken plate in the house. When the doctor asked if she was physically threatened, Florrie said that she was. As well as being a target for the plates, she had once had knives thrown at her and now kept them outside. Also she had the greatest difficulty getting Catherine to take her medicine, because she was convinced that Florrie was poisoning her.

The doctor fiddled with some papers. 'The time has come for her to be removed from your care,' he said. 'Ill-equipped as we are, we'll keep her here until we can get her transferred to Seacliff. I'm afraid her house will have to be sold. Will you be all right?'

Florrie explained that the house was hers. She had held the title deeds for a year or so before her father died, when he and Catherine were living with her. The doctor said he was pleased to hear it but she should get a lawyer and round up affidavits to prove her case. He shook hands with them both and said he would keep Florrie informed by mail and the letters should be held by the lawyer.

They went home via the dairy so they could tell Will and Lucy what had happened, and they, too, told Florrie to talk to a lawyer. They would also be doing so. It was certain Lizzie would be on the warpath again as soon as she found out Catherine was no longer living with Florrie and the dairy had been sold. Florrie wasn't too concerned, because Billy's lawyer had told her that George had done a good job legally and, short of using dynamite, Lizzie wouldn't be able to shift her.

When Kitty and Florrie got back it took them the rest of the day and well into the night to clean up the mess and repair the damage their mother had done. Fortunately, the teapot and the kettle, which were enamel, had survived, although they were both badly chipped. Florrie had managed to throw the cutlery drawer outside so Catherine had had no access to knives. Although the tea caddy was lying on the floor, they managed to scrape up enough leaves to sustain them through what was left of the day. The meat safe, which was outside, had eggs, milk and butter in it. When all was done they sat down to their last cup of tea for the day and enjoyed scrambled eggs, which they ate from the pan. In the morning they would make an inventory and go shopping.

Lucy arrived very early with a large load of things that she no longer needed because their children had left and she and Will hoped to be packed and away very soon. They had to be out in six weeks time, but now they wanted to get away as soon as they could, preferably yesterday. There would be more stuff, she promised. She had just grabbed what she thought would be most necessary for them so they could call off the shopping trip for a few days. She and Will had decided to sort out everything and to pack up the things they wanted to keep. And would they please not let any of the family know about Catherine until she was safely in Seacliff? They hoped to be well away by then. Since the doctor had told them it would take some months before that happened and he had asked them, particularly Kitty, not to visit. Lucy and Will wanted the sisters to help them pack. Anything that neither of them wanted could be sold or given away.

Kitty went back home to care for her animals and to go into town to see if there were any commissions for her. She arrived to find Billy chopping wood. She hadn't heard from him for more than a year and hadn't seen him for three, so they had a lot of catching up to do. She told him she planned to ride into Queenstown in the morning and if there was no work for her, she would go on to the dairy to help with the sorting and packing. Billy said he would come with her but he had nothing to ride. He didn't quite see himself on one of Kitty's wee nags. Kitty refused to rise to the bait. She laughed and told him that if he was such a snob he could bloody well stay home. Or walk. Billy said that if God had meant him to walk He would have given him four legs instead of only one.

In the morning Billy hopped onto Sauce, complaining that he wasn't allowed to carry a crop, and he was surprised at what happened. They were both show-offs, and they enjoyed a bit of fun before they started off. Billy said he was amazed such a small horse could be so spirited. Kitty told him that was good, he was such a know-all about horses.

Billy laughed. 'I know I am. I learned it the hard way. And do you know what? It has always pissed me off that you were born knowing more than I know now! Come on,' and he put his horse into a gallop. He was surprised that gentle Mouse was more than a match for her spirited brother. Kitty said the two horses were equals, it was just that Mouse had the better jockey.

When they arrived at the dairy there was a moment of awkwardness when Will and Lucy saw Billy. Kitty did some fast talking, and Billy was a bit apologetic about his former obnoxiousness. The two men shook hands, and Will said an extra pair of male hands would be very useful. He told Billy they wanted to get away before the dreaded Lizzie found out that they had gone. Billy said he perfectly understood; he owned that he and Lizzie were equally nasty, but he was sure that he himself had more redeeming features.

They got on with the job. Florrie, who was driving her trap, ferried things over to her place for sorting later. The furniture and other goods that Will and Lucy wanted to keep went onto the dray. Kitty was happy to see they were keeping the old kitchen table that George had so painstakingly made before the house was even started.

When they sat down to the food Florrie had brought, Kitty commented on George's table. This led to a flood of reminiscence, but they carefully left out any mention of Kinloch, although Will and Lucy told of their life on the farm during those years. When they were asked about their future they said they didn't know where they'd be. They'd find a wee patch of land somewhere in the sun. Perhaps Nelson? Their stuff would go into storage while they looked but before they settled down permanently. Will wanted to go back to his old home for his first and last visit. They promised that wherever they went they would keep in touch. And they did.

By sundown they had nearly finished. The only things left to be shifted were those Will and Lucy were keeping. It had been arranged that everyone would bed down at Florrie's for the night. Florrie said she now had enough mattresses for an army, and Billy said that as her older brother he was now the head of the family and he would not allow his sister to consort with riff-raff, so it would have to be officers only. And even then, one at a time. She could exchange them as soon as she wore them out. Poor Florrie was embarrassed and horrified. She was not used to that sort of talk. She had to get used to it quite quickly, as her family were a ribald lot, and when Billy produced a bottle from somewhere, he and Will became more so.

The next morning the men rode over to the dairy while the women sorted out the clutter at Florrie's. There were four piles: one for Kitty, one for Florrie, one for sale and one to give to charity. By midday Florrie's house was neat and tidy and better furnished than it had ever been. Kitty's share was on the trap and the other two piles under canvas. Florrie had made bread early in the morning, and now the house was full of the appetising smell. A pot of stew simmered on the stove, and a steamed pudding was waiting on the hob. When the men arrived Lucy was making a rich egg custard.

Will had decided that since they had had such a good time last night and they had been, for the first (and last) time a real family, he and Lucy would stay the night and leave early in the morning. Billy thought it was a good idea because there was half a bottle left and if Uncle Will didn't help him finish it he might get drunk, and Kitty didn't approve of drink. Will said he couldn't possibly leave Billy in the lurch when Billy had helped them so much with the hard work of moving house. They had another wonderful time together, and they all went across to the dairy to say their last goodbyes. Will shook Billy's hand said he was sorry he had misjudged him. He had always thought Billy was a nasty little trouble-maker, and he was very happy to be proved wrong.

'No,' Billy said, 'when you're as small as I am, you have to be a trouble-making little shit to survive. But now I only am when I have to be. When I'm in good company I'm positively charming.'

'And excessively modest, too, to add to your other good qualities,' agreed Will.

They said their goodbyes, the women wept and the men were a bit gruff. They were all having their last looks at the dairy, which, in different ways, had played so large a part in their various lives. Those staying stood waving until the others were out of sight. Then Kitty and Billy took the road to Queenstown, and Florrie went home.

When Florrie delivered Kitty's share of the things from the dairy, she and Kitty set out to sort them and put them away. Among them they found a leather trunk that neither of them recognised. When they opened it they found it to be crammed full of expensive clothes that had belonged to Lizzie. Catherine had cherished and saved the best of Lizzie's belongings as far back as her babyhood, things that could well have been handed down to her younger sisters.

'We all knew Lizzie was Ma's favourite child,' Florrie exclaimed, 'But I didn't realise it was an obsession. Pa tried to make up for it to the rest of us, but he could only do so much, and he had to spend more time with the boys. Evie and I resented having to do the dirty work while Lizzie could choose the jobs she wanted to do. To be honest, we were all taught to be housewives and dairymaids, so I can't say Ma neglected us, just that she was very selective about who did what. Ma had such a beautiful singing voice that it must have upset her that while the rest of us were all in the school choir, Lizzie brayed like a donkey.'

Kitty laughed. 'When I sing I make such a horrible noise that I sang once at school and was expelled from singing classes for the rest of the time I was there, so it didn't come from Pa's side of the family.'

When Kitty wondered aloud if they should try to send the clothes to Lizzie, Florrie snorted and said that Madam would have left them behind because they were out of fashion, and how much more out of date would they be by now, more than ten years later?

So they had a real fun time trying them on, and they decided to keep them, because of the quality of the materials. Both were good seamstresses and could alter the dresses or cut them up. The shoes and boots fitted, and Kitty claimed the expensive leather handbags. Most of the dresses were too big for Kitty, especially in the bodice, but she found one or two Lizzie had grown out of in her early teens, and they fitted her. Florrie persuaded her to keep them, 'just in case.'

When Billy arrived back he was riding a thoroughbred and said he was heading off the next morning. It was time he got back into business. He told his sisters he had probably had the best time in his life just being with them. He had thoroughly enjoyed finding that you could be part of a family that didn't spend its time quarrelling. He carried in the heavy bits and pieces, then asked Florrie if he could spend the night at her place because Kitty's was in too much of a mess. They drove off happily together, a brother and sister who not so long ago had been sworn enemies. Kitty thought that Billy's time overseas had made him finally grow up.

Kitty rode into town to see if there were any messages to be delivered to Skippers. There were, and everything was packed up and ready to go. It was getting late, and there was too much for one horse, so she would be back first thing in the morning. The shopkeeper said he would be open early for her even though there was nothing urgent. The ride to Skippers was uneventful, and Kitty, not in a hurry, was happily enjoying the scenery and stopping to chat to people she met on the road. She felt as if she were coming home.

The Stuarts were, as usual, pleased to see her as were the other women who arrived as soon as the word got around. They came to pick up their orders and to give her their lists for next time. When one of them complained about Kitty being absent for so long, the other women rounded on the complainer and told her how lucky they were to have Kitty's services; why shouldn't she have a break now and then? So Kitty explained about her mother, and they were instantly sympathetic. The woman who had complained mumbled that she was sorry, she just needed the wool so she could finish the jersey she was knitting for her husband's birthday.

Kitty told them about teaching Florrie to ride and Florrie's pleasure in the pastime. For the first time in her life, she could have some time to herself, and riding widened her horizons so much. She was doing so well and could now complete the circuit from Arrowtown to Queenstown via Frankton and back via Arthurs Point, calling at Kitty's on the way. The only problem Florrie had was that she wanted to be married and have children and was now old enough to be considered to be an old maid. The only man who was showing any interest in her had been around for some time. A long time ago he had told her that he admired her but would never live with a mad woman. When Catherine was removed he renewed his interest. He still lived with his parents and too frequently quoted his mother's opinion. His mother disapproved of women riding. This provoked a storm of comment that Florrie should give him the push right now. If he was getting bossy at the beginning of a courtship, what would he be like as a husband? Had Florrie considered that he and his mother might be more interested in the nice little acreage that Florrie owned than in Florrie herself.? What did he do for a living? He was a bank teller. Heads nodded wisely. More tea was poured.

Kitty smiled to herself. She thought of all the warning signs she had ignored before she married John Greig and how her stubborn fifteen-year-old self was blinded by what she thought was love.

One of the women exclaimed, 'I know what! Could she manage to ride up here?'

'I'm sure she could, Dorrie,' Kitty answered. 'I know she'd like that. I'm giving her one of my ponies because her horse is getting too old to pull her trap and might even fall over if she got on his back. I really can't afford to keep all the horses I've got. Business is falling off.'

'I hadn't finished,' Dorrie said importantly. 'Bring Florrie up for the Bullendale Bachelors' Ball. I don't think you've ever been to one either, Kitty. It's a great night. Everyone for miles around comes. You have to be invited, and I know Elsie will want you to come. Single women are especially welcome.'

Kitty laughed. 'You forget I'm not a single woman. You'd be the first to get stuck into me if I took up with another man. I'm sure my husband has one of his mates reporting on me.'

'No, but Florrie's single, and you can be her chaperone. So that's sorted. I'm not trying to marry her off, mind you.'

'Not much you aren't,' smiled Kitty who said she wanted to know a bit more about the ball. The women all excitedly started to talk at once, mostly about what they were going to wear. They easily convinced her that coming with Florrie would be a very good idea indeed. She knew better than to drop it on Florrie suddenly. She would have to get her used to the idea gradually. She decided to tell Florrie about the ball and suggest that they should take some of Lizzie's unwanted finery to sell to the women at Skippers. So that's what they did.

They rode slowly so that Florrie could enjoy the amazing views. She was so struck by the view from Skippers Saddle that she found it hard to turn away. It was a beautiful clear, sunny morning, there was a remnant of sparkling snow on the Remarkables and the whole Wakatipu Basin was spread before them. Kitty pointed out that they could stop again on the way out. Florrie was riding Adam, who was now hers. Eve followed, carrying bulging pack saddles, and Kitty, too, had fat saddle bags. It was a slow trip in, not because Florrie couldn't manage the ride, but because she kept wanting to stop and stare.

They arrived quite unexpectedly at about four in the afternoon. It was only four days since Kitty's last visit. Kitty left Florrie with Heather while she tended to the horses. Florrie's job was to show Heather the goodies, and, as expected, Heather was blown away.

Over tea they discussed prices. The sisters had no idea what to charge and dismissed Heather's suggestions. Not surprisingly, Hamish quickly became bored. 'Auction the bloody things,' he said.

'And if you don't stop talking about them I'll have to go and get my pipes.' That put an end to the talk of clothes – for the meantime.

Early in the morning the message went out – 'Come and see what Kitty's brought!' – and nearly everyone turned up for morning tea. Hamish left for places unknown, taking sandwiches with him and saying he wouldn't be home for dinner but would send an auctioneer in his stead. This person would be necessary to keep things in order in case the women got unruly.

They were all delighted to meet Florrie and to pore over the clothes. Of course, trying everything on took an hour or so. One woman, Ivy, had been at Arrowtown School in her certificate year when Lizzie was in her second year. Ivy said she remembered Lizzie as a primping little clothes horse, even then well aware she was the school beauty. She tried to queen it over the other girls and wondered why she had no friends. Ivy was delighted to be able to think that she herself could swank around in Lizzie's finery. She was not surprised to hear Lizzie was trying to make trouble about George's will, even now that she had made a good marriage and was really well-off. Ivy said that's what you can expect when someone is brought up to be the centre of the universe. Kitty told her that Catherine had been very disappointed in Kitty because she was not the daughter she wanted. But Kitty thought it was lovely for to her to get what she wanted in her second daughter. Thinking of daughters brought a lump to Kitty's throat, and she quickly changed the subject.

Heather, perceiving this, turned to Florrie and asked innocently, 'What about you, Florrie? What are you going to wear to the ball? Elsie said that you two would be staying at her place because she needs your help setting up. It will be nice and convenient for you. Hamish said he would tell her you were here. And here she is.'

Elsie bustled in, saying, 'I hope you've left something for me. And you must be Florrie. I'm very pleased to meet you at last. Kitty, I've got such a list for you to bring next time. All the arrangements are going swimmingly. Has Heather told you that you two are staying with me?' Kitty countered: 'Hold your horses, Elsie! Heather told me about the ball, but she didn't ask me if I wanted to come, and at that stage she hadn't even met Florrie.'

'Oh, come on, Kitty,' said Ivy, 'You're part of our family so your sister must be too. What are you going to wear? Florrie, do you have a young man? I hope not. We've got more than enough men, so if you have, leave him at home. Our husbands have to stand back and let us dance with whomever we want to. Because there aren't enough women to go round, some of the men have to dance with each other.'

'Well, seeing you ask us so nicely, I suppose we'd better consider it. What do you say, Florrie?'

Before Florrie could answer, a plump young woman named Rose asked, 'Do you have an intended, Florrie?'

'Not exactly,' answered Florrie. 'Just more like someone showing an interest. I've known him for a long time, but I've been looking after my mother.'

'What's that got to do with the price of fish? Come, do tell. What's his name? Where does he live? What does he do? Most important, what's he like?' asked Rose.

A flustered Florrie started to answer. 'He lives in Arrowtown and his name is Oliver—'

She was interrupted by a screech from Ivy: 'Not Ollypolly, lives with mummy and daddy, works in the bank in the same job he's had for years. We were in the same class at school. He was always a mummy's boy. She even came to school to tell the headmaster he had to stop the kids calling her baby "Olly" when his name was Oliver. Don't tell me that the old bat has finally let her baby go courting. Wonders never cease. Be warned, though, if you take him on, she'll come along as part of the package.'

The conversation terminated when Hamish came in with another man, whom he introduced to Kitty and Florrie as Morgan Griffiths. He was carrying a fiddle and professed himself sorry to hear that the ladies had concluded their business without warfare. He was obviously very popular and was easily persuaded to give the women a tune before they went home to tea.

The evening meal was hilarious. After they had eaten, the children were allowed to stay up and join in when Heather, Florrie and Hamish sang to the tune of Morgan's fiddle. Hamish left his bagpipes in the wardrobe and Kitty refrained from singing, so it was a pleasantly harmonious evening. Florrie had only once before enjoyed such an entertaining time, and that had been the evening that the Kirks were together as a family.

In the morning the sisters rode out early, promising to be back within the week with all the errands completed. When Heather pressed Florrie to come again, with or without Kitty, she grinned widely and said, 'Try to keep me away.'

'And the ball, Florrie?' asked Heather.

'I think I should give it a go. Pa loved to dance and made sure we all could and did. I just know he would want us to go, and there's been precious little dancing in our either of our lives, so we can go in memory of the best father in the whole world.'

'Amen to that,' said her sister. They mounted up and rode happily home.

Seventh Life
Otto 1896

Chapter Seven

Kitty and Florrie spent a lot of the next two weeks up at Bullendale helping Elsie. Her husband, Mac, a rather gruff, hearty man who was assistant manager at the mine described himself as a general dogsbody who was expected to be everywhere and to fix everything at the same time. He said it was quite nice coming home to be the only rooster in the henhouse, even if the jolly hens never stopped cackling.

Elsie laughed and told him to do his strutting and crowing somewhere else because the hens were too busy to listen to him. It was the day before the ball, and all the women were preparing food for the sit-down supper that would be served at the Phoenix Hotel.

Bullendale was named for George Bullen, who, with his brothers, had made a small fortune in Australia following gold rushes by being early on the spot and establishing stores that sold clothing, footwear and everything a miner needed or thought he needed. It was very profitable because so many new chums arrived on the diggings without any idea of the basics. And even the most hard-wearing gear wore out very quickly on the goldfields.

When gold was discovered in New Zealand, the brothers sold up in Australia and transferred their business across the Tasman. By 1863 Bullen and his brother had stores in Dunedin, Queenstown and Arrowtown. They followed the rush to the West Coast and by 1885 had established stores in Hokitika and Greymouth. They were smart businessmen. By the time the rushes petered out and they had sold their stores one by one, their small fortune had become a large one. The brothers returned to England, and George turned his considerable energy to another form of mining; he bought a share in the Scandinavian mine in the upper Shotover. The place became known as Bullendale, and the mine had its name changed to Phoenix.

The little corrugated iron houses in Bullendale were perched on the steep sides of Murdochs Creek, which ran into the right branch of Skippers Creek. They were built on any small flat surfaces that could be found. Shaded by the surrounding mountains, it was miserably cold in winter, yet women lived and raised their children there. Winter snowfalls averaged a depth of four feet, and when it was impossible to go to school, there was nothing to do but stay in bed all day and try to keep warm.

Social life centred around the hotel and the community hall, which had been donated by Bullen. The hall also housed the library and from 1885 was lit by six electric lights. There was a store, a butcher's shop, a post office and a billiard parlour. The little street boasted twenty electric street lights, courtesy of the mine. Queenstown, so much larger and more prosperous, had no electricity until 1924.

When Kitty was told that Queenstown and Arrowtown guests at the Bachelors' Ball came by coach to Skippers and from there were transported to Bullendale on horseback, she gasped and asked where all the people would stay. She was told that wasn't a problem; they danced until first light, then made their way back home. The ball was by invitation only, and tickets were much in demand.

When everything that needed to be done had been done to Elsie's satisfaction, she sighed happily and said, 'Thanks, girls. Now we can have an easy day tomorrow so we can make ourselves look beautiful for the ball.' How wrong she was!

In what should have been the dark hours the sky was lit up and the peace of the small township was torn by explosions and shouts. The hotel was burning down. Most of the catering that had been done the previous day was destroyed along with the hotel. Someone said the ball would have to be cancelled. 'Not so!' said Elsie.

Elsie's husband made a telephone call to Skippers and asked for help, and the women there responded. They shoved their finery into saddle bags, packed food and crockery onto packhorses and arrived early at Bullendale. Together with the local women, who had emptied their own cupboards, they assembled a substitute supper that could be served buffet-style in the hall. All the horses from both settlements had to be back at Skippers to meet the coaches, and while the men attended to that, the women were able to snatch a few hours' rest.

Both Kitty and Florrie were talented cooks, and they enjoyed the team spirit that disasters bring out in the most unlikely people. Florrie, in particular, loved being in company, something that she had so far missed out on. She was very nervous about one thing, however; Heather had persuaded her to give an 'item' – to sing a duet with her. They had practised a few times to the tune of Griff's fiddle and would have one short rehearsal with piano accompaniment. Florrie told Heather she wasn't nervous, she was terrified.

Catherine had brought her family up to believe that there was nothing worse than a 'show-off', and to her that was anyone who brought attention to themselves. Catherine herself, although she knew she had the best voice in the church choir, had always staunchly refused to take a solo part, nor would she join the local operatic society, because appearing on stage was showing off. And yet she had turned Lizzie into a prancing clothes horse. No talk of *her* knowing her place! Heather told Florrie to get over it – she would be singing for friends and if she was nervous she could close her eyes and pretend they were singing in the Stuarts' kitchen. Heather was a very persuasive lady and Florrie fell into line. Kitty entertained them with the story of Catherine's fury when she was dragged into the circus act that Kitty and George had performed all those years ago.

Finally, it was time for the ball to begin. The band was starting up as they made their way down the steep track to the hall. They passed the still-smoking ruins of the hotel and stepped into the warmth and laughter of the hall.

The first dance was a progressive three-step. The dancers circled the hall to a lively tune, each couple having a few turns together, then each man handed his partner on to the next man. By the end of the dance every man on the floor had danced with every woman, and the bystanders had a good chance to study form. From then on all the women were rushed off their feet. They danced the Maxina, the Valeta and the Gay Gordons, interspersed with waltzes, circular waltzes and traditional favourites such as the Eightsome Reel and Sir Roger de Coverly.

Apart from the waltzes, most of the dances were fairly vigorous, and every now and then the women had to ask for a break. Whenever Kitty or Florrie sat down they were surrounded by men booking up dances, and if and when their dance cards were full, those who were unsuccessful just wanted to chat. To begin with, Florrie was nervous of the attention, but she soon relaxed and began to enjoy it. Single women never stayed single for long on the goldfields; three days was about average. One despairing bar owner asked a friend in Dunedin to find him the ugliest barmaid he could find. He did, and she was *really* ugly but even so, she didn't even last three days before she was claimed in marriage.

Florrie had been warned about this, but she still didn't quite know how to handle the three proposals of marriage she received during the course of the ball. Her duet with Heather was so popular that many encores were called for and they only stopped singing when they ran out of songs. Not realising how animated and how lovely she looked, Florrie was gobsmacked when, at the end of the evening, she was declared 'Belle of the Ball'.

Kitty, too, was surrounded. When one of the visiting women

asked her husband why such a plain little woman was so popular with the men, he told her that it was, firstly, because she was a woman and, secondly, because she made them laugh. When she glanced at her dance card Kitty saw that one name appeared twice. Otto Strohle. She hadn't paid much attention when her card was being fought over at the beginning of the ball, and there had so been so many names called out that she was hard-pushed to fit a name to a face.

When the supper waltz was called, a good-looking, well-dressed man, probably a few years older than she, came to claim her. He took her hand and with a courtly little bow, asked her to dance. When he looked her in the eye she experienced a strange little lift in the pit of her stomach. He led her on to the floor, and she felt that she had been dancing with him forever. Chatting over the buffet supper in the company of other couples, Kitty was conscious all the time of the man beside her. There was nowhere to sit except for the forms against the wall, and because of the nature of the food, most people remained on their feet as they ebbed and flowed around the tables. Kitty, fully aware of her heightened sensitivity and unsure how she should handle herself, was almost glad – or was she sorry? – when the band struck up again and her next partner claimed her.

For the rest of the night, no matter who she was dancing with, her eyes were seeking the man known as the Stroller. Once or twice when their eyes met Kitty felt herself blushing, and she tried to tell herself that she was being ridiculous – she was forty-one, a married woman, not a single, impressionable girl. It didn't work. When the sky started to lighten and he came to claim her for the last waltz, she felt that same lift in her belly.

Together with Florrie and Griff, they walked in single file with Mac and Elsie up the narrow track to their house, where the women got changed to help take the visitors back to Skippers. All six sat down to a quick breakfast, which the men had cooked up while the women were changing. Then, as Stroller gave Kitty a leg up on to her horse and handed her a leading rein, he managed to whisper to her, 'I think, Kitty Kirk, we have some unfinished business, you and I. We have to talk, so I shall call on you as soon as I can. And please call me Otto.' He bestowed a quick kiss on her hand, and again she melted.

She rode back to Skippers with a woman perched behind her and two others on the led horse. All the competent riders were similarly loaded, and a plodding shire horse carried four passengers at the rear of the procession. When they finally arrived and all the visitors had been packed into the waiting coaches and sent on their way, Kitty, Florrie and Heather had a well-earned rest.

The sisters stayed the night with the Stuarts. As usual the two children packed into one narrow bed while Kitty and Florrie topped and tailed in the other. Kitty was restless and squirmed until Florrie, exasperated, told her, for heaven's sake, to lie still. They both had a lot to think about, but they both needed a good night's sleep.

When they arrived at their respective homes they had chores to attend to and life to get on with. And such a lot to think about. The next day, a Wednesday, the bank in Arrowtown was closed and early in the afternoon Florrie had a visit from Oliver, accompanied by his mother and father. Surprised, Florrie, who was in dirty clothes and busy shovelling up manure in the paddock, washed her hands and invited them in for a cup of tea. Oliver introduced his parents as Mr and Mrs Smedley-Jones. Florrie made no apology for her appearance as she arranged samples of her baking on plates to offer to her visitors. There was an uncomfortable silence. Oliver's mother was studying the room carefully and noting the quality of not only the baking but the plates and cups on the table. Florrie, who was a lot more sure of herself than she had been before the ball, began the conversation with a remark about the weather. She was surprised to find that she felt she was in charge of the situation and was actually enjoying herself.

Oliver, noticeably uncomfortable, asked her if she had enjoyed the ball. Surprised, she thanked him and said yes, she had enjoyed it immensely, but how did he know she had attended?

'It was plastered all over the paper,' his mother said. 'Everybody in the Wakatipu knows by now that Miss Florence Kirk was the Belle of the Ball.'

Seeing the way the conversation was going, Florrie commented that she was surprised Mrs Smedley thought that everybody in the Wakatipu was interested in the ball, and why did she think that was such a bad thing?

'Mrs Smedley-Jones,' Oliver's mother corrected her. 'I'm just very surprised that you should choose to cavort with that sort of rough company, that's all.'

'Well, I'm surprised that the Lake Wakatip Mail didn't mention that the Mayor and Mayoress of Arrowtown were there. And the bank manager and his wife. I had a dance with him, and he's such a lovely dancer. Their wives looked as if they enjoyed dancing with the miners. Are they such rough company? There isn't anything the least bit snobby about them or about the station owners and their wives. If you'd been invited you would have been there to see for yourselves. The gowns were really beautiful.'

Mrs Smedley-Jones was taken aback. 'I think Oliver's a little hurt that you didn't mention it to him. I'm sure he would've liked to go.'

Florrie turned to Oliver. 'I'm sorry, Oliver, I didn't realise you had an invitation. And for a charity function like that, the tickets are so very expensive. I've been so busy helping Kitty that I haven't had much time to do anything else. I was very lucky to have been included in her invitation.'

'Well, as Oliver's intended, I think you should have been a little more considerate of his feelings and your own reputation.'

'I'm Oliver's intended? Really? I didn't know that. Why didn't somebody tell me sooner? Or better still, Ollie, why didn't you mention it to me? Apart from your friends, who else knows? Half of Arrowtown?'

Before Florrie could work up a full head of steam she was defused by the arrival of Kitty. When Florrie introduced Oliver's parents, his father said not to call him 'Smedley' because he was plain Roger Jones and please could he have a closer look at Florrie's piano? Florrie told him that of course he could but she feared that it was badly out of tune.

Kitty broke in. 'Is that sad animal at the gate yours? Did you not even notice it had a loose shoe?' Roger Jones said he knew nothing about horses, he had hired it, and sensing an escape route, he said he'd have a look and he followed her outside. After five minutes he poked his head in and announced that it would be half an hour or so before they could leave, because Kitty had started to shoe the horse and she had asked him to hold it for her.

Florrie swore under her breath. She was reluctant to return to the earlier conversation, but Mrs Smedley-Jones was implacable. She said Oliver was a shy lad and he wanted to be sure that his mother approved of Florrie before he made a declaration so he brought his parents to meet her. There were some things she didn't approve of, but she was sure that she and Florrie could sort them out to her satisfaction. Her Oliver had always wanted to live on a farm in the country and she wanted to see him settled. At Florrie's advanced age she was most unlikely to have another chance. It would be lovely to have grandchildren, she said wistfully.

Florrie's anger turned to laughter, and at that stage Kitty and Roger came back in. Florrie, still laughing, told Kitty that she had just learned such a lot. She had learned that she was Ollie's intended, and Mrs Jones had told her that she was too old to have another chance to marry so she should make the best of it and settle down to produce grandchildren for Mrs Jones.

Kitty had another solution. 'What say you and Ollie go out, and you can discuss this in private while he helps you shovel shit. If you do choose him he needs to know what farm work is like, and that's the best place to start. It's the man who does the dirty work while the woman stays in and tends to the kids. It's only fair that he knows about that side of farm life. While you and Ollie are shovelling I'll tell Mrs S. about the competition. She needs to know that you are still considering the three proposals you received at the ball. I've told Roger that our brother Billy is the male head of the family and any suitors will have to ask his permission.'

'Thanks Kitty, but you really needn't bother. I may be old fashioned, but if I can't marry for love, I won't marry at all, and I certainly do not love Oliver. I may be Oliver's intended but he certainly isn't mine. If I do find someone to love I don't want someone with a mother who disapproves of me and only wants to get her son a piece of land and also to get her hands on my fine china. I have completely run out of anything else to say except to thank you for a very entertaining afternoon. Now go. And, Ollie, please don't bother to come back. Ever. I hope you can find another prospective fiancée, but unless you can get away from your mother I don't like your chances.'

Kitty had the horse harnessed and was mounting her own. She announced that she was going to Arrowtown to get paid for shoeing the horse and to give the owner the rough side of her tongue for hiring out a horse in that condition. She cantered off, and without another word the Smedley-Jones family left.

Florrie thought she had seen the last of that family, but the following Wednesday, Roger Jones arrived at her place on Oliver's bike. He told her that Oliver now had to work in Queenstown on Wednesdays. He went in the coach with his mother, who always liked to spend a day with friends. It would now be the best day of the week for him, and please would she make it even better by letting him tune and then play her piano? He had noticed she had no sheet music, and if she couldn't read music he would be happy to teach her. He would also like to accompany her while she practised her singing. A beautiful secret friendship began.

On Saturday morning Kitty returned from shopping in Queenstown to find a strange horse tethered to her fence. She went around the back of her house to let her own horse go and found Otto Strohle sunning himself on a garden bench.

'Hello, my Kitty,' he smiled 'Shall I bring my horse around here, too?'

Kitty stuttered. 'Er, yes, um, are you staying, I mean...'

Otto looked at her levelly. 'I think that rather depends on you, doesn't it?'

Kitty, blushing, answered, 'Um, yes. I'll go in and put the kettle on.' She bolted inside.

When he came in he said, 'we have things to talk about, you and I. Neither of us is young, and there's no point in beating around the bush. You know as well as I do where we're heading.'

Hanging her head, Kitty said, 'I'm still a married woman.'

'I know that. And I still have a wife in Sweden who I haven't seen for more than twenty years. We won't be doing anyone any harm, and I think we have a right to some happiness.'

'I'm thinking... I wonder... do we really want that cup of tea right now?'

They didn't. An hour later Otto suggested that they should take a break for dinner.

Kitty was embarrassed because she had so little to put on the table, but it was all she could afford. They ate what was there, Kitty made scones, they drank lots of tea and they talked and talked and talked.

Otto talked about his life in Sweden. He said that the country was frigid and so was his estranged wife. He would never go back to either. He wondered where Kitty had learned her skills in the bedroom, and she talked about her only previous experience with John Greig and his prudishness, how she had been only fifteen and it had been first love, when she believed in getting married and living happily ever after. She told him about her rude awakening. For the first time ever she talked openly about her tragedies and she cried. She spoke of Annie and her hope of reconciliation and her fear that it would never happen. Then she asked Otto why he had chosen her. There were so many women out there who were more shapely and better looking than her.

He told her he didn't 'choose' her. He said that he had no idea what happened. He was a romantic, and from the first eye contact he knew that she was the one he had been waiting for. It wasn't her appearance that attracted him, it was her spirit, her resilience and her energy. Didn't she think it was time they went back to bed?

Late in the afternoon they emerged again and attended to their animals. They fed the hens, collected the eggs and picked vegetables. They brought in firewood and stoked up the fire. Otto lit the fire under the copper for hot water while Kitty made some pikelets, put on a vegetable stew and started the bread for the morning.

When the water was hot they shared a bath, then had their evening meal. They were still finding plenty to talk about. They went to bed and fell almost immediately into an exhausted sleep.

And so it began. They couldn't live together. Otto had a contract with the mine to do odd jobs when called on. He lived in a hut on his claim, which he worked when he wasn't needed at the mine, and he barely made enough to live on. He had a horse to support and was known to be a dandy, so his wardrobe also needed occasional maintenance. Kitty had her small holding and two horses but was very lucky that Billy had winter feed delivered to her, and whenever he visited he brought meat and stocked up her larder. When she thanked him he said he only did it because he wanted to eat decently while he was there.

Apart from the logistics of the thing, Kitty knew she would lose most of her woman friends when their affair became public. And she knew it would be a scandal that the gossips would get hold of sooner or later. Her position in the little town would become very difficult. But she decided that, in spite of the problems, her relationship with Otto gave her something she had never had before in her life, and it was worth keeping at all costs.

At Kitty's insistence Otto began keeping his best clothes at her place, and she took over the care of them. He would come to her before he went into Queenstown and, although he was already known as a dandy, people began to wonder how he managed to travel from Skippers over that dusty road and still arrive in town so spick-and-span in highly polished riding boots.

Kitty and Otto delighted in each other, but the need for money was always pressing. He suggested that they should clean up the only remaining back rooms of the old hotel and throw down some mattresses. He knew men from the upper Shotover who would happily pay to have somewhere to doss down for the night, because everywhere in Queenstown was so impossibly expensive, especially in summer. They did this, and it completed Kitty's fall from grace. In the eyes of the local gossips she went from having a lover to being the proprietress of a bawdy house and personally servicing her clients. It became customary for a group to come on a Saturday night and bring a few drinks. They would have a sing-song, and sometimes Griff would come and play his fiddle. Sometimes he would bring his Welsh harp and play and sing haunting folksongs from his homeland.

Some of the more charitable townswomen gave Kitty the benefit of the doubt. While unable to deny her relationship with Otto, they decided that considering her truly tragic life in Kinloch, she was a victim of circumstance and was perhaps more to be pitied than blamed. One of the kindest was Mary Jane Mullholland, the wife of the skipper of the *Ben Lomond*. Because of his daily trips to the Head of the Lake, he knew about Kitty's life with John Greig and told his wife. These few women continued to greet her if they passed her in the street, and they didn't tell their children to cross the road if they saw her coming. Her tragic life was either forgotten or ignored.

Kitty's siblings reacted in different ways. Florrie had continued to sing with Griff at dances and weddings. Romance had blossomed, and they were now engaged. Unfortunately, the gossip about Kitty's lifestyle was having an adverse effect on Florrie. Queenstown and Arrowtown are very close together, and the gossips were having a field day. Whenever she went into Arrowtown she saw women who smiled at her, but she heard them whispering behind their hands as soon as she had passed.

Morgan Griffiths had been a foreman at Bullendale for some years and, being very thrifty, he had put away a sizeable amount of money for the day he left the mine. He had intended to leave before his health packed up, and he knew he could make a good living from his music. When he fell in love with Florrie he knew his days at Bullendale were over. One of his intentions had been to buy himself a small holding somewhere in the Wakatipu for a home base. He was a romantic soul, and he was afraid that Florrie might think he just wanted her for her land. They talked endlessly about their future until Florrie was convinced that it could be an interesting life. Griff had enough money to keep them secure, and if they got tired of being wandering minstrels, they had a home to go to, and perhaps then they could think about having children. Griff was a countryman and didn't mind getting his hands dirty, or rather his gloves because he had to protect his hands for his music. He had been brought up a strict chapelgoer and wanted them to be married in Dunedin, where the nearest Welsh community was. They were getting ready to leave when Kitty came to call.

Kitty told her sister and her fiancé that she realised her own way of life was embarrassing to them and she would understand if they wanted to keep their distance in the future. They told her not to be silly, they were family and families stuck together. They didn't necessarily approve, but they were pleased for her sake that she was so happy.

It didn't worry Billy in the least, because he had always enjoyed being disreputable. Whenever he could he came to one of their soirées and joined in the fun. He liked Otto, although he told him that if he hurt Kitty he, Billy, would kill him in the most painful way he could think of at the time. Otherwise, he was very pleased for his sister to find love at last, glad to see her glowing with happiness.

Heather wrote to Kitty, telling her that she wished her all the luck in the world but she and Hamish, regretfully, were leaving the district. Their oldest boy was ready for high school. Apart from that, there was no longer enough work for Hamish as an inspector of mines. There was to be a farewell party for them, and she wanted Kitty and Otto to be there. There would be no unpleasantness from any of the women who had 'turned rancid', as she put it. She'd made sure that she'd seen to that. She'd told them that if they weren't prepared to be nice they were to stay away, it was as simple as that. That lovely newly-wed couple, Mr and Mrs Morgan Griffiths, had already accepted their invitation. Kitty and Otto needn't bother to reply — Heather would take it as a personal mortal insult if they didn't turn up. She said she had hoped to see them at the Queenstown Centennial Ball but fully understood why they hadn't been there, which was a pity because it was such a grand occasion.

Kitty decided to ride up to Skippers the day before the party. Otto met her at Long Gully, and they rode up together to Skippers and beyond to his hut. Kitty had been there before, and they had made it as homely as they could. Otto had brought in a bed that took up more than its fair share of floor space. The hut was a tiny structure that Otto kept meticulously tidy. He had built it to last, and it was as windproof and waterproof as he could possibly make it. Every newspaper he could lay his hands on had been glued to the interior walls and over the years had made a thick layer of insulation. A tiny stove kept the place cosy in the worst of winters. Kitty loved it, but she loved her place in Queenstown more, and it made sense for them to spend more time there, especially because the road was so often impassable when the snow was deep. And Queenstown was so much warmer.

Kitty and Otto enjoyed the party, and as Heather had promised, there was no unpleasantness. Speeches were made, and many of the miners told funny anecdotes about Hamish, most of which were far from flattering.

And of course there was music. Griff fiddled and was joined by a tiny white-haired and bearded Irishman called Johnnie. Heather and Florrie sang solos and duets and everyone in the hall joined in with the chorus of well-known melodies such as 'Goodbye Dolly Gray', the song made popular by the war currently being waged in South Africa. There was no room for dancing because the hall was packed, but to complete the Celtic trilogy, Hamish decided there was enough room for him to march around playing his bagpipes. He was magnificently dressed for the occasion in full Highland fig. Scotsmen outnumbered everyone else present by almost two to one, so he played for a bit longer than a lot of non-Scots would have liked. Hector, who had come up from Dunedin with his wife, resolutely kept his hands over his ears throughout the whole performance. Kitty told Hamish that she really liked the swing of his kilt but wished she could say the same for his music. It was a memorable evening.

Kitty hadn't seen Billy for a while but, as usual, he came and went. Apart from their continuing money problems Otto and Kitty were blissfully happy. Kitty had given Eve to Florrie and Griff as a wedding present, so there was one less horse to feed. Otto had sold his horse and now rode Mouse. He was spending as much time as he could with Kitty, and once when Billy was there, he remarked that they had settled down like a happy, old long-married couple. He said they fitted together like a well-worn pair of slippers.

One day late in 1903, a letter came from Lucy. She and Will had finished travelling and had bought land on the Otago Peninsula. Lucy and Kitty had kept up a correspondence ever since she and Will had left the Wakatipu. Lucy had enclosed two paper cuttings, one from the *Otago Daily Times* and one that had been sent to Lucy with no date or paper's identification on it. The first had been cut from the 'Births, Deaths and Marriages' column and announced the death of John Thomas Greig in Seacliff Hospital. It said that he was survived by his loving daughter Anne Elizabeth, who lived in Wellington. The second rather dog-eared cutting was from Ripley's 'Believe it or Not', which was a popular syndicated column originating in the United States. It was illustrated with a quirky little cartoon and featured one William Kirk, the only one-legged circus clown ever to be charged with assault for beating the Ringmaster over the head with his wooden leg. The crowd had applauded wildly, thinking it to be part of the show. The charges were dropped because the judge couldn't stop laughing.

Kitty had found herself a new source of employment. Fairlight, south of Kingston, was a small town set in fertile plains where grain was harvested in autumn after a prolific but short growing season. Kitty travelled on a boat to Kingston, then she caught a train to Fairlight where she was able to get work as a cook for a harvesting contractor. The work was seasonal, the hours were long and, worst of all, she was away from Otto. Fortunately, it was a good time for him to be working his claim.

Kitty was popular, not only for her cooking but also for her humour and the way she protected her helper, Molly, from the foreman, who was an animal. The days were long and the work was hard, but the pay was good and she was able to start the winter with money in her pocket. While she was away Otto was working his claim, and when he went to Queenstown he stayed at Kitty's place and stored up firewood for the winter.

Unfortunately, there was no longer any work available for Kitty in Queenstown, but in spring Kitty often got work cooking for a shearing gang that covered a large district, reaching from Kinleith as far as Gore. Between the two of them she and Otto managed to live moderately well. Kitty and Otto hated being apart, but unfortunately they needed money to survive.

When they were home the Saturday parties brought in money too. The miners paid for their bed space, and Kitty had told them if they brought food she would cook it for them. She was a very good cook, so they jumped at the chance of a good meal and they always brought a surplus. They brought drink as well. Otto was a moderate drinker, and Kitty didn't drink at all, but there was never any drink left over. The gossips referred to the miners as Kitty's 'gentlemen callers', and of course they thought the worst.

Billy came and went. He always sent bags of oats, and when he came on horseback his saddlebags were always stuffed full of human luxuries. When Kitty told him that she was now a widow, he replied laconically, 'Good'. When she asked him about the Ripley story, he laughed and told her that it was years old and now he was home to stay. One day he would tell her his life story, but at present he was still too busy living it. No matter how hard she quizzed him he resolutely refused to answer any questions about his love-life because, he said, he didn't want to get into trouble. He was now centred in Alexandra, and he was back in the racing business. He rejoiced that Otto had brought his sister lasting happiness.

One unforgettable day in 1906 when Kitty was busy in the kitchen at Fairlight, she looked up to see the usually jaunty Billy standing there. He was white-faced and looked as if the world had come to an end.

'Good God, Billy,' Kitty exclaimed, 'What's the matter? You look like death warmed up!'

He held his hands out to her and said, 'Kitty, I have bad news, I don't know how to tell you this...'

'Not Otto, please, not Otto!' she cried beseechingly.

Billy stepped around the table and took her in his arms. Molly stood with her hands clapped to her mouth.

'I'm so sorry, Sis, there's no easy way to tell you. Otto's dead.'

'No!' Kitty shrieked and, for the first and last time in her life, she fainted.

Billy was picking her up from the floor when the foreman came blustering in. 'Who the bloody hell are you?' he demanded of Billy. 'What's all the ruckus about?'

'Bad news, I'm afraid.' He deposited Kitty on a chair. 'Kitty's man has died. I'm taking her home.'

'No, you're bloody not. She's under contract. Where the hell do you think I can get another cook at short notice. So, her fancy man has died. Tough. It's not as if he was her husband. Well, she can just pull herself together and get on with the job I'm paying her for. And you can get out, you bloody runt, right now.'

Billy's fist shot out. His second punch caught the man on his way down, and he stayed down. Billy told him he could do his own bloody cooking and, picking up the still unconscious Kitty, he carried her across to the station. The train was about to pull out, but they were just in time. Once on the train, Billy worked to revive his sister. After wondering for a moment where she was, she looked at Billy.

'It's not true, Billy, please tell me it's not true! He's only sixty-one. It can't be true.' Billy just looked at her with tears in his eyes and held her closer.

She began to sob, heart-breaking sobs that seemed to Billy as though they would tear her apart. When they arrived at Kingston they boarded the boat, which had been waiting for the train. Billy got Kitty seated and went and got cups of tea. He tried to feed hers to her because she seemed incapable of coordinating her limbs.

'The funeral, I have to say goodbye to him… When… how?'

'Oh, Kitty, he died on his claim, down by his workings. Nobody missed him for a few days. The doctor says it was a heart attack. They had to have the funeral right away. He's in Skippers Cemetery. No one knew where you were. When Griff heard he came down to Alex to tell me, and I got here as quickly as I could. Sis, I'm so, so sorry.'

'Billy, we only had ten years, only ten years. It's not fair, it's just not fair. He had been complaining of indigestion.' She convulsed again. 'We joked about it being my cooking.' She sobbed and spilt the now-cold tea.

Billy pulled a flask from his pocket. 'Kitty, I know you don't, but this is medicinal. Nothing will bring him back, but this will numb you a bit.' She swallowed and gagged.

'I remember the taste. You made me drink it when the girls… Oh Billy, why must I lose the people I love? Don't you ever leave me. Why can't it be me who dies? I can't stand it anymore.' She had another sip or two from the flask, then, worn out, she fell asleep.

Kitty now lived a life of despair. When Billy wasn't there she was desperately lonely. The 'gentlemen callers' still came and still prevailed on her to cook for them. Apart from the charge for the bed, they left food and drink. The atmosphere was friendly but not convivial. Kitty moved like an efficient automaton but it was as if there was no life in her. The men were sympathetic and helped as much as they could by doing small chores. They, too, had lost a good friend in Otto.

When Griff offered to accompany Kitty up to Skippers to say goodbye at his grave and to pick up Mouse, she told him that Otto wasn't at Skippers; he was here with her, all of her waking hours. She told Griff that she would like Mouse to go to him and Florrie because she now needed only one horse. She didn't tell him she had trouble getting to sleep and was starting to rely on the alcohol the 'gentlemen callers' left.

One night when Billy was with her, he said to her, 'Kitty, you can't go on like this. You say that Otto is with you all the time. If that's so what would he think of you now? He told me that he loved you because of your energy and resilience. Where is that now? You are fifty-two years old and healthy. You could live for years yet. He wouldn't want you to give up. I'm not telling you to forget him; I know you can't do that, but for God's sake, pull yourself together and be the woman he would want you to be.'

Kitty was weeping softly. 'I'm sorry, Billy, I'm getting like Ma, am I not? Crying all the time. I'm no company for you. I think it's time for bed.'

'You've got something to cry for, Kitty. Ma used tears as a weapon to get Pa to do what she wanted. There's a world of difference. Bed's a good idea. I'll make a cup of tea.'

'I don't want a cup of tea. I'll just have a wee dram to help me sleep.'

Billy grabbed the bottle. 'Listen, Sis, you've had quite enough "wee drams" tonight. If I didn't know you so well I'd think you were turning into a soak. Now, we'll have a cup of tea, both of us.'

In bed Kitty tossed and turned for a while, then tiptoed out to the kitchen. Billy had hidden the bottle and had left his door open. In the morning before he left, he said to her, 'I don't have the right to preach to you, nobody does. A nightcap is fine, but you and me, we don't have big enough bodies to be able to take too much booze. I know I was a piss-head when I was young, but I learned the hard way. If I want to keep riding I have to keep fit. So for as long as I have to earn a living, I'll have to go easy on the booze. It's an expensive habit, Kitty. Don't let it get you.' And he rode away.

Kitty tried to pull herself together. She was surviving, but she knew she would have to earn some money. She wrote to the manager of the harvesting company, explaining why she had broken her contract. He wrote a sympathetic letter saying he was sorry to hear of her sad loss and said she would always be very welcome. He added that Billy's confrontation with the foreman had been seen and heard and the gang had refused to work with him any longer.

They had given him hell about picking a fight with a helpless wee runt and having no sympathy for Kitty. While he was down Molly had tipped a big pot of soup over him and the men laughed about that. He had managed to leave just before he was sacked, then he had the cheek to write a letter asking for a reference.

So Kitty had a job, starting in two months time. She did her best to limit her boozing, but without much success. She repeated to herself all the warnings her mother had given her about the drink, and she had to admit that Ma had been absolutely right except that Kitty didn't get violent when she'd had too much. She remembered her life with John Greig, the damage alcohol had done to him and to their relationship. She told herself that she wasn't really that bad, she just liked the bit of warmth it gave her and she could give it up if she really wanted to, perhaps when she went back to work.

Then came the dreadful Sunday after a particularly lively Saturday night. She woke up realising there was someone in bed with her. She shut herself in the bathroom and scoured herself with soap and freezing water. She couldn't wash away how bad she felt, how disgusted she felt with herself. When the man came out of the bedroom Kitty felt worse, much worse. She knew him of course. His name was Peter, and he had been a friend of both hers and Otto's, but she had no recollection of the previous night. It got worse still when he spoke.

'Kitty, thank you for a wonderful night. I've never had anything like it. I couldn't believe it when you came on to me. You are an absolutely amazing woman!' He came towards her to take her in his arms and kiss her. She cringed away and muttered brokenly, 'Otto.'

Peter stepped back. 'Oh God, I'm sorry Kitty. You and he had something really special. I guess it might be a bit too soon. We were both pretty sozzled last night, and gin is well known for making you randy. But Otto wouldn't want you to stay miserable. I'll go now. I promise I'll never push myself on you, but it would be great if you could... I'm going now. I'll see you next Friday.'

In the morning Kitty left for Fairlight.

The Eighth Life
Fairlight 1907

Chapter Eight

When she was on the boat she sat outside, punishing herself by sitting in the coldest spot she could find. When she was on the train the rhythm of the wheels repeated in her head, *What have I done, what have I done?* and *How could I do it? How could I do it? Otto, I'm sorry, Otto, I'm sorry*, all the way to Fairlight.

As soon as she arrived she went to find the contractor to see about starting early. He wasn't home, and his wife asked Kitty in for a cup of tea and a scone. To her delight Molly was busy in the kitchen washing dishes and was as pleased to see Kitty as Kitty was to see her. Molly launched into a story about how she had expected to be sacked after she had wasted a pot of soup just as the men were coming in, but they were all laughing so much because they had seen wee Billy flatten that big man, and they laughed even harder when she tipped the soup all over him and he sat up with all those carrots in his hair. The men had been lovely to her and kept the foreman off her. Some of them even hugged her and kissed her. They didn't even mind that there was no dinner. They just got into the cupboards and ate everything they could find and made a terrible mess.

Kitty really didn't want to hear about that day.

Molly said she had been that afraid of getting sacked because she'd wasted a good pot of soup, but Mr and Mrs P. had been that nice. She and Mrs P. had cleaned up the kitchen, then together they had done the cooking until the end of the season. The men hadn't complained once, not even when Molly forgot to put the soda in the duff and it came out like a soggy, pimply black rock.

When Molly drew breath Audrey Patterson took over and added that the custard that she had tried to make to go with the duff was full of lumps and she had also forgotten to put in the sugar. The season had been almost over, and the men were wonderful. One, nicknamed 'Sailor', actually admitted that he had been a cook at sea and came forward to help.

It was just wonderful having Kitty back early so she could do the ordering and stocking up. Audrey wanted to learn how to do it and how to cook and cater in case there was another emergency. Then she realised what she had said and flushed scarlet. She kept wringing her hands and apologising until Kitty quietly asked her to stop and also asked her if they could please move ahead and leave the past behind.

Trying to lighten things up, Kitty told Audrey that she didn't think it appropriate to have the boss's wife as an apprentice, because she insisted on being the boss of her own kitchen and apprentices had to do as they were told. However, if Audrey accepted the situation, she was to get paper and pencils and they would start on the stocktaking right now. Molly, who was illiterate, was to start scrubbing out all the bins and cupboards and tomorrow, when the cupboards were done, she could start on the floors. When there was time Kitty or Audrey would be teaching her to read and figure.

Molly was an orphanage child who, last year at the age of fifteen, had been dumped out, taken to an employment agency and left there. She was lucky that the Pattersons were soft-hearted (or soft-headed as Walter muttered) because when the agency closed for the day she was turned out on the street. The Pattersons took her home. The only thing she had learned to do at the orphanage was clean, and she was slow but useful. But she was a cheerful soul who actually enjoyed cleaning, so they employed her.

Walter Patterson managed three harvest gangs and wanted to start managing his own harvest contracting business, and the time was right because his current employer wanted to sell up and retire. After talking to his wife he realised that Kitty's turning up at this time was serendipitous. He and Audrey could learn from her all the ins and outs of provisioning and food storage and what they needed to look for when employing a cook. To make the business less seasonal they hoped to manage shearing gangs as well. They became aware that Kitty had a drinking problem, but since it didn't interfere with her work they ignored it. Someone had told them all cooks drank, were fat or both. And most of them helped themselves from the stores. So Kitty drank, so what? They knew her as honest and very capable.

Kitty took charge of the provisioning and the cooking, and Molly learned to write her own name. She learned to read by learning the labels on everything. It became the most orderly kitchen that Kitty had ever worked in, and Audrey was an enthusiastic apprentice. If containers were faulty Audrey had them replaced. By the time work started all the containers were painted the same colour and clearly labelled, the floors and benches were scrubbed white, the chimney was swept and the stove and sink were gleaming. The standard of cleanliness and maintenance was extended to the workers' accommodation, which had a common room built next to the kitchen. Walter had built a veranda to provide some shelter where they could clean up before meals.

When some of the old hands arrived back they greeted Kitty with enthusiasm and pretended to groan when they saw Audrey and Molly in the kitchen, but they were delighted with the improvement in their quarters. The next morning a large sign reading *Buckinhum Place* appeared on the common room door. The improvement in living conditions led to an improvement in productivity.

This was the home base for the Pattersons, and there was enough work on neighbouring farms to keep them busy for most of the season. Then it became necessary for the gangs to move on to farms where the conditions were not so salubrious. The men were housed in shearers' quarters, which often hadn't been cleaned out since the previous occupants had left.

Sometimes it was uncomfortable for Kitty's kitchen gang, because they were working in the farm kitchen and the farmer's wife was in charge. Most of them were easy going and were happy to have Kitty take over and enjoyed the company of the other women. Others thought that Audrey was demeaning herself by playing second fiddle in the kitchen or even thought she shouldn't be there at all and were downright rude to her. When it got too much Kitty suggested Audrey should stay home and Sailor should again be put on kitchen duties. Perhaps he could be trained to take on a cooking job instead of a being a labourer. If the Pattersons' plans progressed as they wished, they would need more gangs and more cooks.

One woman was such a martinet that they nicknamed her 'The Dragon' only to find later that that's what her husband called her behind her back. She insisted that she was the boss and it was her kitchen and had to be run her way. Her recipes were the only ones to be used. The kitchen gang was to do everything her way or they would be fired. Kitty told Audrey and Molly to keep their mouths shut and do exactly what they were told and not one thing more. She herself would be doing the same. They could forget about the threat of being fired, because only Walter or Audrey could fire them and would Audrey be likely to fire herself? She said that you had to learn to take the bad with the good, because life wasn't always going to be easy. Molly had been abused in the orphanage but was having a good life with the Pattersons. She owed it to them to work without complaint, because they were giving her a home as well as a job, and the bad jobs lasted no longer than a week.

They did as Kitty had said. They did only the minimum, and one day when the Dragon forgot to tell Kitty to bake the bread, there was no bread. Kitty said she was sorry, but she had not been told to do it, so she hadn't done it. What did the boss lady want her to do now?

'Just do something, Kitty,' she said. 'And from now on make the bread every morning.' Kitty replied icily that her name was 'Mrs Greig' and 'Kitty' was only for friends and family. She was scrupulously polite and asked the Dragon if she had a recipe for Irish soda bread, because they could have it ready for the midday meal. The Dragon had never heard of it.

Kitty made herself comfortable on a chair. She asked politely what the Dragon would like them to cook, as time was getting on. Would she please supply the recipes? The Dragon was furious.

'I haven't time to teach you to cook,' she snarled. 'Do what you like. It was your laziness that caused this problem, so you can fix it. Try to make something edible, and make sure you have it ready on time.' She stalked out. And of course, she was right. Working to rule had given them plenty of time to sit around. Kitty had talked to the men about their problem, complaining because the kitchen staff couldn't join the union unless they were men.

Sailor made the soda bread, and Kitty whipped up some pies from leftovers while Molly boiled potatoes to mash. There was no time to make the usual duff, but Audrey found some stale bread and whipped up a bread and butter pudding, which the men drenched with golden syrup and voted the best pudding ever.

The men were very vocal if their conditions were bad, and if their food was not up to the standard they had become used to, their productivity suffered accordingly. Patterson tried to explain this to the farmers who hired him, and a surprising number listened. One even suggested that he would employ a cleaning gang to sort out the accommodation before his men arrived. The man married to the Dragon said he, too, would happily pay for the service. He said it was a pity about the missus, but if he had to put up with her and her food, so would they. She had complained to him that Kitty didn't know her place and she didn't want her back next year. Walter said that Kitty had complained to him that the kitchen was badly stocked, badly equipped and not as clean as it should be. Her suggestion was that either Walter's gang should do the provisioning and the cleaning before the start of the season or the Dragon should hire her own kitchen gang and do the job herself.

The day of the soda bread the men were delighted with the meal and said so. They said they were happy Kitty had got back into her stride and they could stop complaining about the food. The Dragon, who had come to watch what she had thought was going to be a debacle, slipped out without a word. She couldn't leave it at that. Later she commented to Kitty that she thought only her family and friends were allowed to call her 'Kitty'. Kitty smiled her sweetest smile and said that they were all her friends. The Dragon fired her for impertinence. The kitchen staff downed tools, and when the men heard they downed tools too. All of them went back to work when Walter told the Dragon's husband to keep his wife out of the kitchen. When the season was over Kitty went back to Queenstown with money in the bank and a firm contract for next season.

She found her house clean and tidy, and there was enough firewood stacked to last her a year or more. Some of the gentlemen callers had been staying there while she was away, and the crock where she kept her money was full. Kitty had never taken money from them, they had always put it directly in the crock. But to Kitty the house was empty. Otto wasn't there.

The Saturday parties started again, and once again Kitty sometimes found herself with company in her bed in the morning. She felt that her body was betraying her in finding so much pleasure in something that had been so precious during her years with Otto. She knew that she could regain control only if she stopped drinking, and she always meant to do it but somehow she just couldn't manage it. Every wee dram was going to be the last but never was. Her self-respect was dwindling, too, but there was always money in the crock. She drank less when she was at Fairlight, but she was finding it harder to get through the days.

Early in the harvest season of 1910 Kitty met Teddy Jeffrey. He had been well known around Fairlight for some time, doing odd jobs around farms and any casual work wherever and whenever he could get it. He was a handsome, red-moustached character, a 'gentleman', obviously much come down in the world but still speaking with a posh accent. He was a self-confessed ship deserter, seemingly proud of it, who said he had never been caught because he had deserted from the *Maori,* and on her next voyage back to New Zealand, she was wrecked off Stanhope in South Africa. Something didn't quite add up, but that was his story.

Somehow or other he had found his way to Fairlight, where he had become known for his plausibility and his lack of truthfulness. He was a good worker who had found work on many of the local farms until he was well known, and his reputation made it hard to find work that would provide live-in accommodation. One of the farmers dubbed him 'a gradual thief' because if he saw anything that took his fancy, he would move it several feet. If the owner didn't notice that it had moved, Teddy would move it again. It would take him a week or so to get it to the boundary of the property, and then he would spirit it away. His victims became aware of this and would let him go through the whole process and then move it back just before it got to the boundary fence. Teddy would then start all over again with another quarry. Later they might discover that while they were playing this game, Teddy was actually getting away with something else altogether. And they couldn't prove a thing.

When Teddy had made himself unemployable in Fairlight, he had applied for and got a job as a roadman for the Lake County Council in Queenstown, and that's when he started paying attention to Kitty. He had heard that she owned property there. She was several years older than he was and from a completely different background. Although she had been away from her mother for decades, her speech still held traces of Catherine's native accent. Kitty's detractors said she spoke with 'a rough sort of a burr', while those who were more kindly disposed towards her said she had 'a delightful Irish accent'. She got on well with men, largely because she could make them laugh and she was generous and broad-minded. What she lacked in good looks she made up for in personality.

When he wanted to, Teddy could be absolutely charming, and he wanted to charm Kitty. He laid it on hot and strong with flattery and little gifts. People tried to warn her, but she said that she had always liked stroppy chestnuts.

That winter at home was a disaster. She was lonelier than ever and fell back onto her by-now-well-travelled path of Saturday parties, too much to drink and someone in her bed in the morning. Her self-respect plummeted, and that made her drink even more. She still managed to keep herself and her house clean, but her living expenses were higher than before because though the gentlemen callers were generous, her cash-flow struggled to keep up with her drinking habit.

In the spring Kitty went south again to cook for a shearing gang. Teddy was again in pursuit, and they were married in Lumsden on the 10 November 1910. On the wedding certificate Kitty's age was given as forty-nine, Teddy's forty-two. She was actually fifty-five.

As soon as they got back to Queenstown a life of hell began for Kitty. Teddy began by accusing her of pretending to have a house when all she had was a hovel. Kitty's house was far from being a hovel. It was small but snug and comfortable. It was well furnished and well cared for, but Teddy had obviously expected something a lot grander, and he took his disappointment out on Kitty.

'Do you think I'd have married you had I known that this was what you thought was a house? I expected a roof over my head, and instead I got a lean-to against a ruin.'

'You said you loved me,' said Kitty miserably. 'You told me we could make each other happy.'

Teddy laughed. 'Not a very good start to a marriage when both the bride and the groom lied, is it? Look at yourself, woman. What is there about you for a man to love? You were lucky to get me. I was born to better than this. Now, I expect you to keep me in comfort, because I've made an honest woman of you. Let's have a drink.'

Kitty realised then that she had made the worst mistake of her troubled life.

There was a knock at the door and Kitty opened it to admit two of her old friends. She stood back to let them in, but before she could introduce them Teddy demanded, 'Who the hell might you be, coming in here as if you owned the place?'

Taken aback, they said that they were old friends of Kitty's and they had just come by to offer their congratulations because they had heard of her marriage. 'Well,' Teddy said, 'Now you've done that you can take yourselves off, and tell any of your scruffy friends that none of you are welcome here. I've heard about what used to go on here, and things are different now. Kitty, show them out and then fetch my slippers and pour me another drink. And be quick about it.'

A woebegone Kitty, tears streaming down her face, whispered her goodbyes as she showed them the door. Teddy told her that if any of that lot came back, he'd take it out on her hide. He told her she'd better be afraid of him, because he had a way of dealing with whores and he had heard the gossip in town about her and how she had supported herself. When she asked him what he meant by that, he told her she knew very well what he was talking about and she should think about the date he had left England. Had she heard of Jack the Ripper? Did she realise that there had been no more Ripper murders since Teddy's departure from London? The police were starting to get a bit close, so Teddy went to sea and accidentally fetched up in New Zealand. So she knew just what would happen to her if she went back to her old ways, or if she told anyone else what he had just told her. And to prove he was telling the truth, every night he would tell her some of the gory details of each case.

Occasionally, Teddy would invite some of his friends to call and Kitty would have to wait on them like a maid. Their evenings on their own were spent drinking. Kitty lived in terror and drank more and more. On 13 November 1911, she spent the night in police cells charged with being found drunk in a public place. She was described as being Irish, five foot four tall, with dark hair and complexion and aged fifty-four. She was fined ten shillings.

Again, on the sixth of June, she was found drunk in Camp Street and fined five shillings. Often after that, friends would look out for her so they could pick her up and take her home before the police found her.

In 1913 Teddy was found guilty of the same offence, but he was only convicted and discharged without being fined. Kitty pondered over the injustice of that. Why did it cost more to be a drunk woman than to be a drunk man?

Kitty had the days to herself. As well as his work as a roadman for the Lake District County Council, Teddy did yard cleaning and gardening for some of the local hotels. For this he was paid 'in kind', which happened to be bottles of the cheapest (and worst) grog they stocked. One of the publicans explained that he was saving his time and Teddy's money, because if he (the publican) paid Teddy in cash, he would get the money back anyway. This way Teddy would get his grog cheaper because he would be getting it wholesale. How's that for an example of convoluted logic? One good thing (possibly the only good thing) about Teddy was that he was generous with his liquor and prepared to share it with anyone who would share it with him, which, of course, included Kitty. Liquor and tobacco took most of their money. Kitty didn't smoke, but Teddy smoked enough for two. He also favoured sweet and highly alcoholic cough mixture, which didn't seem to do much for his cough.

What Kitty enjoyed most during the days when Teddy was at work was the company of children. On the other side of the road from her home was a large flat rock where little girls loved to play. Kitty, seeing them there, would go and join them, bringing bread and jam and a pot of tea.

Little Winnie Mulholland told her mother, 'Mrs Jeffrey said she was sorry that there was no butter or milk, but we could have as much sugar as we liked. She told us that our mothers wouldn't like it if she invited us into her house but would we invite her onto our rock? She's lovely, but some of the girls are nasty about her. Vicky said her mother calls Mrs Jeffrey "an old horse" and that's stupid. How can a person be a horse?'

'That's very rude of Vicky's mother,' her mother answered, smothering a smile. 'You must never call a lady a horse. You must always be polite to Mrs Jeffrey, because she has had a very sad life. Once upon a time she had children of her own, but they all died before they were properly grown-up, and that's why she likes being with you.' It was some years before Winnie understood why it was rude to call a woman a horse.

Then the war began, the Great War. It was horrible, but it was the war to end war, and the filthy Huns had to be beaten or there could never be peace on earth. It didn't make sense to Kitty why New Zealanders had to go halfway round the world and fight against the Turks to try to take their country off them when it was the Germans that had to be punished for marching into Belgium, raping nuns and sticking bayonets into babies. Teddy told her to shut up; women didn't have the brains to understand politics, and why the New Zealand government had given women the vote didn't bear thinking about. Thank goodness the British government had more sense. At least the New Zealand government had started the war by taking Sāmoa off the Germans.

'Why does Sāmoa have to belong to us or the Germans? Why can't it belong to Sāmoans?'

'Because they're natives, you stupid bitch. Now they're part of the British Empire they'll be a lot better off. They'll learn to work instead of lying round in the sun all day. I ought to have more sense than to try to explain this stuff to a bloody woman. There's not a brain in the whole tribe of you. Pour us a drink.'

Then came 1915 and Gallipoli. One night sixteen-year-old Winnie Mulholland answered a knock on the door. 'Mother,' she said, 'it's Mrs Jeffrey. She's crying. She won't come in.' Her mother who was also crying, went out.

Kitty sobbed. 'I had to come and say how sorry I am about Jimmy. He was such a lovely young boy. I know what it's like to lose a child and never to be able to say goodbye. They stay with you forever in your heart and mind. You never lose the good bits and the funny bits.' The two women hugged and wept together, and then Kitty disappeared into the dark. Teddy didn't allow her out at night. Although he kept taunting her about her physical appearance, he said he couldn't trust her, because of her immoral past. This night she had managed to sneak out because he was in a drunken stupor.

Teddy was not very well. His cough was constant. Sometimes eating made him ill and then he accused Kitty of poisoning him. He had started drinking before breakfast 'to get myself ready for work'. Often he forgot to eat breakfast. He came home in the evening full of tales about how obnoxious his workmates were and how the boss had a downer on him. Kitty thought he was ill, because his skin had a sort of yellowish cast to it and he never stopped coughing. In order to get some sleep she moved out of the marital bed, but if he woke up he ordered her back. Even an enfeebled Teddy could still manage to terrify Kitty.

One day in 1916 when the gang was working on Frankton Road, Teddy collapsed. One of his workmates put him in a wheelbarrow and wheeled him the two miles to the hospital. He was never to come out again. Kitty walked over to Florrie's and reclaimed Sauce so that she could be the dutiful wife and visit him for the few weeks he had left. It said on his death certificate that the cause of death had been lung cancer. Even dead, he was not finished with Kitty. She was sent a bill for the time he spent in hospital. Some sympathetic person or persons, she never found out who, paid it for her because she had no income and no money. Again she had to rely on her gentlemen callers.

This was an era when often quite vicious tricks of a personal nature were laughed off as 'practical jokes'. No matter if the victims couldn't defend themselves or the following gossip was cruel and malicious, it was still considered to be a joke and laughed about, sometimes for years.

A few nights before he was to be married, a young man who was engaged to a girl from Arthurs Point was taken on the town for the customary stag night. As soon as his mates got him drunk and unconscious, they took him out to Kitty's and propped him up against her gate where his fiancée and her family saw him when they were on their way into town the next morning. The indignant young woman thought the worst, and the wedding was off. The young man's friends finally called on her and apologetically told the whole story. After much begging and pleading the marriage took place, and people sniggered over it for years. Of course no one considered Kitty's feelings.

Some time later, there was a delicious scandal. Of course the gossips enjoyed laying the blame on Kitty. The husband of one of the town's most sanctimonious and straight-laced harridans was found dead in a ditch between Kitty's place and town. There were 'no suspicious circumstances', he was elderly and had died of a heart attack. Then someone started a rumour that sped faster than any wildfire. True or not, it was said that he was one of Kitty's regular callers. Nobody liked the harridan, and the men said that he had been driven to Kitty by his horrible wife. (You did know that it's not only women who gossip?) And what a delicious piece of scandal it was! It didn't do Kitty any good at all, but as always there were some kind women who were prepared to give her the benefit of the doubt.

Since the war began Billy had had a well-paid job travelling the south of the South Island, buying up remounts for the army. The owners had no choice. They had to let their animals go and accept the going rate no matter what their animals were actually worth. Kitty asked why the army wanted horses when all the actual fighting was being done in the deep mud of the trenches. Billy said he didn't know and he didn't much like it. There were some New Zealand and Australian cavalry units fighting in some Arab countries somewhere, but he didn't know anything about that. He didn't like the job much, but it had sounded pretty good when he was appointed to it. He knew he would never be conscripted, because a one-legged dwarf wouldn't be much use as a soldier. Besides, he was fifty. Being appointed to the job was as near as dammit to being conscripted anyway. Except that the pay was a lot better.

There was one good reason for keeping the job. The army wanted stallions for officers' mounts, and Billy thought that could weaken the local breeding stock. When he went to a farm or station looking for suitable horses, he went alone, and when he had bought a reasonable number he would send a team to pick them up. If he spotted a really good animal he suggested to the owner that it should be hidden away or made to look lame with a bit of really bad shoeing. The deceit had to be kept secret, of course, or Billy might lose his job and someone less accommodating might be appointed.

The war ended in November 1918, and in early 1919 every town had its victory parade. Queenstown was no exception. Florrie drove proudly over to Kitty's in her new Model T Ford. She was accompanied by Morgan (Florrie had always preferred to call him that), Billy and her two children. It wasn't their first car, and she was very proud of her ability to drive. It said a lot for Morgan as a husband that he was happy to sit back and let his wife take the wheel. Billy said they had a surprise for Kitty. He brought in a beautiful grey velvet riding habit, which Florrie had sat up all night altering to fit Kitty. He also had a sidesaddle and a flag. Morgan had an Australian digger's hat perched on his unruly Welsh curls. The hat would complete Kitty's outfit.

'Now, Kitty my girl, you are going to ride in the Victory Parade tomorrow. It's time you pulled yourself together and showed a bit of spirit again,' Billy said.

'I can't, I just can't. I'm afraid to show myself in town. I'm so ashamed of what I've become.' Kitty wept.

'You can and you will. You will hold your head up again and look 'em in the eye. A mate of mine is going to ride with you. I'm going to groom old Sauce and Florrie's going to groom you. Him next door is lending me a horse, and I'll be somewhere behind you.'

Florrie put in: 'I didn't sit up all night sewing for nothing, Sis. We will also be following with all the other cars. The kids are looking forward to it, and you aren't going to let the family down. Billy and I will be staying here tonight. Morgan and the kids are going home, but they'll be back first thing. Now we'll light the fire under the copper because we'll all want baths. I'll start on your hair and Billy can get us something to eat.'

'There's nothing in the house,' said Kitty miserably.

'Oh yes, there is,' said Billy, carrying in a box. 'I've been where you are, Sis. You want a drink and you have trouble forcing food down. Well, I know you can't go cold turkey; you can have a drink, and you are jolly well going to eat, even I have to spoon feed you. I'll pour you a drink, have one with you, and then you'll stop fidgeting and let Florrie get on with your hair. No argument.'

To celebrate the end of hostilities, a dignified and magnificent procession was staged. The Garrison Band led the march of veterans, many of whom were on crutches or had lost an arm. It was too soon after the Armistice for the main body of troops to have come home, so nearly all of those taking part in the parade had been wounded in some way. The uniformed men were followed by the proud Boy Scouts and Wolf Cubs. Then came the Mayor and councillors in their best black suits. After their initial surprise the Boer War veterans had welcomed Kitty into their ranks, and she felt good about herself for the first time in years. They were followed by other horsemen and finally the Highland Pipe Band. The motor vehicles, covered in bunting, followed at a discreet distance so they wouldn't frighten the horses. Kitty thought privately that the horses were more likely to be frightened by the bagpipes, but there was no drama. Many of the women among the spectators were weeping. It was an unforgettable day of unforgettable memories. Kitty badly needed a drink.

After the parade when Kitty and Billy were sitting at the table having something to eat and a strictly rationed drink, Billy told Kitty that she really had to pull herself together. He accused her of neglecting her horse and not even noticing that he was past it and had to be retired before he fell down under her. She protested that he was only twenty and should be good for another five years, considering how little work he was expected to do. Billy shook his head and told her to wake up, the poor old bugger was thirty, not twenty, and showing every year of it. He would have to be retired, as of right now. Kitty said she couldn't be without a horse – how else could she get about? She went to bed in tears, and Billy knew she had a bottle somewhere.

Sauce solved the problem himself. The next morning he was found dead in the paddock. The excitement of the parade must have been too much for him. Billy rode into town to make arrangements for the disposal of the body, having flatly refused Kitty's strident demands for him to bury him where he lay. He returned some hours later, driving a small light vehicle with solid rubber wheels, known locally as a jogger. It was drawn by a large chestnut pony similar to those Kitty had owned in her heyday. His own horse was tied on behind. Kitty again berated him for not burying Sauce. He later learned that she had flown into a frenzy and had to be restrained when the knackers came to pick up the carcase.

Poor Billy's patience was wearing very thin. 'Here,' he said. 'Put this away. The pony's name is Copper, but he's called Coppy. Make sure you look after him better than you looked after poor old Sauce. Some feed will be arriving tomorrow. And don't start going on about choosing your own horse. You haven't the money to buy one, so you can just bloody well put up with what I'm lending you. The rig is light enough for you to handle, so you can put it away now, yourself. Now, "Thank you, Billy," would be nice. I'm going in to get myself a cuppa and something to eat.'

Billy stayed with Kitty for as long as he could and tried to talk her out of drinking so much, but like all alcoholics who are monitored, she had become cunning and devised hiding places for her bottles in places Billy would never think to look. He knew she was stealing money from him, and of course she denied it. He never found out where the rest of the bottles came from. But she did thank him profusely, promising that yes, she would stop drinking.

Unfortunately, Billy had to leave. Officially, he was still employed by the army, and he had to report back. There was endless paperwork to be got through before his war was over. Those owners whose horses had been requisitioned had been told that they would be able to buy them back if they had survived the war, and a few of them had survived. This made for endless correspondence. None of the horses that had been in service in the Light Horse Brigade in the Middle East had come home. Many years later Billy met an embittered trooper who had served in that theatre of war and was disgusted to learn that although the men had been told they would be able to bring their horses home, before they embarked they were ordered to shoot them. They had to obey orders.

In 1919 a grand new stone bridge had been built over the Shotover at Arthurs Point. It was startlingly modern, and the only one in New Zealand like it was the Grafton Bridge in Auckland.

Although it was considered to be a marvel of modern engineering, it had a timeless beauty about it, and the inhabitants of the Wakatipu were right to be proud of their bridge. The Spanish Flu hit the district hard, coming so soon after the terrible losses from the war, and it had been decided that something was needed to raise people's spirits, at least a little. The bridge was definitely something worth celebrating, and the best way to celebrate would be another grand parade.

Florrie and family turned up again to get Kitty and Coppy ready to go but, unfortunately, Billy hadn't yet been discharged from the army and his long drawn out paper trail was far from finished, so he wasn't available to help cope with the alcohol problem. The family had decided that Morgan should stay the night to attempt to monitor the drinking, because they thought he would carry more authority with Kitty than Florrie would.

It worked, but his strategy was rather brutal. Instead of letting her go off to bed with her bottle, he persuaded her to eat at least some of the succulent meal that Florrie had left for them, then he started reminiscing about Otto. As a result Kitty cried herself to sleep instead of drinking herself to sleep. Morgan carried her in to her bed and tucked her in, then, knowing that she would wake in the night and come looking for a drink, he bedded himself down on the couch.

Kitty came creeping by sometime in the early hours to go

outside to the loo, and by the time she had come in, Morgan had lit the lamp and was sitting at the table with a half-full bottle of wine, and some bread and cheese.

'Hello, Kitty,' he greeted her. 'I just felt like a wee snack and a wee drinkie. If you'd like to join me, have a bite to eat while I sort out some glasses. You wouldn't want us to drink out of the bottle, now would you? Eat up. I still haven't finished talking to you about dear old Otto.'

After about half an hour he was able to put her to bed again. He put an empty bottle against her door so that it would fall over if the door was opened, then he went back to his couch and was able to enjoy several hours of sound sleep.

Early in the morning, when the Model T pulled up outside the gate, Coppy was tied up in the yard and Morgan was making porridge. When Florrie asked where Kitty was, Morgan told her that Kitty was still in bed asleep. Florrie gasped and asked how on earth he had managed that. He replied that all it took was a bit of Welsh cunning. Just then Kitty came out, rubbing her eyes and looking for a drink. Morgan told her to sit down at the table and eat her porridge while he went to get her one. He also said that she needn't try to dump the porridge, because Florrie would be watching her. 'No eat, no drink,' he said sternly. She ate.

The parade was starting in Queenstown and finishing at the bridge not far from the Arthurs Point Hotel. Kitty wore the same outfit as she had worn for the Armistice Parade. Coppy had a more stolid temperament than Sauce and took everything in his stride. He was very willing but saw no reason why he should cavort and show off. He did what he was asked but with no frills. When Kitty joined the other riders at Queenstown, the men gave a cheer to welcome her, and someone called out, 'Good on yer, Kitty.' Some of them would doubtless have to answer to their wives later, but most men were much more tolerant of Kitty's lifestyle than the women were.

The parade formed just as it had for the Armistice Parade. There were many more returned soldiers but many old familiar faces were absent because of the terrible death toll from the flu, particularly among the children and the aged.

Billy had delegated Wilf, a friend of his and Morgan's, to look after Kitty in his absence, and he rode with her in the parade. As they passed the Arthurs Point Hotel, the barman ran out and handed a tankard of beer up to Kitty. Someone clapped as she tossed it back.

After all the speeches, the ribbon was cut and the Edith Cavell bridge was declared open. When the name of the bridge was announced there was a roar of appreciation from the crowd. The greatest heroine of the war was the most uncontroversial name that could have been chosen. The whole procession passed over the bridge, the Arrowtown people carried on and the Queenstown people turned around and went back again. When Kitty and Wilf were passing the Arthurs Point Hotel the barman ran out again and handed her another tankard which, again, she swallowed gratefully.

Wilf escorted Kitty home, helped her with her horse, then invited himself in for a cup of tea. He explained to Kitty that Billy was paying him to take care of her when Billy himself wasn't able to be there. Wilf was to report back to him if there was anything she needed. He liked Billy, and he owed him, so he would be taking the job seriously. At first Kitty was indignant, then the need for a drink became so strong that she just wanted to be rid of him. He persisted and became a friend who did his best to keep her out of trouble.

Chapter Nine

Despite Wilf's best efforts Kitty went from bad to worse, but he continued to do his best. He made sure she had food and firewood and he kept Billy fully informed. The gentlemen callers, now reduced in number to six, continued with their Saturday night parties, which were not so much parties as mere convivial get-togethers, rather more like club nights for pensioners, the main difference being that one of them would end up in Kitty's bed.

Taking his job seriously, Wilf started going to Kitty's soirées and after the men's initial hostility, they accepted his explanation that he was Billy's mate. Especially when he made it plain that he had no intention of ever sharing Kitty's bed. He was surprised to find that he enjoyed the old men's company and listening to their anecdotes about their lives and the old days when gold ruled. Two of them had followed the rushes from Australia to Otago, on to the West Coast, then back to Australia. They had come back to the Wakatipu because they thought it the best place to end their days, but they were only here because they were too damn old to go to the Klondike. Here they could get the old-age pension, which would be cancelled if they were found drunk in a public place. And they could spend time fossicking or crevicing in the Shotover or the Arrow when the weather blessed them. They all loved Kitty and helped keep her place in order. They grubbed weeds, polished up her jogger and did little maintenance jobs, including taking Coppy to be shod. The farrier never charged for his services. They all drank, but none of them were out of control. Because they knew that Kitty spent the contents of the crock mainly on booze, they kept her supplied with little things like a cake of soap or a pound of butter. They still put money in the crock.

In the middle of 1921 when Billy was finally discharged from the army, the country was full of unemployed returned soldiers. He had never served overseas so he was not entitled to even the miserable gratuity that the returned men received. He was now fifty-six, but like his sister who was sixty-six, he didn't look his age. He went back to what he knew best. The one-legged jockey was riding and winning again.

Florrie had taught him to drive and had given him one of her old used cars, not that it was very old. Her passion was cars, and she always had to have the latest. Her love for cars extended beyond merely driving. She and Morgan had learnt to do their own basic maintenance, and their cars were never kept long enough to wear out. Florrie could change a tyre with the best of them. The roads were not yet maintained to the standard that motorists would like, so tyre-changing was a skill every dedicated motorist needed to learn. Florrie had taught Billy well, although he tended to forget he was driving a car, not riding a horse at a gallop.

Having a car meant that Billy could get himself to more race tracks and could also get to Queenstown to see Kitty more often. Wilf, his faithful lieutenant, kept him well informed. Wilf was courting a war widow in Queenstown, and the local harpies had made sure she had heard about Wilf's 'entanglement' with Kitty. Jessie was made of sterner stuff. She had lost a son and a husband at Gallipoli, each of them having lied about his age to get into the army at a time when the recruiting officers would turn a blind eye if the lies weren't too obvious. When Wilf had talked to her about Kitty and the losses she had suffered that had brought her to her present state, Jessie was full of sympathy rather than blame. She told Wilf that since she herself had never known what it was to be poor, she could only imagine how much harder that would make it to cope with life after the death of loved ones. She got Wilf to take her with him when he went to Kitty's house, and she always took her some small comforts. She managed to get Kitty to do something more than basic cleaning by offering to help her with her chores. And she ignored any malicious tattle from the gossips.

On one of Billy's visits he brought a dog with him. He asked Kitty if she would look after it for him until he could find it a home. When Kitty demurred, saying that she couldn't afford to keep a dog, he told her that he would cover the dog's keep, so long as she didn't teach it to drink. The story he told her was that Scruff had belonged to an old lady who had died. Her son, who was no dog-lover, was going to have him put down, until Billy intervened and offered to find him a home. The man then put a price on the animal. When Billy snorted and started to walk away, he quickly backed down and told Billy to take the damn thing if he didn't want to see it shot. He started to take the dog's collar off until one of the other men there told him not to be such a Scrooge. Someone else had picked up the kennel and put it in the back of Billy's car. When Billy drove off, everyone else departed and the dog's ex-owner was left wondering why.

As Billy had hoped, Kitty soon became fond of Scruff and told Billy that she would keep him. He was soon seen trotting behind her horse or riding beside her in the jogger. He became familiar to the patrons of the White Star, as he was so often seen in the hotel yard doing his duty as the self-appointed guard of Coppy. One patron shouted Kitty a drink and told her he had never seen an uglier dog. Another said that description was too harsh because Scruff could best be described as 'totally nondescript'. Kitty pushed her glass across and said that was fine with her as she had always been totally nondescript, too, and as long as they were buying, they could describe her and her dog any way they liked, but when they stopped buying, would someone please put her back in her rig and point them in the right direction. When she was asked if she had ever been stopped for being drunk in charge of a horse, she replied that that was impossible because if you were as drunk as that, the horse was in charge. She told them that her biggest problems began when she was safely home and she needed to be in charge of herself.

Billy took a position as a trainer and was based in Alexandra. It was a full-time job, and he couldn't get away as often as he had previously, but he came back to be best man at Wilf and Jessie's wedding. Kitty was at the wedding, too, seated between Florrie and Morgan, who later performed at the reception. Not being able to trust Kitty to behave, they had taken her home straight after the service. It was Saturday night, and the gentlemen callers would be there to look after her.

Kitty was becoming increasingly eccentric. The patrons of the White Star bar called her 'a real character, always good for a laugh', but other people weren't so charitable. She was still capable of saddling or harnessing her horse, and she was besotted with Scruff and he with her, so she enjoyed his constant, loving, uncritical company.

She was driving into town one day when she passed a woman who lived near Arthurs Point and gave her a lift into town. She told her that if she had a heavy load to take home, she could come to the White Star and put her parcels in the jogger, then have someone call Kitty out of the bar, and she and her shopping would be delivered all the way home. She didn't take up the offer but later reported that while she was sitting in the jogger, empty bottles were rattling around her feet. When her husband asked why she hadn't accepted the lift home, she told him that respectable people never went near public houses. When he told the story to his mates at the pub, he got the best laugh ever. He didn't laugh at the aftermath. The story, with the postscript about the husband telling it in the bar, went all around the town as good stories do.

Of course that put him in serious trouble when his wife heard the extended version from one of her friends.

As if Kitty didn't have enough problems, her life was now to be made even more miserable. The culture of 'practical jokes' gave some young hooligans a free hand to be obnoxious to the point of cruelty, provided their capers could provide some sort of amusement, no matter how warped it might be. It was all summed up under the heading of 'boys must be boys' or 'boyish pranks'.

Two of the most notorious were Rooster Davis and Hooley Bryant (no relation to the Kinloch Bryants) who were in their late teens and were scions of what were referred to as 'good families'. These two had decided to rid Queenstown of residents that they decided were not the sort of people they wanted in their town. All those they picked on were elderly or eccentric, all were harmless and none of them had influential friends. The first old man that they decided to expel was a foreigner with a poor grasp of English and a slightly dark complexion. He was a devout Catholic. He was living alone and had been in Queenstown for years.

He was easy pickings. A few buckets of water thrown on his kindling wood, stones rained on his roof at night, and he was a nervous wreck. He talked to his parish priest, who, in turn spoke to the ministers of other faiths in the hope that they might put it in a Sunday sermon. He went to the police, who said that nobody had been injured and there was no proof as to who the miscreants were. No real harm had been done, and if the Father was so sure he knew who was responsible perhaps he should speak to their parents. Some of the kinder people in town did speak to the parents, who shrugged it off. The boys were just having a bit of fun. What's the harm in that? What else could you expect from high-spirited lads of that age? They'd soon get over it and find something else to do. The old man was taken to a Catholic old people's home in Dunedin. When his home was sold some charitable protestant suggested that the whole story had been fabricated so the church could get its hands on the money.

The next victim was an elderly Chinese man who had lived there for decades. He was a lot harder for the boys to drive out. He had survived the anti-Chinese frenzy that had swept the goldfields and was living peacefully, growing vegetables, which he sold. Rooster and Hooley decided that although the White New Zealand movement had died out and the 'yellow peril' talk hadn't been voiced publically since Lionel Terry had gone on an anti-Chinese shooting spree in Wellington, Orientals were not wanted in their town.

The wet kindling wood trick didn't work. The old man stored his kindling inside his kitchen. The stones on the roof didn't work either. The next bit of nastiness was to fill his cabbages with birdshot, but his customers objected to that. He sold the best vegetables in town, and while their mums thought it natural for the boys to have fun, they didn't want to shop elsewhere for their vegetables.

Hooley was an expert marksman. His father was a keen hunter and had brought up his sons to be familiar with firearms from an early age. As soon as Hooley was old enough to keep up, he had been taken rabbit shooting, then had graduated to goats and now was hunting deer. He had access to a variety of weapons, so hunting people and scaring them but not damaging them became a delightful new hobby. He developed it while ridding Queenstown of the boys' Chinese candidate for expulsion.

The old man had courage and determination. It took more than six months for them to get rid of him. He spoke to a number of sympathetic locals who said that one day Rooster and Hooley would probably go too far. In the meantime they could do nothing because the boys' parents were much too influential. He complained to the police, who said that they couldn't bring charges, because he had no physical injuries, and suggested that if he was really bothered by a few pranks he should get himself a lawyer and sue them for any damage done, but he would have to prove who had done it to have any chance of success. Because most of the nuisance that he complained about happened at night, it would be difficult to find any witnesses who would stand up in court. And considering who the boys were, it would be difficult to get anyone to speak against them. And after all, they were only boys and would one day grow out of it.

But now Hooley and Rooster were getting bolder. Their target lived a little way out of town, and they were able to find themselves a hideout with a good view of the house. From this spot Hooley was able to ping bullets at all sorts of objects near where the old man was working. Still he wouldn't go. They finally ousted him by shooting holes in his garden water tank right at the beginning of the long hot, dry Otago summer.

One morning they saw him loaded with belongings, waiting on the wharf to catch the *Earnslaw*. As soon as the ship pulled out they rushed to his house. The garden had been rooted out, and every window had been broken. A large bonfire was burning away down the back. When the boys pushed open the door there was a large explosion, and a row of powder led to a larger one that set the house on fire. The Chinese aren't masters of fireworks for nothing.

Public opinion was starting to turn against the boys because the old man had been quite popular with a number of people. The vegetable buyers said that this time the lads had gone too far. The boys themselves were aggrieved because they felt that the old man had turned the tables on them and people were laughing at them. Their victim hadn't left with his tail between his legs, but instead he had got the last laugh, and that rankled. Although they had succeeded in driving him out, they didn't like being the butt of the joke themselves. So they lay low for the rest of the summer and planned their next eviction much more carefully. Their victim was to be Kitty. They decided she 'lowered the tone of the town.' And they wanted to have some fun.

Kitty was still being cared for by Wilf and Jessie, but they had now bought a small grocery shop and simply didn't have the time to visit as often as they would liked to. They delivered groceries to her once a week, and Wilf still went to her Saturday evenings when he could. One of the gentlemen callers had died during the winter, but five faithful still remained. There were still stories told and drinks drunk, and still one of them would stay the night, but the spirit had gone out of it.

Billy was a frequent visitor, and in the winter he occasionally managed to come and stay, but even then there were winter meetings when the weather permitted. And it was the season for steeplechasing. Horses still had to be trained and cared for, but a number were turned out until it was time for them to be brought in again for the spring season. Billy fretted over Kitty's deterioration but told Wilf that he felt entirely powerless. Even when he was there he was unable to prevent her from drinking, and she had got very smart about finding places to hide her bottles.

Then something happened that accelerated Kitty's decline and made some of the townspeople start saying that she was going nuts. One sunny morning she was working in her front garden and Scruff was sunning himself in the dust on the side of the road when a motorcyclist appeared from nowhere. He hit Scruff, fell off, picked himself and the bike up and rode off, yelling abuse at Kitty because her 'bloody dog' had dented his bike. But Scruff was dead. Wilf arrived some hours later to find an almost catatonic Kitty cradling the cooling body of her beloved companion and friend. He dug a grave and managed to get Kitty to give Scruff a funeral. He made a cross with an appropriate inscription, then led her inside to her bed.

The loss of Scruff made Kitty the implacable enemy of motorcyclists. Whenever one was passing she ran out onto the road with her broom flailing and she would try to knock him off his bike. Most of them were young men looking for excitement. Passing Kitty's place and dodging the broom became sport to them. Some of the more accomplished riders were even able to grab the broom and tumble her into the dust. This gave Rooster and Hooley their excuse to start their campaign of terror. No one seemed to think it odd that young men should torment a sixty-year-old woman who lived on her own. After all, boys will be boys, and they were now old enough to take a drink with the men and joke about it.

Night after night they rained stones onto her roof. When they got sick of that they would wait until she went into town, prise up her windows and throw buckets of water into her house. This was most fun in the winter, especially if they could hit the bed. Kitty's doorknob became a favourite target for Hooley, who would lie across the road on the flat rock, taking pot-shots at it and anything else he fancied.

One afternoon, Kitty, covered in dirt and badly bruised, staggered into the police station to complain that Rooster had been chasing her with a stick. But she found that a woman who lived like she did and had a police record for public drunkenness had no right even to try to bring charges against a sober and well-bred young citizen who happened to be a little bit playful. Had she lost her famous sense of humour?

This was too much for Kitty. She screamed threats against Rooster, threatening to kill him at the first opportunity. Senior Constable Peters put her into a cell for the night, and in the morning Dr Anderson was called to certify her as insane. She didn't really have to be certified insane. Being an 'incurable' alcoholic found drunk in a public place for the third time would have been enough to get her locked up for life. Peters was not a popular man and had the reputation of being a bully. He had been waiting a long time for an opportunity to put Kitty away a third time for public drunkenness but, he had been constantly frustrated by Kitty's friends and well-wishers from the White Star, who had been aware of this and had made sure that she got home safely.

Somebody rushed to tell Wilf, who immediately sent a telegram to Billy. By the time Billy received it, a heavily sedated Kitty was handcuffed and wrapped in a wet blanket. She was in the back of the police car, and she and her police escort were well on their way to Seacliff Lunatic Asylum at Waitati, near Dunedin.

Billy drove furiously to Queenstown and met an angry Wilf at Kitty's place. Senior Constable Peters had sent his underling to escort Kitty to the asylum and was now busily engaged in emptying the house. When Billy arrived Wilf was arguing that the horse and jogger didn't belong to Kitty but had been lent to her by Billy. The man who was helping to carry things out wasn't even a policeman. Some of the neighbours had also turned up and joined in the protest. Billy angrily asked, 'Who gave you permission to do this?'

'I don't need permission. I'm the law here. When someone gets sent to the funny farm everything they own gets sold to defray expenses and it's my job to get the house cleared out ready for the sale. Who do you think you are coming here and poking your nose in?'

'I happen to own half the house and a lot of the stuff inside. The horse and jogger are mine, and you had better stop what you are doing right now. Don't I know you?'

'No, you don't. But I happen to know who you are. You're the little bugger who likes to use a king hit to flatten better men than he is. So, have a go at me if you like. The difference is that I'll be ready for you, and with a bit of luck I'll be able to send you to join your loopy sister.'

Wilf and one of the neighbours grabbed Billy before he lost control, and Lachlan, the neighbour, said scathingly, 'I know what he's trying to do, Billy. This is personal. It's some sort of revenge. Don't let him get to you. Remember that oaf called Peters that you had to deal to down in Fairlight? The one that the girl tipped the soup over? This is his baby brother, and he's always boasted that he'd sort you out as soon as he got the chance. Don't give him that chance. He likes a fight, and when he gets a guy in the cells he takes the opportunity to beat him up. Don't play his game. There are too many witnesses here, and we're all on your side. Go and get lawyered up.' The policeman's helper had quietly faded away. Billy got in his car and drove away. Lachlan went to fetch Florrie and Morgan while Wilf and the others settled down to wait it out. Peters went inside the house.

When Billy finally got back he had the local lawyer with him. They tried the door but found it locked. Billy produced his own key, and they went inside. Peters was engaged in bundling stuff into boxes and bags. 'Get out,' he said. 'Can't you see I'm busy?'

The lawyer said, 'I am instructing you to stop right now and get out of this house. You are trespassing.'

Peters burst out laughing. 'Do you think you can scare me?' he sneered. 'You seem to forget that I am the law here.'

'You may not be for much longer. I have just been on the phone to the senior man in Dunedin, and he is not at all impressed with your behaviour. You have not yet received any written instructions about the disposal of this property. This means that it is you who are breaking the law. When I talk to your helper I will, I hope, have some information about any plans you have about disposing of the contents.'

A voice came from the spectators: 'He offered to sell me the pony and cart.'

Quickly the lawyer asked, 'Would you testify in court?'

'My oath I would. There is nothing worse than a crooked cop.'

To add insult to injury, the lawyer asked Peters for a lift back to town, but the man bolted, to the laughter of all present. The lawyer got his lift from Wilf.

Florrie arrived. Billy thanked the neighbours for their support and invited anyone who would like a cuppa to join him and Florrie. He was going to light the fire and make one right now. They all said they had better get back to work, and Lachlan thanked Billy for providing the best afternoon's entertainment in years. All of them, separately, expressed their sympathy for Kitty. They knew that she would never get back home to Queenstown. Some remembered her in her heyday and remembered her tragedies, saying that they could well understand why she had taken to the drink. They also decided to go as a group to the parents of Hooley and Rooster to tell them that they would not stand any more of their 'pranks'.

After church on Sunday the pastor admonished Rooster and Hooley and told them that they had finally gone too far. They must stop taking the law into their own hands and start showing a little Christian charity. Even after this very public rebuke the boys showed no remorse. Rooster said they were satisfied that they had now cleared all the undesirables out of town and could now settle down knowing they had done a good job and had made the town a better place for people to live. For now.

With the help of Jessie and Wilf, Billy and Florrie cleared out Kitty's house. Unfortunately, the title deeds that Billy's lawyer held had only Kitty's name on them because at the time of purchase she had been the one with the money. She and Billy had never got around to updating them. Billy gave Coppy and the jogger to Lachlan, who, together with his wife, had always helped Kitty out when they could. They were also given all of Kitty's tack and her leather-working gear. Florrie and Billy kept a few mementos, but everything else was given away, including Scruff's kennel.

Billy drove away from Queenstown. He felt that an era was over. Neither he nor Kitty was ever to return.

The Last Life
Seacliff 1926

Chapter Ten

Seacliff Lunatic Asylum was a huge, imposing multi-towered building with as many crenellations as could be crowded onto it. It was a tribute to the worst excesses of late Victorian architecture. When the site for the asylum had been chosen in 1872, nine hundred acres at Waitati, thirty miles north of Dunedin, were purchased. It was a time of enlightenment about the treatment of inmates, and instead of being kept confined and brutalised, they were given work to do and healthy food to eat. No longer was being sent to a mental hospital a life sentence, except for some alcoholics. An astonishingly large number of inmates recovered and were able to be discharged. Asylums, increasingly, were built on farms so that the inmates could grow their own food. This provided healthy work with the added bonus of keeping costs down. Seacliff was an unfortunate choice of location for such an institution. Sir James Hector, the director of the Geological Survey, was not convinced of its suitability as he believed the ground was unstable. There should have been more notice taken of his opinion and more research done. The beauty of the site and the presence of an apparently firm clay foundation led the authorities to ignore his warning. It was not long before they had to acknowledge their huge mistake. Within twelve years a Royal Commission had been appointed to investigate, and it was decided that the faults were unacceptable, although it did not conclude that the buildings were unsafe for use.

When Frederic Truby King was Medical Superintendant he preferred to use the term 'patients' rather than call them 'inmates'. He had gardens laid out and a home farm established in the extensive grounds around the asylum. He also preferred the term 'mental hospital' to 'lunatic asylum' and when he had the name changed to 'Seacliff Mental Hospital', similar institutions throughout New Zealand followed suit. Unfortunately, it took decades before the name changes were accepted by the general public, who continued to refer to them as 'loony bins', 'funny farms', 'nut houses' or simply 'the asylum'.

By the time Kitty was admitted to Seacliff in the mid 1920s, the hospital was falling further into decay and there was gross overcrowding. Patients now numbered more than a thousand, and the population was increasing. The building was becoming more and more unhealthy. Because of the nature of the land and the gradual deterioration of the building itself, the drainage and sewerage systems were continually failing and the physical health of the patients was suffering. These conditions naturally made for a rapid turnover of staff. Every attempt was made to adhere to Truby King's principles, but with an overcrowded decaying building it was very difficult.

When Kitty was admitted she was suffering badly from what was then called the 'DTs' or, more properly, delirium tremens. She was trembling and hallucinating. She kept asking where she was and wouldn't stop screaming for a drink. The young constable was reprimanded for the way she been treated, and he in turn passed the blame on to his superior. He removed her handcuffs, grabbed her wet blanket and departed in a hurry when he was told that the Queenstown police would be reported for their treatment of Kitty.

Kitty was very cold and very dirty. She had to be sedated so that nurses could put her into a hot bath to clean her and warm her up. Her hair was so tangled and knotted and there were so many bits of leaves and sticks in it that they had no choice but to cut it very short. And she was badly bruised. When she became conscious she had to be kept under restraint in solitary confinement. She refused to eat anything but kept on screaming for a drink. Her withdrawal symptoms lasted for three days. When she became aware of her surroundings she was very indignant about her haircut so they told her about her condition when she arrived. They asked her about her bruises and thought she said a rooster had done it. That set them wondering about her state of mind until she was able to to tell them how she had been treated. They still wondered until the doctor talked to Billy who had come to visit as soon as could after she had been admitted. Billy told the whole story of her life and Joyce, a young nurse from Queenstown, was able to confirm the part about Rooster and Hooley.

Billy came to visit as often as he could, and every time she brightened as soon as she saw him and asked if he had come to take her home. He had to explain that it wasn't possible. He had been to see the Superintendant and had also talked to his lawyer, but the police had stitched her up beautifully. Peters had written his report, which had been endorsed by Doctor Anderson, the doctor who had certified her. He was a new locum and anxious to please. He said that she was a habitual drunk with two convictions for being found drunk in a public place, and another was pending for the day she was arrested. She had become a danger to herself and others and he described her attacks on motor-cyclists without mentioning her dog. Also, he said that she was suffering from delusions. She believed that two young local men were tormenting her and, in the hearing of the police and others, had threatened to kill one of them. If, and when she was to be released from Seacliff she would be charged with threatening to kill, which, if it didn't send her to prison, would certainly send her back to Seacliff. Billy explained to her that if she were to go back to Queenstown she wouldn't be able to go back to her house because she wouldn't be safe from

Rooster and Hooley. He didn't tell her that the house was to be sold. His lawyer was investigating the legality of the sale. Because of Billy's and Florrie's itinerant lifestyles, Kitty couldn't be released into their custody. 'Sorry, Sis,' he said, 'I'm afraid you're stuck here. I can't do anything about it. At least you don't have to worry about food or anything and I don't have to worry about you getting into the drink again.'

'Billy, all I want is to go home. And yes, I do want a drink. Will I ever stop wanting one? Ma was right wasn't she? I wish I had never started. They look after us well in here, but there are just too many people, and it rains too much. When it's not raining it's misty. The building's damp and cold and it's falling to pieces. I'm a Wakatipu woman. I love the dry, hot summers, and even though the winters are cold, they're dry. And when I die I want to lie beside Otto.'

Billy couldn't bring himself to tell her that she would never go home. He excused himself, promising that he would come and see her whenever he could, and he kept that promise.

The patients all had jobs. Men worked on the farm or in the beautiful gardens. Women did domestic duties, and after Kitty had had enough of scrubbing floors and hanging washing, she wandered into the kitchen, where she started making herself useful. She told the cook that she had cooked for large gangs of harvesters and shearers, and when one of the nurses came to shepherd her back to her proper job, the cook refused to let her go. 'When I tell her to make something she makes it. I don't have to tell her how to do it. Take one of the others instead. Now go. Can't you see I'm busy?'

Kitty began to realise that she was actually quite happy. The sexes were segregated, so there was no outdoor work that she could do, but there was a beautiful park with lovely gardens especially for the women, and they were encouraged to spend time there when they were not working. On Saturdays there were sports and entertainments. In summer there were picnics, and in winter there were fortnightly dances. Other entertainments were magic lantern shows and concerts provided by visiting groups from Dunedin or by staff members. Other amenities were a billiard room, a games room, a reading room and a library. Truby King's doctrine was that good diet, meaningful work and time spent outdoors made a healthy body which, in turn helped enormously to manage and in some cases cure mental illnesses. These regimes were introduced all through New Zealand. Kitty never stopped wanting a drink. When she confided in a senior nurse, the nurse told her sympathetically, 'It's not your body that wants the drink. It's a couple of years now, and the booze is well out of your system. It's your brain that won't let go. What was so great about being a drunk? Did it make you happy? Did it make people like you better? Whenever you start craving the demon drink, just ask yourself these questions.'

Kitty felt lost. She didn't believe that she would never go back to Queenstown. The garden had a row of flowering cherry trees that were so beautiful when they were in blossom that Kitty spent much of her spare time just sitting, gazing at them. She collected seeds from them to take home and plant in her own garden. Her mind wandered back to her early childhood in Dunedin, to a time when she and her mother loved each other and spent nearly all their time in each other's company. She remembered Catherine's early teachings and her fervent belief in God and wondered if there might be something in it. She thought that she had experienced both heaven and hell in her own lifetime and wondered what she had done to deserve it. She knew that she had indeed been a sinner and started wondering what lay ahead for her. Was there an afterlife? Had Catherine's warnings about hellfire actually been right? One day while she was sitting in the garden enjoying the sunshine and the beauty of the flowers, she was joined by an elderly gentleman who introduced himself as Father Byrne. He was a Roman Catholic priest.

Kitty found herself talking to him about her mother and how Catherine had been forced to deny her faith but found it again when she became demented while still in her fifties. It had been a great comfort to her. Kitty had finally found someone who would listen to her. Over the next few weeks she confided her whole life story. Father Byrne was a good listener and not at all judgmental.

Kitty told him about her mother's early teachings and her own worries about an afterlife. When he told her that sins could be forgiven she eagerly embraced the Faith and, like her mother, derived great comfort from it. It brought her a sense of belonging that she had never felt before. She wondered why, at this stage of her life, she kept harking back to the faith her mother had tried so hard to teach her when she was so young. And why, after all those years of skeptical Protestantism, she had a longing to learn about the beliefs that had given her mother such a mixture of hope and fear.

She knew that she had been a sinner, but she hoped that the Lord would forgive her relationship with Otto, because she could never think of it as a sin, but then again, could that be why he was taken from her? Father Byrne explained that children who were raised in the Faith until they were seven years old almost always came back when they were old and needed the comfort the church could bring. He taught her about confession and the forgiveness of sins.

Kitty was now working full time in the kitchen and was in charge of cakes and puddings. Christmas cakes and puddings were always made in the winter when it was grey and foggy outdoors and damp and miserable inside. It was warm and cheerful in the kitchen, which was the busiest and happiest place in the institution. Kitty had a good team working with her, and they loved to hear her tell stories of her childhood and the horses she had handled. For so many cakes and puddings, endless hours had to be spent creaming butter and sugar, and storytelling made the hours pass more quickly. Kitty supervised the brandy being poured into the mix but was not allowed to touch the bottle herself. It took six weeks to two months to get all the cakes baked and all the puddings boiled in their bags. Then they had to be properly wrapped and stowed away until Christmas. In July 1930 the job was done for the year and the workers sat, having a cup of tea before they went to their beds. Kitty thanked them for their good work. She started to stand up but crashed to the floor. The last word that she spoke was 'Otto'. She didn't get to lie beside him at Skippers but was buried in the cemetery at Waitati. She was seen off by Father Byrne, Billy and Joyce.

On her death certificate it gives her age as fifty-five when she was actually seventy-five. She would have loved that.

Kitty is still remembered in Queenstown. Her legend has grown, and she is spoken of more kindly than she had ever been in her adult life. After her death people emembered her years of tragedy and her years of achievement. Mostly they passed over the drunken years and talked of the way she had struggled to survive in hostile times. Oral history records her as being a 'victim of circumstance', 'a living indictment of hard times.' The last word must go to Winnie Mulholland, who described her as 'an unsung heroine of Wakatipu history.'

AUTHOR'S NOTE

Kitty's story was told to me by Winnie Mulholland over a lot of afternoons during 1976 and 1977. Her mother, Mary Jane Mulholland, had asked her to 'get Kitty's story out', and Winnie had decided that I was the person to do it. At the time I was living in Queenstown, working as a postie. I knew I wasn't going to be there much longer as my children had all left home, and I didn't mind much if I lost my job. So I constantly broke one of the sternest rules. Mail had to be put in the mailbox and nowhere else. But if it were raining or snowing, if the recipient were old, I would knock on the door and hand it to them. Disgusting behaviour, I know. When one of the ladies told me how much she appreciated the service and was going to write a letter to the postmaster and tell him, I had to explain the situation and swear her to silence.

Winnie invited me in for a cup of tea, so I called in one afternoon when I had finished my shift.

I was very interested to see that she had a contemporary poster of the Battle of Omdurman. Always having been interested in history since my father sat on my bed and told me history stories instead of fairy stories, I asked Winnie where the poster had come from and she told me she had an uncle or great-uncle who had been in the cavalry, who had fought there, but she knew nothing about the battle, where it was fought or why. I was able to tell her, and from that peculiar beginning, our friendship flourished, but always formally. She was Miss Mulholland, and I was Mrs Mills, but we did become very good friends.

Winnie told me the story of Kitty, most of which she had from her redoubtable mother and some from her own memory. Her mother, Mary Jane Mulholland, was an amazing woman. Today she might have been called a feminist, but the word hadn't been invented then. In 1893 she was one of the first women on the electoral role and one of the first to vote in the general election, in the electoral district of Wakatipu. According to her daughter she gave a lot of time to good causes, and I can't imagine how she found the time, because she had nine children, the youngest of whom was Winnie, born in 1899.

Mary Jane was born in 1855, the same year as Kitty, and she died in 1936. After Kitty's death in 1930, she told the whole story to Winnie, probably thinking her thirty-one-year-old spinster daughter was now mature enough to hear it. It was Mary Jane who had invented the expression 'gentlemen callers'. Because her husband had been the captain of the various ships that serviced Kinloch she knew about Kitty's life at the Head of the Lake. So, my story is founded on oral history, and because oral history is not always very reliable, there will be errors.

When I first heard the story there were still other people in Queenstown who had known Kitty or heard her story from their parents, and when they heard from Winnie that I was 'getting the story out', they came and told me what they knew or thought they knew.

That was forty years ago, and I have forgotten many of their names. At the time, my elder son was working in Dunedin, and he spent time in the Hocken Library in Dunedin ferreting out what facts he could find out about the story, but a great many interesting people never have their stories told in books or newspapers. The upshot was that I wrote twelve pages for Winnie, but I never forgot Kitty. Some time after I left Queenstown Winnie passed the story on to Lel McBride, whose forebears had had a hotel in Queenstown since the very early days. She, in turn, passed it on to the Lakes District Museum.

When I, too, became old and unable to spend as much time in the garden as I had done, I decided I needed to start using my brain instead of my body, so I thought I would write a book, wondering whether I would get it finished. But I did, with so much help and support from many people whom I shall acknowledge later, but the stand-out star has to be Anne Maguire, Archivist at the Lakes District Museum. She has stopped me from making many mistakes and sent me so much useful information. Many thanks, Anne. Finally, I have done my best to fulfill my promise to Winnie Mulholland. I hope I have succeeded.

The historical passages have been researched as thoroughly as possible, and any errors are mine. For the oral history, I have to trust those who told the stories, and those stories are remarkably similar.

Margaret Mills

REFERENCE BOOKS

Golden Days of Lake County. F.W.G. Miller
Skippers: Triumph & Tragedy. Danny Knudson
Road to Routeburn. Doreen McKenzie
'Unfortunate Folk': *Essays on Mental Health Treatment*. Edited by Barbara Brookes and Jane Thompson
Register of St Peter's Anglican Church, Queenstown
Accessed via *Papers Past*

ACKNOWLEDGEMENTS

Trevor Darvill, my partner. Without his getting up and getting breakfast, giving me an uninterrupted hour or so in the mornings, I simply could not have managed. Also for the time he has spent correcting the manuscript. I am a techno-cretin and a terrible typist, so he has had a lot to put up with.

Barry Woods, a friend for more than thirty years and my sternest critic. Barry is a retired printer and proofreader. He has not retired from being a poet. When I asked him for help and criticism, I asked him to pull no punches, and I have had black eyes ever since.

Anne Maguire, who did her best to make sure that I had the reported history (as opposed to the oral history) correct.

Brett Mills, whose remorseless research caused me to throw out some perfectly good fiction and replace it with (hopefully) the truth, meaning that one whole life had to be rewritten.

Heather and Graeme McKay, for information about the Mulhollands.

David Robie, for encouragement and advice.

Mike Lynch, for believing in me for so long.

Sacha Paddy, who insisted the story should have a happy ending. It doesn't, but I did my best to keep her happy. And she did a fine job of editing.

Jane Scheib, for her finishing touches.

Greg Hepworth, for the beautiful cover

James Darvill, my literary executor, who has taken so much interest in Kitty since he read the first draft and who has helped me so much with my battles with the computer.

And Jonell, Loris, Graham and all my family and friends, who have contributed in so many ways.

My grateful thanks to you all.

Margaret Mills